in
DARKNESS
we
BREAK

SHADOW JOURNEY SERIES
BOOK FOUR

Praise for the Shadow Journey Series

The Shadows We Make – Book One

"A beautifully crafted SF dystopia, boasting relatable characters and a skillful plot." *BookLife Reviews*

"…high stakes adventure…strong emotional themes." K.C. Finn – *Readers Favorite* – Five Stars

"Ash captivates the reader throughout…poetic… dramatic… suspenseful…" *BookTrib*

"Loved it…an amazing read." Sally Atlass – *ReedsyDiscovery*

The Thrice-Gifted Child – Book Two

"…imaginative…suspenseful…memorable…" *BookLife Reviews*

"…a page turner…intricate…gripping…doesn't allow your attention to waver for a single moment." Pikasho Deko – *Readers Favorite* – Five Stars

The Sleeping Myth – Book Three

"…fascinating action…imaginative plot twists. I highly recommend it." K.C. Finn *Readers Favorite*

"…stellar storytelling…magical, inventive, and thrilling." *Book Commentary*

in DARKNESS *we* BREAK

SHADOW JOURNEY SERIES
BOOK FOUR

JO ALLEN ASH

Potter Street Books
Zionsville PA
2024

This is a work of fiction. Names, characters, places and incidents are the product of the author's imagination or used fictitiously and any resemblance to persons living or dead, locales, businesses, or events is coincidental.

All rights reserved. No part of this book may be used or reproduced in any matter whatsoever, electronically or otherwise, except with the express written permission of the author. Please do not participate or encourage piracy of copyrighted material in violation of the author's rights.

ISBN: 979-8-9870681-9-9

© 2024 – All rights reserved

Printed in the U.S.A.

Potter Street Books/Robin Maderich Publishing

Cover design by Robin Maderich

This book is also available in digital format.

a journey ends, the next begins

Grace

Chapter One

A lantern, heatless and utilitarian, pushed back the darkness deep underground. Rolling a little on the solid surface beneath me, I stretched my fingers toward Duncan's and found only cold stone.

Duncan sat cross-legged on the cave floor out of reach, his lean body hunched forward, his dark head tipped in my direction. His turn to keep an eye on me, then. I'd woken several times to find one companion or another staring at me from beyond the small light. No one had admitted setting themselves this task when I questioned them, but I recognized their purpose. They waited for my instability to show itself once more.

Ignoring Duncan's scrutiny, and desperately missing him at my side, I closed my eyes again. The shielded illumination from the kinetic torch glowed against my lowered lids.

They're afraid of you, Grace, Skelly taunted me

from the crystal inside the bag around my neck.

They are not afraid, I silently snapped back. *They are worried.*

Pretty much amounts to the same thing.

Hardly, I answered, yet I supposed he was right.

I heard another noise from him. A snarky condemnation.

My thoughts went to what he'd been before. Before he became…this. Back in the facility on Emerald, when he'd been just another inmate. An inmate with an addiction, yes, and a propensity for unpredictable, even violent, behavior, but essentially one of us, the five who had escaped. He had died, horribly, on the prison planet's surface. Killed by the mutated creatures who haunted the perpetual twilight. I still didn't understand what had happened, what had made him *other*. Still unpredictable. Still violent. And still, in some ways, to be pitied.

He stirred in the crystal. I ignored him.

We had all survived the passage through the Sleeping Myth but I had changed, too, as surely as Skelly had on Emerald. But not like him. I wasn't like him.

Whatever makes you feel better.

Cloth rustled nearby, followed by a shuffling boot on stone.

"You all right there, Grace?"

Duncan's voice, oddly gruff. Duncan, sweet Duncan, braving my new, erratic nature to come nearer, after all. Tears pricked along my lids. I sat up, dashed a hand across my eyes. Duncan's boots clomped twice in rapid retreat. My heart plummeted.

"I'm okay," I said, dropping my hands to my lap. He remained standing, backlit by the torch on the floor.

"May I sit with you?"

I drew a deep, ragged breath, let it out. "Please," I said. "I would like it if you did."

He dropped down beside me. Only a day ago, or was it two? he might have bumped his shoulder against mine in camaraderie. Now, he maintained a small distance. Inches only, but there.

"I know I've asked before, but I'm asking again," he said. "Isn't there anything I can do?"

He tensed at his own words, expecting me to lash out in anger. Because I had. This time, I merely shook my head. "I don't know. Not right now. Not until I figure out exactly what is wrong with me."

Liar.

Skelly, shut it.

Is it easier to not tell him the truth? What would he think of you if he knew you'd rather lie?

I'm surprised you care, I said.

I don't.

I grunted in response.

Duncan eyed me askance. "Is he talking to you? Shane?"

"Yes."

Duncan pointed toward my upper garments, toward the place where the bag hung hidden against my sternum. "Would it help if I, you know, took it? Carried it for a while?"

Let him. Oh, yes, please let him. That would be loads of fun.

"No," I said, "it wouldn't help."

Duncan nodded, shoved his arms over his drawn-up knees, folded his hands together. I studied the shape of them in the dark, the lamp highlighting skin and bone structure, dirt and healing cuts and the fraying bandages still covering his damaged right. I wanted to reach out and take both his hands in mine, hold them close, tell him how sorry I was. For everything.

Tell the guy who betrayed you how sorry you are? You're pathetic.

A wretched sound escaped me. Duncan turned to me again. "Grace?"

"It's nothing. I'm fine."

Particles from his breath misted in the chill air. He dropped his hands to his sides. A moment later, he lifted his arm, circled it about my shoulders, pulled me up against his side. "Is this all right?"

I bit my lip. He hadn't had to ask before. "Yes."

We sat in silence. I listened to the others breathing in the shadows beyond the lamplight. Carina and Mika lying so close together they made one shadow. Resa, sprawled as if she'd fallen in a dead faint. Brand hunched like a sleeping animal, his blanket around his ankles. Hannah and Ren had been left outside the Sleeping Myth. Despite Hannah's last actions, I worried about them both.

"You'd think all the stuff crammed into your head now would include an instruction manual," Duncan whispered.

I laughed, cut it short. "I know."

He pointed at my chest again. "We're no closer to getting rid of him."

"I know."

"Or finding out who is behind all this. Because it's…it's someone."

"I know," I said yet again, feeling patience slip in a manner it never would have a short time ago. I reminded myself to focus on my warrior's training, no matter what else bombarded me now.

"Someone with the ability to rally all these

different factions together and to fool them into believing each one has a chance to be on top when this is over," he went on, nearly repeating what I'd said myself at some point. "Because I don't for a minute think it's going to be any of them. It's like they're allowed to think they're doing the dirty work for their own benefit, but it's really for his."

"Or hers," I said.

"Or hers," he agreed. "Whoever it is, they have to possess a lot more charisma than the mere likes of me."

"Power," I said. "Mage."

Dipping his head, he nodded.

"That would make sense," I agreed.

Beneath frowning brows his eyes remained averted, his anxiety at bringing up the subject obvious. "And after what we saw in Landing, where they were clearly mage…" Duncan's voice trailed off. The way he said 'mage' startled me. The word carried a certain distaste. I couldn't blame him for feeling this way. Nothing good had come from such association. I should have told him something to comfort him, but I sat on with my mouth closed, studying the light's meager reflection over the cave walls. After a moment, he went on.

"They were afraid, the people in Landing. That would mean someone with more power than they had, right? And that scares me. They…they had gates that vanished and guards appearing out of nowhere…" Again, he fell silent.

"I understand," I said, "and it could be you're right."

"And that…that might mean, there's a reason you…you…" His voice failed once more. I knew by the stubborn set to his mouth he intended to stay silent now.

"The prophecy, Duncan, that's what you're hinting at?"

He nodded again.

"I've been wondering about that myself. Of course, I have. How could I not? But it's of no help to us. No use. I possess gifts the purpose of which I can't even imagine, but I have no training, no guidance. I've spent most of my time since going through the Sleeping Myth trying not to explode."

His arm across my shoulders tensed, fighting the impulse, I supposed, to pull away. "Not literally, I hope?" he mumbled.

I said nothing.

"You'll be better once we're outside," he went on. "We all will. This traveling underground is getting old."

Snorting agreement, I shifted my body, providing him the excuse he needed to drop his arm and adjust his position. I'd felt better with him close against me, but I couldn't burden him with the responsibility. I needed to be myself again, with or without him.

"I'm sorry," I whispered.

"You haven't hurt any of us, if that's what you're worried about."

"Yet."

"You won't." His mouth twitched. "I thought you would kill me when you found me on Emerald, though. You know that, don't you? Instead, you forgave me."

The stupid, foolish tears broke out again.

"You became my friend," he said. "My best friend."

A low groan emitted from Brand's prone form, followed by his voice. "You two're killin' me."

I narrowed my eyes at Brand and his crumpled blanket on the cave floor.

"All this kissy-kissy stuff—"

"Excuse me?" I snapped. "I haven't kissed—"

"Yer ignoring the underlyin' issue here. Ya need help. Ya got all this power, yeah? And no idea how to control it. We're followin' you. We need to make sure that's the right thing to do."

My brows arched. "I'll find answers," I muttered.

"You've said that before, Grace," Duncan reminded me.

I bowed my head, took several slow, deep breaths. He and the boy from Trill kept their eyes on me, waiting for me to react.

"We're not ganging up on you," Duncan added quietly. "These are the facts. We need to figure it out. All of us together."

Swiping at my eyes again, I looked away.

"I'm not faulting you, Grace. None of us are. Not accusing you in any fashion. Of anything. It's just...well, you might not ever get the exact reply you seek. Not anymore. It seems things have gone beyond, you know? You might have to work it out over time, based on what's been given you."

I nodded, not quite committed to what he said. After all, time didn't appear to be on our side.

Brand spoke, muffled by the blanket now wrapped around his shoulders. "You know what animals do when they're not runnin' or huntin'?"

Glancing in his direction, I frowned. "What's that?"

"They rest."

"Point taken. I didn't mean to disturb you."

"Not what I meant. I only meant you should stop talkin' and go to sleep."

"You need it," Duncan said.

"We all do," Brand muttered. He rolled on the ground, away from Duncan and me, away from the light.

"It's hard to shut the thoughts off," I whispered to Duncan.

"Carina can help you with that," he whispered back.

"I don't—" I began, realizing only then that Carina had materialized from the shadows in the way she had, moving so gracefully, so quietly, she could sometimes be unseen. I raised my hand. Not quickly enough. They must have been waiting for this moment to catch me unaware. Carina's tiny fingers swept across my brow before I could stop her. My consciousness vanished into the dark.

Chapter Two

When I awoke, the stiffness in my limbs, especially my not quite healed thigh, indicated a long, motionless slumber. I listened to the small noises around me. Morning had come, or morning such as we estimated inside the cave. I turned my head, rolled over. Only the light from the torches illuminated the cavern around us. My companions were packing up remnants from breakfast. I noticed they had set within reach a cup and several bits of whatever they'd cobbled together from the meal for me. I pulled the cup close, lifted it, drank thirstily. For the moment, food held no allure.

"How are you feeling?" Mika asked from a small distance. "How's your leg?"

Mika, the physician's son. He wanted nothing to do with his father, but what he had learned from watching the man had been invaluable during our journey together.

"It'll do," I said. "I'll do. Sleep helped. It really did. I'm sorry for the way I've…been."

Mika shrugged, not quite exonerating me. This recent day had been hard on them, I knew. Many days had been hard on them. They had survived—we had survived—but sometimes barely.

"Grace, we're ready to move on," Duncan said, standing not far behind Mika. In the past, no one had to prod me in reminder. Since my injury in the mountain village, I'd needed more rest, found myself sleeping through noise that should have woken even the heaviest sleeper. I knew the body needed extra sleep to heal. I supposed the mind did, too. Bodily injury had been one thing, this new knowledge something else entirely. I suffered from the recognition I had changed.

I stood, folded the blanket, tucked it away, stretched, considered my new self. Wondered if I cared for her or not. Mostly not, if I had to be honest. I lifted the battered metal plate from the floor, picked up the food with my fingers, shoved it into my mouth, chewed, found the bits and pieces tasteless. I could barely swallow. Hastily, I washed the remaining crumbs down my throat with the last dregs from the cup. I stowed both plate and cup in my pack.

"Ready," I said.

The cave floor here ran rather smoothly, large enough for two to move side by side. Duncan strode with his sister, and Mika and Carina together, of course. Brand brought up the rear. I walked in front, still in front, but alone. I had not minded this position before, had taken it up as mine deliberately, intentionally, maybe proudly. Always, though, I could count on Duncan appearing at my elbow. Not now.

I missed Chauncy and the other two *conjures*, too, their steady presence, their protection and strange, natural knowledge. Even the stink from their heavy, oily hides. Leaving them outside Landing had been difficult. I had never planned not to return for them. Their absence inside this cave was fortuitous, however. They, with their huge bodies and lengthy single horns, would never have been able to maneuver along the narrow passageways or over rock fall, even if they would have survived the transit through the Sleeping Myth.

My *lathesa's* loss hit me hard, too, but in a different way. My weaponless right hand seemed naked.

Abruptly, a longing for my home, my family, surged to the fore.

"Mother," I whispered.

"What's that, Grace?"

I glanced back at Duncan, who had drawn as near as he could manage with Resa beside him. "I miss my mother," I said.

"I miss mine, too." He sounded surprised by his admission, as well he might. After a moment, he added, "I miss Gran more, though."

"I'm sure you do."

"Maybe one day I could introduce you to her," he suggested, an awkwardness to his tone. My cheeks flamed.

"Me, fly up to Riley?" I scoffed. "I'm never letting my feet off this planet again." At his silence, I added, "But she could come down, couldn't she? We could gather at my home, all of us together. You all could meet my family, too."

Even as I spoke those words, my ruined home appeared in my mind. I had no idea if the image were true or merely a figment caused by worry. I had not heard from or about my family since the day Stone Tiran and his soldiers took me away. My thoughts turned to the other offspring spirited from my community that day and Tiran's threat to kill them all if the tribes rose against him. His threats hadn't stopped my people, maybe even spurred them on. How loyal were Tiran's troopers? Would they have murdered children in cold blood when he gave the order?

"Grace?"

"Sorry," I said. "Just thinking."

The passages we followed and had been following were unlike the ones we had found in the past when in other underground places. Those had been cleared by machine and other means rather than environmental and geological processes. This cavern appeared to be crafted only through nature's decree, by ice and water and shifting stone. We had to climb, we had to squeeze, we had to choose between one rock-strewn corridor and another. I continued onward, following the ways outlined in my head through Resa. Led by what seemed a dream, yet Resa moved in the same direction, lured by the same ways. I fought down my dread, the fear we might become forever lost if the dream misled.

"Do you hear that?" Mika asked. We all stopped, listening.

"Sounds like water," Brand said.

Yes, clearly liquid dripping on rock.

Duncan nodded. "I suggest we find it and replenish our containers. Grace?" Deferring to me. Pretending I still led them.

They would be better off without you. You know that.

I squeezed shut my eyes for a moment, resisting the urge to shout out loud at Skelly. "Good idea," I said to Duncan. "Can you tell where it's coming from?"

Brand waved a hand. "This way."

We trailed after him, still in the direction we'd

been headed until we reached a side passage and he paused. "Down there," he said, pointing. The water sang loudly now, splashing from ringing stone to ringing stone.

Duncan spread his hands, gesturing with curled fingers. "Everyone, hand over your containers. Brand and I will go down."

The entrance looked narrow. Brand was small and Duncan leanly built and determined. I nodded in agreement, fetching my container from my pack. The others did the same.

"Be careful," I said.

Duncan lowered his right eyelid in a wink. "Natch."

Metal containers clanking, he and Brand disappeared into the void, the kinetic torch Duncan carried shooting light in all directions as they climbed downward. Eventually, the illumination faded to a glow, the noise disappearing into watery sound. I kept my eyes on the faint light barely visible in the opening. If the small gleam vanished completely, I was going down after them. We all would. I didn't like being separated from Duncan. From any of them. We'd been divided more than once. I refused to risk it happening again.

Mika made a sudden noise, a small exclamation, and darted past me to the narrow tunnel. He crouched before it. "I think I hear Duncan."

I hurried over and dropped down beside him, my scarring thigh protesting such hasty action. "What's he saying?"

"I don't know."

"Duncan!" I called.

Words filtered up from below. I barely heard them over the water.

"I can't understand him," I shot at Mika. "Can you?"

"No." He started to shirk off his pack, preparing to climb down. I put a hand on his arm.

"Wait." I nodded toward the growing light. "They're coming back up."

A minute later, Duncan's head appeared. He scrambled out beside me.

"I think you'll want to see this." He looked around at the others before snatching his pack and Brand's from the cave floor. "I think you'll all want to see this."

To manage the opening, we had to climb with our packs in hand. I took Resa's together with my own and one by one we began a surprisingly easy descent. As we neared the bottom, I spotted Brand with his torch. Small as he was, he still helped everyone down onto the slick, stone floor. I lifted my head. My breath rushed out.

Though insignificant in the vast chamber, the torch light glittered on water sliding over the rock face on all sides except where we stood. The water frothed in a vast pool before us with a thundering echo. Rainbow color arced through the misted air.

"Beautiful, eh?" Duncan whispered.

I nodded, speechless.

"That's not the best of it."

"No?"

"No. Take a breath. A big one."

I did so, and then another. My mouth curved. "That's fresh air."

He grinned. "Yup."

"Where's it coming from?"

"Don't know yet, but we figured you should all come down here so we can go find out."

Suddenly giddy when I'd been so hounded by dark thoughts, I hurried to pass the filled containers to everyone. We donned our packs once more as soon as the water containers had been stowed inside. Together, we faced the direction from which the air appeared to flow. Only then did I consider the path we'd been following above, the one in my head. I spun to look at Resa. She had lost the intent expression she'd been carrying for some time now, and instead had reverted to her usual preoccupied appearance, indicative her inner eye had moved on to some faraway place.

I took her hand in mine. She accepted it. We trailed after the others who had, quite oddly, taken the lead.

Fresh, chill air drew us onward, filled with the scent of snow and open spaces. I found it strange, recognizing snow's particular smell when I had been born and raised in the desert. But we'd been trekking through frozen precipitation for many days except when underground. I suppose I'd become attuned to it.

Beside us, the pool stood dark as ink beneath the high chamber ceiling. We had left the bubbling froth behind and only the occasional ripple on the water's surface reflected the lanterns we carried. My gaze kept straying to the blackness. I imagined I saw things there. Undulating things longer than my body, shimmering yet barely discernible from the darkness around them. Looking straight at the water, I saw nothing. Nothing but the black pool.

"I see them, too."

I glanced at Carina beside me now. She'd whispered as though afraid to speak louder. I looked back to the water.

"Not when you're looking," she said. "When

you're not."

I swore. Duncan glanced over his shoulder, paused, took a step back in our direction.

"Grace, what's wrong?"

I nodded at the water. "There's something in there."

He turned, studied the surface through narrowed lids. "What? What does it look like? What do you think it is?"

"I don't know what it is," I said, tersely, and apologized. "I can't see them directly, but Carina has seen them, too."

"Them?" This, from Mika. He and Brand had joined us. We stood at the water's edge in a tight knot.

Right at the water's edge.

"Back up!" I cried. "Back away!"

Too late.

Chapter Three

Three of them rose up from the murky depths. Three creatures I'd never seen before, never imagined, never dreamed. They possessed long appendages, pale and silky smooth, extending from bodies reminding me of the slugs in my mother's moist, well-tended garden. Slugs crave the wet. They didn't live underwater, though. They never could.

My gaze traveled upward to the creatures' heads. Slugs didn't possess teeth either. These did. Inches in length and needlelike in their opening mouths. We hastened back toward the cave wall, away from the lashing appendages. Not far enough. A curling end caught Carina's leg, yanked her down to the ground and then up into the air. Mika darted forward with the glass cutter from the mines freed from his belt. The thin, brilliant beam sliced through fleshy membrane and whatever lay beneath. I caught Carina as she dropped. A scream filled the air, high-pitched and wordless. Not Carina. She wasn't even wounded.

Resa broke free from her brother and rushed toward the appendages still thrashing the air around us. Resa who moments ago had been unaware of the here and now. Resa who could not hear the screams. Resa who would administer untold damage. She raised her arms. I ran to her, still clutching Carina.

"Stop her," I said. I circled my left arm around Resa's waist as Carina's fingers came down onto her shoulder. Resa slumped. I scooped her up against my hip like a small yet unwieldy sack and hustled both her and Carina back toward the others, where I shoved Resa into her brother's arms.

"Run," I said. "I'll hold them off."

"Not alone," Duncan growled.

"Duncan..."

"Not alone." He passed his sister to Mika and then whipped out both blade and glass cutter. Mika stood a moment in indecision before grabbing Carina's hand and dragging her onward. Brand did not follow. He broke out the odd implement he used for hunting, fitted it with a stone from the cave floor.

"We should back away," he said.

Duncan didn't turn from the creatures' extremities dancing overhead. "What?"

"We ought back away. They're not attacking now."

"But we don't—"

"Are you gonna eat that?" Brand pointed at the severed piece still writhing a bit on the ground and weeping a milky liquid. "No reason to kill 'em if you're not. Back away."

I longed for my absent *lathesa.* I could have diverted the creatures' attention without destroying them. Enough to keep them busy while the others moved on. Brand was right, though. They no longer appeared to be on the offensive. The legs, or whatever they were, slashed through the air but made no move to pluck one of us up as they had Carina, nor did the massive bodies move nearer. Perhaps Mika's defense had been enough to warn them off. Or perhaps violence had never been their intent.

"Brand," I said, "your gift is weather and animals, right?"

"Aye," he answered.

"Can you read these creatures? Do you know what they're after?"

"Never seen the likes. Could be tryin' to figure out what we are. Could be curious. Could be hungry. I can't imagine they get much meat down here."

"Not making me feel any better," said Duncan.

"Keep your eyes on them," I said, "and back away, like Brand says."

We did so, heading to where Mika, Carina and Resa waited. The creatures dropped into the water and followed, again only visible peripherally in a perplexing camouflage. I heard them now, though, moving through the black pool, a liquid susurration. Soon, it began to sound like voices, or something did, but not a language I understood.

"Can anyone else hear that?" I asked.

Mika frowned. "Hear what?"

"The voices," said Brand. "I hear 'em, too."

Duncan glanced toward the water. "From in there?"

"Maybe," I said. "I think so. Carina, do you hear anything?"

She shook her head, her transmutable eyes blazing yellow as flame.

"What are they saying?" Duncan persisted.

I swallowed, listening harder. "I don't know."

"It could be water and echoes tricking the mind, couldn't it?"

"I suppose," I said.

"But it's not, is it?"

"No."

Duncan swore, paired words that made me grin. It felt odd to my face, grinning, as though scowling had become a permanent expression this past day or two. Quite possibly for longer. Longer than we'd been in this cave system. Longer than our march from Trill, or our time in the City of All Dwellers.

"It's all right," I said, pushing down the dismay threatening to return. "Animals communicate. You know that. Maybe what Brand suggested about them being curious is true. We must keep moving though. We can't let them distract us. We—"

"Watch out!"

With a huge, sucking noise, the creatures rose from the water again, this time appearing taller, bigger, rounder than before. How was that possible? The shortened appendage on the one had already healed. My right arm came up, fist clenching in remembered grasp around an absent weapon. Hand empty, I opened it palm out, willing the rosy light to appear. A heatless flickering grew into a massive ball, illuminating the creatures, the water, the cave walls behind with pink hue. The color calmed me somehow. Not so the unnamed creatures. They reeled back in what appeared to be fear.

"Keep moving," I hissed over my shoulder at the others.

"Grace—"

"Keep. Moving."

I focused on the creatures now they were upright and visible, and backed away, following the shuffling made by everyone's footgear behind me. Why hadn't I seen this danger? Sensed it, somehow, with my newfound gifts? What use was the burden of mage without any assurances? I would gladly have given it all back to be what once I had been.

You were always this, Skelly whispered. As usual, in crisis I had forgotten him. I pulled my mind away.

"Grace, come on!"

"Right. Coming," I called back to Duncan, realizing my feet had stopped. Something hypnotic existed in the appendages' movements, as though they wove words into the air the way Resa did with her fingers and hands. It seemed the patterns were meant to tell me something. I didn't know how to listen, though.

Fingers closed around my arm. Duncan. The pale light in my hand went out.

"Now, Grace!"

Yanking me hard, he pulled me to where the others had momentarily paused. Once beside them, we all moved as swiftly as we could manage on the damp stone. The creatures kept pace in the water, darkly shimmering at the corner of the eye. Brand muttered something. Duncan reacted to it with uncharacteristic savagery in his tone.

"They're not hurting us yet but they damn well will!"

"Not hurt," Brand snapped back. "Herd. They're herding us."

I whipped my head around to the dark pool. The instant I did, the gigantic, slug-like beasts rose again, liquid dripping almost musically onto the water below from their pale, fleshy bodies, the waving limbs.

"They look like they'd pop if you squeezed them," Duncan said in disgust.

"Maybe they would," said Mika, "but I'm not interested in finding out."

"Stay here," I instructed and darted back the way we'd come. Immediately, the creatures shot forward, their membranous limbs flung across my path. Dodging the nearest, I hurried back to the others.

"You're right, Brand," I said. "Herding us is exactly what they're doing. They don't want us to turn around But, to what end?"

Brand shrugged.

"I know you don't have an answer. I'm only trying to make sense of their behavior. We were heading this way, anyway. They had only to follow us, or snatch us all at once."

"You may be counting on an intelligence they don't actually possess," Mika said.

"No matter what," Duncan interrupted, "we can't stand here doing nothing. I still smell fresh air. We keep going, but be prepared to fight them if we have to. Yes?"

"Yes," I said with a short nod.

We rushed on. The slimy beasts dropped into the water and dogged our movements, the strange communication between them continuing. Mika and Duncan took turns carrying Resa, who had not yet wakened. At Mika's side, Carina's eyes constantly sought the water. Her iris was now so black the pupils had disappeared. One by one, we lost our footing on the slick stone, regained it. The creatures matched their undulating, swimming pace to ours.

"I thought this was just an underground pool," Duncan whispered. "It seems to be a lake."

I grunted agreement, still catching the low shimmer moving alongside us beneath the water. Under our feet the rock was unusually smooth, like glass, its slippery surface an impediment to faster forward momentum. The path neither rose nor dropped but ran on a level course. I feared it might end before we ever reached the place from which the fresh air flowed. End and leave us stranded in a place we could not defend. Those things had multiple limbs and unknown intent. I didn't even have a weapon. Not one I trusted. Not one I understood.

Abruptly, I held my hand out to Duncan. "Let me have your dagger."

He eyed me sidelong, his hesitance minimal, but there. Still distrustful deep inside, my Duncan. A little piece of my heart peeled away.

After all you've been through, Skelly said with more than a little sarcasm.

A breath rushed out my nose. "Enough."

"You're not talking to me, are you?" Duncan asked as he removed the glass dagger from its makeshift sheath.

"No," I said. "Sorry."

"So am I." He laid the wrapped handle across my palm. The blade, a jagged, hefty piece from the glass mines, glittered in the light from the torches. I swung it in my grasp, making the air whistle. Duncan shied away and then returned, nodding at me, mouth curved.

"You've always been a little bit scary, Grace," he said. "You know that, right?"

Dolt, Skelly muttered.

I forced a smile back at Duncan. "I'll try not to be as scary as I've been recently, okay?"

He bumped his elbow against mine. "Sounds good."

In time, the stone path narrowed, forcing us to go single file. The rock wall to our right rose straight up four or five times my height, ending at a shadowed ledge, hidden in darkness. Though not smooth, the sides showed no visible handholds. I dropped back.

Duncan took the lead. Everyone had their weapons out. Brand handed Carina several stones from the bag he carried on his belt. Her aim with a thrown stone could be as accurate and effective as his slingshot. He had promised to make Carina one of her own. When we reached the outside world again.

Brand was odd, and kind, and brave. My gratitude for his presence among our group surged. We would survive this. We would all survive this. I swore it, in my heart, in the very fiber of my being.

You saved me once, but in the end it wasn't enough.

I swallowed, blinked back unexpected tears. I had a sudden image of Skelly, what was left of him, back on Emerald. Inside my head he began to scream.

I'm sorry, I said. He didn't stop. He couldn't stop. My mind filled with the noise. Blocked out the acoustic vibrations around me from my friends, from the water and the creatures trailing us. I felt Skelly's brutal cries surging through my very blood. Felt them moving through tendon and sinew and muscle. I clamped my teeth together, fighting their escape. Pain and fury threatened to rip me apart. My head tipped back. Raw emotion choked me. Vision dimmed and my body went rigid. My mouth opened wide, releasing Skelly's agony into the cavern. The creatures from the black lake rushed in to take me down.

Duncan

Chapter Four

It happened so fast. The scream startled us all, stole precious time. My heart rebooted as I spun with the glass cutter glowing, but Grace was already gone. So were the creatures, the only sign they'd been stalking us the eddying ripples on the dark surface.

"Grace!"

My shout echoed back at me. I ran to the water's edge where last I'd seen her, jerked my arms free from my coat, swapping my weapon from one hand to the other while I did. Fingers tugged my sleeve. Turning, I found Resa at my side. I glanced around for Carina to retrieve her. I had no time for this.

"I'm going in," I said to no one in particular. I didn't care who listened or didn't. I needed to get Grace back. I needed to save her. Kicking my coat away, I prepared to dive. Carina's voice cut through.

"Don't!"

She grabbed my arm. I shook her off and leaped in a clumsy arc into the cold, cold water. Blackness surrounded me. Beneath the surface there was no visibility at all. I rose with a gasp, shook the hair from my eyes, whirled toward the yelling I heard from the pathway. Suddenly, I rocketed into the air. Resa's name tore from my throat in a strangled cry.

Far below me the lake's water was pushing back, swirling away on a cyclone wind, curled like a living wall. Unlike the pathway, the lake bed was neither smooth nor unobstructed, but filled with jagged, giant rock. No sign of Grace. No sign of the creatures.

Spinning in the updraft, I jerked my head around again and again, checking the turbulent water wall for them. Each time I spun, I spotted Carina beside my sister, clearly undecided. If she halted Resa's actions now, those rocks below spelled death for me. Dropping from this height, I couldn't imagine it ending any other way.

It occurred to me Carina must have read Resa's intentions. Why else would she have tried to stop me following Grace into the water? Now I was stuck, and Grace had vanished.

"Grace!" I called again. Desperately. Stupidly. The word got snatched away in the powerful air currents. I caught sight of something pink before I was spun away again. Those things were sort of pink. A sickly, fleshy gray-pink. I glimpsed them in the arcing tide pushing toward the direction we had been headed, not circling ceilingward with the water behind. When I cycled back around on the whirlwind, I no longer saw them.

"Hell's bells," I ground out, a Gran saying I hadn't thought about in years, let alone uttered. I didn't even know what it meant. With a grunt, I shifted my body, spread my arms, attempted to move downward against the pulsing atmosphere. Little by little, I made my way, losing ground and fighting for it again. Carina stood with her hands to her mouth and away from Resa. Mika and Brand seemed to be encouraging me, waving their arms, and calling out with words shredded by the wind.

I worried my slow progress wouldn't be enough. Resa would change her mind the way she did, and I would drop like a weighted sack onto the rocks below before the water could rush back in to cushion my fall. Although it might drown me. There was always that possibility. It seemed the likelihood might arrive sooner rather than later.

I heard the rushing water before I saw it, and certainly before I felt it. The huge wave slapped me with such force I found myself flying head over heels, heading for the gods knew what. Not down. I understood that much and braced myself, covering my head with my arms. If I managed to get up when I landed, I needed my brain intact.

Somehow, I hit something softer than stone before impact, allowing me to thump down with only a few bones jarred. I glanced around dazedly for the others and spotted them huddled together at a distance, so far away I couldn't make out expressions. Their faces were nothing more than indistinct ovals in the light from the kinetic torches. How had I landed here? Wherever here was. Not in the water. I heard nothing but a few last drips from my clothing after the lake crashed back into its boundaries. That, and my companions rushing nearer, calling out. I felt a little dizzy. They might have been shouting *run*.

Bloody hell.

"Language," said a voice.

I realized I'd spoken aloud. I also realized whose voice it was chastising me. I jerked around and to my feet, swaying where I stood.

"Ren!" I shouted and threw myself at him, wrapping an arm around his neck. My friends hadn't been shouting 'run.' They'd been shouting Ren. Ren, whom I'd hated upon the instant I'd met him. Maybe not hated, but I sure as heck held no liking for him. Those emotions had changed after the glass mines.

"How did you get here?" I demanded, holding him at arm's length. He looked somewhat battered. I wondered if it had been his body I'd struck on my way to the ground.

"The long way around," he said. "Well, apparently not as long as your way. Over the top and down again."

I stepped away, trying to wrap my mind around that piece of info, forcing it aside for the immediate as my head cleared. "We have to find Grace! Those things in the water took her."

"She's fine," Ren said, jerking a thumb over his shoulder. "She got out of the water back there."

I stepped away, looked past him where I saw nothing but darkness. "I don't understand. Did you…did you make them let her go? How did you know where to find us?"

He shook his head. "Not me. Long story. I don't even know how to begin. You all just need to follow me. Can I borrow your light? I almost broke my neck back there."

Grateful to know Grace was all right, I handed over my torch, which had somehow remained strapped to my wrist.

The other four caught up, exclaiming at finding Ren among us once more. Except Resa, of course. Yet she looked at him, really looked at him, and I would say there was recognition before she disappeared back into her own mind. No one asked the obvious question. Not even me.

But I thought it. Was Hannah with him?

Brand handed me my discarded coat. I shoved my arms into it gratefully. Although the water soaking the rest of what I wore had been stripped away by the buffeting winds, I shivered in my damp clothing. I expected Grace would be in no better condition. Without wood to build a fire, we wouldn't find any relief.

The lights danced over cave walls uneven and slick with moisture. Ren trudged ahead, favoring his right leg a little. Again, I wondered if my impetus had been slowed by a collision with him. My good luck and a very strange coincidence. I don't know if I'd have survived otherwise.

The Universe. The Universe didn't want me checking out quite yet.

Ren glanced back. "Those beasts of yours. The *conjures*. They're waiting outside the caverns."

My lips curled up. Grace would be thrilled. She'd bonded not only with Chauncy, but with every *conjure* we'd come in contact with.

Behind me, Carina finally asked the question. Probably because she could sense it loudly bouncing around in my head.

"Ren, is Hannah with you?"

Hannah the betrayer, I wanted to add. I brought myself up short. I'd been guilty of betrayal once, too. I'd been forgiven.

"Yeah," Ren answered. "She's with Grace."

"How'd you get away from the soldiers?" Mika questioned him. With suspicion, I thought. Couldn't blame him there. It seemed unlikely he, Hannah and Valeah would have eluded capture. Not in the vulnerable position I'd last seen them. I slowed my pace, waiting on the answer.

"As soon as you disappeared, Valeah led us back the way we'd come. We just managed to get away without being seen. After, we gathered supplies and headed out."

Something didn't sound quite right. "Is Valeah with you?"

"No. She stayed behind with her family. Things are not good in Landing, as you know."

Of course, I knew. We'd known as soon as we'd arrived. I persisted in my interrogation. "How did you know where to go? Where to find us?"

"We didn't."

I stopped dead. Brand stumbled right into me. "I don't understand," I said.

Ren halted, too. Spun to face me. "You don't listen, do you? The *conjures*. They came up to us outside the gates. Hannah insisted we go with them. I mean, they weren't about to let us do otherwise, but okay, it was a smart move."

"They brought you to us?"

"Pretty much. To the outside entrance to this place. The rest we had to manage on our own."

"And how, exactly, did you manage that?" Mika drawled.

Ren's yellow brows arched at Mika's tone. He smirked. Same old Ren, despite everything. Closing his eyes as if he'd reached an end to his patience, he shook his head and pivoted on his heel. "Quit stalling. Let's go."

I looked around, exchanged glances with the others. They nodded silently. We went on.

I'm not sure how far we walked. The further we went, the more I wondered how Ren had happened to find me, moving through the dark the way he'd been. There was much I didn't understand. I supposed he could have seen the torch I'd managed to hold onto. Watertight, it had remained alight. Fine. He'd been moving in the *near*-darkness, then, over a slick surface with Resa's whirlwinds racing through the cave, water spiraling everywhere and echoing, cacophonous sound. Easy-peasy. Sure. I believed that.

"Look, Ren," I said to the back of his head. "How did you come to be at the right place at the right time when I came plummeting down?"

Ren spun once again, walking backward now. He lifted a hand and pointed. At Resa. "Her," he said.

My mouth dropped. "What?"

"She's in my head. I want her out."

Ren had always been afraid of my sister. His eyes glinted with something more than fear, though. Anger? Very likely. And a bit of desperation. I would have given anything to have Resa in my head. For a little while, at least. I might understand her better. Know her better. Know her at all.

"I don't have any way to do that," I told Ren. "Maybe Carina—"

"No," he interrupted. "Not yet. I don't remember how I got here, exactly. I need help getting back."

Turning, he stalked onward, holding my torch high above his head in an arrogant, Ren-like display. I frowned at his back as I followed, my thoughts on Resa and this latest manifestation of her so-called gifts. If she'd done something like this before, I had no awareness. How could I? So much about my sister remained a mystery to me. Carina and Grace possessed closer, more secure relationships with her than I did. Or could.

I felt a sudden grip on my fist, forcing it open. I

looked down, saw Carina pressing my sister's fingers into my own. Using both hands, she closed mine around Resa's and stepped away, giving me a nod, a smile. Carina, stealer of thoughts. Or at least, a spy on them. I thanked her.

We followed Ren along the smooth rock shore. The water lay still beside it. No monsters beneath the surface. The ripples from the water's crashing into its basin had vanished, too. The lake reflected our lights like a dark mirror.

"What are those things that grabbed Grace?" I asked.

Ren barely turned his head to respond. "Beats me."

I found no comfort in his answer.

"Don't make me regret being happy to see you," I muttered at his back.

"Stuff it, Oaks."

Yeah, liking this less and less. In my bandaged hand, I grasped the glass cutter tightly, having clung to it even after landing. The tool had hit the rock pretty hard though. I had my doubts the thing would activate again, especially given its dunking. I hoped I was wrong. My only other weapon, the blade made from a narrow chunk of mine glass, I'd given to Grace. I had no idea if she'd managed to hold onto it.

"What are we walking into?" Mika whispered, having come up beside me.

"Dunno. Be ready, though."

He grunted at the obvious. Carina stood directly behind him, Brand at her side. Very small for their ages, the two of them. Resa, too. It seemed like an odds-beating kind of thing. Something the gamblers back on Riley would have loved to bet against, how many short kids they'd likely find in a group of misfits fleeing across the lands.

Carina's hand shot up and buffeted my sleeve in a sharp slap. Right. How could I possibly forget her mental eavesdropping? No one reacted to Carina's slapping me. To be honest, I barely felt it. So, we trudged on, silently, warily. Ren dropped his hand with the light to his side, bouncing his shadow across rock and beneath his feet. Always the lake at our left, a narrower passage now, easier to see across as the cave walls on the opposite side closed in, reflecting our lights. Reflecting us.

I continued to scent fresh air, sharper now, overriding the water-smell. Silvery drops came down from the ceiling, plopping onto the surface and sending out ripples. I eyed the ripples with misgiving, not trusting they were merely that. Brand spoke.

"Hear voices," he said. "You?"

He had keen ears, Brand did. He and Grace had mentioned hearing voices from the watery depths before. From those creatures. I halted, peered hard at the tapering lake.

"No," said Brand, spotting where I looked. "Ahead."

The bouncing water droplets confused sound for me. Still, I turned front, listening. Yes, I heard them now, too. "How far?"

Brand shrugged.

"How far?" I said again, louder, directing my question to Ren. He either didn't hear me or didn't want to be bothered answering. Resa tugged my hand. I glanced down and found her eyes, dark brown eyes, eyes like our father's, staring straight up at me. She tugged again and picked up her pace, dragging me along. I decided not to thwart her by digging my heels in. She knew things I didn't.

"Where are you going?" Ren asked as we passed him. The others followed on my heels, leaving him to trot to catch up.

"Don't you know?" Mika mumbled. "I thought Resa was in your head."

Lifting my hand, I activated the cutter. Or tried to. Clearly, it had been damaged, either by the water or impact. Hopefully it only needed to dry out. "Weapons ready. And could someone give me a replacement for this thing?"

No one had put their weapons away. They all still clutched whatever they possessed or, in Carina's case, been given. Mika handed me his glass blade and stored my broken cutter in his belt. I supposed he planned to try repairing the cutter from the mine at some point. Physician's son and thief of fine machinery, he could probably figure it out. Given enough time.

"Enough time for what?" Mika asked.

I glanced aside at him. "Was I talking out loud again?"

"Yep."

"Sorry. It was nothing."

His brows dipped into a frown, but he returned his attention to what appeared to be our destination, a fissure in the stone through which a faint glow shone. Sunlight or lantern, I couldn't tell. The light was rather dull, despite the darkness surrounding us. I supposed our own lamps discharged enough illumination to keep the narrow, uneven line—like a crack in the midnight sky—looking minimal. The voices Brand and I had been hearing took on a certain clarity the closer we got, like wind and words together.

Ren hustled back into the lead. "Almost there.

Hurry up now."

He really hadn't changed. He'd shown himself braver, yes, and kinder, too, but basically, he remained a pompous ass.

"Or maybe he's just struggling to prove he's not what you think," Carina whispered.

My face contorted. "Not likely, and stay out of my brainwaves, Carina." Making a small noise like a nasal bird, she dropped back a little and said nothing more. "Sorry," I apologized after a moment.

"No worries," Mika responded for her. Interesting. She must be quite angry. Or hurt. I felt bad about both, but not that bad. She really had to stop listening in on my thoughts. For some reason, she zeroed in on mine more than anyone else's. Or considered herself freer to comment on them.

Looking again at Ren hurrying before us, presumably still at Resa's direction, I wondered if Resa had developed or learned this ability from her time with Carina, how to delve into someone's thinking. I didn't think she'd had it before, but what did I know? In truth, Carina didn't project herself into someone's head and manipulate them. She merely heard thoughts in full context or drew conclusions from what she sensed there. I glanced down at Resa at my side. My chest pinched. Would I ever understand my sister? Should we all be more afraid?

Ren halted and turned. "Okay, I know where we are now. Can you make her stop?"

I shrugged a shoulder. Resa wriggled her hand from my fingers. Ren's mouth twisted, his eyelids tightened and loosened before opening wide. I heard his exhalation where I stood.

"Better?" I asked.

He nodded. "Yeah. Thanks."

"I didn't do anything.," I said. "But you're welcome."

"Got it." He jerked his head. "Through here."

The light from the fissure cut along the stone, brighter now and revealing an uneven, narrow tunnel leading toward it. Ren climbed in. I stayed close to him, worried, wanting to give the others a chance to flee back toward the lake, if necessary. Brand took the rear. Ren stayed resolutely silent, feeling his way along. Checking his footing. Never once looking behind. Typical Ren behavior, and yet...

Without warning, a visible, pearly force blasted along the walls and straight into us all. What light there had been vanished as surely as though I'd gone blind. Later, possibly a long time later, I heard swearing and opened my eyes again. It occurred to me the rapid-fire speech came from my mouth and nowhere else. Except for my breathless expletives, all was silence.

Lurching forward, I snatched a fallen torch and raised it high, checking on my companions. Ren didn't move. Behind me, I spotted Brand pushing up from the ground. He reached a hand to Carina, who startled as if she'd been shocked from some strange state. She immediately reached for Resa, who had managed to get up onto all fours. I poked Mika. He grunted and sat. Okay. Awake, all of them. I scurried over to Ren, touched his neck. His hand whipped up and shoved mine away. Fine. Conscious, too.

"Is everyone okay?" I asked quietly. Whatever that had been, I didn't want to instigate a repeat performance. "Ren, what was that?"

"I...don't know."

"Stay here."

Ren opened his mouth. "Don't argue with me," I

said. "I mean it." Climbing over him, I headed toward the opening.

About two strides away—not el strides, which was an Emerald measurement, but the length of my own—I became aware of breathing. Harsh, rapid breathing. The way it echoed caused me to glance around, but I remained alone. For once, Ren had listened to me. He had gone to the others, who were still struggling to regain perception. I crept forward into the light from beyond, glass dagger in hand.

I saw Grace first, standing immobile on the opposite side of the boulder strewn floor. Her brown face was pale as sand, the tattooed symbol on her cheekbone a dark slash, her green eyes sunken in shadow. Beside her, Hannah's condition was no better. I didn't need Mika's opinion on this one. Shock. They were in shock. Before darting across to them, I followed Grace's gaze in prudent search for the cause. My lungs emptied.

What I thought had been rocks were bodies. Dozens of bodies. Dead? I didn't know and didn't wait to make a determination. I rushed around and over them, straight for Grace. When I grabbed her, she crumpled. Wrestling her upright, fingers digging into her upper arms, I shook her repeatedly, calling her name.

"Stop," she finally gasped. "I'm okay."

I turned to Hannah next, eased her onto the ground. She dropped her head forward between her knees and drew a deep breath. Assured she wouldn't pass out, I returned to Grace. "What happened here? Who are these people? Are they—?"

"Dead? No. At least, I don't think so." She tossed my hand from her arm and strode forward. Bending to the nearest, she touched the face, felt the throat for a pulse, and straightened before moving onto the next. I followed after her.

"What are you doing?"

"Checking to make sure they still live," she whispered.

"How did they get this way? Did you see?" My mind went to the energy pulse, wondering if the thing that had made it lingered nearby, if it might be the creatures from the lake. I had not seen them. Water lay quiet and black beyond a low rock wall close to where I'd located the girls. Clearly it had been formed by hand not nature. I assumed the water was from the same underground system.

Crouched beside an inert form, Grace looked up at me. Her green eyes shone in the illumination filling the rock chamber. The light came from a source I couldn't locate, making shadows deeper and more confusing. The stark horror in Grace's expression sliced knife-like through my guts. She took my fingers in her frigid digits, squeezed them, let them go.

"I did this, Duncan. Me."

Chapter Five

My ability for speech abandoned me. With a narrow-eyed look at my open, silent mouth, Grace returned to checking for life signs. More than two dozen bodies remained to be examined. I trailed beside her, stooping, and then standing once a pulse was found. The others came through into the chamber as we worked. Ren ran to Hannah. Mika joined Grace and me in our efforts. Brand and Carina just stared, open-mouthed, Resa at Carina's side. Shock still had me in its grip. Grace had done this. Grace.

I noted something about the unconscious as I moved along in Grace's wake. Something unusual. There was not a male in the bunch. Every one female. Every one armed. "Grace," I said, glancing about to be sure no one had yet started to rise, "who are these people?"

She paused, looked up, looked away. "I don't know."

"How did you—"

"I don't know."

I studied her ashen face, lowered my voice. "Why did you?"

Her shoulders slumped, caving in on themselves.

"Fear. Anger."

The clipped syllables reverberated through my head like the massive bell in a tower in Citadel I knew no longer existed. I had seen it fall. I had heard the bell's final echoes. Grace's response stunned me no less. I dropped down onto one knee at her side.

"There are only a few more to check," I said. "I'm sure they're all fine. We should get going. Now."

She shook her head, lurching away from my hand on her arm. "No. You should go. They came for me. I have to find out what I can."

"Then I stay as well, Grace. You know that." I stood, bumping my elbow right into someone else. I whipped around and found Mika there.

"We all stay," he said. "Well, maybe not those two." He tipped his head at Ren and Hannah. "Up to them."

Grace rose, too. "You can't."

I stared at her in silence before turning to signal the others to come nearer. I explained to them quickly what had taken place, Grace's part in it, her half-baked plan to engage in conversation the armed warriors she'd just attacked.

"Duncan," Grace growled warningly. I ignored her.

"Grace does have to stay," Ren said.

"What?" I nearly sputtered. "What are you talking about?"

Ren raised his hand and pointed at my sister. Again.

"She told you? In words?"

"Not words, so much. Ask her."

"How?"

Ren frowned. "The finger-hand thing. Have you forgotten?"

I swore. The reminder irked. I caught Resa's attention and began to ask about her bringing Ren to us, about the creatures, about Grace staying in this place, about anything I could. Probably too quickly. Probably without making sense. Resa's gaze grew frantic. Her hands came up. Not to answer me. I dropped to my knees and took her fingers in my own, drew her close until we were eye to eye. Slowly, I spoke to her, hoping she would get the gist from facial expression, if nothing else.

"I'm sorry, Resa. It doesn't matter. We'll figure this out later." Twisting at the waist, I looked back at Grace. "We're staying with you, Grace. No argument."

She said nothing, her eyes on something behind us.

"Grace?"

"They're waking up," she stated. "Follow me."

With purpose, her agility returned to her. She leapt over the nearest warrior and headed toward the place I'd found her and Hannah. She stayed away from the water and instead took a stance with the wall at her back. We followed, arraying ourselves beside her. On the floor, the warriors turned, groaned, sat up. Some even stood. No one looked at us. Not yet. They appeared dazed. As we had been, and we'd had thick stone between us and the force of whatever Grace had thrown at them.

Light in the cavern grew. I jerked my head up. Sunshine poured like liquid over a lip in the rock far above. Beside me, Mika stirred. He exhaled and whispered something I didn't catch.

"Mika?"

"Look," he said.

The water creatures had returned, standing up

from the surface and reflecting the sunlight. In that reflection, I witnessed far more than I had before. Beneath the gelatinous, gray-pink, mounded, and misshapen flesh, existed something else. A form not dissimilar to ours. Genderless at this distance, but legs, torso, arms, heads with eyes that watched us.

"I feel awful," Mika said.

"For what?"

"Cutting off its arm."

My stomach turned. Only a little. Unlike the rest, I'd been involved in the battle at Trill. I'd seen a lot that day.

So, there we stood, these creatures on the one side and nearly thirty warriors in front. They turned to face us, the warriors did, weapons at their sides, expressions wary. Good. A little caution on their part was what we needed. Beside me, Grace drew a deep, slow breath. Her head lifted. She shook the damp hair back from her face with a small movement. The warriors waited. As they should. They'd all just been laid out across the cave floor by…by whatever Grace had done to them. I eyed Grace's profile in curiosity and wonder.

"Stop staring," she whispered before taking a step forward.

The warriors shifted, backed away, more as though they prepared for the unexpected rather than planned to run. Those in our group who possessed weapons still held them, but we'd lowered them, without thought, without discussion. I raised mine again, tightening my grip.

Grace spoke. "I'm sorry if I harmed any of you. I had not intended to do so."

Okay. Not what I'd anticipated. I straightened my spine, eyeballed the female warriors arrayed in what I realized now was a semi-circle. Good positioning for an attack. I had to give them that. One made her way forward. Carefully. Limping. Crap.

She looked old. Well, not *old*-old. Maybe my mother's age. So, at least old enough to know better than to put herself in the direct line of Grace's fire. And yet she kept coming. Grace watched her. I saw Grace's tongue poke out for a quick swipe at her lip. She glanced at me and away.

What do you want me to do? I thought at her in a desperate, silent, mental shout. Because I really didn't know. Grace didn't hear me like that, though. Carina did, and sidled closer. I shot her a look and told her to stay, like a disobedient pet. She narrowed her eyes at me but stopped behind Mika. Dutifully, she held tight to Resa. I would always be grateful to Carina for my sister's care. Always. If we survived this, I would tell her.

"Thank you," she whispered.

I met her mutable eyes and nodded, then swung around to focus again on the woman approaching.

She dressed in an odd assortment of clothing, looking to me like a combination of the Sisters who had once cared for Resa and the residents of Trill. A belted, gown-type thing covered her to mid-thigh. Below it she wore trousers and boots. Warm boots to protect the feet in the harsh mountain climate. The quilting inside folded over the outer layer. Her cloak had been manufactured from animal hair. I recognized the make, shorn from a beast, then felted. The man who was my father had worn something similar, but lined with fur. I looked to the others with her. All were dressed similarly. All kept a weapon sheathed in their belts while holding another in their hands. A strange kind of thing. I couldn't quite make out what it might be. Still, I had no doubt it would be deadly.

The warrior stopped a short distance away. The others with her remained where they stood. Brave, this woman, or else foolish. Beneath a hood her hair had a color like dust. She met Grace's gaze.

"You are newly come to your power," the woman said.

Grace's right shoulder gave a jerk. She swallowed. I heard it. "What makes you think so?" She sounded defiant, fearless, and yes, maybe a little uncertain. I figured I recognized the last because I knew Grace so well. I only hoped the warrior did not notice.

No such luck. The woman's brow furrowed and her mouth twisted. Whether in amusement or impatience I could only guess. She took another step nearer. "Grace Irese," she said.

Oh, hell. Not someone who knew who we were again.

I held my breath, tightened my grip on the glass blade, my eyes shifting to take in the other warriors. I was fed up with strangers knowing who we were, hunting us, casting a net that always caught more than the three from the supposed prophecy. For designs of their own. Nothing more. Still, I was glad we'd all been captured together. I never wanted to be separated from Grace, from my sister, from Carina. We belonged together, all of us. And yet at times we had been split up. Violently and with deadly intent.

"Enough already," I said. Out loud. Bad habit. I didn't care.

The woman's head snapped in my direction. "You do not speak."

"Oh, yes I do," I answered. "Clearly, I do. You just heard me."

Grace hissed something through her teeth. Two words: *shut up*. Not this time, Grace.

An object sped through the air, slicing it, whistling. Almost before I registered the sound Grace's hand had come up. A thin, needle-like blade vibrated in her closed fist, red blood trickling from the flesh.

The woman whirled about with a harsh word. One I didn't recognize. The girl she addressed bowed her head nearly to her chest and remained in that position. More slowly, the dusty-haired woman turned to face Grace again. She most definitely commanded this lot. I could see that now.

"My apologies for the actions of my daughter," she said. To Grace, not me. "She will be duly punished."

Grace opened her fingers, flipped the narrow blade around and handed it to me. I shoved it in my belt. She wiped the blood from her hand on her trousers, leaving a rusty smear. I don't think I'd ever seen her look so hard-edged. Almost cold, like stone. She addressed the woman standing before her.

"You know who I am. You probably know who we all are. I would have your name now."

Even her voice sounded different. Emotionless. Scary. Blood continued to drip from her hand. One, two, three tiny drops, falling to the wet stone at her feet. I recalled the almost invisible movement that had snatched the blade from the air. Inches from my face. Dragging my gaze from Grace, I returned it to the warriors in their half-circle.

"Neala," the woman said. "My name is Neala. I am chieftain of my people."

"And who are your people?" I asked. I should have remained silent. Not a single eye turned my way.

Neala's daughter, head still bowed, snorted into her cloak. Grace sucked in a short breath and let it out.

"Who are your people?" Grace echoed. Behind her, our companions remained silent. Apparently, they were smarter than I was proving myself to be.

"We are the Fianna," said Neala. "Surely, you have heard of us."

I opened my mouth to say no, but Grace lifted a blood-smeared finger from her side in warning, stealing the word from my tongue. I chomped my teeth together, waiting.

"I have," Grace said. "In tales. Legends. Myths from a time long ago."

Neala stared at her, saying nothing. I leaned closer to Grace and whispered a question, hoping not to have another blade flung at my head. "Who are the Fianna?"

Grace turned her head slightly toward me, keeping her eye on Neala and the others. "An ancient female warrior race, come from another world, or so the stories go. They died out, longer ago than history can clearly recount. I've never believed the tales."

"Maybe you should," I said. "Think about it. How many others have we found out were true?"

Grace's glance lashed at me like a dagger. I almost ducked. But then her gaze softened, became thoughtful. She nodded, turned back to the warriors. "Neala," she called, "have you proof of your claim?"

The woman's ashy-blond brows lifted. The sunlight struck her eyes. She winced, drew her hood closer. "Come with us," she said, "and I will show you."

"I don't like the sounds of that," Ren muttered.

"Wait," I said, wheeling to face Neala directly. I didn't care if I got skewered. I needed an answer. I jerked a thumb at the creatures still standing in the water to our right. "Did you send them to attack us?" Something I couldn't understand gnawed at me.

"It becomes obvious you do not know your place," Neala said. "But I will answer you. No."

"To bring us to you, then," I persisted.

"No. The *prair* are their own. They do not communicate with or obey the directives of my people."

"Whose then?"

Neala's daughter lifted her head. "Mother, why do you bother responding to him?"

Neala spat a word at her. Her daughter dipped her chin again. I turned and looked at Resa, wondering at Ren's story, about Resa being in his head. Was this somehow all her doing? Or was it a misunderstanding? Maybe even an illusion? Could these grotesquely formed creatures be responsible?

I turned back to Neala, my head spinning. "Who can command them? Is there someone?"

"As I said, the *prair* are their own."

Not an answer, Neala, I thought.

"How many are there?" I pressed.

"The underground lakes are filled with them."

Neala's daughter glanced up again at her mother's answer and smirked at me. I could only imagine what my face displayed at hearing there were more than these three. "Can they leave the water?" I asked.

The warrior woman took her time in answering. "They have in the past."

I had a bad feeling about this. A godsawful bad feeling. "Then we will come with you," I said.

Grace gasped, probably remembering the time I shouted out 'sanctuary' back in The Wilds. Me, making snap decisions for us all. That hadn't turned out well. But this time was different. This time—

Water surged across my boots, roared through the air, thundered down on us all. Neala's warriors turned as one to face the lake, their boots hitting stone with a unified sound. Blindly, I reached back, snatched my sister's hand from Carina's.

"Run!" I shouted.

Yeah. This time, it was different. This time I wasn't wrong.

Chapter Six

They moved fast, the creatures, considering their bulk and buoyancy's lack on land. They also made a noise that unnerved me despite the adrenaline coursing through my blood. I didn't look back to view their locomotion. I imagined it was quite as nightmarish as it sounded.

I soon realized about half the warriors had turned around to face them, the rest surrounding us as we raced through bucking shadows. Neala was not among them. She had taken up a stance with her warriors. I visualized her staggered gait and slowed my own. Grace had already done so, turning, nearly coming to a halt. I knew what was in her mind.

"Grace, if we split up, the rest go on with this lot, and who knows what their intent is."

"But I can defend Neala and the others from the beasts."

"How can you be sure? Do you even know how you leveled these warriors? Or if it would work again? On those things? Sorry. Being practical here."

And yet I had stopped, too.

Beside me, Grace drew a glass blade from her belt—my glass blade—and swiped it through the air.

"There are other ways."

Without her *lathesa* she had no other weapon. She could physically fight even weaponless, tossing people left and right with annoying ease and order. But these creatures? I doubted it.

"Okay, then," I said, my tone grim even to my own ears. "Let's go lend a hand."

"No!"

I spun around to find Ren behind me.

"No," he repeated. "That's what they want."

"Who?" I asked. "The Fianna ladies?"

Someone nearby growled. I'd spoken without thinking. Perhaps insulted them. They'd shuffled to a halt, too, the warriors. Neala's daughter was not with them. She had remained by her mother's side.

"The *prair*," Ren said. "That's what she called them, yes? The *prair* want us all back there. They know we won't let you go alone. They want us all. Well, most of us."

"Where are you getting this info?"

"I don't know. I can't be sure. But we can't go back there."

I frowned at him. "Then you stay with the others. Keep them safe. Grace and I—"

Once again, I found myself interrupted. By Carina.

"No," she said. "Ren is right. I know, too. In here." She tapped her temple.

What were they saying? These creatures, like the mutants on Emerald, employed mind-control? Or at least the muddling interference that had nearly been my undoing back on that cursed planet?

My mouth twisted up at one corner. "They want you three." I nodded at her, at Resa, at Grace.

"More than just us," Carina said. Her voice

echoed along stone in a sudden silence. I glanced back the way we had come, toward the open chamber, the lake, the battle taking place there. Except I saw and heard nothing.

"We move," said the nearest warrior. "Now."

So, we turned around yet again and picked up the pace. After several minutes I heard footsteps following. Footsteps, not slushy, slimy scrabbling. Not flopping and heaving. Whoever remained to Neala's troops was catching up.

I peered over my shoulder. Neala's daughter and another held onto their leader between them. Neala's legs dragged. Her head drooped. I ran back and shouldered my way between them, putting my own arm around Neala.

"Don't you dare touch her," her daughter ground out.

I shot her a look. "Shut up."

Neala felt like bones inside her clothes. Without so much as an excuse-my-impertinence, I swung her up into both arms and hustled away with her. Her warriors stampeded after me.

When I reached Grace, she gasped. "What are you doing?"

"I think she's dying," I said.

"Where's the wound?" Mika asked, swerving closer.

"I...I don't think there is one. I think it's something else." My thoughts went to Levon. Emaciated, ingratiating, not quite sane Levon. A strange sadness swirled through me at the memory. He'd revolted and angered me, but in the end, he'd proven himself a hero.

Trying to make up for what he had done, I supposed. Still, I was grateful.

"What are you doing with her?"

I glanced aside at Neala's daughter. "What's your name?"

Her lips compressed. She didn't answer.

"Fine. I don't really care. I don't need your name to tell you your mom is pretty sick. However far we have to go, she's not going to make it on her own. I'll carry her."

The girl, a very angry girl, inclined her head grudgingly in acceptance. The remaining warriors closed around us. Mika looked them over, as if counting their number or checking for injuries.

"Is anyone hurt?" I asked on his behalf since I still had my face after telling the warrior queen's daughter, or whatever she was, to shut it. "Have you left anyone behind?"

Murmured negatives came from those closest. I looked at them all, assuring myself no one pointed those odd weapons at me. They still had them out at the ready, but not directed at anyone in the group. In my arms, Neala's body had grown limp. I suspected she had lost consciousness. She still breathed, though. I could hear it over all the noise we made.

Suddenly, I sensed someone staring at me. My eyes went to Neala first. Her lids remained closed. I glanced then from side to side. Calmly. Not as though I felt unnerved by it. I wouldn't give anyone the satisfaction. My gaze fell on two silvery eyes watching me as she bounced along on Ren's far side. Hannah. I realized I hadn't as much as said hello to her. I was still unsure, I guess. Still pissed off.

I had to admit, she looked terrible. The dark

circles I noted earlier lingered under her eyes. Her carefree haircut appeared flat, untidy, almost dusty. None of us looked all that good, but we sporadically ran a hand through our hair, shook out the leaves, plucked the occasional stray animal follicle from it. She seemed to have stopped caring. The hollows in her cheekbones had grown more shadowed in the past couple days than I remembered, too. Had she given up eating? Or had they not found anything to eat?

"Brand," I whispered. He came over to me, keeping pace at my side with his low, sloping stride.

"Yeah?"

"Can you give those two something to eat? Ren and Hannah, I mean. I'm not sure they've had anything. I'll replace your supplies with mine. My hands aren't exactly free."

He bobbed his head in agreement and headed straight over to them. I could hear him explaining as he shirked off his pack to dig down inside it. He handed them something I couldn't see and continued along beside them. Hannah's eyes sought mine across the short distance. I deliberately looked away.

She liked me in a way I couldn't reciprocate. I felt oddly responsible for that in a situation anything but conducive to such drama. The anger simmering inside me was for an entirely different reason, however. I still believed she had been trying to betray at least Grace, if not everyone. I ignored her aggrieved study, reminding myself I had more immediate problems. Like the woman I carried, a woman who might very well die in my care with her warriors an arm's length away. Especially her daughter. That one had been willing to fling a dagger into my eye merely because I spoke out of turn.

I looked down into Neala's face. Her color appeared okay. By my standards, anyway. Anyone who wasn't white from blood loss, gray from pain, or red from raging fever gave me hope they'd recover. Even those who didn't look like they'd make it survived. Grace came immediately to mind, striding on my right with only a slight indication her leg injury still pained her.

Sudden blood-stench filled my nostrils in recollection. My memories didn't usually include odor. My mind didn't play those tricks. Eyes jerking down, I searched Neala for evidence a wound lay hidden beneath her clothing. I turned my head to call Mika over to help and smelled the iron tang again. Real, and nearby.

Beside me, Neala's daughter stumbled. When she straightened, I spotted the sweat on her face, the awkward way she held herself, the translucence to her skin. I did call Mika, then, loudly. Brand, too.

"Help her," I said. "She's hurt."

The girl snarled at me. Literally snarled. I don't think she had the wherewithal for words right then. I arched an eyebrow, sympathy vanishing.

"Then you two, instead," I snapped at the warriors closest to her. "Help her."

Surprisingly and in silence, they obeyed. Each slipped an arm behind her shoulders. She wrapped her own arms around their necks and held on. The fact she didn't protest their assistance spoke volumes.

As for me, I found myself starting to flag. Neala's wasted body, though light in weight, dragged at my arms and shoulders as she wavered near consciousness. I hoisted her up higher, ignoring That One's wordless objection. I would have to get Neala's daughter's name from her somehow. 'Daughter' and 'that one' were starting to wear thin inside me.

"Alwyna. My name is Alwyna."

I inhaled, choked on spit, turned to look at the pale, sweating warrior slung between her mates. She'd spoken as though she'd heard me, heard my thoughts. Oh, please, I begged silently, let there not be another one doing that.

"Don't look so surprised," Alwyna went on, her tone angry and strong despite being held up by her cronies. "You were talking out loud."

Crud. Of course, I was.

Carina called back to me. "How did you manage to con anyone, when you let slip such things for all to hear?"

I grimaced at her and made no reply. I'd been good at my job. I'd been really good at it. I wanted to be good at something else now. However, this recent tendency to speak my inner thoughts to the world was something I needed to get under control. I had no idea when the shift from tight-lipped to unaware blabbermouth had occurred, but I had a feeling it had somehow started with Grace.

I looked at her again. At Grace. I caught a crooked smile dissolving on her face. Naturally, she'd overheard the whole exchange and been amused. Why not. I would have liked to be something more to her than a jester, though. I would have liked to be what she was to me. A hero.

A sudden murmur made its way through the warriors behind us. I tensed, ready to pick up my burdened knees and run faster. I heard instead a rushed exclamation.

"They've gone! They've fallen back!"

Relief burst from my lungs in a heavy breath.

"Are you sure?" Grace asked.

"Yes," the same voice replied.

Another voice, faint, rasping, responded, "Not surprised. They can't be long from the water. And the ways are getting too narrow for them to pass."

I gaped down at a conscious Neala. Her open eyes looked at me, then around. In the dancing light I saw how yellowed and bloodshot they were.

"You can put me down now," she said to me. "I can walk."

"No, m'am," I said, with a deference I reserved for very few. "I'll keep this up until we get where we're going."

Neala snorted.

I smiled, lips closed, grim. "How far is that, anyway?"

"We'll be there soon. You'll know we're there when you see it." Her eyes closed again. Her body sagged, unconscious once more but breathing.

From nearby, Mika whispered, "Still alive, then."

I nodded. We exchanged a look, a worried look, a what-will-we-do-if-she-doesn't-survive look. Because honestly, if the warriors, these

Fianna, decided to place blame somewhere, we were outnumbered almost four to one. Sure, Grace might be able to repeat her recent performance and Resa might take it into her head to send them all skyward, but I really didn't want to have to rely on either action. I wanted this all to end well. Period. We all needed a break. Some time to recuperate, get our bearings, really figure out what to do next. Gran had an expression: flying by the seat of one's pants. As far as I could tell, it meant operating without a plan, a goal, a choice. That's what we were doing, what we had been doing since the beginning. It had to stop.

Our race away from the sun-filled chamber near the water had taken us further from the light as well. Our torches and whatever the warriors carried were the only things illuminating the underground passage we traveled. The dancing lights distracted the eye. Confused the mind. Or was that something else?

Swearing, I glanced around, looked back, misstepped and stumbled and righted myself with Mika's help. To either side I saw faces in the shadows. Deep-set eyes stared back at me, observed our progress.

"Do you see—"

I didn't even get the question out before Mika and Grace answered in unison. "Yes."

"They are our ancestors," Alwyna said. Sinking into delirium. Not a good sign. The watchers surveyed us from both sides, greater in number, greater in size. Like—

IN DARKNESS WE BREAK

"Giants," Hannah said, the word no more than a breath. I swore once more into the whispering echo from Hannah's statement.

Grace

Chapter Seven

"Not giants," I contradicted Hannah. "Statues."

Beside me, burdened with Neala, Duncan gaped around again. "You're right."

"Our ancestors," Alwyna repeated. "The greatest warriors of old, from whom we are directly descended."

Presumptuous, boastful, but likely true. The warriors had slowed their pace and, therefore, so had we. I glanced at the statues nearest, barely discernible in the dark, called the pink light to my palm and raised my hand high. Seeing this, Hannah produced her own. Rose and golden hues ran like liquid over beautifully carved stone. Someone drew a quick, quiet breath. Carina.

Every figure, female. Strong, proud, fashioned in wondrous detail. The clothing altered, as did the weapons in their hands, but warriors all.

"Who carved these?" Duncan asked, but not as though he expected to receive a reply. Good thing, because he didn't. I glanced back at Neala still cradled in his arms. Her golden skin looked nearly translucent.

IN DARKNESS WE BREAK

I strode close enough to hear her shallow breathing and shot a look at her warriors nearby, wondering if they understood how sick Neala was.

Unlike the desert tribes, these warriors possessed no tattoos to note their accomplishment in training, in life. If they truly were the Fianna, a race long vanished into legend and rather unbelievable to consider, they might be able to help me understand what I had become. It had been said…

A lot had been said, embellished over countless years in retelling. How true might it be? How could they exist after all this time, unseen?

I recalled the dragon in stunning flight, its appearance in the cave, the broken claw in Duncan's pocket. Well, yes. More did exist to our world than I'd ever known. I drew in a deep, long breath, closed my eyes, opened them.

"You okay there, Grace?" Duncan, rather breathless. He'd been rushing along with Neala in his arms for quite a distance.

"Fine," I said. "How about you? Need a hand?"

"I'm good."

I didn't argue. He had nothing to prove as far as I was concerned. He'd done so much for all of us. If he faltered, we would help him, but he appeared determined. He might even win these warriors over with his persistence. Alwyna had given him her name, after all, deigned to speak with him. That was something. More than something. Among the Fianna, if they truly were Fianna, males were considered lesser beings, or so the tales would have us believe. Even if they were not Fianna, their attitude toward Duncan and the others had been obvious from the start.

From her awkward position, Alwyna ordered

several warriors forward. She had taken temporary command.

"Where are you sending them?" I asked.

"To open the gates."

I nodded. Wherever we were being shepherded, we were nearly there.

"The moment of truth," Duncan whispered to me.

Indeed. Whether good or grave intent, we would shortly know. Again, I yearned for my absent *lathesa*. The original weapon, made for my hand and marked by beautiful symbols, had been taken from me before my imprisonment, but the makeshift ones had served their purpose with equal efficiency. I had Duncan's glass blade, but the balance, the grace of use, the effectiveness was far from the same.

You possess other means for fighting.

I hissed through my teeth at Skelly's words. I knew I had other ways to defend us. The recent aftermath was fresh in memory. Try as I might, I couldn't bring to mind what I had done to lay the warriors low when they had come upon Hannah and I. An automatic, semi-conscious response, perhaps, yet not one I wanted to repeat with my friends close enough to be hurt. I had to retain control of my thoughts, my reactions, my fear and anger. My warrior training had been completed, with honors. The ability to control my emotions, my behavior should be easily attainable. Yet, it wasn't. Not now.

My gaze slid to Ren and Hannah walking side by side. I hadn't asked Hannah how she found me, where they'd come into the cave system. I hadn't had time. They didn't appear to be with the warriors, so must have entered another way. That would certainly be important if we required an escape route.

However, I had no desire to go anywhere near the

water creatures, if it could be avoided. Something about them unnerved me. They seemed to possess a sentience that belied their sluglike appearance. I'd fought them beneath the water, expecting to be killed, but they had another intent I didn't understand. If I hadn't managed to escape them, dragging myself from the lake near Hannah, I don't know what would have happened. Yet, after waiting patiently in the lake they attacked the warriors. I wondered which was the danger here. Those calling themselves the Fianna or the *prair*. Although the *prair* differed as species from those who wanted to claim the gifts we shared, if they in fact had the intelligence to recognize the value, would they seek us for their own purposes?

My teeth ground together. My muscles tightened.

Had enough, Grace? You know what to do.

No, I shot back at Skelly. *I don't know what to do.*

I pushed him down, then, with a concentration that made him groan.

"Grace, you okay?" Duncan again.

"Fine."

"You're sweating. It's not even warm in here."

I swiped the hand clutching the blade across my brow, held it away, narrowed my eyes at the glistening moisture on my skin. "I'm fine."

"If you say so."

Something clanked hard ahead, sounding like iron on wood and causing a booming reverberation over the walls. Another sound followed this one. Chains? Light broke through a narrow crack. Within moments it spread through the cavern toward us. I narrowed my eyes against the glare and subdued the no longer needed light on my palm. Daylight poured in, revealing everything. The tall statues, the warriors all around us, the opening gate's vast size. Beyond, constructed into the rock under the mountain and lit by the sun through a huge, jagged opening above, were numerous structures on the cave walls. To be honest, it was not what I had anticipated. The legendary Fianna of old resided in the forests, in colonies led by females. The males had their lesser roles. The Fianna reveled in sunlight and green, living things, cool water and changing seasons. If anything about those tales were true, at what point had they moved underground with only a glimpse of the sky?

We passed through the gates, also carved, not with statuesque warriors, but with trees and flowers and animals. The things the Fianna would have remembered. The things they had loved. Perhaps I needed to set aside my doubts about the identity of these warriors. We had found stories from legend to be true in one fashion or another before.

"It feels abandoned," Carina said under her breath. Mika nodded in agreement beside her. I felt it, too. I heard our footsteps, the rustle of our clothes, the muttered voices all around, but beyond us all, I heard nothing except the wind rushing by in the cold sky far overhead. I recalled Yunlen, the abandoned village which had almost been my undoing. A place of warding. Hannah recognized it as such. Rumors were, it might be Duncan's grandmother—his father's mother, not his mother's—who had set the warding. The forcefield surrounding Landing, too. She couldn't have done it alone, we were told, without help.

The desert world where I was raised, where I had learned to fight, had been a safe and limited place. Spread out over great distances, desert society had still been a haven for us. I wondered if any tribal elders had truly known what existed beyond its boundaries.

As warriors, such knowledge should have been part of our teachings, rather than as the tales we shared.

Looking to place blame for your shortcomings, Grace?

Skelly's voice startled me. I slowed my stride until I fell in once more beside Duncan and the woman he carried. We trod a narrow road through the small city's center while behind us several warriors pulled the gate shut and lowered a mammoth cross bar into place. I looked back several times at the mechanism used. If we required a hasty exit, it wouldn't be through the gate. I turned my eyes front, scanning the area for another way out.

Beside me, Duncan addressed Alwyna. "Where is your physician? We'll go straight there."

Her face twisted. "We have none," she said. "Our healer is gone."

"Gone, as in dead?" Duncan responded, looking alarmed.

"Gone, as in she turned her back on us and went into the outside world."

Duncan grunted. "So, dead to you." I pivoted and eyed him askance. He ignored my look.

"Who tends to your mother, then?"

She said nothing. Her unwillingness to speak on this matter disturbed me. By her uncertain look, I figured she struggled with it, too.

"Stop here," Alwyna instructed.

We did, waiting. She loosened herself from the warriors' grip and stood straight, wincing. Blood stained her trousers, smelling strong, but from what I could see through the rent in the fabric, bleeding from the wound had nearly ceased. Only a thin, crimson trickle ran along her flesh. She turned to address Duncan.

"Relinquish the Riona to these others. They will see her home."

Riona must be Neala's formal title, I decided, especially when two warriors stepped forward and removed her from Duncan's arms. I had thought Alwyna to be no more than my age, prone to temper and somewhat rash, but she acted now as someone mentored to take command in her mother's place. I studied her with newfound respect.

Alwyna started off in a different direction despite her wound, tossing her head for the warriors to follow. "Come with me," she said to us.

"Where are we going?" I asked.

"To be fed," she answered, jerking her chin toward Duncan. "That one's guts are louder than thunder."

"Duncan," I said. "His name is Duncan."

"She can call me Chauncy for all I care," Duncan whispered to me, "as long as we get something to eat." He bumped my arm with his. "They're outside somewhere, the *conjures*. Ren said so."

I smiled, heart leaping. Suddenly, I felt them, all three of them, out there beneath the sun. Grunting, circling, grumbling, waiting. Faithful. Protective. A part of me, somehow. Or I had become part of them.

Alwyna directed us to halt before a low, rounded stone wall, behind which stood a building constructed almost entirely from wood on a stone foundation. Some wood had been cut and sawn, but most of it remained living. Branches curved upward toward the sun and arched over the roof. The roof itself was made of a material I did not recognize, pierced in three places by small glass or vitrine domes, providing light to the interior.

Alwyna pointed at Mika, Brand, Ren, and

Duncan, one at a time, then swept her hand in a broad motion. "You four, you will go around back."

"For what reason?" I asked. "We stay together."

"You cannot. It is the way things are."

"What do you mean, it is the way things are?"

Alwyna's jaw tightened. "The lesser kind will not dine inside. It is not permitted."

The smile lingering on my face vanished, something hard replacing it. "We all eat together," I said. "Wherever you are sending them, Carina, Resa and I will go as well."

"Then you will not eat," Alwyna shot back.

"Grace, really," Duncan whispered, "it's okay."

"It's not okay." I swung around to Alwyna. "As much as we appreciate your offer, Alwyna, we will be on our way now. You will not ostracize my friends no matter your reasons. You have your traditions, your beliefs, your laws. I respect that, but my friends and I will not be separated because of them."

The warriors still standing by shifted their stance, eyeing me.

"You need rest," Alwyna said, as if I required reminding, "and sustenance."

"Thank you," I said. "And we will be grateful to have both. Together."

Alwyna shifted her weight over her uninjured leg and held it there. "The entry of lesser into the inner chamber violates its sanctity."

"You would have me believe you take meals within sanctified halls?"

"Yes," Alwyna said. "I would. It is in this hall where warriors meet and dine in observance of certain auspicious occasions. Such as your arrival."

"Our arrival?" I echoed.

"Of course. You and certain among you. Not all."

Anger sparked in me. I tamped it down.

"Ask her how long it's been since the hall has been full," Carina whispered to me, her eyes, a strange, muddied yellow now, focused on Alwyna. I did, without hesitation. If Carina read something in the warrior's head and felt it worth passing on to me, I trusted the information's importance.

Alwyna blinked, her set expression otherwise remaining unchanged. "It doesn't matter," she said.

"Of course, it does," I answered. "How long?"

She huffed out a breath, petulance, I thought, until I realized it might be pain.

"Why don't we sit down?" I nodded at the various benches set outside the hall. I didn't want to point out her need to get off her injured leg. She seemed prideful, stubborn. "We could all use a rest while we discuss this."

Alwyna nodded agreement and moved to the closest seat. Several warriors gathered behind her, still standing. She waved the rest away. They moved off slowly, looking back as they went.

I lowered myself onto a bench nearby. Taking their cue from those standing opposite, my friends took a stance behind me, making the point we stood united. For a minute or two no one spoke. Even Duncan's stomach remained silent. I could see Alwyna gathering her thoughts and, perhaps, her strength. She needed that leg seen to.

Finally, Alwyna drew a breath, bit her lip, shifted her shoulders. Although she spoke quietly, her voice carried. "We have lived here many years, but it was not always so. I do not remember any other place, but the eldest among us did." She lifted her hand, indicating the buildings. "My people took what you see for their own when they retreated from the outside. The hall was built in recent memory. I watched its construction when I was very small."

"And what about the people who lived here?" Duncan asked, struggling with his tone. I wondered the same thing, had probably drawn the same conclusion he appeared to have done.

"The Fianna were not responsible, if that is what you are implying," Alwyna snapped at him. "We are not thieves and murderers. The inhabitants had died off, over time."

"Same as all of you are destined to do," Duncan muttered.

I jerked my head around. "Duncan!"

"The lesser one speaks and his words do not matter," Alwyna said, lips twisting into a smirk, a smirk that faded before she spoke again. "But they are true. Partly true. Our numbers have dwindled. Many in the passage of time have integrated themselves into the outside world. They have entered it in secret, abandoning their sisters, leaving their gifts and knowledge behind. More recently, others have taken up arms under other banners, now war has come again. The young among us, the littles ones, may be our last born as Fianna. The lesser have gone. They tired of the old ways, no doubt."

"Imagine that," Duncan said. She threw him a sharp look, saying nothing. Duncan subsided, took a small step back. Ren whispered something to him I didn't catch. I felt suddenly sorry for Alwyna, for her kin and her people. Their prospects as she described them would be most unpleasant. It didn't have to be that way. Maybe the time had come for them to integrate into the outside world, too.

I stood. "Thank you for telling us this. I think you might need your leg seen to. I know you said your healer is gone, but there is one among us who has some medical knowledge. He is not a doctor. He has, however, tended to our needs many times. He saved my life."

Duncan made a quiet noise, still in denial about how close it had been. I wasn't a fool. I saw the truth in Mika's eyes every time he looked at me, questioned me as to how I felt, watched me when he thought I didn't see. I would be forever grateful for his intervention, his care.

Alwyna stood, as well. "I'll see to my leg myself. It's stopped bleeding, I think. In the meantime, you may all eat together. Out here," she added, her gaze spotting something that irked her on Duncan's face behind me. "Your food will be brought out."

She sent someone inside with that message, then turned on her heel, stumbled, righted herself and went on. Three warriors took up a stance on the benches' perimeter. The rest of her immediate group followed. As soon as they vanished from sight, my companions sat on the aligned benches, Duncan at my side. The two warriors watched us as if waiting for something. I couldn't imagine what.

"Stay vigilant," I said.

Carina grinned, her eyes a fiery red. "Always."

"Do you recognize the trees on the hillside?" Duncan asked me.

I looked to where he pointed, observing the twisted growth, trees not much taller than I. The fissure overhead provided them sunlight through the day. This time of year, nothing grew on them, however.

"Fruit trees," I said. "My mother nurtured several in her garden." My voice caught. I cleared my throat. Duncan pretended not to have heard the catch.

"I remember them around the Quadrate in Citadel," he said. "Before they were blasted by fire. I stole the fruit when times were lean."

His stomach rumbled, no doubt in memory. I snorted, looking for further agriculture. I spotted gardens, mostly barren in this season, mulched over, although green and leafy plant matter filled one large square.

Duncan's empty belly growled again. Hunger had become standard fare among us. I hoped they'd feed us soon. On impulse, I fished around in my pockets. After a moment's search, I pulled my empty hands out. We had all gotten used to me carrying snacks, scant though they were, to keep us going on the road. Duncan looked disappointed, childishly so, yet I couldn't blame him.

"Sorry," he said.

"Don't worry about it."

"I hate being hungry. Back home, Gran made the best food. Even with those long hours she worked. Once I came down from Riley to start plying my trade in Citadel, I had to fend for myself."

I made a sympathetic noise in my throat.

"Still," he went on, "those meager meals I'd mustered up were feasts compared to what we've been consuming most days these past months. I should be used to it by now, I know."

"It's all right, Duncan," I said quietly. "We all feel the same. Our stomachs just aren't quite so vocal as yours." I punched him in the arm. He caught my hand and held it a moment before letting go. The guards—yes, I could only assume they were set to make sure we did not attempt to leave—eyed his action with disdain. I crossed my arms and stared at them one by one until their gazes dropped.

Footsteps sounded behind me. I looked over my shoulder. Two young boys, perhaps Resa's age and laden with trays, made their unsteady way down the steps. A woman followed them. Beneath her coat she wore a simple tunic, trousers, and serviceable boots. The way the boys kept glancing up at her, seeking approval, I thought she might be their mother. The way she looked back at them I figured I was right.

I rose from my seat. The woman met my eye. At home we had a servant living with us. Ella. She'd been much more than that to me, to our entire family. I, however, used to do battle with her to allow me to help her, for her not to serve me, for her to share her time with me like a friend. It had taken many attempts and many years for me to realize how much pride she took in her job. I had no business denying her that. So, I sat down again and waited, my hands folded in my lap, the inside of my cheek clamped between two molars.

The boys approached cautiously, holding the trays out at arm's length. We took what we wanted from each, setting the wooden plates and cups down on the benches beside us. We thanked them and their mother. Pleased, they went back inside.

Beside me, Duncan tried his best not to shovel in his food. On his other side, Resa quietly consumed hers. Carina and Mika sat on another bench, feeding each other from their plates. I looked away each time I saw them doing it. Once, upon spotting them at it himself, Brand caught Duncan's eye and rolled his, causing Duncan to chuckle. Brand ate on a bench apart from the others.

Brand hadn't been with us since the beginning, or even in All Dwellers. He didn't carry with him that invisible badge of camaraderie shared by those who'd started this journey on Emerald. When the residents of Trill, including Duncan's mother, his father, his younger brother, prepared to abandon their homes and flee, Brand had opted to accompany Duncan. According to Brand, he had no family. I wondered, though.

"Brand, enjoying your meal?" I called over to him.

Brand merely nodded his head and lifted a hand holding something resembling bread before returning to consuming it. I noticed no meat existed in what we'd been served. No matter. We'd been operating on feast or famine for some time now. We'd make do.

"What are our plans?" Duncan asked before taking a swig from the wooden cup in his hand. My cup remained full while I ate slowly, avoiding bloat.

Duncan sucked in a quick breath, choking a little on the liquid in his throat. I whipped around to check on him and followed his gaze.

Alwyna approached. So did her warriors. She stopped a foot or two away, favoring her uninjured leg. We all stood, Duncan reluctant to set aside his meal. He scooped in another mouthful before placing the plate and his utensils on the bench. Alwyna eyed him with an annoyed glare, then turned to me.

"You will come," she said. "Now. You, and that one."

Chapter Eight

It felt a little strange, Mika striding beside me. In all we had been through, this had never been his place. No particular reason why came to mind, except we had all fallen into a pattern, like soldiers, like warriors. Something my friends were not. And yet in this way we had survived.

"Mika," I whispered, "don't worry."

"I'm not worried," he said.

Liar, hissed Skelly.

Stop it.

I know him better than anyone.

Honestly, I thought back at him, *I don't think you do.*

Even so, I figured Mika was trying for a brave front, perhaps believing any failure on his part to identify Neala's ailment, treat it, would result in a decision to dispense with him. I had meant what I said, though. He didn't need to worry. No harm would come to him or to the others so long as we stayed together. I would not permit it.

Duncan had always said I possessed power in my promises. Maybe he had seen something I didn't, understood something I had not. Not this mystical revelation moving in me, but something in who I had always been. I held onto that, because these new gifts I did not trust at all.

Think, Grace. Think back. You know.

I prodded Skelly from my mind, the half-truths in what he said as well. I couldn't allow confusion to drive me. I didn't believe we were safe here, but I did believe we could gain some benefit by staying. For a little while, anyway. Unlike my hopeful, perilous decision to seek knowledge in The Wilds, these females were in many ways like me. They could help me, help us.

We trailed after Alwyna in silence, my friends and I, because I'd refused to be parted from them. Alwyna had surprisingly given in. The warriors who'd been watching us while we ate followed noiselessly behind, all armed. Only one carried a staff resembling a *lathesa.* The rest kept their less traditional weapons stashed about their clothing. A small voice in my brain told me I should be afraid. A very small voice, a voice easy to be ignored.

I determined the outcome as to what they wanted from us would be balanced by what we needed, and received, from them. Yes, I didn't much like who I'd become, yet pragmatism wasn't exactly a failing. Not with what we all faced, all we stood to lose before we ever made it home. I refused to use the word "if." We would go home. To my home, if the others wanted to. Duncan, of course, would return to his Gran. My heart ached at the thought, a twinge quickly stifled.

The sun from overhead warmed my hair, the curve to my skull, the tips of my ears. I suddenly longed for my home, for the desert, my family. A blade, an invisible blade, cut deeply into my chest. It took me a moment to realize Alwyna had spoken. I looked to her. She stood before me with her hand raised. I stopped walking.

"We are here."

She had halted before an ornate door with unfamiliar symbols. The door fit flawlessly into the rock surrounding it. A small line of light shone out along the bottom, highlighting the flat stone at its base.

Alwyna turned to Mika. "You will come with me."

I moved forward with him, as did my companions.

"Not all of you," Alwyna said.

"Since Neala is not well," I said, pretending to misunderstand her, "I quite understand why you don't want her warriors following us inside." Behind me, Duncan sucked in a breath. Alwyna's cheeks reddened.

"They will remain outside," she said, "with—"

"Very well. Lead the way." I ushered my friends forward. Alwyna looked very much as though she wished to argue. I know I would have. But in this I would not relent. It was imperative we stay together.

Giving in, Alwyna opened the door. Once we had all entered, she closed it behind us. She leaned the staff she'd been using to aid in walking against the wall, maintaining the short dagger in her belt. At a tangent, I admired the fine craftsmanship on the hilt, metal worked into symbols akin to those I'd seen outside.

"Mother?" she called.

I bit my lip at her tone, remembering my own mother. Something touched my hand. Duncan's fingers curled around mine. I lifted my eyes to his, recognized understanding. I'd forgotten how much emotion my face could sometimes show. Indeed, I had never realized my bouts of transparency until Duncan pointed them out. Usually with a witty remark, or, if he couldn't control himself, a quote recalled from his Gran. I squeezed his hand and let go. The unbroken left. His right had been damaged so many times now it didn't look to ever heal properly short of surgical correction, despite Mika's careful tending. But the bones had knitted in their fashion, the best they could. Duncan had told me they didn't hurt anymore. I knew he lied.

Alwyna signaled us to follow. We traveled down a short hall lit at intervals by small lamps. Alwyna entered the chamber first. I halted, putting my hands out to stop the others. I wanted to hear what Neala said before she knew we were there.

"Where are they?" Neala asked. "Are they secure—"

"They are here, Mother. With me."

Neala hissed something unintelligible. I moved forward, Mika with me, the others close behind, entering a room dimly lit by a small device which seemed to have no power source. I supposed it likely the same as what they had carried in their hands, much the same as the pink light I could now produce, though more brittle than fluid, sharp rather than soft. It etched deep shadows across Neala's face and up the walls. She lay in a bed propped on pillows, her weapons and her outer garb across a nearby chair. Dark smudges colored the skin beneath her eyes.

"This is Mika," Alwyna said, indicating him with a flicking finger. "He has some medical knowledge."

"No."

Alwyna stared at her mother's stony expression. Her own turned impatient. "We lost our healer how long ago, Mother? Don't be foolish."

"How dare you?" Neala shot back, trying to push herself up on the pillows and failing. Whatever her ailment, it appeared to have a rapid ascent. Perhaps not permanent or she would not have been able to accompany her warriors to find us. Something recurring, then? I stepped forward.

"As I told Alwyna, Mika saved my life. I don't know that he is able to help you at all, but I can't see the harm in letting him try."

"I will not permit him to touch me," Neala said, her throat tight, words clipped.

I inhaled, released the air slowly. "Then he won't. But he can ask questions and you can answer him, yes? Whatever physical examination needs to be performed, he can instruct me and I will do it."

Her lips compressed. After a brief contemplation, she nodded her head. Alwyna sighed in relief, indicated Mika and I should move nearer the bed. Mika looked down at Neala, who avoided his gaze as though it might burn her. Her behavior provided her no benefit and demeaned us all. I began to lose my patience. Again.

"Look at him," I said.

"Please," Mika added, trying to diffuse my annoyance.

Reluctantly, Neala turned her eyes in his direction. He asked her a few questions. Interesting questions, I thought, as I would never have chosen them as the right ones on my own. But she answered them, answered him, until she began to voluntarily describe her symptoms. He nodded and encouraged, asked more questions, and moved infinitesimally closer with each one until I was staring at his back and she at him while she spoke. My lips curved.

Mika, thief, and doctor's son. Both talents had proven invaluable in our journey. I wondered if he understood how much.

I watched and listened, my friends standing near my back. Alwyna observed the process, too, her shoulders dropping, tension easing away. She glanced at me with a small nod and back to the bed where her mother lay speaking. In time, Mika called me forward with a small gesture.

"If it's all right with you," Mika said to Neala, "I'll have Grace help me, now."

"No," Neala answered. "Do what you must. Grace will stand by. The rest of you, turn away."

I had expected her to insist they leave and found myself glad not to have to argue the point with her. Everyone spun where they stood, facing the opposite wall, Resa following signed explanation from Duncan. Alwyna took her mother's hand.

Mika's examination was based, I supposed, on the information Neala had provided him. He checked her pulse—the only objective I recognized—and then gently poked and prodded here and there. In time, he straightened and wiped a thin sheen from his brow, his pale face set.

"I am no physician, no healer," he said, and I knew his next words would be carefully considered. Likely unwelcome. He pointed a steady finger at an area on Neala's abdomen he had previously spent time probing. "Were you wounded? Here?"

Neala nodded. "Many years ago."

"I can feel something there. Possibly scar tissue? I don't know exactly what it is or what should be done. But it appears to be the source of your pain, which I think you already knew. I remember...I remember my father saying once that scar tissue in the abdomen can sometimes adhere to the abdominal wall and organs." He bit his lip. "If it is scar tissue," he added.

I tipped my head to get a better look at Mika's face. "Is there nothing you can do?"

Mika shook his head. Alwyna shoved her way between us to confront him. "Are you saying—" she began. Mika cut her short.

"I'm not saying anything. I'm only saying it's beyond me. I can't be sure what I feel beneath the skin, not really, and I certainly can't do surgery. I'm not qualified. I'm not trained at all. I just paid attention, watched my dad."

This was the first time I ever heard Mika refer to his father as 'dad.' The few times he mentioned the man, his tone had been neutral, almost cold, as if warding off a deep anger, and never once did he call him anything one might construe as sentimental. I couldn't blame Mika. Knowing his story, I couldn't blame him at all.

Alwyna spoke again. "Can't you try something?"

Mika's eyes did not leave Neala's. "No." Neala dipped her head in a barely perceptible nod at Mika. Alwyna did not see. Instead, she stared at Mika with her fists clenched against her thighs. I did not know what her gifts might be, did not know if the warriors here possessed any but the most rudimentary. Still, I refused to take chances. I placed my body between them, the way she had between me and Mika, forced her to look at me. She took a step back.

"Are you all right?" I asked.

She scowled, looked away and back again. I guessed her to be somewhere around my age. She couldn't have been much older. And yet, she faced the prospect of taking her mother's place. Not readily.

First and foremost, such a succession meant the loss of her mother. Responsibility's weight would be heavy at any time, but more so for that.

I think we all saw it in Neala's visage. Mortality. I wanted to put my arms around Alwyna and comfort her. I knew she would never allow it.

"The boy is a healer," Neala said. "I sense it. But he cannot help me. It is not only scar tissue in my abdomen. I have known this."

Alwyna's mouth twisted. Tears shone in her eyes.

"You have suspected as well, my daughter."

"I don't care," Alwyna protested. "I won't believe it."

"You must," said Mika.

I snatched away Alwyna's weapon before it contacted Mika's face. Alwyna gasped and thrashed her hand through the air, missing the object entirely. I might have believed she didn't truly want it back, if not for the anger in her glare. After several moments, her gaze dropped, and then her head. Her shoulders slumped beneath her cloak. I held her weapon out. She didn't reach for it. I lifted her hand and pressed her fingers around the handle. Neala reached from the bed and circled her daughter's other hand.

"It will be all right," she said. "You are ready. You have always been ready," she added with a short, breathy laugh. "Remember that I am very proud of who you have become."

Listening to Neala's words, I blinked moisture from my lashes.

"But you must do one thing for me, daughter," she went on.

Alwyna lifted her head. Her own lashes were wet, as were her pale cheeks. "What is that, Mother?"

"Respect and honor your heritage, but also

recognize that hope exists beyond the old ways."

Alwyna's shoulders jerked. "This is not what we have been taught. What you have taught."

"And perhaps I was wrong," Neala said with a long glance at her daughter. Alwyna lowered her head in acknowledgment. Neala's pain-clouded eyes slid toward Mika and on to the others standing behind. "We will not survive without change. These…boys," she said, forcing the word out, perhaps avoiding one more discourteous, "do not stand for Grace. They stand with her, as equals. I think I understand why."

About time, Skelly snarled from within, startling me more with his sentiment than his voice. Odd, he should feel this way, when he viewed all my friends with such disdain. Even back on the Emerald when so few remained after the purge prior to my arrival, Skelly Shane maintained his animosity. Yet, he had followed us into the outside world. A world he feared in a manner reducing him to paralysis and hysteria while still incarcerated. Why had he come? He would have been safer had he remained in the facility. He would have been alive.

I prodded him, wondering if he might now answer my question. But he remained silent. I could feel him simmering. I felt something else, too. Something prompting tears to be blinked away again.

Don't feel sorry for me, Grace. I've told you I don't want your pity.

I know, I responded. *I know what you've said. I don't believe you.*

"Grace?"

I startled, finding Duncan leaning toward me, his face close to mine.

"We should head back outside," he said. "I think Alwyna and her mother want to talk."

I nodded at him. We all turned as one, heading for the door. Alwyna stopped us. She walked up to Mika, held out her hand. Mika hesitated before taking it.

"Thank you," Alwyna said.

Mika inclined his head, withdrew his hand, looking shocked at the fact she had both touched and thanked him. I'm sure he expected a more violent reaction. Alwyna, however, appeared to have calmed down.

"Wait for me at the front door," she instructed.

I assumed she meant everyone, not only Mika, and responded accordingly, leading the way. Even if she meant only Mika, we were staying together. Upon opening the door, I found the warriors blocking our path.

"Let them pass," Neala called from her bed.

The warriors backed against the wall. I smelled a sweaty tang on the nearest. Fear? Yes, it seemed to be. I met her pale blue gaze as I passed her. She quickly lowered her eyes.

Did she fear me? Perhaps so, given what I had done to them by the underground lake. She wouldn't be quite so afraid if she realized I had no idea how I'd brought them all down. Then again, such unpredictability was cause for anxiety on its own merit. Mine and theirs.

We waited bunched together by the closed front entrance, Alwyna and her mother's voices drifting low along the corridor, the words indecipherable. The warriors remained still, not speaking. They watched us, though, two, like the one who appeared fearful, glanced sidelong while the others stared.

"Let's go outside," I said.

"But—" Hannah said, and stopped.

I glanced at her. She stared at the warriors with eyes wide. I snatched her garment between finger and thumb and shook my head. "I don't care," I said.

With a jerk on the handle, I yanked the door open and stepped out. The sun had moved a little in the rocky opening far above, slanting its light at new angles. I walked straight into the nearest beam. Stood there, immobile, my face lifted to the sky, my eyes closed. I recalled the desert wind, the delicate sound made by the sand as it shifted. I recalled my family's voices, Ella's, as well, and Mara's, their tones sweet and sad in memory. And then I shut them out, willing myself to feel only the sun and its warmth on my shoulders in the cold air.

The ground beneath my feet vibrated slightly at the others' approach. I stayed where I was, gathering what comfort and serenity I could from the beloved sunlight.

"Grace?"

Duncan again, softly, loathe to disturb my bid for tranquility.

"They're coming, too," he whispered. "And more. I think they were told to stop us, maybe?"

I reached back for his hand, but instead I found Resa's. She seemed to be expecting it, slipping her fingers into mine. I looked down into her brown-eyed gaze. She didn't often look anyone directly in the eye. When she did, it meant something.

"Get behind me," I said and spun to face the oncoming warriors. In my free hand I found I held an object I recognized. A *lathesa*, or something akin to one. The last I had seen this weapon it had been in the pale-eyed girl's hand. I realized now she did not fear me. She feared her own actions. Somehow, in that minute exchange, glance, and glance away, she had given her weapon to me and I had not even been aware. Maybe such was her power, her gift, distracting the mind. If so, she could be formidable indeed. But she had passed her weapon to me. To me. I imagined many reasons why. Only one made sense.

I stepped forward, Resa still clinging to my hand. Seeing this, Carina hurried to stand on Resa's other side. Abruptly, the warriors halted, exchanged looks, settled their collective gaze on we three.

The warrior, the witch, the thrice-gifted child.

In all this time, I hadn't fully recognized—hadn't wanted to—the power we shared, Carina, Resa and I. Suddenly, I did.

Duncan

Chapter Nine

A shiver radiated from my spine's bony ridges out across my flesh, raising the hair follicles like miniscule flags. The sensation made breathing difficult. I shifted my gaze left then right, checking if Mika, Ren, Brand, Hannah were having the same reaction. Finding them in what appeared a similar state, I turned my attention back to the girls.

They resembled one unit right then, Grace, my sister and Carina. One very formidable unit. Neala's warriors recognized the same thing. I half expected them to turn and run. Perhaps they might have, if Alwyna hadn't appeared supporting Neala at her side. Neala lifted a hand.

"Stand down," she said. When they didn't immediately respond, she repeated the command. Louder. Pushing away her weakness. Her warriors complied in a manner reminding me of Tiran's army, taking up identical stances, feet apart, hands behind their backs. To be honest, the mirrored action creeped me out. A lot.

I wanted to kick myself. Why hadn't I been

looking for a way to leave this place from the second we were brought inside the gates? There had to be other exits, maybe not as grand and imposing, but quicker, quieter. More accessible to me and my friends.

"Grace," Neala said, "I ask you to stay calm. I want no one to be hurt here."

Did she threaten Grace? How short was her memory?

A moment later I realized Neala's words were a plea, not a threat. She came forward with Alwyna's help, holding her hand out, palm up. The term *supplication* came to mind. The words *don't trust her* popped up right after.

I didn't say them, though. I had a feeling this all had to play out. For better or worse.

In preparation for worse, I patted around my waistband for the narrow blade, Alwyna's blade, Grace had given to me earlier. Instead, I bumped my oddly distended pocket.

Oh. That.

I yanked the dragon claw from my pocket, judging its utility for defense. It fit well into my hand. Good grip. Nice, sharp point. I raised it toward the sun, checking it for cracks and weaknesses. The pearly surface gleamed, arrowing brilliance into the shadows.

Someone exclaimed, followed by another. I looked around, my brow twisting into a knot. Alwyna and her mother stopped short.

"Where—how did you get that?" Alwyna stammered.

"From the beast itself," I said, confused at her tone. "How do you think?"

She stared at me. For the first time, I noticed her

eye color. Green. Not Grace's green, but muddied through with brown. The sun highlighted the mixed colors. "To be honest," I said, tossing my head, "I ran back to save Hannah from it. It stepped on her ankle and the claw broke off. So, I kept it."

"You...you are brave."

I shrugged, not much caring for the shock in her admission. I lowered the claw to my side. "I try to be. If you want brave, Grace whistled to distract the dragon and it went straight at her. Passed her, sure, but it's not like she knew it would. Passed her and flew away."

Her gaze went to Grace and returned to me. "But you," she said, still not bothering to hide her astonishment. "You went back for your companion."

"Well, yeah." She seemed to think my actions greater or at least more surprising than Grace's. Why? Because Grace was warrior and expected to behave in that fashion? Or because I was male and expected not to. Disgusted, I turned away, looking to Grace for our next move.

"You are brave," Alwyna repeated.

And you're annoying and repetitive, I thought. I turned to her again, jerking my head around at my friends. "We all are. Not one of us deserves your contempt."

She inhaled, released a slow breath, nodded. "Understood."

I suppose she read the astonishment in my facial contractions. For a moment anger replaced her brief humility, and then her expression changed once more. Oddly, she looked relieved.

"Grace Irese," Neala said, "would you speak with me?"

The woman's body trembled beneath her winter

cloak. I wasn't surprised. The temperature in the open felt frosty.

"I noticed a fire pit near the benches. Could we light a fire there, and sit?" Grace suggested gently, despite her stance. Neala nodded, signaled for it to be done. Several warriors headed in the hall's direction.

"Walk with me?" Neala said. Grace nodded in her turn and she, Carina and Resa took a place on Neala's right side. With a slight movement of her head, Grace indicated we should join them. We moved to Grace's right and Neala's warriors surged toward Neala's left. It made for a crowded walk across the stony ground toward the hall. Due to Neala's condition, a slow walk, as well. By the time we reached the bench area, the fire had been lit and flames licked along the wood, the heat from it already steaming in the frigid air. Alwyna lowered her mother onto the bench nearest the flames. Grace took a seat beside her. Alwyna, Carina with Resa, stood at their backs as if they'd done this many times before. It made for a strange, yet oddly familiar, tableau.

"Please," said Grace, "can't everyone just sit?"

With hesitance in varying degrees, most did. Too few benches existed, so some seated themselves on the ground in proximity to the fire. My sister and Carina remained standing at Grace and Neala's back. Brand and the others followed me over to them, where we sat on the ground beside the bench. We received disgruntled glares for our seating choice. I didn't care. I stared right back. We belonged where we were. Together.

I shifted as a small stone dug into my butt cheek. Two warriors on the bench nearest brought their weapons up and quickly lowered them again. This was going to be a joy. I supposed I needed to take care with a nose itch, too. The sooner we left this place, the better.

"You have questions," Neala said to Grace. "I do, as well. You begin." She smiled, weakly. I looked to Grace, wondering where she would start. I possessed my own questions. The invite had not, of course, been extended to me.

For one, I would have liked to know more about the Fianna's move into the mountain. Call me nosy and perhaps prone to jump to conclusions, but it seemed like they were hiding. What caused them to conceal themselves from the outside world? Generations ago, according to Alwyna. Might it have been the war that destroyed All Dwellers? Olympian, as it used to be called? Grace had spoken about it, about the history and the tales. So had the Lyoness. Fleeing such devastation made sense. Hmm. Maybe I didn't need that question answered, after all.

"First," Grace said, "I would like to apologize to you all again for what I did. Harming you in any way hadn't been my intent. I have not been quite myself since…since our passage through the Sleeping Myth."

"So, it's true," someone whispered. I couldn't see who. Neala echoed the warrior's words.

"Yes," Grace answered, "it's true."

"We have heard many tales," Alwyna said, "of those who seek the Sleeping Myth for answers, to commune, to gain wisdom, but none who pass through survive. How did you?"

Good question. Grace had told me what she believed had occurred when I first regained consciousness afterward. I glanced aside at Hannah, Hannah whose motives remained unclear, and leaned forward, waiting on Grace's response.

"I possessed something which aided me. Aided

all of us, since we were physically connected. A talisman. It is gone now. I lost it in the passage through. It disintegrated."

Hannah gasped. I barely stopped myself letting loose an even more telling exclamation. Grace was lying. Outright. The problem with that? Grace didn't lie.

A second later I corrected my thinking. She had lied before. Yeah, Grace had lied to me. I supposed I should understand this time, too, and keep my big mouth shut. She had a reason then, and no doubt had one now. By the suddenly interested, maybe even greedy look on several faces, I figured she had a darned good reason.

Yep, lost the darned thing. I'd bear witness to it if I had to. Hannah crept up beside me, wriggling on her knees across the ground.

"Duncan…"

"Shh," I said. "Not now."

She subsided onto her heels, pushing her straggling red hair back with her fingers. Her proximity made me uneasy. I remembered how she used to feel about me. I had no idea if that had changed. It didn't much matter. Either way, infatuation or disenchantment, I had no desire to stir up those coals again.

"Duncan," she whispered, "I need to explain."

"Shh," I said again. Several pairs of eyes turned our way. Grace's, also. Her expression made no sense to me. She turned back to Neala and her daughter.

"And now?" asked Neala. "What are you plans?"

I listened for that answer, too. I wanted to get out of here. Quickly. Without fuss would be preferable.

"We came to the Sleeping Myth seeking answers, as Alwyna said. We came out the other side with more questions. Or at least, I did. I don't know that you can help with those. I am...something else now."

A murmur ran through the gathering. It sounded like rustling leaves beneath the noise from the crackling fire.

"More immediately," Grace continued, "we need to rest a little longer before moving on."

No, we don't, I thought, despite the fact we did. However, not here would have been my choice.

"Yes," said Neala, "you have been running for a long time."

Grace inclined her head in acknowledgment, her shoulders stiff. "You seem to know something about us, me, and my friends. I don't understand how word travels so quickly, but I accept it. There are many things I do not know or understand. What I need is a mage's teachings."

Another murmur rushed around. Heads turned, tipped together. Neala raised her hand in an unspoken command for silence.

"I don't suppose you have one of those secreted away here?" I asked her.

Grace's lids lowered. She shook her head, opened her eyes, raised them skyward. Annoyed, I knew.

Neala sat up straighter. A muscle in her jaw spasmed, perhaps in reaction to pain. Or to me. "We do not," she said.

"How do we get back outside?" I went on, feeling suddenly bold and reckless and disinclined to be treated like a thing to be squashed beneath someone's feet. "Because Grace does need those answers and we, of course, will travel with her. Where are we now in relation to...anywhere?"

Neala's breath whistled out her nose. "Your tone is offensive. This side of the Halcyon Range belongs to us. It is our domain. If you are suggesting we cower here inside the mountain, you are wrong."

The muscles in my stomach performed a rather nasty jerking, like they suddenly reached back to grab my spine. Still, she protested rather loudly what no one had specifically said. I tried for a levelheaded tone in response. "I made no such suggestion. I asked a question. A reasonable question. Because we haven't any idea where we are. Not really."

Neala attempted to stare me down. Because of her weakened condition, she looked away first. She addressed Grace.

"We are gifted in many ways, but we are not what you seek. We are not mage."

Grace rose. "Then perhaps we should move on now. Your hospitality as well as your help with the...*prair*, I believe you called them, is appreciated."

Neala nodded toward the vacated bench. "Sit, Grace. I believe you had other questions. Questions I can answer."

I decided on another tactic. I couldn't let the moment go. "May I speak?" I asked.

Grace's jaw clenched, then twitched into a small smile. Neala indicated I could go on.

"The *prair* took Grace deliberately. Does this sound like something they would do?"

Neala's brows lowered until they were a straight line above her eyes. Grace glanced at me. Worried.

"Tell me more," said Neala.

I continued. "Ren here told me my sister led him in his mind to me, maybe both he and Hannah to our general location? Resa—my sister," I clarified, "has never shown that gift before, so I—"

"I'm not lying," Ren interrupted, surly as always.

"I didn't say you were," I shot back at him.

Neala cleared her throat warningly, impressive despite her weakened state. "Your sister passed through the Sleeping Myth, did she not? As did you all."

"Well, yes, but I—Oh."

I turned my gaze to Resa with a renewed sense of…what? Awe? Disbelief? Fear? I couldn't be afraid of my sister. I wouldn't be afraid of her, despite what I knew. And yet, there it was, trepidation if nothing else, niggling in the sensitive place at my nape.

She'd been powerful enough, daunting enough, before our foray through that strange, organic-and-yet-not-organic mechanism. If word of this found its way into the cosmos or whatever generated the legend machine, we'd never be without greedy fools chasing us down.

"Far-Seers have many skills, many gifts. Perhaps hers were enhanced by the Myth," Neala said.

I whipped my head back in her direction. "Far-Seer?" I echoed.

"Yes, you ninny," Hannah hissed from somewhere off to my right. "What did you think?"

This, from the girl who had been scared witless of my sister. Who seemed not to understand her power at all. Had she been faking that, or had everything fallen into place for her at some point later?

"You knew a Far-Seer," I said to Hannah, remembering. "She sent all of you after us. Pointed us in the direction of the Sleeping Myth." I frowned. "According to you, anyway."

"Enough!"

I jumped, literally jumped as I spun on the ground to face Grace. I found her standing. Dark pink slashed across each cheekbone. She was pissed. Oh, boy, was she.

Grace addressed Neala. I took the hint and remained silent while she spoke. "If Resa is one of these Far-Seers," she said, "is it common for them to reach into someone's thoughts and direct them?"

"No," said Neala, her tone cautious, "I've not heard of it, but since she did pass through the Myth—"

"Are there many Far-Seers?" Grace cut in. I knew why she asked. When Hannah had first mentioned communicating with one, Grace had been startled by the reference. Far-Seers hadn't populated the countless desert tales she'd learned. Yet, the name made perfect sense, considering what I knew about Resa's troubling gift. She saw and heard—in her head not through her ears—things occurring in distant places, not like a vision of future events, but as they took place. I wondered if all Far-Seers were the same. If so, that would be frightening, because Resa's gifts didn't end with her ability to witness incidents transpiring in locations beyond her.

"Pardon me," I said, trying to sound deferential to appease both Neala and Grace. "My sister is referred to as the thrice-gifted child. Do you know what her three gifts are? Before this one, this new one," I added, although I wasn't entirely confident it had been Resa leading Ren through the caves. Something else could have been doing that. Someone else.

The sense far more was at play crept around inside me again, chilling my veins, slipping into my brain and out through my skin pores. I tightened my muscles to prevent a shiver.

"Besides being a Far-Seer?" Neala said. "The prophecy states she is powerful indeed. We have heard rumors she can lift and toss about objects, people, with her mind. Is this not true?"

I said nothing.

She gave me a tired, suspicious look, taking my silence as admission, I suppose. After a moment, she went on.

"And there is your sister's symbiotic connection to certain, fearsome individuals." She glanced at Carina and Grace. My brow puckered. Carina, fearsome? Grace, I could see, sure, and Carina had her mystic gifts, but fearsome? Anyway, how could that be part of it, when Resa had only met them a relatively short time ago and had been afflicted for nearly her whole life? Gods, I didn't understand this. It made sense in one way, but in so many others, it didn't. At all. My head started to ache trying to figure it out.

"Why did you and your warriors come to the water?" Grace asked.

Yes, good question. Sensible question. I focused on Neala, on her answer. I saw the words forming on her lips, eyes revealing a certain thought train before she spoke. Explaining the coincidence which had brought them to the lake at the same time Grace had arrived there wouldn't be easy. Couldn't be straightforward. More than likely, not coincidence either.

Right. Not coincidence.

I stood. My friends followed me upright. So did Neala's warriors. Alwyna rose, too, leaving her mother seated. Neala reached up, touched her hand. She shook it off.

"We were directed," Alwyna said.

"What?"

"Directed. We were directed to go there," Alwyna repeated.

My eyes went to Resa. Resa who stood with her

gaze cast down, lost in the goings-on inside her head. Suddenly she stooped, lifted something small from the ground and held it up. A minute winged and colorful creature. I wasn't sure how any of us had missed it lying near her feet on the chilled, drab stone.

I took a step closer, a weapon in each hand, not to use against this little thing, but because of necessity. No matter what Neala and her people wanted us to believe, we were surrounded by hostile intent. And yet the creature drew me in as if nothing else mattered.

"Beware," a voice called out.

I ignored the odd warning, dropping to one knee beside my sister, bending closer to her hand. The creature had burrowed into the cup formed by her palm, delicately breathing, wings fluttering half-closed along its back. Light flashed along its many colors.

Scales, I realized.

Yes. Scales.

A dragon. The thing was a tiny, tiny dragon.

The air above our heads erupted into flame.

Chapter Ten

I threw myself on Resa, dragged her down, rolled beneath the nearest bench. I heard desperate shouting, startled screams, feet thudding, bodies dropping. I saw their shadows crawling elbows to the ground for safety.

Someone shoved into our hiding space. I turned to find Ren's yellow hair nearly in my face. Resa struggled against my grip. I willed her to be calm with everything in me, despite knowing it hadn't worked in the past.

"Where are the others?"

Ren shook his head. "I don't know. Out there."

"What is going on? Are we under attack? Did you see?" Had someone's army discovered us? Decided if the girls couldn't be captured and controlled, they may as well kill us all and be done with it?

"It—it was one of them," Ren stammered.

"The Fianna?" Shock made my voice squeak. I thought I'd grown beyond that years ago.

"N-no. D-d-dragon."

I glanced aside at the tiny thing still clutched in Resa's hand and back at Ren, whose pale face had turned to mine. "Wait," I said. "Like the one in the cave?"

Ren nodded.

"Did it knock something over? Where the hell is the fire coming from? Not from it?"

"The building," he said. "It knocked the roof in, I think."

I swore colorfully. "We have to get to the others. We—"

The bench shielding us lifted straight into the air. Whirled away. I looked up into smoke and flame and ash. Arched, like a domed ceiling. As if something held it at bay. I stretched my neck, turned my head, and saw Grace.

Despite the immediate heat, my body went cold all over.

Grace, my brave Grace. She'd faced down the *conjure* before it knew her. Taken on a contingent of the mutants on Emerald alone. Marched straight into Stone Tiran's encampment to save Resa. Confronted the Lyoness in a room surrounded by her armed fighters. But this was a bold, new Grace. She held back the flames in an inverted bowl above our heads with a power she hadn't had or hadn't known she possessed back then. Sweat beaded her brow in concentration. Her raised hands glowed. Her limbs quivered. But the spell or the gift or whatever it was, held.

I'd made jokes about Scary Grace. Scary wasn't the word for her anymore.

"Resa, no!" I cried as my sister wriggled to face Grace and broke away from me. I scrambled up after her, leaving Ren cowering on the ground behind. An instant later he appeared at my side, rushing me from a low position, grabbing my coat.

"Wait!"

"Get off!"

He yanked harder. "No, Duncan. Wait."

He'd called me Duncan. My head spun in confusion. Extending my arm, I grabbed his collar and jerked him upright, pulled him along beside me as close to Grace as I dared. Resa had joined her. Carina, too. Mika and Brand and Hannah crouched at a short distance, gaping in the direction from which I'd just fled. I followed their gaze.

Atop the hall, the hallowed hall where I, Mika, Brand and Ren were unwelcome, a dragon stood, its claws embedded in the roofing material, white wings spread wide. Flames shot fitfully from the dark and battered roof, leaping up here and there. Stone and broken wood littered the ground. I heard cries from within, remembered the two little boys and the woman who had served us our meal earlier.

"Go."

I glanced back at Grace. She spoke again through clenched teeth.

"Save them."

I don't pray. My family isn't like that. But I did right then, grabbing Ren again, hurrying across the open space to the crumbling doorway. We pounded into the flame-lit darkness. Footsteps echoed behind us. Brand encouraged us to speed as he raced to catch up.

I heard a female voice echoing his, recognized it. Alwyna. She and three others charged into the damaged building. I half expected them to try to stop us, to keep our kind from fouling the sanctity of the hall, but they passed us by, urging us on toward the building's rear.

"The preparation areas are this way," Alwyna

said. "They'll be in there."

Little light entered the space now, the flames confined to the front. Where the domes had likely admitted sunshine there was now only shadow as the beast's great hulk blocked them. Even so, I could see where the roof was giving way beneath the dragon's weight.

"Faster," I said.

I tried not to think about Resa, Grace and the others still outside. The imminent roof collapse over our heads. The fact a dragon—a dragon, *again*—had entered our midst undetected, damaging the hall before anyone even noticed it.

"Here!" Alwyna cried.

We pushed in over already accumulating debris to dark space. I made out a gleam here and there from metal and glass. Remembering the kinetic torch in my jacket, I pocketed a blade and yanked the torch out. Activating the beam, I pointed it around the room.

"Over there," I directed, holding the light steady. "In the corner."

The woman, the two kids, huddled beside a huge hearth. They were helped to their feet. Brand asked if any others were hiding. The woman shook her head. I didn't want to rely on someone in shock and started looking around myself. Ren had his own light out now, shining it into the space immediately around them. Alwyna and one of her warriors followed me.

"Hello?" I called. "Is anyone else here?"

Hearing debris shift, I whipped my torch around. Nothing. And yet…

"What's that?" I indicated a shadow with my pointer finger, my weapon clutched tight in my palm.

"I don't see—"

"Right there."

Alwyna's breath whistled through her nose. "How did that get in here?"

"What is it?"

"A *dollywop*. They live in the cave systems. Harmless, but they avoid people."

"Let's get it out, then," I said.

"No time. We need to move."

Despite being torn, expediency seemed best, and I started to turn away. One of the boys called out from the darkness. A name, I thought. Something strange to me, but the creature answered with a small bleat. I spun back, ran in its direction. Behind me, Alwyna uttered a word I didn't know, but understood. Too bad. This thing was the kid's pet.

As I neared, it started jumping erratically, stuck somehow. From the vast front room, I heard crashing as more roof fell in. "Help me," I said to Alwyna who, for some strange reason, had followed me.

"Idiot boy," she mumbled. She didn't leave me, though. Instead, she bent beside me and, despite her injured leg, grabbed the log obstruction and began to pull. I did likewise, snatching the creature as soon as it came free. Claws dug into my sleeves. And my pants. And my coat, heading for my face.

Something fell over it. Alwyna's cloak. She grabbed my arm and tugged me away. I wrestled the *dollywop* into submission beneath her garment and together we scurried toward the rear door, meeting the warrior who had accompanied us.

"They're outside," she said. "Hurry."

Flames had entered the kitchen. I felt their heat at my back, saw the orange light shimmering over the walls. Clutching the clawed and frightened animal to my chest, I burst into the open. The noise out here appeared even more horrendous than it had beneath the failing roof. One of the boys raced over to me, arms outstretched. I pulled away the cloak covering the creature and held it out. Hairless black skin reflected the firelight. Long claws stretched and clicked on the two legs bursting up from confinement. I hesitated to release the thing. It looked like it could tear somebody to shreds.

"Beatrice!" the boy exclaimed. My eyebrows shot up. Beatrice. I handed Beatrice over to someone who obviously loved the ugly thing. The animal wrapped all its long, skinny legs around him and clung on. Pivoting, I handed Alwyna's cloak to her, readying to run. She grabbed my wrist.

"Well done, idiot boy," she said.

Her words made my face heat. I shook her off with a nod and a thanks and hurried back to Grace.

At first, I couldn't see her, or my sister. I spotted Carina's head, though, her white hair lifting in the heat from the fire, swirling like smoke itself. Spread out behind her and to the sides in an uneven half circle, everyone stood immobile, staring. At what? Not up, not toward the roof. My eyes went there, though, wondering how they could ignore the animal destroying the hall. Flames still rose from the wrecked building, but the dragon squatting up there had gone.

I pushed my way forward to Carina's side and stopped short, head turning. My heart paused with a solid thump. As did time. Just for a second. Everything, or perhaps only me, felt frozen, and then my mouth opened. A word popped out.

"Grace."

I started toward her. Carina's hand came up, touched mine. Not in her mystic's way, to shut me down, but merely to stop me. I obeyed of my own accord. It would have been very dangerous not to. I understood that when clarity finally reasserted itself.

"Don't move," Carina whispered.

An unnecessary command. I'd already figured as much. I realized after a second that she wasn't speaking to me, but to Brand and Ren, who had appeared behind.

"What the—" Ren began, hushed by something Brand said to him in a harsh undertone. After that, silence reigned among those gathered. It made the crackling flames in the hall seem overloud. That, and the deep-bellied breathing, in and out, of the dragon positioned before us.

And right in front of it, Grace, and my sister.

The skin beneath my clothing prickled like it might dance off my bones. My clenched jaw like it would pop. My heart like it would never beat normally again. *Grace*, I said, inside my head. I didn't dare utter her name out loud.

They stood side by side, Resa and Grace, almost beneath the dragon's arching neck. Its head inclined right above theirs. Only an arm's length existed between. I fought the urge to charge the creature, to attack it, to snatch my sister and Grace away. Provocation would be deadly, especially now we all stood exposed.

Resa's arms slowly lifted. Good, good! I thought. Blast the thing away. Yet that was not her intent. Her hands were not turned palm out, but palm up. When my tiny sister had extended her reach as high as she could, Grace took over, lifting her into the air. Right up to the dragon's mouth.

Grace! What are you doing? My screams were silent, contained to my brain. I didn't speak, didn't move. Trust. I had to trust her. To trust them, together. Carina, too.

I felt pushed to the outside suddenly. Not a physical push, but something deep inside. Displaced. That was it. As if my place among our group had changed.

I continued watching the peculiarly elegant motions before me. They seemed almost ritualized. Which was nonsense. One didn't prepare for something like this. One didn't anticipate facing down a dragon. Was that what they were doing, though? I didn't think so. It seemed something more.

I spotted movement in Resa's hands. Colorful movement. Winged movement. The tiny dragon she had found on the ground. I noticed something more, as well. The dragon's white back held color, too. Along the spine, brilliant, shifting color. Living things moved there. Mini-dragons like the one on Resa's palm. Dozens of them.

Babies.

My jaw unclenched. My mouth dropped open. Fearlessly, Grace and my sister returned offspring to parent, allowing the apparently flightless little beast to scurry along the dragon's face to join the others on its back. So many questions raced through my brain. How had the baby gotten here? What had led Grace or Resa to understand this was what the larger one wanted? How had chaos ceased and this stillness settled? Would the dragon just fly away now? Why hadn't the creature killed them both? Killed us all?

"It's all right," Carina whispered to me. Calm filtered through my frantic thoughts. For once, I didn't rebel against her listening in.

There was a zoo attached to the casino where Gran worked. For the families who visited Riley. Not usually for the ones who lived there. Yet, I'd been to it a few times. I remembered the *ondoids*, short-legged animals with long, ugly snouts. They carried their babies on their backs for months, until they were old enough to forage, to run, to hide. Good parents, my Gran pointed out. The cruel reminder in her statement had been unintentional. She apologized after.

Grace lowered Resa to the ground. With a hand on my sister's shoulder, Grace backed away, Resa at her side. The dragon turned, head and neck first, followed by body, its long tail lashing the building. Wings arched, it beat the air and lifted from the ground. Grace dipped protectively over Resa as the rushing air pushed my sister back. The dragon rose in a spiral, heading not for the opening to the sky, but toward a ledge on the rock face far above the last habitations carved into the mountain. Folding its wings along its side, the dragon scuttled inside. I spun to the nearest warrior, demanding to know if they were aware a dragon lived in their midst. The warrior happened to be Alwyna.

"Yes," she said. "They are kept away from the dwellings by a barrier created long ago by those who had the gift. The barrier has always held, as it was designed to do. The dragons stay away from us, coming and going through the sky-rill." She pointed to the wide gap far above our heads before glancing around at the damaged hall, the burned vegetation. "I don't know how this happened."

"Dragons?" I echoed. "There are more than one?"

"Of course." She tipped her head to the side. "Where do you think the babies come from?"

I narrowed my eyes at a question which seemed a cross between insult and flirtation and turned away, hurrying over to Resa and Grace. I threw my arms around them both. My limbs shook.

"It's okay, Duncan," Grace said. "We're all

okay."

I nodded against her. "How did you know what it wanted?"

"I didn't. Resa did."

A small breath exited my nose. I released her and stepped back. "I don't get it. I don't get it at all. Resa is changing. I know we've all seen it. But she really is, isn't she?"

"Yes," Grace said. "She is."

"For better or worse?"

Grace lifted her gaze to mine. "I don't know."

Yes, that was the problem. None of us truly knew anything. We were all guessing and flying, as Gran so often said, by the seat of our pants.

Boots sounded on the ground behind me. I turned. Neala's warriors approached. They looked oddly formidable with the hall burning in the background. It took a moment for me to recognize their weapons had been stowed away. They strode with their arms at their sides, hands empty and open. Alwyna walked in front, straight up to us. Mika, Carina, Ren, and the others stood off to the side, watching in uncertainty.

"What is it?" I asked. Maybe I made the wrong choice, being the one to speak, but I'd grown tired of having to dance around them, not knowing which time I opened my mouth was the one allowed and which wasn't, which time might get me skewered and which might get me a casual taunt from Alwyna. With Grace and the others, I knew where I stood. We all did.

"Will you come with me, please?"

Please. That was different. I glanced at Grace.

"Where?" Grace questioned, not moving.

"To my mother. She's over there." Alwyna indicated a point beyond her shoulder.

We followed her. Alwyna's limp had become more pronounced. Grace's, on the other hand, seemed non-existent. I knew Grace's wound still pained her but she appeared to be mastering it. Alwyna's was fresh. When she stumbled, I almost reached out to her. Common sense stopped me in time. Saying please was one thing, being assisted unasked in her weakness by me or any other "lesser" folk would be something else. I glared at the back of her head.

Catching my expression in her peripheral vision, Grace whispered, "You need to calm down, too."

"I am calm," I said.

"And thank you," she added.

"For what?"

"Saving the boys and their mother."

"No problem," I said. "Where is the man in her life, do you think? I mean, if the kids are hers..." I quickly recalled my own father. "Absent, I guess."

"I suppose so," Grace responded, sounding like she wanted to drop the subject.

Okay, fine. She was as much in the dark as I. It wasn't the time for this discussion. I got it.

Neala sat on a bench, her clothes disheveled and dirty, a red smear across her forehead. Blood, but not much. The other benches around her had been overturned, some broken. A half dozen warriors flanked her, equally as dirty, cloaks tangled and torn. Grace strode past Alwyna and approached the woman, bowing her head.

"Are you unharmed?" Grace asked her.

"I am," Neala answered. "Sit beside me."

Grace did, still holding the staff that had appeared in her hand. Well, not appeared, but one minute her hands had been empty and next time I looked at her after leaving Neala in her bedroom, they weren't. I'd nearly forgotten, what with the dragon attack. Question for later, not now. I stood by in curious silence.

Neala studied her interwoven fingers. Grace glanced around. "This place reminds me of Landing somewhat," she commented.

Neala's breath went out. She lifted her head. "There may be a reason for that. They were built at the same time, I believe. When our ancestors found this place after the last War, it had been long abandoned, the residents rumored to be long dead."

She said war like that, as if the word needed a capital W. As I supposed it did.

"The war which destroyed Olympian," Grace said, for clarification. I don't think any of us needed it. We all—except Brand—had been to The Wilds, seen the destruction not quite hidden beneath the vast forest, been captive in the reconstructed city, heard the tales. Mika, Ren, and I had been treated to a firsthand glimpse of the glass mines. I checked my reflexive shudder in recall.

Neala nodded.

"Are we to be held prisoner here?" Grace asked bluntly. Leave it to Grace, fearing nothing, not even words and what they might invoke. It seemed to me the other warriors stilled, listening, waiting perhaps on Neala's reply. I slid my fingers closer to the cutter, casual-like, as if I might only be placing a hand on my hip. Someone hissed behind me, cut short. It had to be Carina. I couldn't keep my intent hidden from her.

"Why would you think so?" Neala finally replied.

"Your question is not a response. I would request that you answer me."

I eyed Grace sidelong, remembering how often I'd witnessed her not backing down, not accepting evasion, standing up to some truly frightening people. Neala must have recognized the same thing I and my companions had come to understand without reservation. You didn't mess with Grace.

"You are not a prisoner. None of you are. Our Far-Seer—yes, ours," she said to me, even though I hadn't spoken, "has been gone these past two months. She left with the last group of warriors who departed. She spoke of watching you cross the lands. She had knowledge beyond her kind, because she knew you would come here. And today…"

"Who called you to the water?" Grace asked.

"Not called," said Neala. "Directed. It was the last instruction from the Far-Seer before she left. That we should go to the Black Water on this day and wait for you there. But you arrived before we did."

This last surprised her, concerned her even, I could tell. I looked at Ren. He'd been listening with brows lowered, his eyes going to Resa and back again. He believed Resa had led him and Hannah to us. But what if he was wrong? And what about the *prair*? What part did they play in all this?

Grace brought the latter up. "Those creatures you call the *prair*," she said. "They took me by force to the place where you found me. Hannah," she added with a toss of her head in Hannah's direction, "was already there waiting for me."

I thought rather suddenly of Mika's game. The one he carried everywhere in a box under his arm on Emerald. The one he played obsessively. The various pieces being moved here and there toward a definitive end. An end not meant to be gleaned by an opponent. Not until it was too late. Not until the game was over and you had won.

A chill surged over my skin, lifted every hair on my head. "We have to go," I said loudly, way too loudly. "We have to go now."

Grace

Chapter Eleven

I rose, spun at Duncan's words, his tone. His fingers reached toward me as though he didn't realize what his arm was doing. Nearby, Alwyna's expression turned odd. Perhaps, she thought I would chastise Duncan for speaking out. I wouldn't. Why would I? I trusted Duncan. Trusted his instincts. I stood, took his hand in mine.

"What is it?" I asked him. "What do you know?" I'd asked him this question many times before. Not only him. Carina, too. Hannah. Anyone who might be aware of information eluding me. They all counted on me and I had none of the answers.

"I think this is all planned, plotted, playing out," he said.

"All what?" Hannah, appearing silently at Duncan's side. I'd almost forgotten how stealthy she could be. I'd almost forgotten her attachment to Duncan, too.

But her question was appropriate. I repeated it.

Duncan pulled his hand free, waved it around. "All of this. Our coming here. Meeting the Fianna. The *prair*. Hannah and Ren finding us. That should have been impossible, but it wasn't. Ren blames Resa for it, but I don't think that's what happened, and neither does he. Not now. Do you?" He glanced back at Ren, who shook his head in a slight movement.

"I've been feeling like something is off," Duncan went on. "Like maybe we're being manipulated. Like this is a trap. Not set by your people," he said to Neala, when she opened her mouth to protest. "By—"

"The Darkness," I said. "Whoever that might be. Whatever it might be."

Silent now, he nodded.

"We, too, have heard of the Darkness," Alwyna said.

Neala agreed, adding, "It is why so many or our warriors have gone into the world. To stop it."

"You're not safe here, anymore," Duncan said to her. "Not in this mountain. Not while we are with you. Maybe not anywhere."

I grabbed his hand again, lifted it to my face and held it there. My warm breath circulated over his chilled fingers and back against my skin. "You're sure?"

"Of course, I'm not sure," he said. "Which makes me more afraid than if I were."

Oh, yes, I understood that feeling. I certainly did. The strangeness he experienced had somehow affected me, as well. But who possessed such power to cause this, to influence us all?

I addressed Neala, asked her that very question.

"I believe you know the answer to that, Grace."

I stared at her.

"Dark Mage. Beings out of legend and unwritten history."

"They don't exist," I said.

"Neither did we as far as you knew, until you met

us."

My stomach knotted. I fought down bile and the churning food from our meal. I would not be sick. I would not allow myself the weakness or the luxury.

"This is what Kerrick told me, too," Duncan said, referencing the man who had helped him and the others after they escaped the glass mines. "About the Darkness, I mean. That he or she was an old being, somehow new again. A dark mage. I didn't want to believe him, though."

Mika and Ren, who had been with Duncan then, started asking questions, their voices tangled, overriding each other. I raised my hand.

"Not now," I said. "Please."

They subsided.

"You didn't tell me that part," I said to Duncan.

He looked away and back again. "I know."

Alwyna moved to stand beside her mother. She lowered her hand onto the woman's shoulder. "We know who you are," she said to me. "We know what you are. You escaped the Emerald."

"*We* escaped the Emerald," I corrected her. "Which would have been impossible, if not for Duncan and Mika."

"You have defied those who sought to kill or use you, stole the thrice-gifted child—"

"Resa's my sister," Duncan interrupted. "We saved her, we didn't steal her."

Alwyna continued as if Duncan hadn't spoken. "You took her from the usurper and defied the Lyoness in the City of All Dwellers. Destroyed the city itself."

I shook my head in fierce denial. "We didn't destroy the city."

"It was only part of the city," Duncan said. "And

yeah, that was Grace and Resa."

"Not helping," I said to him, dashing my lifted hand toward the ground. Pink light splashed like liquid, glinting off stone until it faded. Silence followed my unintended demonstration. I drew a deep breath, steadied myself, let the air escape. Duncan was trying to make a point, I knew, but it wasn't helping. Alwyna and her sister warriors wanted to believe so much more than what was true. Duncan, unwittingly or not, had fed into it.

"You recount these actions as though they were deeds in a glorious tale," I said. "It is not so. What we have been through is real and not at all what you imagine or have heard. We have fought hard, have been afraid, have made mistakes. On many occasions since escaping Emerald, we have had unexpected help. My friends are far more than brave. They are heroes. Yes, they are heroes. But not the heroes this prophecy would make of me and Carina and Resa. Together we are strong, *all* of us, but we are not that."

Alwyna looked as though she might argue. I delayed any speech by going on.

"I agree with Duncan. Our being here puts you in danger. Which is nothing new. It happens everywhere we find friends or aid or hope. If you might spare us a few supplies, we'll move on."

"No," Alwyna said.

My chest tightened. "No?"

"We will go with you, Grace. You will lead us."

I heard Duncan's muttered exclamation behind me. I had all I could do not to laugh. Not at him. Not at her, either, nor at her earnest belief. No, at the role into which she sought to put me.

"I cannot lead anyone," I said. "I am no leader."

"But you are," Carina whispered.

My breath caught. A sudden warmth coursed my skin, moved through my blood. I had stepped into a function like leadership to keep my companions safe. Maybe that was all this was, too. A function required by these warriors in their tribe. But Alwyna had to tread that path when her mother no longer could. Not me. I said as much.

"I am not ready," Alwyna declared. "No matter what my mother may think, I am not. And where we are going, out there, into battle, requires someone tried and true."

"Battle? We—my friends and I—aren't going into battle."

"You are," she said. "You must."

I shook my head.

Alwyna scowled. "You have been trained for it."

"I am a warrior. I am not a commander."

Aren't you? muttered Skelly. *Think about it.*

Not now! I shot back. I didn't need his badgering. Now, or ever. "I am nothing," I said, "except a danger. Whatever it is I have become, without training, without guidance, I may as well be this Darkness."

"Grace!" Duncan yelped, horrified.

Neala pushed herself up from the bench, took a step toward me. Dark smudges stood out beneath her eyes. A tremor shook her. "We will give you what you need. And directions to one who might help you. She is called Enid and lives alone in the forest. A hermit's life. She has been for more years than any among us can remember. When the time comes, the Fianna will join you. I do not expect I will be there, but if I can, you will find me at your side."

* * *

IN DARKNESS WE BREAK

We took our leave from the Fianna in the morning, following a much-needed rest after helping them to clear away the debris from the ruined hall. I'd heard the dragons in the night, a mournful keening echoing along rockface from nest to nest. Several warriors had been set to stand guard, to give warning if another came down. None did.

I thanked Alwyna and her mother again for the provisions we'd been provided. Our sacks replenished with water and non-perishable foodstuffs, we prepared to follow a path pointed out to us, one I wouldn't have noticed otherwise. Brand, however, observed it with a smile, asked no one in particular how he had missed it when we first entered the huge chamber. Duncan held the map given to us by another warrior, a cartographer. Duncan admitted he once held aspirations for mapmaking. Why he'd chosen the con artist's path, I didn't know. We'd never talked about it. Not in detail.

Those who had torches, lit them. We were leaving the sunlight behind once again, striding in single file into a passage much narrower than those we'd been following before our descent to the dark lake. Duncan mentioned claustrophobia more than once. Jokingly, I thought, but I understood why the term framed itself uppermost in his mind. Elbows had to remain at sides in many places to avoid collision with stone. The taller among us were frequently forced to duck our heads. My forehead and crown acquired several bruises before long. I don't think I was the only one, given the intermittent exclamations.

I finally handed Carina the staff the unnamed, blue-eyed Fianna had given me. Carina kept it upright in her small grip as she walked, calling out warnings when the cave ceiling dropped below a certain height.

I didn't miss the staff in my hand. The weapon had never truly been mine, after all. Even if it had been, no room existed to use such a defense here. I would make it mine, though, once we regained the freedom presented by a more spacious landscape. In honor of the warrior's gift and because I needed a weapon, I would prepare it for weight and exacting grip. Once *lathesa*, makeshift or otherwise, even a staff would become a critical ally.

"How's it going back there, Grace?" Duncan called.

I had taken a place at the rear, guarding our flank. Duncan walked just behind Mika and Carina, Brand in front of them, making sure we stuck to the path. Resa was squeezed between her brother and Carina for obvious reasons. Ren and Hannah filled the space between me and Duncan. We hadn't really discussed placement, but had fallen into position in unspoken recognition. An odd positioning, really. Not what we'd held in the past, although what was necessary at this point in our journey.

"Good," I said.

"Nothing following us?"

"Not that I hear. We're making so much noise, though, it's not likely I would."

He laughed, cut it short, and we all started taking more careful steps, reducing conversation to bare minimum. Even Carina stopped her warning calls and merely tapped the uneven ceiling to let us know when to duck.

"Oh," said Ren suddenly, turning to look back at me. "Those hairy creatures you're so fond of are outside waiting for us. They brought us here, me and Hannah, to this side of the mountain."

The *conjures*. My heart leaped in a light upward

beat. I nodded at Ren in gratitude for telling me. A moment later, uncertainty had me in its grip. I couldn't help but wonder if whatever—whoever—appeared to be manipulating events could have an effect on Chauncy and the other *conjures*, as well.

No, I decided. Deep inside, I knew this couldn't be true. The consciousness of *conjures* existed in a manner above and apart from such as we. They were other. They were original. They were *more*. I had learned this since Chauncy attached himself to me. We all had seen the evidence. With the *conjures* we would be kept safe.

Once we left the mountain, they would find us. Had the cavern tunnels been wide enough for passage, they would have tracked us inside. Chauncy had followed me underground in The Wilds. Since then, he and the others had defended us, steered us from danger, protected us from frigid cold. Despite the fact their hides smelled like bog mire and sulfur combined, no better champions could be found.

"How much longer before we reach the outside?" I asked.

"Not far," Brand called back quietly. "I see droppings. Creatures 'ave been in an' out."

"What size creatures?" Hannah questioned in a voice raspy with nerves.

"Small 'uns," Brand replied. "No worries."

We lapsed into silence again, our movements accompanied by the noise from rustling clothing, boot soles slapping on rock, Carina's sharp tapping with the staff above our heads. In time, I spied a pale glint on certain stones. A shimmer, a blink, and then gone. I squeezed my lids together, opened them again, making sure my eyes weren't fooling me. Duncan's question negated the possibility, unless he'd been similarly affected.

"Does anyone else see that?" he asked.

"Those lights? Yeah," said Ren.

"Me, too," Hannah chimed in.

"What is it?" asked Carina, lowering the staff and pausing. Brand stopped as well, looking back.

"Flowers," he said.

"What?"

"There's moss all along here," Brand explained, pointing his finger at a rocky ridge running perpendicular to the floor. "With flowers. The lights're activating 'em. Makin' them open. Glow. I figure the sun comes in at some point. We must be close to getting out."

For Brand, that was a lengthy spate. Duly warned, we avoided brushing against the stone and the growth there and continued walking.

"If they glow like this," Ren ventured to ask, "doesn't that mean the plants are trying to attract something, like food?"

"Yep," said Brand. "Insects, I guess. Too small to eat us."

"Glad to know it," Ren muttered.

"Paid attention in lessons, did you?" Duncan taunted Ren. Good naturedly, considering their former relationship. Ren glanced at him with a snort.

Within a short time, sunlight began to reach us, dimly at first, but growing until it saturated the rock walls like water. I had an urge to hurry everyone along, to place myself firmly in the daylight, face lifted to the sky. It occurred to me we had no idea what lay beyond, and my urgency altered. I called out to Brand, warning him to be cautious, and proceeded to squeeze around the others to join him, taking the staff from Carina as I maneuvered my way past. I spotted Brand's Y-shaped weapon in his hand and nodded in approval. I knew he carried stones to fit into it in his pockets.

The tunnel widened out slightly. Beyond, I saw a brittle blue sky and harsh reflection. Narrowing my eyes, I made out trees, mountains, more snow. Brand and I waited for the others to catch up. They paused behind us. Duncan moved up close. He raised the map to the sunlight.

"There's supposed to be a path once we're outside," he said. "I guess we'll find out."

"How far do we have to go?" I asked.

"A half day, maybe more, maybe less, depending on what we find out there. And if the *conjures* find us."

I grunted. "They will."

"What did you think of the Fianna?" He threw the question out in a casual manner that didn't fool me. "If...if that's really who they are."

"I guess we have no reason to doubt their heritage," I answered him. "As to what I think of them, I don't know. They are warriors. Some of them may even be gifted in other ways. They all could make light. That's something. But if you're asking what I think of Neala's promise, I can only hope they will be at our side when needed. Because I believe it will be when, not if."

Duncan's head moved in a short nod. Brand eyed me sidelong. The others still stood far enough back they didn't appear to have heard our conversation. That would do for now. I didn't want everyone worrying. Too much.

"So, you trust them," said Duncan.

"As much as I trust anyone but all of you," I said.

Together, Duncan, Brand and I stepped out onto a

ledge. The mountainside dropped in steep descent. Rocks and trees marked the terrain, some ice-covered. Silently, I wished for an end to this freezing landscape. I'd had enough. Looking right and left, I saw trodden trails visible beneath the snow in each direction.

"Which path?"

Duncan double-checked the map before jerking his head left. "This one."

The track was wide enough for two to move side by side. The mountain formed a boundary on our left and trees and rockfall some protection from a misstep on the right. Jackets were fastened, hoods pulled up, gloves tucked into sleeves against the biting gusts. Although chilly compared to a temperate desert night, the caves had at least shielded us from wind and blowing snow.

Duncan tapped the map. "I don't really know what the distances are. The Fianna seem to have a different term of measurement. I've tried to estimate based on the distance we've come through the tunnel. It's the best I can do. If the lines aren't accurate, well..." He stowed the map in his coat.

"We'll be fine," I said. "Are there landmark indications? Place names?"

"Landmarks, yep. Not many names, though. Settlements may be few and far between. I don't expect to come across anything large, do you?"

I shook my head in response. I knew nothing about this part of the world except for the continuing visualization in my head of a looped bearing. We needed to see this Enid Hartshorn first. I had a feeling, a feeling I determined to nurture, that she could help me. Help us.

The path ran straight for a time before veering

downward. Wicked weather had caused trees to fall across the track here and there. We shoved some barriers away and had to climb over others. The trail beneath remained clearly defined, however, for which I was grateful. It wouldn't do to get lost in this terrain. If the path disappeared, the map would be useless.

And where were the *conjures*? I had expected their arrival as soon as we exited the mountain. They, especially Chauncy, possessed an uncanny sense of *us*. Or perhaps only me. It didn't matter. They always seemed to be in the right place at the right time.

Maybe this was the wrong time.

Or the wrong place.

I swore. Duncan stopped dead.

"What's up?" he said.

"Where are Chauncy and Vigor and Bell?"

"I... Not here yet."

I spun to face Ren and Hannah. "How did you two get into the mountain? Where?"

Ren opened his mouth but didn't speak. He looked perplexed, glanced at Hannah, who appeared equally as befuddled and shrugged.

"I don't remember," she said, then turned to study our surroundings. "Somewhere above here, I think."

"But you're not sure," I pushed.

"No."

I swore again, a virulent stream. Hannah's pale eyes widened, went moist as if she might cry. "Think hard," I said. "Did you really come here on the *conjures*?"

"I—"

"Yes," interrupted Ren. "I know that for sure. You can still smell their stink on my clothes." He rushed forward, holding up his arm and pushing his sleeve toward my face. I leaned toward it, took a deep whiff. Duncan did as well.

"Yeah," said Duncan, "I smell them. You do, too, right?" he asked me.

"I do, too." I let my breath out.

Something had interfered with their memories. Could it be the *prair*? Not likely. They had their own agenda deep underground. Ren and Hannah stumbling upon us seemed to come from a greater influence that happened to coincide with whatever the *prair* had intended. Frightening, whether deliberate or not.

I peered around through the snow-laden trees. "Then where are they?"

"I don't know. We should keep moving, though. We have no idea what else exists out here."

"Right," I agreed. I led the way.

Everyone listened for signs of movement in our surroundings, not speaking. Eyes sought the cause to every sound. Weapons had been taken out. Brand had a stone at the ready for his slingshot. Carina's pocket bulged with her own stones, small enough for her hand's wicked aim.

At a distance down the mountain, we came to a crossroad. Not a road, exactly. The worn track continued straight and another extended to either side, both free from debris, making their course obvious. A small statue marked the place on a narrow plinth. I reached into my pocket and pulled out the talisman Hannah had given me. The Crone. They were very similar.

"You said you lost it!" Hannah exclaimed. "I heard you."

"I lied," I said.

"Why?"

"Because I didn't want it taken from me." I

pointed at the statue and addressed Duncan. "Is this on the map?"

"No mention of the statue. But there's a crossroads. Here," he said, showing me the paper. "So, we go left. Downhill."

"Are you positive?" Ren asked.

"Look," said Duncan, holding the spread map up to Ren's face. "The mapmaker marked the route. There's not another crossroads showing until down here." He tapped the aged paper. "Not before, only well after. And the marked route doesn't go in that direction, it turns here. This has to be the way."

He sounded very definite. Maybe too definite, as though he were trying to convince himself. Yet, I could see the markings made by the warrior and they appeared to indicate exactly as Duncan said. We moved on, descending toward an unseen valley. I assumed the closer we got to the valley the less snow would lie on the ground. We were a long way from my desert home, but I would welcome green growth underfoot. Sand would be better, but I had no idea when I'd see the desert again. Citadel had possessed lovely green spaces, though, lawn and trees and flowers. Parks, they were called. Parks which had all been burned to ash.

My imprisonment in Citadel's Quadrate, the mock trial, my sentencing, all came back to me in a rush that made me gasp. Duncan's part in it, too. I eyed him askance, calming my galloping heart. Sensing my gaze, he turned his head and studied me.

"Grace?"

"I'm fine."

"You sure?"

I nodded, prodded my thoughts away from memories and back to our situation. What was done was done. I knew now Stone Tiran was a small player in a bigger game. He probably didn't know it, though. I don't think any of them did. They all thought they were—what did Duncan call it? Top dog. Strange name, but appropriate. It most definitely formed an image that put them all into perspective. Snarling and brawling for position at the heap's pinnacle.

I hated them all. I hadn't been one for hate. Annoyance, yes. Dislike, disappointment, disdain, certainly. Hate wasn't something I'd been taught. But I'd learned it. The feeling had only gotten stronger since passing through the Sleeping Myth. I needed to overcome hatred. I knew this. Recognized the truth in it. Hatred would not triumph over whatever awaited us. It would cripple me.

Brand called us abruptly to a halt and silence. I lifted my yet unaltered staff into a position for defense and listened.

I heard nothing. Brand, with his attuned hearing, had turned around to face the direction we'd come, his head cocked to one side. He lifted a hand, the one with the stone curled in the palm, and raised his pointer finger into the air.

"What size thing?" I asked.

"Large enough," he said. "Walks with care. Not those beasts o' yours."

"Crap," Duncan growled.

Before reaching Trill, a pack of some low-to-the-ground, long-toothed animals had hunted us, charging in for the kill, and might have succeeded if we hadn't kept chasing them back with stones and snowballs. Draig's fortuitous arrival with his troop had turned the tide. I'm not so sure we could have on our own, even with Chauncy's help.

"How many?" I said to Brand.

"Only one. Not sure."

I went to stand beside him. "Get behind us," I said to the rest. "Be ready." A second later Duncan appeared on my other side. The rest complied, crowding together at our backs.

"Can't you just knock it out?" Duncan said at my ear.

"I told you. I don't know how I did that. Think about Resa and how she is. Things happen. Like her, I can't necessarily control them."

His expression turned grim. "Okay."

I heard the animal coming now. We all could. As Brand had said, unhurried, stealthy, not small. It strode with some delicacy, though. Step, pause, step, pause. Closer and closer. Still, I couldn't see a thing.

"Brand," I said, "where is it?"

"There." He sounded breathless, awed. I followed his pointing finger. My own breath rushed out, left my lungs deflated.

Duncan stirred. "Where?"

I couldn't speak. Instead, I directed his gaze with the staff as the creature separated itself from the snowy backdrop. Nearly as white as the snow itself, as tall as Duncan or I at its shoulder, possibly weighing more than half of us combined, it took delicate steps toward us on long legs. Its hooved feet were dark in comparison to its pale hide, a russet brown, beautiful in hue. The animal had a wide, tapered head, ending in a pinkish muzzle where its nostrils flared, testing the air for our scent. Atop the head grew solid, wood-looking protrusions, branching out like a small, leafless forest from its skull.

"What is it?" I finally managed to stammer. "Brand? Do you know?"

Brand cleared his throat. "I've not seen the likes.

Similar beasts, though. With ruddy hides. Smaller antlers. Usually only two of 'em." He wriggled a finger on each side of his forehead.

"It's a Singer's Hart," Duncan said.

I turned and gaped in surprise at him, then quickly angled my gaze to include the beast still approaching. "How do you know that?"

"A picture in a book. A real book. An old one. My mom brought it to Gran's and left it there. She planned to read it to me, she said. She never got around to it before she took off again. I picked the book up myself, sometime later. I loved that picture. I thought it was from a fairy tale."

"Hey," said Ren. "Isn't the woman we're going to meet named Hartshorn or something like that? Funny coincidence."

"Not necessarily," I said. "Maybe her tribe or her family or whatever took their names from local beasts."

"Is it dangerous?" Hannah asked.

"Don't think so," said Brand. "But make no sudden moves, hear?"

I lowered the staff to my side. We all stood stock still, watching and waiting. I had never seen anything quite so beautiful, nor so ethereal despite its obvious gravity in its surroundings. The animal bore an intelligent, solemn look in its eyes. Without conscious thought, I bowed my head to it. It snorted, a mere breath, tossed the great, antlered head from side to side.

"Resa, no!"

Calling out to her was useless. Duncan knew it. Shock had compelled him. With all eyes on the hart Resa had slipped past us. Duncan started forward. I put out my hand, held him back. "Wait."

He shook me off. "Are you crazy?"

Brand grabbed his sleeve next. "Wait. Like Grace says."

Resa stood a single stride from the animal. The hart lowered its soft muzzle to within inches of her face. Resa reached up, lay her palm against the regal brow. Her fingertips slipped between the antlered forest branched out above her dark head.

"She has the animal gift," Brand whispered. "Like me."

Duncan exhaled. "Like you, too," he said to me. "That dragon didn't harm either you or my sister, and it so easily could have. Grace, the *conjures,* they *know* you. I think it's the only reason they tolerate the rest of us. What does this all mean?"

"I don't know," I said. But I needed to find out. It seemed more crucial than ever to get answers. Get them before it was too late.

Too late. Yes. Two words I should never use, even in thought.

Chapter Twelve

The ship's engine thrummed the air. It flew somewhere still beyond our sight, blocked from view by the trees that stayed green in winter. Conifers, they were called. Sometimes evergreen. Fortunately, they blocked anyone seeing us from above.

I grabbed Duncan's arm, turned him toward the others. "Get everyone under cover. I'll grab Resa."

I walked up to her slowly, despite the moment's urgency. I held out my hand. The huge white animal standing before her lifted its head and looked at me. Due to the eyes' placement, the sidelong gaze seemed almost contemplative.

"I have to take her with me now," I said, sliding my fingers into Resa's, warm from her contact with the hart's head. I was glad to know the beast gave off heat. I had vaguely feared it might be a construct of everyone's imagination, some manipulation by this Darkness about which we knew so little.

I moved my head in such a way as to indicate to Resa where the others had gone. She walked alongside me without resistance. The hart strode behind, close enough its breath moved across my neck, ruffled my hair. Did the beast plan to follow us now? I did my best to ignore its proximity as I hurried toward my companions with Resa. Above, the airship drew nearer, still hidden from view by snow-laden branches. Hopefully the craft did not possess an ability to track us through the growth and its operators relied solely on sight rather than a heat signature or something similar. Otherwise…

I didn't want to think about that.

I found my friends grouped beneath several huge branches hanging close together, almost like a tent or dome. They stared at Resa and me and the hart at my back as we approached.

"Grace," Duncan said, pointing.

"I know," I answered. "Your Singer's Hart followed us."

"No. No, it didn't."

My brow puckered. "What?"

"Turn around, Grace. Turn around now!"

I whirled about, pushing Resa behind me to safety. The staff whistled through the air in my hands. Abruptly, I dropped one tip to the ground, held it there.

"Who are you?" I demanded. A woman stood where the hart had been, the animal now waiting at her back. The woman wore white from head to toe, lowered hood, coat, pants, footgear, and her long, pale, silky hair shone like mist. Strands blew in the wind across her nut-brown face. My mind went to the Darkness unidentified and I raised my weapon once more. "Answer me."

"I am whom you seek," she said.

Duncan spoke, echoing my thought. "The Darkness?"

The woman shook her head. Her eyes seemed to

shift color like Carina's, from gray to brown. Yet, perhaps it was only the lighting beneath the trees.

Duncan stepped forward. "Are you—"

I held up my hand to stop him providing her any information. "What is your name?" I asked. "How are you called?"

"I am Enid," she said. "Enid Hartshorn, or so I am called by many. The name suits. I do not mind."

Duncan shook the map he somehow still clutched in his hand. "We are nowhere near—"

"I came for you," Enid interrupted him. "I am aware of everything in this forest. It is mine. Mine to protect. The ship has come many times in the past two days. It disgorges its soldiers to search the land. They return to the ship after, and fly off. They will not stay in the forest overlong, as well they should not. It is dangerous. To them, anyway."

My shoulders relaxed. "But not to us?"

She smiled again. "Not to you or to your friends. We must move on, however, before the ship sets down in the clearing."

She made her way around me, the hart trailing behind, walking past the place where Carina, Mika and the other three remained standing. She paused a short distance away. "You'd do well to come along," she said. "And you," she added with a nod at Duncan. "Stow that map away. You won't be needing it."

My lips curved. I liked her. I felt suddenly and totally at ease in her company. And that worried me. But not enough to stop me from touching Resa's shoulder and striding after the woman, Resa at my side. The rest fell in behind. Following Enid and the Singer's Hart, we wove our way downhill.

* * *

Enid's stone dwelling was circular and not very large. It had windows at various compass points all around, glazed with thick panes against the cold. The sloped roof overhung the structure by a good bit, shielding the windows from ice accumulation and, perhaps, the sun's reflection, giving me a clear view into the outside world. Or as clear as could be, with the trees closely grown all around. I stood with my hands folded at my back, listening to the conversation behind me. Enid only had two chairs for her small table, so most sat on the floor enjoying the meal Enid had provided. Enid neither ate nor prepared meat, she explained before dishing out a very satisfying vegetable stew. I'd already finished mine. From a deep armchair against the wall, Enid watched me. I sensed her eyes on me and finally turned in her direction.

She smiled. It seemed she did so often. Too often? Maybe. "I know why you keep watch, Grace," she said, "but they won't come here. They can't."

"But I can hear them," I said.

I could. Men shouting to one another. I saw none beneath the trees.

"They are not able to come here," Enid said.

Hannah had been observing us speaking, head swinging back and forth, an empty spoon held in the air. "Is it a warding?"

"Not a warding," said Enid, with a stern glance. "A warding is harmful."

"Don't I know it," Duncan mumbled around the semi-masticated bread in his mouth.

Enid's gaze turned his way, the curiosity in it fleeting, then went back to Hannah. "You might call it a charm. A beguilement. It is a barrier for those whom it is intended to keep out, but not for others. Also, the soldiers will not comprehend it, merely experience an unconscious decision to turn away, to believe nothing of import is beyond."

I didn't like what she was saying. It sounded too much like mind control. Yet, it appeared to be necessary to safeguard her and us. I tamped down my objections and stayed silent, turning back to my study. The hart grazed quietly outside on what appeared to be moss. Not the insect-eating kind, I presumed. No flowers, anyway.

"Maybe we can just stay here," Hannah piped up in a wistful voice. Enid said nothing. Neither did anyone else. We all knew better.

Enid's chair creaked. Light footsteps crossed the floor. Enid stopped beside me, her focus out the window on the forest. She stood at a height a little below my shoulder. I glanced at her boots. No heels. Her true height, then. She had that in common with Carina, too, although Carina was much smaller. Still, Enid's size, her nearly white and unusually smooth hair, her changing eye color, might indicate shared ancestry.

"You can trust me," she said. "I know you are worried about this."

Perhaps more like Carina than I suspected. "You're reading my thoughts," I said.

"No. Your body language."

I nodded, not quite believing her. She sighed. A dead giveaway, even if Carina hadn't suddenly said:

"Come and have more stew, Grace?"

"I'm good, thanks," I called back to her, duly warned. I returned my gaze to the hart ripping up moss.

"Whether you trust me or not," Enid said, "I trust

you. You and your friends. That's important."

"Yes," I agreed. "Trust is very important."

Her mouth curved again, her nose wrinkling. "I understand your reservation. You've been through a lot."

I huffed out a breath. "How does everyone know what we've been through? How does word fly so quickly?"

"The usual lines of transmission," she said. "They are still functioning. Not everywhere, but where it is necessary, I suppose. Also, word of mouth. Communication of the Far-Seers. Other ways. Quieter ways. More secretive."

"Why?" By the sudden silence behind me, I realized my tone had altered. I lowered my voice. "Who are we that everyone should be so interested? I know what I have heard. I know the rumors and the prophecy. I know what gifts we possess. But those things are not enough to warrant having everyone we've met know who we are, or to be sought by those we don't even know."

Enid's chin tilted up. Her eyes lifted to where a creature flew, a bird with a wide wingspan and dusky brown feathers, making its way over the rooftop. "Isn't it?" Enid questioned casually. "Enough, I mean."

Tears pricked my lids. A sudden and complete exhaustion dragged at my limbs. I looked accusingly at her.

"It's not me, Grace. This is how you truly feel. You need to rest or you will break. All of you. And you cannot break. You are counted on."

I thought back to Hannah's recent question. "Can we stay here?" I asked. "For a little while. I won't turn my back on the world we've all left behind, but I need help with who I am now. I need to learn. Can you do that? Can you help me? Help us?"

Enid stared at me. Her eyes went from icy blue to a green like my mother's. Like mine.

"Of course, Grace. To all of it."

When evening fell, we all bedded down in our usual positions in proximity to each other on the floor. But this floor was warm due to the heater Enid used. She said the heat was derived from the sun, but a flame burned inside the box, smokeless and hot. I didn't know the mechanism and after puzzling over it for a while, let it go, slipping into a deep sleep.

In the morning, I rose before the others and made my way to the window where I'd been standing for so long the night before. Intermittent winds battered the eaves. Flying snow circled in sunlight, whether fresh from the sky or off the trees, I couldn't tell. The hart had gone, but I didn't suppose it had gone far. They seemed connected somehow, the Singer's Hart and Enid. Like me and Chauncy.

My thoughts went to the *conjure* with fierce longing. Pressing my face closer to the block glass, I peered from side to side into the small clearing around the dwelling. I spotted a few *ken* pecking at the soil beneath the fresh snow layer. At least, they looked like the birds Mara's uncle kept. A whole flock from which he daily collected eggs, selling the excess to neighbors and at the market. Memory jumped out at me of a morning spent watching him perform what he called "candling" to make sure the eggs did not hold young *ken* inside. Did Enid use the eggs for food? My mouth watered recalling the taste. Ella prepared them often for the family at home. I had not contemplated such small and pleasant memories for a long time. I had not allowed myself the luxury, or the pain.

Perhaps Enid had access to a transmission device I could use to contact my family, to let them know I still lived, that I would be making my way home to them.

After, of course. Yes. After.

We, or at least I, had something more to do. No purpose would be served in going home if we had nothing to go home to. Any contact from me—if it could even be managed—would endanger family and tribe. Showing up among them would be worse. Besides, with the rumors about us spreading everywhere, news, no matter how convoluted, had already reached them. Silence would be better. For now.

Not exactly comforted by this bitter conclusion, I continued looking for the three *conjures,* hoping to find them hulking in the shadows beneath the trees. The shouting soldiers had disappeared before nightfall, presumably back to the ship. However, if Enid were correct, they would resume their search today. I had no idea why our pursuers believed we had survived passage through the Sleeping Myth and had found our way out from the mountain. I supposed they might only be seeking to make certain. Unless…

I turned, frowning at Ren and Hannah's sleeping forms. Hannah lay with her mouth open in slumber, as if she had not a care in this whole, wicked world. Ren, on the other hand, slept with his brow furrowed. Bad dreams? Probably. He had plenty to haunt him. The fact any of us slept without bolting awake in screams astounded me.

Could those two have betrayed us? Maybe not without persuasion, but they'd both suffered greatly at the hands of the Lyoness and I could understand if they succumbed to more recent threats or mind control. Ren and Hannah had been confused about the events leading them to find us, suggesting disorientation, and even before our sojourn through the Myth Hannah had tried to wrestle from me the very thing from which I was trying to keep her and the rest safe: Skelly and the crystal securing whatever he'd become.

Letting out a long, low breath, I returned to the window. After a moment, I slipped into my coat and boots and snuck out the door, shutting it quickly to keep the chill air from disturbing my companions' much needed sleep.

Cold seared my nostrils, bit at my cheeks like tiny teeth. It had been very warm inside Enid's home. Warmer than anywhere we'd been in a long while. Since our days in Trill at least, although I seemed to recall even there the rooms had contained a certain dampness. I suppose my desert blood caused me to feel it more than the others.

Enid had showed us the boundaries of her beguilement. The placement was impressive, going well beyond the circular clearing surrounding her home, out into the woods, at ground level and above. Since it wasn't set against me, I could have walked straight through the charm without knowing. Thus, I stayed within the cleared area as I walked. I didn't want to accidentally betray our location to those who hunted us by straying beyond.

Something made a noise nearby. I spun in a swift, defensive movement and spotted the hart. The beautiful Singer's Hart, raising its head from a mossy patch it had uncovered beneath the snow. It looked at me with a lingering gaze through eyes the same russet brown as it's hooves. I might have expected an animal with no discernible color in its hide to have equally colorless, perhaps even red eyes, but they were dark and penetrating.

"Good morning," I said.

The beast snorted, tossing its head from side to side. The antlers with their forest of branches caught a tree limb, the crystalline snow showering over its body sparking in the morning light. I walked slowly over to the creature, stopping an arm's length away. I lifted my hand as Resa had done. The hart bowed its muzzle toward the ground until my fingers could slip into the oddly long fur across its brow.

"I'm homesick," I said. "I can admit that to you. I'm worried. I'm afraid. I'm uncertain. All the things I will never say to my friends. They count on me to be strong." Blowing a breath out my nose, I tried to gather my courage, my determination. A light footstep fell behind me. The hart jerked its head away, stepped back with another snort, but it didn't flee. I closed my eyes, swearing silently.

"All right there, Grace?"

"I didn't hear the door," I said to Duncan. "You were very quiet."

"So were you."

He came closer, stood beside me. His arm lifted, settled on my shoulders. I leaned into him, despite my inclination to stay strong.

"I'm homesick, too," he said. "And worried, and afraid, and uncertain. We all are. That's why we stand together and not alone."

"I love you, Duncan," I whispered. "I know I've said that before. It doesn't change things between us, does it? We're still friends first, right?"

"And what? Lovers later?"

I jerked my arm, digging my elbow into his stomach. His breath whooshed from his mouth. He dropped his arm and doubled over with great exaggeration. I hadn't hit him that hard.

"Not funny," I said.

"Wasn't meant to be." He straightened. "It wasn't meant to be, at all."

My cheeks heated. He couldn't say things like this. The last thing I needed was distraction. I didn't want to think about entering a territory I'd really not given much thought to before our growing friendship. Certainly, I'd had passing "fancies" my mother called them, about…well, about Mara, mostly, but they'd been unformed, really rather juvenile when I looked back on them, especially in comparison to who I was now. Because I'd changed since I'd been forced from my home. Perhaps not entirely for the better. Yet for the most part, I felt no shame in who I'd become.

Reaching back, I slipped my hand around his, feeling the rough bandages against my bare, chilled fingers. Bandages and the heat from Duncan's skin. It seemed he always ran a few degrees hotter than I did, like an engine on overdrive.

"No matter what's ahead, what is in our future, we will always be friends, Grace. And I'll always be grateful for that."

I blinked, sniffed, turned my gaze to the trees. "Don't make me cry, Duncan Oaks. Because I will take pleasure in kicking your—"

He slapped his hand over my mouth. I tried to pull free, not amused, but then I saw the hart prancing fretfully, saw it rear and drop down onto all fours again, its great forested head tossing. Duncan yanked me away, hurrying me back toward the house before abruptly veering off to shelter beside a nearby shed. "Don't say a word," he whispered in my ear, easing his fingers from my lips, fisting them, pointing with

one to the shadows made by the morning sun.
    The shadows were moving. And when I glanced back at him, Duncan was gone.

Duncan

Chapter Thirteen

I heard Grace screaming. Woke up to it. Tossed the blankets across the floor before I even realized I was standing. Had my coat on before I reached the door. Snatched my cutter from the table where I'd left it and shoved my way outside without my boots, stumbling in the stone-filled pathway leading from Enid's cottage. Swearing, because the rocks hurt my feet through my socks. Swearing, because I couldn't believe what I saw.

Swearing, because I knew I was too late.

Grace had gone beyond Enid's barrier. She stood alone with a stick in her hand. A stick, not a *lathesa*. A damned twig. She held it like a weapon, though. Like she thought it something else. In her grip, possibly it could be more than a small and brittle branch, but I couldn't see how. I raced across open ground in her direction, ignoring sharp stone and bitter cold. Grace was not alone. More than a half dozen dark shadows surrounded her. Closing in for the kill, most likely. She didn't appear to see them. Her gaze went from the ground to something in the distance, a middle distance between me and her. Pain. I witnessed pain in her expression. Surprise. Struggle. Fear.

I shouted for the others, hoping they would hear me, and grabbed a hefty branch, a branch ten times as thick as the one Grace clutched. Switching on the glass cutter in my other hand, I ran at the mutant creatures from Emerald with a battle yell ripping from my throat. Grace had saved me from these beasts back on Emerald. I owed her one.

When I crashed through Enid's charm, it hurt. I hadn't expected it would. My skin burned, pricked, felt like it bled. I didn't bother finding out. I ran straight up to Grace and backhanded her in the face with the fist closed around the cutter. We didn't have time for niceties. I needed her to snap out of it before I, too, succumbed to the creatures. These creatures and their ability to twist a mind like fabric in the wind. If we both became ensnared, then we were both dead.

Grace's head snapped back from the blow. Her eyes flared with shock, then filled with fire. She raised the stick, the puny little stick, bringing it down like a blade toward my neck. At the last instant she turned and stuck the thing straight into the eye of the nearest beast. It drew back with a howl I heard in my head, and likely not elsewhere. These creatures were mostly silent except for occasional mimicry and the torment they inflicted inside you.

"Get behind me," she hissed. "Your back to my back. And give me that blasted club."

I did. She began swinging it. Sounds from impact made my gut wrench. I started applying the blade in the efficient way my uncle had taught me on the fly back in Trill. I remembered that day and the blood not my own and then tendrils of memory began to drift, pull away, shred, until my arm, my body, tried to follow.

"Duncan, don't give in," Grace ground out through her teeth.

My thoughts slipped away again. I heard my name spiraling into darkness. Someone calling me. Not Grace. No, not Grace.

Suddenly, I smashed facedown onto the ground. I tasted salt blood spurting from my lip. A weight landed on my back. I lashed out behind with the blade, waving it wildly, not wanting to end up like Skelly. Not wanting to remember the horrible way Skelly's life had been torn from him. Not wanting anything but to be back home again. Back on Riley. With Gran. Yes, with Gran.

What about Grace? I asked myself in a strange, filtered way.

Grace. Right. I lashed out again. Save Grace. Save Grace.

Something tugged my feet, my legs, dragged me over the cold, hard, forest floor. I bounced roughly, tried to kick out, get away.

"Hold on!"

Someone had my arms now. Mika. It was Mika, clinging to one outstretched arm. Ren had the other, and a leg. They shoved me against the nearest trunk, bark cutting into my face.

"Hold on!" Mika shouted again, wrapping my arm tightly around the tree. He and Ren grabbed on, too. Just in time. Our lower bodies lifted from the ground. Charged with static, the wind buffeted us from side to side, up and down until my teeth rattled, my bones popped. The noise filling the volatile atmosphere nearly deafened me. An abrupt clarity returned to my mind. I remembered.

"Grace!"

"Over there," Ren shouted above the din. I followed his gaze. Shock struck like a chill blade through my intestines.

The legendary three stood side by side. Resa, Carina, Grace. The thrice-gifted child. The witch. The warrior. Above their heads, circling in a maelstrom filled with debris and ice, the creatures from off-world rose higher toward the sky. Clearly, the beasts were no longer animate. Whether killed by the thrashing winds or something more direct and sinister, I couldn't tell. Below them, as if sheltered by calm, my sister stood with Grace and Carina. Resa and Grace's arms were upraised, Carina with a steady hand ready if needed. Eerily, their hair and clothing drifted in gentle contrast to the thrashing winds. Branches cracked and spiraled away with the creatures. Tiny now, they spun into the distance over the treetops, mere specks against the sky. Abruptly, the wind died. The spiral collapsed in on itself, raining debris all around. I plummeted to the ground. Despite the short drop, air burst from my lungs.

I struggled upright and ran toward the girls, swiping blood off my face and mouth with the back of my hand. Mika and Ren pounded after me. I had no idea where the other two had sheltered and only hoped they and Enid were unharmed. Grace turned as I approached. Severe concentration vanished from her face. I was met by a smile instead.

"I'm not a monster," she said.

"Of course, you're not."

"I'd feared I'd become one."

I put my arms around her and pulled her close. My limbs were shaking. All I could see in my head were the mutants, thrashed and discarded. Despite their terrible nature, their danger to all, the necessity for their destruction, I couldn't stop that image replaying in my mind. Couldn't stop the contradiction I felt, between the Grace I knew and the Grace the image presented. When she'd battled the beasts before, I hadn't really seen it. I'd been too out of it, remaining forever grateful for her rescue and for the not remembering. To be honest, she was covered with much less blood this time than the first, which maybe meant less brutality required. Even so, a certain unease threaded through my veins.

"I am not a monster," Grace repeated in my ear, as though she recognized my thoughts. "But I am a warrior. That cannot change."

She seemed comforted by her words. I held onto them, held onto her, seeking the same solace, until I heard Enid speak from somewhere nearby.

"Back inside the charm. Everyone back inside the charm. Breakfast, and then training."

As if nothing she'd just witnessed troubled her at all.

* * *

Not trusting anyone had become my stock in trade. Even before the events thrusting me into Grace's life. Back on Riley, once I'd taken up with the Grif-Drifs, I hadn't much choice. I'd developed the no-trust attitude because no one could trust me. I just had to make them think they could. Meeting Grace, betraying Grace, had changed me. Well, maybe not changed me into something different, but had caused me to shed the con-artist persona. But by being honest, truly honest, I found myself expecting the same from everyone else. Finding the world filled with people who lied with deadly consequences had been a brand-new eye opener. So, although I trusted me, trusted Grace and at least most of our immediate friends, my distrusting everyone else had only increased. It was therefore no surprise I watched Enid now through a jaundiced eye.

They all wanted something from us, from the three. The question uppermost in my mind? What did Enid want. Because she wanted something. I felt it in my bones.

By a mutual, silent agreement, we all helped with making the morning meal. We'd been doing so for too long to change our routine. The difference when we were somewhere food existed in quantity was only the amount to be prepared, doled out, eaten. We had eggs boiled in water, dried fruit from a cellar beneath the house, an oddly sweet tea, toast with cheese. No one complained about the taste or the fare. This was what I missed most on the run. A full belly every day. That, and a safe place to rest. And a comforting routine. And, yeah, Gran. I wouldn't admit that last out loud, but it was true. Even after leaving Riley to ply my trade in Citadel, I'd missed her. I'd liked my life with Gran. My chosen career had finally called me elsewhere. A promise of better targets.

What a mistake.

My gaze slid to Grace as I slowly chewed the toast in my mouth. Grace was not a mistake. Grace had saved me, in more ways than she would ever know.

Enid drifted toward the door, glanced back. "Training," she called, and exited as if she expected us all to follow. Which we did after piling the dishes in the sink, donning our outdoor gear, me with dry socks now inside my boots. As I'd pulled them on, I'd thought of my mom. She'd given them to me, back in Trill. Supplied us all with extra clothes. Begrudgingly, it had seemed, but she did it. I couldn't recall if I thanked her. It wasn't likely I'd ever get the chance now.

Resolute, especially after what had happened earlier, we all trooped out into bitter sunshine. I couldn't help but recall the one training session we'd had with Grace on Emerald Penal prior to escape. Grace had thrown me around quite a bit to make a point. In retrospect, I told myself she'd done so in order to instruct. At the time, though, it hadn't felt that way. More like payback. I'd still been feeling guilty about betraying her. Still did.

My gaze kept straying to Grace. Grace had confessed to having experienced some sort of delusion leading up to her encounter with the mutants. Rather than the disorientation these creatures usually imparted, a false scenario had been playing out in her head. She didn't want to talk about the details, dismissed them, but she kept glancing in my direction. The delusion worried me. Really worried me. Because maybe, just maybe, it hadn't been the mutants' doing at all. And it had seemed to involve me.

I eyed Enid and dismissed her as the culprit. Who, then? The Darkness? That was scarier still.

My focus turned to Grace. An odd sheen coated what I could see of her bronze skin. She looked tense. Too tense for training activity. Grace had counseled relaxation's importance during our single session. To loosen up before getting to the physical stuff. Of course, I didn't expect anything exceedingly physical would take place in Enid's training. From her position at the fore, the woman studied us one at a time.

"What I witnessed today was extraordinary," Enid said in general address.

I bet, I thought. Although I'd witnessed them in action before, Resa, Grace and Carina, I still couldn't quite wrap my head around the recent display. I hadn't witnessed what took place in All Dwellers with Resa and Grace, but I did see them hold back a dragon and its destruction only two days ago. This morning, though, had been shocking. And maybe a little terrifying.

Who was I kidding? A lot terrifying.

While Enid recounted what we already knew, I allowed my gaze to slip toward the forest, empty now but for small animals one might expect to find there. We were lucky to have survived the earlier encounter. Those who had been on Emerald understood more than the rest how unlikely an occurrence that was. Grace had mentioned her suspicions the mutants might have been dropped here by the ships. She was probably right. I couldn't imagine them getting this far on their own. They were being planted like an evil seed to hunt down not only us, but whatever, or whoever, crossed their path.

I shook my head, trying to clear troubling thoughts. Glancing at my friends, I found Carina watching me. I couldn't read her expression, but assumed she was, as usual, poking into my head. Beside her, Resa stared fiercely at the ground. At something by her feet.

Crap.

My gaze shot to the sky, searching for a dragon's broad wingspan. As with the Singer's Hart, Enid's charm might not keep dragons out, either. Seeing nothing resembling a winged beast even in silhouette, I quickly joined Resa, crouching to see what had her attention.

My brows drew down. The thing wasn't an animal, or plant matter. Not even a seed. It resembled a small, multi-pointed—very pointed— star made from some material I couldn't identify. Not metal. Not glass. Not wood. Perhaps stone, but the item possessed a translucence like black water. I reached for it. A sound came from Enid, stopping me dead.

She hurried to my side, her soles sliding a little on the frosty soil. "Everyone, look around for more of these," she said, indicating the one by Resa for everyone's edification. "Don't touch them. Alert me to where they are and I will gather them up."

I lifted my head. "What are they?"

Her mutable eyes, so much like Carina's, flashed from gray to red. "Something that should never have gotten through my shield."

Chapter Fourteen

I exhaled. Okay. Whatever the thing, from Enid's tone I knew it was not good. I signed to Resa not to touch it. She folded her arms across her chest, continuing to stare, but made no move to pick the star up. The rest of us checked the charmed area around Enid's house. Four more dark, star-like objects were located. Enid retrieved a canister from inside, shook heavy, off-white powder from it, which dropped to the ground leaving smoke-like trials in its wake. I wondered what mage stuff this might be, until I spotted the word "flour" clumsily printed on the side in black ink.

Using a fabric strip to protect her fingers, Enid gathered the stars and dropped them inside the container. She tossed the cloth in after. Murmuring to herself, or to the things inside, she fit the lid back on and tucked the canister beneath her arm.

I pointed at the container, couldn't help asking, "Does the flour have some magical properties?"

Enid glared. "Hardly. It was the only thing I could quickly grab. I'll have to get another. I can't use this one for flour anymore."

"Why not?" I pressed. "Is the canister contaminated now?"

Her eyebrows arched. "Yes. As a matter of fact, it is. I will seal this with some melted wax. It cannot be opened."

My breath went out again.

"What are they?" Carina ventured.

"Yeah, what?" prompted Hannah impatiently at Enid's hesitation. I noticed Grace still said nothing. Her green eyes went from the can to Enid's face without a question, as if she held some undisclosed information. Something she wasn't sharing. If she knew, I needed to know. We all did.

I tried to catch her eye. She looked away.

"We should leave," Grace said to Enid. "Now."

Enid shook her head. "No. Not yet. Not necessary. There is still time for me to help you before you go."

I exploded. My whole being exploded, like a vegetable in Gran's oven once. Meant to be pierced before cooking, but I'd forgotten, it had blown its insides all over the rack.

"Would someone please tell me and the rest of us who obviously know nothing about anything just what the hell is going on?" I shouted. It felt good to yell. Hurt my throat, but the release was worth the discomfort.

Grace and Enid turned to stare at me. Brand gave me a look I couldn't decipher. The others merely gaped.

"You can't keep secrets," I said. "We're in this together. We've been running because we've had to. Escape after escape. We can't go home. Not yet. So, we keep running. Seeking answers. Not getting much in the way of those, by the way, but now—" I paused, drawing breath, and went on after a moment in which no one said a thing. "Now, we are being drawn, or herded, or bamboozled toward something more dangerous than anything we've encountered. And yet, we don't even know what it is. And the two of you are sharing some hidden info that would probably benefit us all to hear."

Still, no one spoke. I pointed at the canister tucked neatly against Enid's ribcage. "Let's start with that. What are they? No enigmatic answers, okay? I've had enough. Grace, I'm pretty sure you already know, don't you."

Grace bobbed her head in a reluctant nod. "They're part of a cross between mage work and...technology, I guess. I learned about them during warrior training. As part of history's lore. They were last used more than a century ago, I think. I've never seen one in person, but I've seen images."

I gave Enid's canister another glance. A wary one. "And what do they do? What are they used for?"

"Tracking," Grace said.

I felt like I'd been punched, right in my mid-section. "What?"

Grace went on. Reluctantly. "They are imbued with blood knowledge. They seek out whoever's blood has been imbedded in their making."

"And whose blood might that be?" I asked, my skin crawling now.

"Except for Brand, we've all been imprisoned at some point," Grace reminded me quietly. "It could be any one of us."

I swallowed. Hard.

Enid cleared her throat. "They were used to hunt down refugees who'd fled Olympian in the last war.

Outlawed afterward. They can be cast in wide dispersal from—"

"A ship," I finished for her.

"Yes," she said. "A ship. From there, they move on their own, searching."

"Move?"

"Through air, along land, yes. Move," said Enid.

Ren piped up with a question. "Why are they shaped like that?"

Enid inhaled, exhaled, her expression grim. "Some points are barbed, like a seed would be, so they can cling and be carried along if necessary. Other points are needle sharp. For testing. For defense."

Ren made a face, as if sorry he'd asked. I pushed on. "You recognized these things, though. How?"

"I started finding them several days ago, out there." She jerked her chin toward the forest. "I looked them up afterward."

"On a computer?" I asked hopefully. I'd always been good with computers. I could use one right about now, to check on the state of things if nothing else.

Enid shook her head. "In a book."

She had shelves lined with books, old books, their bound spines tattered. I'd wanted to take them down, look through them. I knew I never would. Not if they held secrets like these. "What were those words you spoke when you put the star things in the canister?"

"A mage spell. Because Grace is correct. They are a cross between dark magic and science. I wanted them deactivated."

"Gods," I muttered. "We're really screwed."

Grace reached out, patted my arm. Like I was a kid in need of comfort. I gritted my teeth. She seemed to recognize the mistake in her gesture and whispered,

"Sorry."

"No problem," I said, scarcely getting the two words out.

Mika stirred. "What do we do now? If these trackers are locked onto our blood, or even just someone among us, how do we avoid them once we leave here? They got through your—your charm or whatever you call it. There are probably more coming, yes?"

Before Enid could answer him, Grace spun on her heel, looking toward the rocky, snow-covered peaks rising above the forest. "What if the trackers have gone into the mountain, have found Neala and her people? Because we were there, wounded. There must be traces of our blood inside."

Enid held her hands up in a placating gesture. "Please. Be calm. From what I know, they will only follow their intended targets. They may seek in places you've been, may even test the blood of those who have harbored you, but if it is, in fact, you they are after, then it will only be you they follow."

"Not reassured," I said.

Enid's eyes slid to study me. "I will alter the beguilement for as long as you are here, strengthen it, if you will. So long as you remain inside the perimeter, they will not detect you."

"But they already have," Mika argued. "I'm assuming some kind of signal is returned to those who sent them out. They know we're here. Right here."

"And we were all outside the perimeter a short time ago," I reminded Enid. I glanced at my sleeve still smeared with the blood I'd wiped from my face, and held it up for Enid to see. She nodded. Her nearly white hair caught the light.

"Understood." She looked around at the others.

"Who else has wounds?"

Hannah raised her hand, as did Ren and Mika. Grace studied her own fingers and arms, slowly lifted her hands, as well.

"Very good," said Enid. "Since we don't know whose blood has been imbued in their making, I'll take it all."

"Excuse me?" Ren. Eyes wide. I don't think he had quite grasped Enid's intent. But I had.

"How will it be carried?" I asked. "The hart?"

Enid smiled. The first real smile she'd given me. "Smart boy," she said.

I arched a brow at her.

"But not the hart," she went on. "Something with the advantage of flight."

Within seconds, she began instituting her plan. Even those who had no fresh cuts on their person pricked a finger with a thin blade Enid provided. We flicked crimson drops onto leaf bits and seed pods and whatever natural detritus lay about on the ground. After, she swept them all up into a cloth square and loosely tied it. Giving a piercing whistle, she searched the skies. I cringed and looked upward, half expecting a dragon to answer the call. Instead, a bird, a large, hook-beaked bird, swooped down and landed on a nearby branch in a tree within the charm. Enid spoke to it, tied the small, makeshift bag to its leg, and spoke to it again. With a mighty flap exposing the bird's white underbelly, it took off again, sailing out across the forest, bits of debris fluttering from the bag's opening as it disappeared over the trees.

"That was amazing," Brand murmured.

Enid winked at him. "A bit," she said. I snorted. "All right," she added, looking at me, "more than a bit. And now we've addressed that problem, let's return to training."

I unfolded a finger from my fist, pointing the digit into the air, seeking permission to interrupt. "I'm thinking maybe it would speed things up if you only dealt with the girls. It seems more trouble than it's worth trying to train us in anything to do with, you know, mage stuff." I indicated myself, Mika, Ren, Brand with a wave. "Unless you mean combat. Grace's kind. We could use some of that."

"When events make it necessary, that would be Grace's responsibility. However, you all have a part to play. You did not come together merely by accident. There is a design. One I can't see in its entirety. But you each have a strength, a gift, which will be sorely needed. You will train, and you will learn, and you will be…magnificent."

I actually blushed. I rarely did, couldn't recall to mind the last time. Probably in response to something Grace said. Never, when speaking to a…well, a woman of Enid's age. It was almost embarrassing.

I lowered my lashes, stole a look at Enid from beneath them. I really couldn't explain the heat to my cheeks. My no doubt stupid expression. But I'd never been told I could be magnificent. Maybe by Gran, but that didn't count. Not the same at all.

"Duncan Oaks," Enid said.

I opened my mouth to stall her. To cut her off. I didn't want to hear any more praise from her. She spoke before I got a word out.

"You must believe in yourself. You must have faith in who and what you are."

Crap. Sweat broke out across my forehead. I wondered if she could be causing this somehow. Intentionally. Forcing my idiotic reaction.

Grace turned her head. Her eyes widened. At my

expression? At the salt drops dotting my brow, despite the cold? I wanted to explain to her, but there was no point. I'd only dig myself in deeper. Instead, I focused on Enid's eyes, which had turned a pale gold.

"Duncan," she said, "do you know who you are?"

"Of course, I do," I stammered. "As you said, I am Duncan Oaks. I...I am son of Marcella and Aeron, brother to Resa and Toma, true friend to everyone here with me. Does that work for you?"

"But do you not know who else you are? Grace knows. She has seen it."

Grace shook her head, rapidly. "I have seen something. I don't understand it."

"Yet you believe he keeps it secret from you," Enid said to her.

"Keeps what secret?" In my growing agitation, Enid's effect on me lessened.

"Not secret." Grace spun on her heel to face me. "You're not keeping it secret, exactly. I think it's something you haven't recognized yet, have not wanted to talk about. The Darkness, Duncan."

"No," I said, appalled at the accusation. "I only know what Kerrick told me, which was scary enough. He said this Darkness, whoever or whatever it is, is binding together all those who seek power through this war. He didn't know how or who. And I don't either. I would have told you, Grace. You know I would have. Is this what you have seen? Is this what you believe? That I'm a liar?"

Grace stared for a moment. She drew a breath and darted forward, throwing her arms around my neck. She scrubbed her face against mine. "No, Duncan. I don't believe you are a liar. Not for one minute."

I tightened my grip on her. "Then what? What

have you seen?" Grace trembled. My breath hitched. Held.

She stepped back. "After we came through the Sleeping Myth, I kept seeing a shadow beside you. In my mind, not in reality," Grace hastened to clarify.

"Do you still see it?" I asked, remembering the shadow circling around Grace and me. The shadow that was Skelly before he was called into the crystal. My voice remained steady. Remarkable, considering.

Grace glanced over her shoulder at Enid before settling her gaze back on mine. "Yes."

"Do you mean like right now?"

"If I close my eyes."

"And?"

"And it's like you. A shadow of you. A double of you in shadow form."

"I don't understand," I said. My knees started to shake. I wondered if they would give out.

"The shadow is not you. Not exactly," Enid said.

I dropped my hands to my side, turned to Enid. "Perhaps you could explain this better, then. You seem to have some idea what Grace is trying to say."

"There is light, and there is darkness. You, Duncan, here and now, are the light."

"What? Wait. Here and now? You aren't saying I will somehow grow to be darker. Bad, somehow?" My hands flew out in front of me. I backed up. Shock shuddered through flesh and bone. Revulsion. Fear.

"Don't be ridiculous," Mika spat angrily, attempting to dismiss the concept outright. "We know you, Duncan. This lady is just trying to scare you for some reason."

Grace dogged my movements, her hands lifted toward mine. "Duncan!" she cried. "No! That's not it at all."

"How much time do I have? How long before I'm not me anymore?"

Somehow, Grace managed to grab my hands. She pulled me down onto the snowy soil, leaned in, pressed her forehead to mine. I wanted to shove her away. Instead, we knelt, knee to knee, brow to brow, hand in hand, both of us shaking.

"I don't think it's you. It seems to be a shadow of you, but I think it's someone or something else," Grace whispered.

"Like what?" I managed.

Boots came into my peripheral view. Enid dropped to her knees, too. She peered closely at me.

"Like your mother's firstborn," she said.

My stomach rolled over. My blood chilled. "I am my mother's firstborn."

"No, Duncan, you came into this world second. Nineteen minutes after your brother."

My breath caught in my lungs, as if clumped and solidified. Suddenly, I understood something I'd always known inside of me, something that had been hidden in a strange, hollow place.

I had another sibling. Another besides Toma and Resa. A brother I'd missed like a phantom, alien limb, a limb you weren't ever meant to have, but once removed, you never forgot. There'd been an absence in me making me search in everything I did for an answer I didn't know I sought.

A twin brother. I had a twin brother.

And *he* was The Darkness.

Pulling myself free from Grace's grasp, I veered sideways and spewed hot vomit over the ground.

Grace

Chapter Fifteen

An odd, pervading silence rang in the clearing. A silence loud enough to drown out birdsong, the wind, the sobbing breaths I took. Duncan. Poor Duncan. I held him from behind where he crouched on the ground, his back curving against my chest, his shock shuddering through his body and into mine.

I had seen this. Deep inside after passing through the Myth, I had seen this without it making sense, being definitive or real. The knowledge had lurked in me, unsettling me, twisting my emotions, making me angry, making me afraid. Making me lash out at my friends. I'd never forgive myself for the latter.

"Duncan," I whispered. He raised a hand from the ground in warning, shutting me up. I continued to hold him, biting back my words. I pressed my mouth against his shoulder, his jacket's soft texture. Fur. In another life, I would have objected to it, but within the context of our present existence I would never complain.

Many feet moved over the frozen ground. It seemed many more than our number, yet when I lifted my head and looked around, I saw only my companions. My companions and Enid.

"Is anyone else here?" I asked.

"Not in the sense you mean," Enid said. "But there are others around us."

Along with the shuffling footsteps, I heard whispers, too. I sucked in a breath and nodded.

"What? Like ghosts?" Ren asked, face pale.

Enid didn't answer him. Neither did I. "I don't like what I am now," I said to Enid, for the first time out loud. "I want it to stop. I want to give it all back."

Foolish notion. That could never happen.

Enid crouched down beside me and Duncan. "Grace, this is what you have always been. You know that. You've considered it, at least. The Sleeping Myth didn't change you. It awakened you."

"I can't do this," I said, tone stubborn, like I was five years old again.

Clapping her hands on her thighs, Enid straightened, stood, looked down at me. "You have to."

"No. I don't. I am a warrior."

"Yes, you still are that. As I said, you are what you have always been."

I stopped myself shouting back at her and rose, hauling Duncan to his feet, holding him upright, my arm hooked through his. I spoke quietly, trying for reason. "I am changed—"

"Awakened."

"Changed," I repeated. "This is all too much. If I truly possessed any of this when I was younger, why didn't I react to it? Sense it? Use it? Question it? How did I control it? Keep it shut away?" My voice rose despite my intention to remain calm. Power surged through my blood, unbidden. Beside me, Duncan gasped, slipped his arm from mine, took a step away.

"Something in your mind protected you from release, from recognition," Enid said. "Now that you know, you must relearn control."

Duncan stepped toward Enid. "Then teach her," he said, his voice harsh and flat. "We need Grace now more than ever. I need Grace now more than ever. I've just found out that I share the same blood—gods, the same birth date—as the Darkness. He has all the power of our ridiculous partial-mage origins, and I have nothing. What am I supposed to do with that?"

I shut my eyes, trying to wrap myself in composure, trying not to speak. Not yet. When I lifted my lids, I found everyone watching me. I turned to Duncan, took his hand. He held his fingers stiffly for a moment before closing them around mine.

"What's his name?" I said to Enid. "Duncan's brother. The first thing we can do is reduce the fear induced by such a term as 'The Darkness,' can't we?"

Enid's lips curved. "Yes, that is a good step to take." Her gaze swiveled to Duncan. "The name given to your brother before he was taken away by your grandmother—your father's mother—is Moros."

Ren sniggered nervously and tried to utter an apology. "Sorry. I just—"

"Don't bother," Duncan said. He leaned forward, looking into Enid's eyes. "Why didn't she take me, too? Not that I would have wanted that. I'm only wondering."

Beneath her cloak, Enid's shoulders shifted. Her eyes changed yet again. Her lips curved, only a little. In sympathy, I thought. "Good question," she said. "Your grandmother did not know your mother carried twins. Quite soon after you were born, your father secreted your mother and you away."

"To Gran," Duncan said softly. "My Gran. The only Gran I care about."

"Yes," said Enid.

Duncan's mouth worked. "Not quite the story my father or mother told me. They didn't mention Moros at all."

"Are you surprised?" Mika whispered from the place where he stood next to Carina and Resa. Hannah had positioned herself in his shadow. Her pale, silver-blue eyes watched Duncan, her mood subdued, her thoughts shuttered. I wondered again if she still felt the same about him.

"I am," Duncan answered. "Thinking back on those last few minutes I spent with them before Brand and I came after all of you, I am surprised they didn't say something. Oh," he breathed.

"What is it?" I asked.

"They are with her, the Lady. That's where they went when they fled Trill. All of them. To her. To her court, or whatever it's called. To the woman who raised the Darkness." He stumbled forward. I thought he might collapse again. I caught him around the waist, held him up. He dashed a hand across his eyes and straightened.

Mika stirred from thought, lifted his head. "Does that mean they're with your brother, as well?"

No one had an answer to that, of course. Even Enid remained silent. Duncan stared into some place in his mind, his face pale, the flesh beneath his eyes dark with shock. I tightened my grip on him.

"Since this seems to be our destiny," I whispered, "we'll find them, Duncan. I swear to you we will."

Brand turned to me. "So, it's the Darkness—Moros—we're headin' toward, yeah? The danger we all agreed to face in following you."

I nodded. My stomach knotted a little. "Appears that way, yes."

"And he's Duncan's brother, a guy his age, with power enough to manipulate all sorts of people. Bad people. Am I right?"

Releasing a long, slow breath, I nodded again.

"Okay. I just wanted to be sure." He bent and started picking up stones, shoving them into his pockets. Amusement twisted my lips.

"We're not leaving right this second," I said.

He glanced up at me. "Never hurts to be prepared."

No. It certainly didn't. Whatever help Enid was offering, we needed to take advantage of it right now.

* * *

In what Enid called training, she talked, mostly, and we listened. Out here in the cold. We could have been inside where we'd been warm. Perhaps this was an essential part, fighting the seeping cold heightened by inactivity. Maintaining patience. Listening to every word while our minds, our eyes, our ears, sought out signs we were being watched, that something was coming nearer, that we weren't alone.

Enid discussed history, facts and tales and legends. She insisted we, me and my friends, were inextricably connected to what had passed before us, what was coming now, and to each other. We had, she said, been drawn together for a reason beyond our obvious misadventures. No matter how many times she said it, my doubts remained. I couldn't deny the fact we all needed each other, relied on each other, had become far more than friends chance met.

However, under the scenario she tried to present what, exactly, were we all?

Some mystical unit, Brand suggested, when I voiced the question aloud. Enid pointed at him and rapidly bobbed her head.

"Correct," she cried with a smile. I'd had a teacher like her during my warrior's training. Enthusiastic when a point was recognized. Impatient when it wasn't. I kept my mouth shut, hoping she'd say more. Quite like that same teacher, she did not. As I recalled, we always had to work it out for ourselves. This didn't seem like the right moment for such a lesson, since we sorely lacked time. The threat from the Darkness—from Duncan's brother—loomed large. Closing in or lying in wait, I couldn't tell. Too many disparate factors existed. Too many operating under his influence with cruel, self-absorbed intent.

"I think we need a clearer explanation," I finally said. "How are we connected? I've no wish to endanger my friends based on supposition."

"I'd hope not at all," Ren muttered, making a wry face, collecting himself when he noticed mine. "Not that you ever have. On purpose. You always tried to protect us. Sometimes…well, sometimes it was the other way around. Or we worked as a team."

I bit the soft flesh inside my cheek. It had been his choice, his and the three with him in the beginning, to waylay us. After the events at All Dwellers, Ren and Hannah had fallen in with us and yes, we'd worked together. Not always easily. But we had. I inclined my head at him in agreement, because truthfully, situations had arisen again and again which we'd never have gotten through without us all being together.

Yet the implication in Enid's speech indicated

something deeper. Our friendships ran quite meaningfully already. How much more might there be? She had agreed with Brand's statement, though, about a mystical unit, as though we were bound by something we didn't understand. A connection beyond the undeniable link I shared with Carina and Resa, a link which had been developing well before we got to The Sleeping Myth. Something affecting all of us.

Are you going to let her know now, Grace? About me? About how I helped you back in that wicked city?

No, I said.

I swallowed hard over the constriction in my throat. Breathed deep into my lungs. Threw back my shoulders. Forced him down with all my might. A time was coming when I'd no longer be able to keep him under control. I knew that. Perhaps this is what I needed Enid's help with most of all.

Oh, she'd be happy to help herself to me, I'm sure.

My gaze shot to Enid at Skelly's sly words. Her eyes, pale as smoke now, looked back into mine.

Go ahead, Skelly said. *Ask her what her intent is. I dare you.*

You're lying, I shot back at him.

Am I? Am I, Grace? I may be many things, but a liar I am not. You know that.

Enid's glance moved past me, touching slowly on each companion. "I think the time has come for me to stop talking and show you what you're up against," she said.

I glanced around at my friends and found their eyes on Enid in anticipation. All except Hannah. Her focus was on the place where the crystal lay hidden in its drawstring bag beneath my clothing. I hadn't forgotten Hannah's attempt to take the bag from me before she shoved us all into the Myth. I had not yet asked her why she'd acted as she did. I needed to. I had no idea what was stopping me, except that despite her behavior before the cave's great maw, I still wanted to trust her. Because if I didn't, if I couldn't, then she shouldn't be here. And didn't that run counter to what Enid said about belonging together?

My jaw tightened. My eyes narrowed, watching Hannah's covetous expression. Greedy, yes, greedy for something she hoped might bring her power. She possessed through her diluted blood certain, small mage skills. She wanted more. Perhaps a betrayer held a part in this great, cosmic plan. Was this what Enid meant?

"Grace?"

My head jerked like a puppet's. I blinked several times to clear my vision. In my head, Skelly chuckled in dark amusement, no doubt enjoying my distrustful turn of thought.

Is this your doing? I asked him. *Making me feel this way?*

Not me.

"Grace," Duncan called to me again. "Are you all right?"

"Fine," I said.

He growled, low in his throat. "You don't sound fine."

"Well, I am."

"And petulant, too," Ren mumbled. I spun on him, enraged. Something pulsed beneath my skin, making it feel like it would peel right off. Immediately, I found myself face down on the cold, hard ground.

"Get off!" I yelled, trying to kick my way free from the weight on my back. I lifted my head, glared at every face watching me, realized it was every face watching me. Even Enid's. Yet, I couldn't move, couldn't shake off whatever pressed down on my spine, my hips, my shoulders. In delayed recognition, I noted Enid's arm held out before her, her hand open, palm down. A soft glow like morning light emanated from it, from the skin and her fingertips. Influenced like Carina's quiet gift for giving sleep, I began to relax beneath Enid's mage craft. I struggled against it for several moments before giving in. My forehead dropped, touching trampled ice.

"Let me up," I whispered. "I'm all right now."

A hand fit itself into my armpit, lifted me to my knees. Duncan. Of course, Duncan. Always Duncan. I sent warmth his way before I even realized I had done so. That I could do so. His mouth twisted. He looked back at me in surprise. Clearly, he'd felt it.

Enid stepped closer. "We can go inside now. I'm sorry to have kept you all out in the cold. If things had gone bad, however, the house would not have contained the energy. You understand that, don't you, Grace?"

"If things had gone bad? What are you talking about?"

But I knew. Naturally, I knew. She meant if I'd lost control. "Are you causing this confusion in me?"

She shook her head. My hand crept up to my coat, to the place where the bag hung on the silk cord beneath my shirt.

"It's not that either," Enid said with a nod toward my hand fisted near my throat. "Not the entity you call Skelly."

I gasped, but I should have known Enid would sense him.

She went on. "Someone or something is

attempting to manipulate your emotions, your mental condition. All of you, really, but the brunt is borne by you."

"Why?"

"Because you are, at this point, the strongest, the most dangerous. That role used to be Resa's, but you've surpassed her. You, Carina, and Duncan's sister are a threat to be reckoned with. But you three could not be what you are together without the others in your group. Especially Duncan."

"I don't understand."

"I don't either," said Enid. "Not entirely. I can't see through every mirror."

"Mirror?" Duncan echoed.

"This is what it's like, when I reach out. Reflections everywhere."

I lightly pounded my sternum with my palm, bouncing the bag against my flesh. "And this? Him? How do I get rid of him without endangering my friends? How do I save him, if I can? What am I supposed to do? This…this is the answer I've been seeking…" My voice trailed off. I dropped my hand down onto my thigh. "Help me."

Enid's expression softened. "That burden cannot be taken from you, Grace. I'm sorry."

I recalled the subcutaneous tracker I'd wanted excised from my arm on Emerald, how desperate and horrified I'd been. How determined to see it gone. I refused to accept Enid's response. Glared at her, a retaliation forming in my mind. Her expression changed again, hardened.

"Don't do that, Grace," she said. "You won't win."

I caught myself, my damaging thoughts, and exhaled. "You can feel what I'm thinking?"

"Right now, we all can."

I looked around at the others, noting fear, concern, resolve. I turned back to Enid. "Can you help me with this, at least? Please?"

Enid strode forward, arms outstretched, put them around me, pulled me close. "That, I can do," she whispered. I caught Carina's approach peripherally. Too silent, too swift, for me to stop it. Small fingers touched my chilled wrist below my sleeve. Consciousness swirled away.

* * *

When I awoke, the world outside had lost its color. I could see the sky through the windows, the trees muted, nearly black. Night had fallen.

I sat up. Unlike the many other times Carina had enforced sleep on me, my head hurt. I brought my hand up, pressed it against my browbone. A scent filled the air. One I hadn't smelled in a long time. Flowers. Unavoidable tears pricked my eyes as I recalled my mother's garden. I smelled something else, too, something underlying the floral fragrance. Herbaceous. Smoky.

"You all right there, Grace?" Duncan asked. I spied him not far away, shadowed, propped against the wall with one knee pulled up and an arm across it. Keeping watch. Beyond him, shadowed too, lay the others beneath blankets and coats, seeming to be asleep. I couldn't be sure they were. Would I be, with me nearby?

"Yes," I said. I cleared my throat. "I was out a long time."

"You were."

"Because?"

"It was necessary."

I nodded, compressed my lips between my teeth. "And now?" I asked after a moment.

"How do you feel?"

I gave his question due consideration. As I should. As he deserved. As they all did. Except for the fading headache, I felt…lighter. Relaxed. Not exactly unburdened, but perhaps separate from my problems. In a good way, not an uncaring way. Sleep could do that, I knew. Rejuvenate a person. This seemed like more, though.

"Ah," I said.

"What?"

"My thoughts feel like my own. The inside of my head isn't a battleground."

Duncan performed a funny sideways shifting with his posterior across the floor until he reached my side. His arm came up, slipped around my shoulders, pulled me nearer. "Good," he said. "Because I was worried. Really worried."

I leaned into him, rested my head against his collarbone. "You don't need to worry."

"Oh, yes, we do."

"Well, maybe not so much now. What did Enid do to me?"

A quick breath ruffled my tangled hair. "She just said to let you sleep and then after we all had dinner—which you missed. Sorry. Anyway, after we all had dinner she started some weird activities, burning herbs and talking to herself…or maybe to you. Mage stuff? I don't know. Whatever she was doing, it relaxed us all, I think."

"And the flowers?" I asked. "Where did she get

those?"

"Flowers?"

I sat up. "I smelled them as soon as I woke. I still can."

"I didn't see any flowers. I don't smell anything except those herbs."

Although the scent had begun to fade, I breathed in again the light fragrance drifting through the air. So much like the garden at home.

"Mother," I said.

"What?"

"This is the second time I've smelled flowers like hers since we've been running."

Duncan squinted at me in the dark. "Really?"

"Yes. And I wonder."

"Wonder what?"

"If she's reaching out to me somehow. I mean, my mage blood comes from somewhere, right? I'd always thought I possessed none, had no reason to think otherwise, but since the revelations of the Myth, I've been trying to figure it out. That it came from someone in my father's lineage made sense, but perhaps it's from both sides. My mother's heritage is…ancient. Beyond the desert. Something older."

Duncan said nothing. I wrapped my fingers around the hand he'd rested in his lap.

"Don't worry. Just thinking. Thinking like me, not under any other influence."

"Okay," he answered. Still dubious.

I shifted and settled back against him. "I promise."

His breathing slowed. Tension left him and his

spine curved, bringing him closer to the wall at his back. Bringing me closer to him, too.

"Grace?"

"Yes?"

"Can you look at me a second?"

I did, lifting my head, turning my face to his. He had long lashes, Duncan did. Some light came in through the window, casting their deeper shadow across his face and eyes, hiding the latter from me. "What?" I asked.

"This."

He kissed me. No questions asked. No hesitation. I sucked a breath in but didn't pull away. In fact, I decided I liked his mouth on mine, lips warm, unaggressive, testing my response. I kissed him back in a way that shocked me. Him, too, I think. His whole body tensed again. He held me tighter. The rushing air through his nose whistled across my cheek, followed by a noise in his throat, one I couldn't recall hearing from him before. Ever.

A voice spoke in the dark. "There's a shed outside if you two need some privacy."

Duncan jerked away, pushing me back a little. "Ren," he said.

"I'm not the only one awake," Ren shot back. "Just saying."

A few mumbled agreements issued from various places on the floor. I squirmed further away from Duncan and scrubbed at my eyes, my heated face, with both hands. "Who actually is asleep?" I asked.

Mika answered a second later, presumably after a headcount. "Looks like no one."

"Well, hell," said Duncan.

Ren laughed. "Sorry to ruin your moment."

In the shadows behind him, Hannah's head lifted, her spiky red locks recognizable even in the dark. I couldn't tell if she looked at me or Duncan, but the dismissive sound she made before dropping back down again said all I needed to know. Duncan pulled his knees up to his chest, wrapped his arms around them.

"So," he said, "since we're all awake, what now?"

My lightly vibrating body lapsed into sudden and absolute stillness. For several heartbeats, I didn't even breathe, studying the faces in the shadowed room before pivoting my gaze back in Duncan's direction. He appeared to be avoiding mine.

"What now?" I asked. "After my long sleep, I need the bathroom."

Pushing up from the floor with an abrupt movement, I headed in that direction through the dark. My vision had long since adjusted to the nearly non-existent illumination and I managed not to bump into anything along the way. Once inside, I shut my eyes as light from the motion-activated lumi-bar filled the small room. I stumbled forward to the sink, where I washed my face and drank some water from my cupped hands. After relieving myself, I stood with my hips against the sink basin, arms crossed over my chest, contemplating what had just happened. Would I enjoy a repeat? Yes. Yes, I would. Could I afford the distraction? No.

With a disgusted expletive, I spun and washed

my hands. Fingers still dripping, I ran them through my hair. Knuckles rapped lightly on the door. "Duncan," I said on an exhale. I reached for the handle, yanked the door open.

Not Duncan.

Not anyone I knew at all.

Chapter Sixteen

My arms flew up in preparation for defense, my right leg kicking out at the door to slam it shut. I refrained though, yanking my leg back, remembering my friends were all outside the room and may need me.

"Who are you?" I demanded, looking the stranger up and down, gauging strength, possible weaknesses, the downfall of position in the narrow hall. She—or he, I couldn't really tell in the dark—had a very strange appearance, pale to the point of near translucence, yet still formidably solid. Not solid, though. The facial features relocated as they would in speech when it answered.

"Do you not recognize me?"

"No," I said. I had to get to Duncan and the others, make sure they were all right. In the short period I'd been gone, anything could have happened. We'd all experienced mishap, danger, separation with lightning speed.

I brought my rampaging thoughts up short, took a few deep breaths while still maintaining my position. I did not plan to be overpowered, no matter what the stranger's intention, but I also had no desire to be fooled again by whatever sought to manipulate me. I reminded myself this was, perhaps, no false vision. I heard no outcries, however, no struggle. Whoever this was, Enid had likely let the being into her home. I resisted the temptation to reach out and poke the pale skin, and asked again, "Who are you?"

"Ah, quite right," it said. "You have only seen me in my other form."

I bit back another oath. "Your other form?"

"Your friend—Duncan, I believe? named me as a Singer's Hart. True enough, in that body. By day, that is what I become. I am thankful for the long winter nights, because it provides me more time with my wife as I truly am."

"I...what?"

"Cericia?" Enid's voice called through the darkened house from the room in which she slept, and not alone, apparently. I frowned. Shapeshifters. I'd heard tales about them, too, but never countenanced them as truth. I knew I shouldn't be surprised to find these tales also had definite roots. Yet, somehow, I was.

Enid appeared in a long, white gown. I slept in something similar at home, shorter in length. Back when I had clothes to change into at night. Or any time. "So," she said, spying me in the oblique light while she shoved her arms into a robe, "you've met my partner. The others did earlier, while you slept."

So much for Enid living as a hermit. Apparently, her relationship remained a secret. At least to the Fianna. Realizing I still stood in a defensive stance, I dropped my hands and arms. "A pleasure," I said, struggling to mean it. Shock continued to hold me in its grip.

"May I?" said Cericia, pointing to the tiny room at my back.

I stepped quickly from her path. "Oh, yes, of course."

She moved inside and quietly shut the door. Not wanting to linger outside it, I headed back to the main room. Enid trailed at my heels.

"Grace."

I glanced at Enid striding a pace behind me. "Please tell me this isn't another hallucination."

"It isn't. Search inside yourself. This is different than what you have been experiencing. This is real."

Right. Real. A creature changing from an enormous white hart to an icy-looking, semi-human female, wed to our host. Enid was right, though. I recognized the difference. Sensed reality and accepted the truth, no matter how bizarre. For now, doubt and underlying confusion fled. "I didn't know," I said. "I didn't mean to be rude. I'm sorry."

"No worries," she responded. "Under the current circumstances—"

"I still should not have been rude."

"Well, yes, but I'm sure Cericia understands."

I didn't know if I would have. This was her home, after all, hers and Enid's, and now populated with a misfit pack being hunted by some very dangerous people. No reason at all to accept or understand my behavior.

In the common room, everyone had plainly overhead the exchange between me and Cericia. They were all sitting up, Hannah's small mage light propped on a table near her head. I had noted before her need to have the light close by to keep it burning. Mine had different physical characteristics. Proximity didn't appear necessary. On occasion, I'd managed to splash the pink flames around like water. I wasn't quite sure how I managed to do so, but it seemed the action worked in tandem with my mood. Not the safest criteria for its use.

"Duncan," I said with a small nod. He continued to look uncertain regarding his reception after our recent interaction. I'd reassure him later nothing had changed between us. It would be a lie, of course, but a necessary one.

"All alert, are we?" said Enid, her tone unreasonably chipper, given the hour—whatever time it was. I returned to the place where I'd awakened beside Duncan. He slid over to provide me extra room. Space I didn't need or want. Enid waited until I had settled before speaking again.

"The sun will be rising soon."

I started. How long had I been asleep? Conversely, how long had Duncan been awake, watching over me? I slid my eyes in his direction, the night's silver illumination highlighting his face. More precious to me than ever, Duncan's face. Everything about him, in fact. This could become a problem. Cause me to make mistakes, alter decisions. I turned my attention back to Enid. Duncan stirred.

"I was going to tell Grace what we talked about," he said to Enid. "I figured she should know."

Enid's nearly white eyebrows lifted, looking like two pale caterpillars on her brow. Her eyes modified their hue, changing to something misty, like fog. "You were supposed to wait for me," she said.

Duncan shrugged, meeting her gaze. "You're here now."

"I am indeed."

Cericia entered the room behind Enid. I sized her up again, noting a height I had not when standing inside the toilet room. I realized now her forehead had been hidden by the lintel on the doorframe. In the light from Hannah's sphere, Cericia's hair was as white as Enid's and Carina's, sticking out in all directions around her head in triangular tufts, like the hart's ruff and brow. Beneath her clothing, the woman possessed muscular shoulders and upper arms, strong thighs. I could almost imagine her bending forward to touch her hands to the ground, transforming to the Singer's Hart before my eyes.

She caught me watching. A dark gaze, deep brown, met mine, eyes large and very beautiful and spaced wide on her face to either side of a broad nose. After a moment she nodded and moved away, lowering herself into a chair in the corner. A chair nearly too small. Knees bent up to her chest, she wrapped her arms around them, her focus settling on Enid and staying there.

Enid faced me. "Would you like details, or the nucleus? I suspect you are already aware in some manner what we discussed while you slept. Perhaps you only need clarity or confirmation."

I let out a breath. Enid did like to talk in circles. "I don't know anything for certain," I said. "Can you condense what was said in some summarizing fashion?"

She blinked at me and laughed. "I'll try. So much goes on in my head at one time, it's often hard for me to articulate what I want or need to say. Cericia could confirm that, I'm sure."

The shapeshifter nodded silently in her chair, mouth curving. Enid dropped to the floor at Cericia's feet in an oddly Carina-like flow, graceful and mesmerizing and making me wonder anew about her full heritage. The woman tucked her feet close, wrapping her gown around her legs.

"Grace," she said, her tone now abnormally solemn, "your exposure in the Sleeping Myth was intense. What was thrust upon you is something uncovered and disciplined through years in training. As you know, a mage's instruction is always performed in isolation for obvious reasons. Mages continue to remain apart because learning is lifelong. Sometimes they do not ever master what you have attempted to work through by yourself in these past few days."

"You mean control?" I managed to ask.

"More than control. The extent of your gifts, which is a huge and perilous unknown."

My stomach rolled over. This conversation was not headed toward a cozy conclusion. Not for me, not for anyone. "Then it seems I must I go on alone, after all. Leave my friends behind."

"Goodness, no," Enid cried with a bell-like laugh, cutting off Duncan's sputtering retort. "Breathe and stay calm, young warrior. They merely need to learn to protect themselves from any mishaps coming their way, as well as from those who deliberately wish them ill."

"Like my brother, you mean," Duncan said.

Hannah shot him a look, pivoting to Enid with wide eyes. "Is that even possible?"

"It is," Enid answered.

"How?" This from Mika, who always preferred the definitive explanation.

"And," Duncan interrupted a reply, "what would stop others from getting the same skills? Skills to avoid not mishaps, but, you know, a deliberate action?"

At his question, everyone fell silent. Enid studied

Duncan's face. She tipped her head to one side. "It is possible, but not probable, Duncan. Would you like to know why?"

"Sure," he said, less than politely, "why?"

"Because they are not you."

Duncan's brows lowered. "I don't understand."

"They are not you," Enid repeated. "Not any of you. They can never be exactly you, separately or together. What you learn from me for protection will be the sum of everything you know, everything you feel. No one else is the same. You will be like a key to a lock that can't be picked, can't be broken. A key which cannot be duplicated."

Above Enid's head, Cericia's lips curved. She reached out, stroked Enid's hair, folded her hands with their russet-edged, blunt fingers back down around her knees. Enid shifted on the floor like a bird settling into its nest. They looked content, the two of them. Attuned. Happy. I glanced at Duncan and away.

"There will come a time when you must operate as one unit even more than you do now. One mystical unit," she added, pointing at Brand, who had earlier said the same.

Mika released Carina's hand. "Okay, I get it. I mean, I've come across a lot I never considered real. My eyes have been opened. Agreed. But I'm not sure I can believe what you're saying."

Enid strained forward. "You must believe. If you do not, you fail, and the fault...well, the fault is yours."

Duncan swore, looked at Mika, then at me. Hastily, he apologized to Enid and her partner for the exclamation. They waved the offense away.

"How can you not believe?" Duncan asked Mika. "You've *seen*."

"Yeah," Mika answered. "I have. But I'm not like the rest of us here. I'm...ordinary. Sure, I've seen plenty. Things I would have denied or laughed off as nonsense at home. I know they're not nonsense now. When I say I don't believe Enid, it's not that I'm doubting everything we've been through, everything we've witnessed. I'm doubting what she believes is in me, what I'm capable of. Because it's not. I'm not. I don't share the same blood as the rest of you. I'm the only one who doesn't."

"I am not mage, either," Carina whispered to him.

"But you are a mystic," he whispered back. "You have power."

She took his hand, lifted it, held it to her lips. It was the most demonstrative I'd ever seen her, despite all their physical closeness. Unmistakably intimate.

"So do you," she said.

"Mika Donnell," said Enid, "physician's son, listen to her."

Mika's head jerked in Enid's direction. I twitched a little myself. Surprised. Perhaps a little ashamed. All this time together and I had not known nor inquired about Mika's surname. I didn't ask myself how Enid knew. I was well beyond asking. Some things just were.

"Is not the ability to heal a gift?" Enid asked him.

"It's not the same," he said.

"The sum of everything you know, everything you feel, Mika. No necessity for mage blood."

He met her gaze and after a moment reluctantly nodded. I doubted he'd been convinced. Mika was a very logical sort. What we were being told, nearly everything we'd encountered, defied logic. Belief was not always logical. Belief, backed by science or not, was faith. I had learned that long ago. Mika, unfortunately, had not. Glancing at Duncan, I saw even he struggled with Enid's words despite his questioning Mika's doubt.

I looked around at the others, at their expressions, trying to read them. An ability to intuit my friends' thoughts had increased with the influx from the Myth, but it waxed and waned and I was not, in any way, Carina. Nor did I want to be. But right now, I could have used a touch of her abilities.

"This is what Enid means," Carina said to me, having delved into my mind. "Together we have what we need for whatever it is we must face."

Enid smiled, speaking gently. "That is correct, Carina. All of you together."

"Even Ren and Hannah?" asked Duncan. "Is that how they found us?"

"They were already on their way," Enid explained. "They needed a little help from me to get to you inside the mountain."

"I thought it was Duncan's sister who did that," Ren said. "And then I wasn't sure."

"And I thought it might be Grace," said Duncan.

"What about the *prair*?" I asked.

We all stared expectantly at Enid, waiting.

With a sigh, Enid stood. She reached back for Cericia's hand. The shapeshifter took it and left the chair, standing beside her, her head so much closer to the ceiling than Enid's. "There are many forces working for and against you all," Enid said. "We tend to get in each other's way. Battles occur in places you cannot see, do not know. You are only aware of the aftereffects."

I frowned and rose, too, a chill lump in my abdomen quickly spreading through my blood. "Then, is there no hope?"

Enid moved toward the door, Cericia with her. "There is always hope, Grace," Enid said as she touched the crystalline knob, turned it. The darkness outside had altered, seeping into the shadowless time before dawn. Tree trunks and green needles possessed a dulled, nearly colorless appearance, the snow a light gray, the soil, a darker shade. Not quite night, not yet sunrise. I yanked on my footgear and followed them outside. My friends trailed behind, shoving into their coats, stuffing feet into unclasped boots. I didn't look to see in what order they exited the dwelling. I only knew Duncan was closest to me. I recognized his footfalls, his breathing, his energy, his gravity.

I stopped walking several strides short of the place where Enid and Cericia stood. He came up beside me. "What are we doing out here?" he asked.

I inclined my head at the couple. "I'm not sure, but I expect we're going to see something amazing."

"Oh, yeah? What exactly?"

At a small distance, just inside the perimeter, Enid and Cericia turned to face each other, hands clasped. Cericia bowed her head until her brow touched Enid's. Her breath smoked, spiraling into the air above them. They spoke together softly, too softly for anyone else to hear, lips barely moving.

Suddenly, Cericia drew back, tossed her head, her white locks catching the sun, the newly risen sun. I saw what happened next, yet saw nothing at all, as though my vision blurred with tears. One second, the large and formidable woman with the unique build and wild hair stood there. An instant later, the Singer's Hart bounded into the forest and Enid stood alone.

"That," I whispered.

Duncan stared after the hart, speechless. Once she'd disappeared beneath the trees, he turned to me, shaking his hair from his eyes. "Holy crap. You were expecting *that*?"

"Yes. Weren't you?"

"Gods, no. Why would I?"

I squeezed his arm. "You met last night, right?"

"Well, yeah, but she was just a…an unusual looking woman." He twisted his mouth up to one side, talking out of it and not clearly, thank goodness. "Like, she's not quite human. I had no idea."

"Clearly, Cericia is not human," I said, observing Enid. Enid remained watchful, barefoot in her nightdress in the cold, her gaze on the path Cericia had taken. The shapeshifter was lost to sight, my sight anyway, in the shadows and snow. Enid exhaled, bent and lifted Cericia's clothing from the ground, straightened. She squared her shoulders. Her chin lifted. Slowly, she turned and made her way back to us, her white gown shimmering beneath her robe, her expression pensive and sad.

"She'll be back tonight," I said in an attempt at comfort. Enid's look altered. I sucked in a breath. "Won't she?"

She paused. "Cericia has taken on a mission. I do not know when she will return. It may be some time."

Walking past, Enid strode into the house. We

trailed after like herd animals. At the door, I placed a hand on Duncan's elbow, holding him back. He let the others file in past him wanting, no doubt, to get warm, prepare breakfast. Take what relief they could before our daily existence again became hard.

Carina turned and closed the door, leaving us outside, her changeable eyes going from my face to Duncan's. Behind her, Resa stared at Duncan with singular focus before the barrier clicked into place.

I took Duncan's hand in mine. A bit awkwardly, now, due to what had passed between us. I didn't like feeling that way. Self-conscious. Hesitant. We were still the same, Duncan and me. Nothing had changed. But everything had changed.

"Duncan," I said, "do you think she knows? Resa, I mean. She can see other places. Do you think she has seen—"

"Moros?"

"Yes."

He shrugged. "I hope not. He's her brother, too. I'd rather she didn't know what he is."

"Understood," I said. "Is it possible he could somehow reach out to her?"

"Not according to Enid. Resa's special gifts keep her immune."

It seemed they had touched on that, at least, in their nighttime discussion. "What else did she say?"

Duncan hunched his shoulders. "It's cold out here."

"I know."

"We can talk inside after we eat." He slapped his hand against his coat, giving it a squeeze in his belly's general area. I didn't hear his stomach growling. He was trying to fend off my questions through gastric subterfuge.

"Tell me, Duncan. Tell me now."

"She referred to the last days," he said.

"That doesn't sound good," I murmured.

"It's not. All those skirmishes we've avoided, heard about, been involved in, are leading up to it. She said it's not a repeat of the ancient war that destroyed Olympian, forged the glass fields and mines from sand and rock, set people to living in small sanctuaries. But it's more like, well, the last grasp for power of those folk who survived the time since. Not those who'd like to just live in peace. But for the rest."

I hadn't really understood the bigger picture before. I suddenly felt weighted down, overwhelmed, and rather insignificant. "Those who'd like to rule the world," I said, my sarcasm lost in truth.

Duncan nodded.

"Like your brother."

"I suppose so." He looked grieved by the admission.

"And in all this," I said, "am I a danger to you all?"

"No. You heard Enid. She says not anymore. Especially once we work on our 'connection.' But…"

I shook his arm. "Tell me. Tell me now."

He grunted. "We don't have much opportunity to get that done, to solidify the link she says we already have. The main thing Enid stressed last night is…" He sputtered to a halt like a flame snuffed by the wind and looked at his feet, not wanting to go on. I shook his arm.

"Duncan!"

"Fine! We're out of time, okay? Just like you thought. We are out of time."

As if on cue, we heard a hum in the sky and looked up. The ships were back.

Despite the shielding from Enid's charm, instinct took over. We hurried inside, mentally prepared for the worst.

Duncan

Chapter Seventeen

We worked in the common room. Practice made perfect, Gran always said. I couldn't keep my mind on it, though. I kept an eye on the windows instead, watching for the ships. One had passed directly over Enid's home without pause, which should have reassured me her charm worked. She had another word for this magic, something I liked better than charm. Charm sounded weak, like a token on a string. Beguilement. That was it. Beguilement. Something to fool them all.

Telling myself Enid's beguilement had strength, I returned my attention to the lesson, noticed everyone's eyes were closed except mine. I quickly shut them. Stopped listening for the ships, for sounds in the woods, for distant shouting. We were safe here. We had to be.

But were we? I thought a moment later. My lids popped open. I found everyone watching me. Enid's pale brows made two, level lines above her eyes. Not happy.

"Concentrate, Duncan."

"I'm trying," I said.

She grunted. From her, it sounded soft, gentle. Still, I read disapproval loud and clear. I shifted my position, fully turning my back to the world outside. I still felt it, though, the threat. The danger. The unknown.

"Duncan."

"Yes, m'am."

I knew what she wanted us to do. I needed to concentrate. Become one with the universe or some such rubbish. I suppose that was the problem. My condemning her efforts as nonsense. Even though I knew better. I mean, hadn't I given Mika a hard time for his doubts? Hadn't I witnessed as fact more than I could ever imagine? Yeah. Buckle down, Duncan Oaks. This is important. This could save lives.

Could? Would.

Therein lay the crux. My fear what Enid was trying to teach us couldn't, wouldn't, save anyone. I didn't want to lose my friends because I wasn't strong enough. Because I didn't own inside me what Enid thought I did. No matter how many times she said it, I found myself unable to see her truth.

But I had to. Had to or else we were doomed to failure. Doomed to die.

At my brother's hand. Or at least his direction.

I swore out loud. All eyes turned my way once more. "Sorry," I muttered.

Maybe deep down, I didn't want to fight him. Maybe I wanted to save him. Fat chance of that. From what I'd gleaned, he could wipe me off the planet without batting an eye. Or maybe with batting an eye. I didn't really know how his nasty powers worked.

"Duncan."

My name with emphasis. This time from Grace. I looked at her. As much as losing any of my friends would hurt, would fill me with grief and guilt, it was Grace's demise which would kill me. Literally. I knew it would.

"Sorry," I said again. How many times had I apologized since we'd been at this? Too many, I figured. By the look on everyone's faces, way too many.

Carina turned to Enid. "Can we hold hands? I think that would help."

"Like we're all going to be able to stop in the middle of who the hell knows what and hold hands," Ren said. Sneered, even. Showing a bit of his old self. Frustrated, I knew. I think we all were. Frustrated by me more than anything.

"I don't think that's what Carina means," said Enid. "She's talking about now, while you learn. If you learn this well, physical contact won't be necessary. Right now, it would help. Carina is quite correct."

They exchanged a smile, Carina and the woman who shared so many similarities with her. Perhaps Enid possessed some island blood. And mage blood. And the gods only knew what else. I had to remind myself I had mixed blood, too. Enid had hinted at promise because of it. I only knew I had no gifts despite a father with mage running through his lineage, a sister with powers I still didn't understand, and a crazy, formidable twin who either called himself or allowed himself to be called "The Darkness." Pompous ass. I wanted to meet him just to tell him so. Mostly, though, I had no desire to meet him at all. Ever.

Rustling clothing alerted me to everyone's movement. Arms lifted. Hands extended. I grabbed Mika's hand with my still bandaged right. Carina sat on his other side in the circle, Resa after her, followed by Grace and then Ren. Fortuitous positioning, that. Except for Ren clutching Grace's hand. I wasn't too keen on the smug twist to his lips as he looked across at me, but I had to ignore it or I'd never be able to concentrate. I reached out to my left. A hand smaller than mine slipped into my fingers, squeezed hard. I glanced aside at Hannah, her pale eyes staring up into my own with an expression I did not care to read.

Refraining from swearing again, at least out loud, I turned and looked to where Enid sat between Ren and Brand. Her gaze moved from Hannah to me with mild amusement. I kept my expression stoic, ready to move on.

"Lower your clasped hands to the floor," Enid instructed. It occurred to me Resa might not do well in this experiment and, if not, we were all in a precarious position. Enid, however, perhaps reading my thoughts, allowed her gaze to move to Resa and rest there, clearly untroubled. Okay, I thought. Your funeral if this doesn't work out.

"Dun*can*." Carina's turn to call me out. Yeah. Of course, it was. I sighed.

"Close your eyes," Enid said. "Focus behind your lids as if viewing a small point near the bridge of your nose or somewhere close to it."

I obeyed. Weird, but the tactic worked. After a few minutes, I felt something change in me. Shift. In my head. I heard Enid's voice in there, too, whispering words I didn't recognize. When I did finally understand, she said she was backing out, would be watching, and that we must all reach along the connection we'd made, first to one person, then to two together, and continue until we concentrated on all.

What are we concentrating on? I asked. Dreamily. A strange sensation, because I understood all could hear.

No specifics, she said. Only each other.

Got it, I thought, and proceeded as directed, first one, then two, three, four, until I sensed all. The others moved through me as well, drifting around, all of us like leaves on a stream, swirling, touching, floating away and back again. Without real identity. Only knowledge.

When I traveled into Resa's mind, really into it and not just a glancing pass, the serenity faltered. She was looking at me, physically looking at me, at my solid manifestation sitting in the fading light, my head bowed beneath my dark hood, hair longer than I'd ever worn it.

Crying out, I snatched my hands away from Mika and Hannah and bolted to my feet.

"No," I said. "*No.*"

Everyone blinked up at me as though rudely awakened from a nap. "What is it?" Grace asked.

"Moros. They're connected. Resa and Moros."

"It's all right, Duncan," Enid said.

"No, it's not. How can it be? I—"

"Duncan, sit. Please. Sit back down. Breathe."

I didn't. I wouldn't. Not even the breathing part. My mind raced, swinging between yanking Resa off the floor and running with her—which would never have ended well—or—I don't know what. Too many scenarios clashed in my head. Images like rapid-fire lightning flashes. An arcade on Riley had a game like this. Baffling, confusing, sometimes damaging. I sucked air into my lungs, my body forcing me to take a breath. Fingers slipped over mine. I looked down, saw Resa at my side. Dropping to my knees, I put my arms around her waist, pulled her close, turned my head to Enid.

"How do we stop her?" I asked. Begged, really.

"There's no need," Enid answered.

"But—"

Enid raised a hand, silencing me with the gesture. "She sees him, yes. She's been seeing him. But he can't see her. Your sister is special. He will never see her. Not like that. He cannot influence her, either. Breathe deep, Duncan. You're hyperventilating."

Enid's tone, her voice's cadence, soothed me. I inhaled, exhaled, slowly, regularly. My heartrate steadied. I released Resa and she went back to her place between Carina and Grace.

"Okay," I said. "Okay." Twisting at the waist, I looked around at the others. "Did you all see him, too? In Resa's mind?"

"I made no direct contact with anyone's mind," Grace said. "I only felt the connecting flow."

The murmured consensus from the rest echoed Grace's response. I would have thought at least Grace and Carina, or even Enid, might have seen what I did, but they merely looked at me, waiting for me to go on.

"And?" Grace finally prompted. "What did you see?"

"It was me, but not me, of course. Sitting alone in a room. Thinking."

"About what?" asked Ren.

"I have no idea. How would I?"

Ren shrugged. I bit back an angry obscenity, addressed Enid again. "Can he see us?"

She shook her head. My shoulders relaxed.

"Not complaining, I assure you," I said, "but why the heck can't he?"

Enid's gaze shifted to Resa. She nodded. "Your

sister shields you all. Your brother and those he influenced have been casting mage craft and science like seeds to the wind in a pitch-black night. Occasionally, something finds its way, but for the most part you and your friends have been protected."

"By Resa?"

"And occasionally others." She smiled in a self-satisfied manner, then winked at me. As it had done before, my skin warmed. I didn't like the sensation. Not at all.

"It doesn't really feel like we're protected," I said. "Just…you know. Saying."

"Understood." She lifted her hands, curling her fingers in invitation for everyone to reconnect. "Sit down, Duncan. It's not going to get any better. We need to do this and do it now."

I returned to my seat on the floor. "And do it right," I said. Beside me, Hannah laughed and quickly shoved her fingers into mine. Surprisingly, I managed to control my urge to shake her off.

* * *

The sun had started to dip behind the mountains. Long shadows stretched across the room. We had worked through the day, initially with the hand-holding, and after a time without, but constantly enabled by Enid or Carina. I knew it. We all knew it. We wouldn't always have Enid with us, but we'd have Carina. We'd better, because we hadn't enough time to learn how to do this on our own. I didn't think even Grace had the necessary gift. I sensed the truth behind my consideration in a heightened way, sensed the time slipping away. A knowledge facilitated, I supposed, by our exercises in the whole connection thing.

"Enid," I said, "when we're no longer here with you, can we do this without help? I mean, like if Carina is knocked out or something." I didn't want to suggest any other scenario, anything dire or irreversible.

Enid's eyebrows lifted in the way they did. A way that made a person cringe. Or at least me. "You are assuming she is holding you all together," she said.

I took a second before answering. "Sometimes you, sometimes her."

Ren and Mika nodded their agreement to my assessment. Brand said nothing. He'd said very little since the process began. The girls remained silent, too.

"And you won't be coming with us," I added.

"You are very presumptuous, Duncan Oaks."

"No," I said. "At least, I don't think so. Will you? Be coming with us, I mean."

"That remains to be seen. It's possible, but—"

"Not probable?"

She snorted. "We shall see. I guard this ancient forest. But if all danger follows you, I will not need to stay behind."

My breath whistled out my nose. The idea all danger might be following us wasn't exactly unfathomable, but not something I wanted to contemplate.

"Enid," said Grace, "where did Cericia go?"

I grimaced, looked at Enid. Words popped from my mouth tactlessly. "Into the danger."

"Yes, Duncan," Enid responded with a frown. "Into the danger."

"But those creatures," Grace pressed.

Enid waved a hand. "She will not succumb. She is immune. As will you all be if we can just get back to work."

We did, continuing into the night. When we finally stopped, we all assisted in preparing a late meal. Seated in our various places on the floor and in the few existing chairs, I watched Enid while we ate.

"You're worried," I said.

"Of course," she answered.

"About Cericia."

"About everything."

I lowered my spoon back to my bowl. "Why is this all happening?"

"I don't know."

She either lied, or the answer was too complicated to express. Both, I supposed.

Hannah spoke up in a beseeching voice, small and whispery and slightly whiny. "Why can't we all stay here with you?"

Ah, yes, Hannah. The weakest link in the chain we attempted to forge.

"Or some of us?" She glanced at me. I looked away from her.

Enid's smile was brief and oddly sad. My heart skipped a beat. "It's all or none. This is what I have seen. And you cannot stay here. I am sorry."

Hannah quickly bowed her head over her soup. The spoon in her hand went from bowl to mouth several times in brisk succession. I thought she might be crying. A moment later I saw I was correct. She scrubbed at her eyes with her wrist. Ren reached out and placed a comforting arm around her, surprising the heck out of me.

"This is hard on all of you, I know," Enid said. "To be chosen like this—"

"Chosen?" Mika interrupted her. "By who?"

"By the universe," I said, my sarcasm evident.

But inside, I wondered if this might in some strange way be true.

Enid flipped her own utensil in her fingers, pointing the scooped end at me. "Don't scoff, dear boy. We are none of us alone and more exists than you will ever know."

Carina leaned forward between Mika and my sister. "Do you know?"

"No," said Enid. "Not everything. In the vast realm enfolding possibilities and truths, uncertainties and mysteries, I basically know nothing."

"A grain in the desert sands," Grace murmured.

"Precisely," Enid agreed.

Brand looked up from his meal. "But we're to trust you."

"Yes," said Enid.

"'kay." He went back to eating.

For some reason, with Brand's casual acceptance, I relaxed, returning as well to the hearty soup in my bowl. Yet, even in respite, I felt the heavy weight hanging over us. More than an awareness. I knew if I possessed the proper vision, I'd see it, like a metaphysical blanket or something.

I wondered if this was what Grace experienced all the time now. My sister, too. And Carina. Were we all gaining something from our connecting practices? Did I really want it?

"How much more time do we have?" I asked. "Before we need to leave."

"A day," Enid said. "Two at the most."

I didn't ask her how she knew. Her answer would be something cryptic anyway. Besides, I think I already did know, and that scared me. I was changing. We all were.

*   *   *

I knew better than to stare at Grace while she slept. In any other setting it would be creepy. In this setting, too, I supposed. But I had nowhere else to look. I had wakened from a nightmare and needed to be grounded. Grace always steadied me. Always. But she sensed my gaze. Her eyes flew open and her hand to the staff she had not yet finished preparing. It whistled past my ear before cracking down onto the floor.

"What the hell, Duncan?" she whispered fiercely, lifting her head to glance around, making sure she hadn't woken up the others.

"I didn't mean to…"

"I know," she said. "What's wrong?"

I said nothing. What could I say? I wish I'd made different decisions? Too late.

She let out a breath, released the staff and reached for my hand instead. "Mind if I move a little closer?" she asked.

I rolled onto my back. She wriggled her way across the floor, blanket, and all, and lowered her head onto my shoulder. The staff caught up in the fabric poked me in the ribs. She pulled the blanket around us both.

"It'll be all right," she said.

I grunted without comment. With her so close to me, I could almost believe she wasn't wrong. But a big gap existed between believing and knowing better. A gap filled with doubt, confusion, the images from my nightmare. I needed to tell her about those. Sure, I did. Determined not to, I clamped my lips together to keep the words in.

"We didn't ask to be involved in any of this," she

said.

"Nope."

"And your brother… You have no responsibility there."

"Right."

"I'm serious, Duncan. We're in peril, I know that. People behave as if we are destined in some fashion to bring this whole conflict to an end. I don't understand how that can be true. I only wanted help with Skelly. But everywhere I've led you all has only involved us deeper in something I'm not sure we can or should face. Especially not you. It's your brother they're talking about."

I said nothing.

"It isn't fair."

"No," I said. "It's not. Doesn't matter. We do what we have to do."

"Maybe we should just go home."

Hearing that from Grace surprised me. She knew the danger to our families if we did. Likely, we wouldn't make it anyway. Something or someone would stop us.

"We can't," I said.

"I know."

"Then why did you say it?"

"Because, wouldn't it be nice if we could?"

I heard the catch in her voice. I thought I hadn't forgotten how much more Grace bore than the rest of us, but it seemed I had. For a moment, I had.

"I'm sorry, Grace."

"Thanks." She snuggled closer. "And don't be. Sorry, I mean. None of this is your fault."

My abdomen tightened. "Isn't it?"

"Not how you mean. Besides, I'm a warrior. This is what I was raised, trained, to do, to face."

I pressed my lips to her hair. "I don't think you ever expected this, precisely."

She snorted. "No. I didn't."

"And you're not only a warrior. Not a mage warrior, either. You're a mage with warrior training. I have a feeling there's a big difference."

She didn't answer. When her ribcage expanded and contracted against me, accompanied by soft, steady breathing, I realized she wouldn't. Grace Irese, the most formidable person I knew, had fallen back asleep in my arms as though safe there. As though I could protect her.

Staring grimly into the dark, I remained awake, waiting for the dawn. I, too, had become warrior, but of a different kind. Grace always said her duty was to protect rather than harm. She'd killed the mutants, yes, but as far as I understood, she'd never taken the life of another human being. I had. Or at least I thought I likely had. Fighting amongst my uncle's warriors, I'd done what I had to do, what I'd managed to do with the quick, on-the-spot training I'd received. The experience had horrified me, grieved me, shredded me. Had altered me down to a cellular level. I couldn't turn back the clock.

This is who I have become, Grace, I thought silently at her. I will protect you. With everything I have in me now, I swear I will.

By the time dim gray light crept through the thick vitrine blocks in Enid's windows, my thinking had swung one-hundred and eighty degrees. I left Grace's side. Left her lying on the floor where we both had been, breathing with her mouth slightly open, my blanket and hers snug around her shoulders. My heart felt weighted, like the organ had filled with lead. I had to force each breath I took.

IN DARKNESS WE BREAK

The nightmare hadn't left me. It clung to my mind's twisted surfaces like poisoned honey, shrouding light and common sense. I knew we all had to stay together. Enid wasn't lying. But I wanted to run. Not away. Toward my brother. Without my friends. The only way to keep them safe would be to end it all before they had to go near him. I wouldn't hurt him, though, Moros. Didn't seem likely I could, even if I wanted to. But I didn't want to. I wanted only to stop him. Nothing more, nothing less. The means were obscured, hidden away in fear of failure.

Even here, we did not unload from our packs those things necessary for journeying. The varied catchalls were lined against the wall, ready to be shirked up onto backs at a moment's notice. Mine already rested against my spine, with slow-to-perish food items added to the essentials. I had seen the others do the same when they thought no one watched, stow away boiled eggs, dried fruit, hard bread, readying themselves despite the comfort and safety we'd found under Enid's protection.

I said a silent goodbye to all my friends from where I stood. One by one, to those I could see and to the humped blankets disguising the others. I hoped we'd all meet again, but I doubted the chances. Lastly, my eyes went to Grace, her tousled dark hair shadowing her arm. I remembered the day she'd had her long braid cut off for a shorter style similar to Hannah's. She'd said it would be easier to care for. I suppose it was. I could still picture Grace standing beside the pond at All Dwellers with her cropped hair and in that ridiculous getup she'd been wearing. I'd laughed. Or maybe I'd tried hard not to. I wasn't sure, anymore. She'd looked awkward. Uncomfortable. A little angry. Tentative. Strangely adorable.

Adorable. Grace would kick my ass if I said that word out loud to her.

I sucked in a shaky breath. My stomach juices burned my guts. My eyes stung, too. I dashed the moisture away on my sleeve. Crying. I'd become a clandestine weeper. Maybe having Grace throw me around a bit wouldn't be a bad idea. Snap me out of it. I was supposed to be brave, after all. Needed to be.

Right.

Pushing away all misgiving, I headed straight for the door. I couldn't spend a second longer contemplating departure. I had to get the hell on with my plan. Reaching for the clear knob, I hesitated. Not in indecision, but because a large shadow stepped from the darkness surrounding the doorway.

Not one shadow. Two. Brand and Mika. Apparently, there'd been nothing under their blanket-y lumps.

"How long have you been awake?" I whispered.

"Long enough," Mika answered. "Going somewhere?"

"I'm leaving."

"Yeah," muttered Brand. "We noticed that. Saw ya gatherin' your stuff."

"I didn't see you," I said.

Mika lifted a shoulder. "We were already up."

"Doing what?"

"Checkin' on things," said Brand.

"Things?"

"Enid," Mika said.

"Enid? Why?" The answer suddenly hit me. "You don't trust her."

"Do now," said Brand.

"And why is that?"

"We found proof she's been helping us," Mika

said. "Maps. Physical maps where she's been keeping track of our location and those following us. Notations all over the place about spells, maybe? Things she's done to aid us. Not directly, but by stopping when she could whatever was after us. She writes a lot. Even keeps a…a…" He worked his hands a bit, trying to come up with the word.

"A diary," Brand interjected.

I squinted at him. "What's that?"

"A book with blank pages."

"A physical book?"

"Yeah, where you write things in. Your thoughts an' your plans and things ya've done. My mom had one when she was alive."

"My mother, too," said a fourth voice. "She always keeps a journal."

I jumped, whipped around. Grace stood there, rumpled, sleepy-eyed, but still somehow wide awake.

"All about her flowers," Grace went on as though she hadn't caught us in the middle of a very telling conversation. "The species, sketches of them, even flattened, dried blooms. Makes notes whether they liked direct sun or shade. How much water to give them. When they flower. What fruit the trees bear. The recipes for preparing those when we didn't eat them fresh." Her lips twisted, pained by the simple memory.

"That's nice," I said, trying to hide the pack behind me. She jerked her chin toward my back.

"Where are you going?"

"He thinks 'e's leaving," said Brand.

Reaching around me, she jerked the pack from my grip and off my shoulders. "Not today," she said, the sack hanging from her hand. "Or if it is today, then we all go. But I think we still have some work to do."

"We are meant to be together." This came from Carina, appearing beside Grace. In the pre-dawn light, she looked otherworldly. Resa, Ren, and Hannah were the only ones still sleeping. I didn't expect their slumber to last much longer. We'd stopped whispering a while ago.

"He thinks he will save us all by going on alone," Carina added to Grace.

"How often have I thought the same thing, Duncan?" Grace said. "And acted on it. I was always wrong. You know that. We go on together."

"Or not at all."

Enid.

I closed my eyes, opened them again to study Enid's face. "Do we have a choice?" I asked.

"Naturally," she said. "We will let your final hours here take their course."

I didn't like the sounds of that. However, it seemed to me we'd already decided right then and there, standing in the shadowed entryway. Grace, Mika, Brand, and Carina would never let me go on my own. Made sense, really, but I didn't like it. Still, having the decision taken from me settled things down inside. I felt right again. Balanced. At least as right and balanced as I could be.

Grabbing my pack from Grace, I returned the carryall to its place by the wall. I spotted Resa's head on her pillow, her dark, beaded braids pulled into a single clump with a cloth strip. She appeared calm in her sleep, her brown skin slightly pink across her cheekbones. I wondered if she would have seen me in my travels had I gone on alone. I wondered, too, if she had perceived me in the past. She'd displayed no surprise after we'd located her in Tiran's compound once Carina had quieted her down. Then again, she didn't often display any strong emotion. Had she known I was coming?

Squeezing my quaking fingers into fists, I decided to keep any speculation to myself. Silently, I joined the others away from the sleepers. In a low voice Enid instructed us in physical exercises to reduce the stress we all felt. Without speaking, everyone began stretches and breathing, much like Grace had tried to teach us on Emerald. Well, Carina and me. Mika hadn't joined in and Skelly had walked out in a huff. That had been the first and last time Grace engaged us all in that manner. The ionic storm had come soon after, changing everything.

Seemed to me another storm was on its way.

Skelly

Chapter Eighteen

The clod looks worried. As well he should.

Interesting development, his brother. I wouldn't want to be Oaks at this point. His family is a never-ending source of surprise. A freak for a sister, a little brother he hardly knows, a mother who—well, did what mine did. Only mine waited a little longer to do it, and didn't give me over to someone like Oaks' Gran. As for his father? I hadn't really been able to get a read on that oaf. I sensed a disturbance in him, though.

Maybe now I know what it is. Yeah, I'd be a bit disturbed, too.

And Grace? Nearly shattered Grace is pulling herself back together. She's scaring me a little with that. I worry she might not let me out when the time comes. She has to. Because this Moros—

IN DARKNESS WE BREAK

dimwit's twin—is someone I want to meet.
   He's my kind of guy.

Grace

Chapter Nineteen

Enid took me aside, away from the others. They remained in a circle, the *ken* pecking around the soil uncovered by our maneuvers. A small, mock battle had been our afternoon training, a battle in which we all remained mentally—spiritually—connected while we fended off Enid's attack. She didn't hold back. It needed to feel authentic to us.

The bruises on my body throbbed. The salt-iron taste from the blood in my mouth made me nauseous. The latter was my fault alone. I'd pulled back at the last second, afraid Enid would be hurt. In our connectedness, everyone faltered, even Resa. Enid had sent us all flying to the ground. Had the fighting been real, I would have lost my friends in that moment. Every one of them.

"Grace," she began, when we were beyond earshot.

"I know," I said.

"Do you?"

"Yes."

Her gaze held mine. Not comfortably. I looked

away.

"Grace," Enid said again.

"I *know*."

Enid released a short breath, nodded. "Out there, away from my protection—"

"I know."

"When you are fighting independently, the decisions you all make are your own. The consequences are to the individual. When you are connected, you must remain unified. Even if you are physically apart."

A situation where we were separated and yet connected hadn't truly occurred to me. I'd been visualizing us all together, side by side. Never parted. A sudden, panicked tremor coursed my body. I swore.

"Sorry," I said.

"For your intemperate word, or your failure?"

Anger flared and died like an ill-fed spark. "Both."

"You must not let that happen again."

"The swearing?"

Her expression turned hard. "No jests, Grace. You know what I mean."

"Of course, I do," I said, short-tempered, tired, frustrated.

Scared.

Enid reached out, touched my arm. I drew back, expecting enforced peace or something similar. Instead, I only felt her fingers' light grasp.

"You are doing well," she said. "So much better than many twice your age with years of training behind them. All of you are."

My cheek muscle twitched. "You need to tell them that."

"No," said Enid. "You do. It is you who lead

them."

I opened my mouth to protest, snapped it shut.

"You do, Grace. You have from the very beginning. But they do not blindly obey. You are, as the yellow-haired one said, a team. Each with their strengths. Each with their weaknesses. Harness the former, lessen the latter. The connection running through you all is greater than you realize. You must accept it."

"But they're my friends," I whispered. "I don't want anything to happen to them."

"It already has. To them. To you. You've fought hard to stay alive, on your behalf and theirs. So have they. Whatever comes now will come. You cannot hide."

"I don't want to hide," I said.

"Good." Enid turned, looked back at my friends staring at us from across the yard. "Go and speak with them. This is the defining moment. This is when you will all decide. This is when you break or stand strong."

I gazed at my friends, studying their expressions. My stomach twisted into a knot. If we did not unanimously agree on our next action, we would be splintered. Weakened. I knew what I planned to do, despite what I had said to Duncan about going home. I could never do that. Go home. Not yet. Not until whatever I was supposed to accomplish was done.

"Once I passed through the Myth," I said, "I understood where I had to go. It had not been my original intent. I only wanted to know what to do about this." I pointed at my coat, at the bag where Skelly lurked, unusually quiet. "A destination started haunting me straightaway. I had to go there. I don't know why."

Enid dipped her head in the bag's direction. "Maybe for the solution to what you've been seeking since the moment you called the entity down into the crystal."

"Is it not Skelly?"

"I don't know. I have no answers for you where the entity you call Skelly is concerned."

Still, Skelly remained silent, leaving me to flounder. "I can't see finding resolution there. I haven't, from my first thoughts of the place I envisioned so oddly. There is something else."

"What is it that troubles you, Grace?"

I swallowed, took a short breath, let it out. "Everything."

"Narrow your focus. What troubles you most?"

"Endangering my friends."

"You are all in less danger together than you are apart."

"But we are still in danger."

"Yes."

I scuffed my boot in the dirt, thinking. Thinking hard. Trying to formulate words to make sense.

"Why us?" I finally asked, keeping it simple.

"I have no response to that, either. But I am not the only one to have foreseen this, as you are aware."

"Quite aware," I muttered. Across the ice-crusted yard, my companions continued their observation. I could tell by the change in Duncan's stance he was considering coming over. I held up a hand, silently asking him to stay put. He nodded, eyeing Enid warily, wondering, no doubt, what she had to say to me away from them. My hands clutched into frustrated fists at my sides.

"Grace..." Enid whispered warningly.

"Don't worry," I said. "I'm fine. I just...need to

know. What are we supposed to do? What are we expected to do? Against an army. Against Moros. Against who knows what. What makes anyone think we can?"

Enid tipped her chin up, gazing at the cloudy sky. She stayed in that position so long I thought she meant not to reply. But then her voice came, quiet, and calm, and fiercely certain.

"I have no idea what you are to do, what you will do. That is not for me to see. It is a matter of belief. For some, belief is fear, for others, hope. For you and your seven companions, it is who you are. Channel that and don't let go."

Turning my head, I spat bloodied saliva onto the ground. "Very well. I'll do my best."

"Do better than your best, Grace Irese. It is time for you to speak with your friends. To make the decision that cannot be altered."

"Cannot, or must not?" I asked, taking a first step back in their direction.

Enid smiled at me. "It amounts to the same thing."

* * *

We left the next morning. Nothing more could be done. Sanctuary and learning were at an end. We'd taxed Enid's strength and her supplies. She did send us off with water, food, a final word or two in advice, and some very odd weapons dug out from her shed. They looked ancient, although carefully stored and preserved.

"Where'd you manage to get these?" Ren asked. Not one for respect, he managed to ask the questions we wanted answered.

"They are mine," Enid said. "Or were. I have not always been a peaceful, powerful hermit."

"I wouldn't say you're much of a hermit, either," Ren responded with an inappropriate and expressive lift to his yellow brows. I wanted to throttle him but Enid only laughed.

"Where has Cericia gone?" I asked Enid, prompted by the exchange with Ren. "What is her mission?"

I thought perhaps I had been too bold. Enid turned to me, however, with a reply.

"She is searching for the *conjures*. It is odd they are not here, when those two—" she twitched her fingers toward Ren and Hannah, "left them outside the mountain before entering it."

"Why is that important enough to send Cericia looking?"

"Because it's important to you."

I was touched, until I realized she probably didn't mean those words in a personal manner, but more in reference to our mission, mine, and my companions. "Have you ever physically seen one?"

"To be honest," Enid answered, "I have not. But I look forward to it when we meet again."

I wriggled my shoulders, redistributing the weight from my pack against my back. "Will we meet again?"

"Of course, we will," she said, turning to check on the others. Not quickly enough. I caught the shadow darkening her eyes.

"Enid?"

She lifted her hand. "Hush. Your friends are ready. It is time."

We all gave our packs one final check. Our pockets, too, and the weapons we carried. Carina retained the staff gifted to me from the pale-eyed warrior and I clutched the one from Enid's cache. Not a staff, but a true *lathesa*. The balance was so perfect, it almost seemed made for my hand. I suspected it had not been Enid's. The length was wrong for her. I didn't ask, though. It might have been Cericia's. It might have belonged to another. Whatever the history, Enid had given the weapon specifically to me, pressing my fingers around it with a brief, near silent, incantation.

At the perimeter to the beguiled area around Enid's cottage, we all paused. Enid handed me a small, drawstring bag similar to the one holding the crystal. It, too, had a cord for wearing around the neck. "What's in here?" I asked, reaching to take it.

"Nothing. Put the talisman in there and wear the bag beside the other. It'll help."

Don't you dare, Skelly said, breaking his prolonged silence. If I'd had any doubts her words were true, they fled at Skelly's panic. Taking the Crone from my jacket pocket, I dropped it into the bag, slipped the cord over my neck and tucked the bag inside my shirt. Although similar in size, the contents felt very different in weight. After a moment, they balanced out.

Skelly? I called. He answered, angrily but distantly, not filling my brain. I grinned at Enid. "Thank you."

"My pleasure. I couldn't help you with it, I mean him, directly, but at least I could do this." She stepped away to address us all. "Remember, the trackers have been led a merry chase, but that doesn't mean they can't pick you up again, or that more won't be sent out. Keep to the trees to avoid detection from above. As for those mutant creatures—"

"Block 'em and then those three will see 'em gone," Brand said, jerking a thumb toward Carina, Resa and me.

Enid winked at him, a habit she possessed. An odd habit. She reserved it for the boys, who always blushed a little in response. "Yes, more or less. Remember to practice connecting as frequently as possible until it becomes second nature."

"Will do," he said.

"And how do we know where we're going?" Hannah asked, for the tenth time.

"Through Grace," Enid said. "As I believe has been discussed. She's still carrying the calling in her head. It hasn't left her. Duncan's sister, too."

"Fine," said Hannah, sounding sullen. "So, she'll give us a heads up when we get there?"

In the past few days, there were times I wanted to leave her behind with Enid as she had asked. This was one of those times. Yet, I knew we couldn't. We had to remain together.

I huffed out a breath. "Believe me, you'll know."

"That doesn't make me feel any better," she mumbled.

"Hannah, you agreed to go," I reminded her. "Are you wanting to back out?"

She bit her lip, shook her head, her red hair bobbing in the morning sunlight.

"Good. Because we need you. I need you. We'll do our best to keep each other from harm. All right?"

She nodded, her eyes sliding toward Duncan. I wished she hadn't. If her only reason for joining us in this danger was Duncan, then the threads binding us were weakened by something tenuous and destined to unravel.

I pushed those thoughts aside. Too late now. Straightening my shoulders, I turned and shook Enid's hand. She clasped her other hand around mine and hers and pulled me close, releasing her grip to put her arms around me. I had to bend and she had to reach up, but we managed a farewell embrace.

"We will see each other again," she said. "I promise."

With a nod, I strode closer to the perimeter, my friends gathered at my back. I stood immobile, reflecting on how much I valued every single one. The vagaries of fate had brought us together and now drove us onward. Together.

"Together," Carina whispered behind me.

"Together," murmured the rest.

Striding beyond the perimeter, I breathed deeply the frosty, perilous air outside Enid's charm. A biting fizz coursed over exposed skin, crackled in my hair. One by one my companions appeared beside me, seeming to experience the same sensations, the same sentiment regarding the first steps taken on a journey into darkness. Because it wasn't just The Darkness, not only Moros, but a palpable, burgeoning shadow determined to eclipse hope. Odd, that I wasn't more afraid.

Or maybe not so odd. My friends were with me.

Chapter Twenty

I doubled over with a stitch in my side, legs still pumping. Normally, I could run for hours. Back in the desert, during my training, I'd been expected to and had, with ease. None of us could hold this pace for much longer, though. Despite adrenaline. Despite desperation. To be honest, I hadn't anticipated the need to run anywhere so soon. But when the snow rumbled down off the mountain behind us, we'd been taken by surprise, could only run. The thunderous onslaught was nearly on us.

Spotting a rocky outcrop off to our right, I pointed, called on the still-unrecognized gifts in me. Called silently to Resa, too, hoping she sensed it. Tossing those mutants had been one thing. Holding back nature another.

Exactly, said Skelly, his voice still faint, struggling to be heard. Fighting to be heard, and for good reason. He was giving me a reminder. I couldn't hold back nature.

But I could do this.

With a bellowed cry, I jerked my friends high into the air and propelled them like wingless birds toward the ledge, unable to provide them ability to land unbroken. But Resa had heard my silent pleas in her way and understood. Nearly obliterated by the spewing snow, a sphere appeared around her and the others, cushioning their descent from my messy attempt to get them to safety. Spinning to face the onslaught, I knew I had no chance to survive. Still, I would do my best. Huddled on the ground, I gathered the power around me, hoping to stave off shattered bones, a killing blow, suffocation. I reached out to my friends in what might be our final connection, not wanting them to know my fear, only how much I cared. I had no clue if I was doing it right. I had no conscious perception how to do anything at all. It was utter nonsense. Unspoken wishes without cohesion. Frantic stabs into the dark.

Something hit me hard. Bit down into flesh and bone like tearing teeth. Only my heavy outer garment prevented agonizing breakage. The blow lifted me from the ground, threw me sideways, ran away with me with bounding, slamming, brutal force. Downhill. As it would. Gravity ruled the barreling snow wall. Gravitational laws could not be circumvented. I would ride this tide until the life was beaten from me.

The ground shook beneath my body, faster and faster. My spine jarred again and again. I expected it to snap, to suddenly not feel my legs, my arms, my beating heart. What had happened to the protective barrier I'd called? Or was it holding, a slim boundary between life and death?

No longer curled into a ball, my legs flapped without restraint, the one arm not snared wrapped around my head in an instinctive shield. If I got out of this alive, my skull, my brain, needed to remain intact. Foolish thought. A functioning brain and a shattered body. Mika could not help heal such wounds. Those injuries would be beyond him.

Suddenly, I sensed their thoughts again. Everyone together. Like Enid had said. I felt surprise, shock, fear, gratitude. They were alive. I love you all, I thought fiercely into the connection.

Open your eyes, Grace.

I sucked in a moist breath. It dragged across my tongue, blood-tanged, filling lungs from which the air had escaped almost too long ago. *Who is that?* I asked. I received no answer, but did as bade, forcing sticky lids apart.

Rather than bright, impending doom, I beheld darkness, moving darkness, lifting, falling, rising again. My body shifted when it did, leaped when it did. I still heard the roar from the cascading snow and debris, yet the noise was somehow muffled. Nearer sounds reached me. Grunting communications. Accompanying them and the shadowed dark came a nearly overwhelming stench.

I cried out, disbelieving and joyous. The *conjures* had returned.

One had my arm in its dangerous, toothy maw. Another, I realized now, had managed in the last few seconds to grab a thrashing leg. The largest, Vigor, galloped alongside black as night, growling as flying stone and ice struck his body. *Conjures* could be unbelievably fast given their bulk. The impetus of certain death if they faltered had provided them a speed unsurpassed.

"Thank you," I rasped as I held tight to consciousness. I could do little else. The *conjures* had me in their grip and I wasn't about to risk them letting go.

* * *

"Look at you, Grace."

I smiled up at Duncan, feeling a certain crooked pull in the action. My face on the right side was slightly swollen, the flesh stretched tight. "That's not exactly possible," I said, lips barely moving.

"You're in one piece, though," he said. "We all are."

I nodded, wincing. Duncan sank to his knees and pulled me close. "Ow," I said. He let go, sat back over his heels.

I'd only been upright for a brief time. Prior to that, I'd been on my back where Chauncy and Bell had dropped me, subjected by Mika to a lengthy examination. After, the boys had slid me onto a blanket and dragged me inside. The place I'd thrown my friends had proven to be more than an outcropping. It had opened into a fissure forming a shallow cave. For now, we were camped inside it.

No fire, though. Smoke would be seen by day curling out the cave mouth. After our ordeal, everyone sat without moving, wrapped in their blankets, the kinetic torches set at intervals. Weapons, Enid's and our own, lay near to hand. Somehow, strapped to my back, her *lathesa* had survived intact. It was a beautifully crafted object. I would have regretted its loss for that as much as my need.

"The *conjures* have settled down outside," Duncan said, gazing in that direction. "It's good to have them back with us."

I laughed, touched my cheek, groaned a little. "That's an understatement."

"Yeah. Well." He looked me in the eye for a long moment. He didn't have to say anything more.

Without the *conjures* fortuitous arrival, I'd likely not have survived, or at least not for long. My companions would never have found me under all the snow.

"It's all right," I said. "I'm here."

He snorted, yanked his blanket back up around his shoulders, turned his gaze to the cave floor.

"Duncan?"

His head snapped up. "Don't ever do that again."

"Do what?"

"Don't separate me from you."

"If I hadn't—"

"Don't," he said. "Just don't. Save the others, sure, but I stay with you."

My eyebrows arched at his words. Painfully. "Duncan…"

"I'm serious."

I shook my head. "If you're expecting me to apologize, that's not going to happen. If you're expecting me to agree, that's not happening either."

"Grace."

"No." I shifted on the hard ground, tucked my blanket around my aching legs. "The *conjures* couldn't have grabbed both of us. Who do you think they would have chosen?"

"They might have done," he answered stubbornly, ignoring my question.

"Perhaps," I agreed. "Which would have slowed them down, and they and we would be gone now. Dead."

A muscle twitched in his jaw. "You didn't know the *conjures* were nearby when you did what you did."

"True, I didn't. But what I did know was you were all safe. That's what mattered most to me. It always will."

IN DARKNESS WE BREAK

His hands clenched into fists on his knees, then opened as he smashed his face down onto his palms. His fingers curled into his dark, tangled hair. His shoulders shook. The sudden noise from his sobs filled the stone hollow. The others reacted to the sound with an odd paralysis. Except Hannah. Swiftly recovered from the shock, she started to get up. I mustered my way through pain and beat her to it, kneeling beside him and pulling him into my arms. Hannah continued past to the cave's opening. Glancing aside, I saw her silhouetted against the pale sky beyond.

"Duncan, shh," I whispered against his temple.

"It's my fault you're here."

"In this cave?"

"In this life," he spat. "If not for me, for my testimony, for my ridiculous choices in my own life, you'd still be with your family, still be in your home, still—"

"Shut up," I said, choking on the words. "Just. Shut. Up. It's not that simple. Stone Tiran would have seen me imprisoned or dead with or without you. You were his tool, sure, but if you'd failed at it, or had decided not to cooperate, he would have just chosen another. And it wasn't even a decision for you. He had Resa, remember? Besides, if we hadn't both been in that damned facility on Emerald, Mika and Carina would still be there. Right? As for after that, yes, it's been—what's your Gran's saying? Out of the frying pan and into the fire. Out of many frying pans and into bigger and bigger fires. But everything that's happened has apparently been for a reason. I don't like that. I don't like thinking our destiny is laid out for us, but it seems it is. No matter how I feel about the universe or whatever you want to call it sending us into the biggest fire of all."

He grew quiet, raised his head, smeared the tears off his face. He didn't look at me, though.

"Duncan, all of us here, everyone who has traveled with us through this mess, is here for a reason. The cosmos? Maybe. Friendship? Oh, yes. The need to make things right? That seems to be our inclination. A force for reckoning? I don't know, but you've seen us in action. Maybe we're just a bunch of misfits—"

"Speak for yourself," muttered Ren with a small laugh to take the edge from his statement.

"—who want to do what's right. Who have half a chance to actually do that."

"Wow," said Hannah. "That was quite a speech."

I hadn't heard her come back. I looked up at her over Duncan's head. She clapped her hands slowly together in mock applause. Outside, the *conjures* grumbled at the sound.

Leaning forward from his place between Carina and Resa, Mika spoke. "What's your problem, Hannah?"

"She's just being Hannah," Ren said.

Hannah shot him a look, mumbled several unintelligible words. Ren appeared to understand them. He stood.

"Enough," he said. "You came voluntarily."

"Enid said we needed to be together," Hannah shot back.

"She did, and we do, so act like you're a willing participant, will you?"

"I am willing. I just thought..." She didn't finish the sentence, but her eyes went to me and Duncan on the cave floor.

"Hannah," Duncan said, "you know how I feel.

That hasn't changed. I care about you. You're my friend. Only my friend."

Her head jerked. Pivoting sharply on her heel, she stormed back to the cave's entrance and outside, giving the *conjures* a wide berth.

"Is she leaving?" Brand asked. "Some'n might want to stop 'er. She could give us away out there." Not waiting for a volunteer, he jumped up and strode after Hannah. Carina rose and neatly folded her blanket.

"I'll go, too, in case any intervention is necessary. She won't survive if she decides to head off on her own."

"Neither will we," I said, so quietly only Duncan heard.

"Do you really think so?"

I shrugged, but inside my head I knew so.

Between them, Brand and Carina calmed Hannah's hot-headed reaction and brought her back inside. Everyone agreed we should continue to rest and recover, spend the night hidden away from prying eyes and any unexpected weather.

"Especially you," Mika reminded me. As if I needed reminding. Every movement made me grind my teeth to prevent swearing. How I hadn't managed to break a leg, an arm, or my skull, I couldn't imagine. Despite their haste and the risk, Chauncy and Bell had managed to carry me without furthering any injuries. I still had plenty. Superficial, but painful.

After a meal and before darkness fell, I made my slow way out to the *conjures*. They rumbled in welcome. Knowing I couldn't help but retain the stink in my clothes, I still hugged each one in turn. The man who had released Chauncy to me would have been astonished by the relationship which had developed.

Not only between me and Chauncy, but all my friends and the three *conjures*. A symbiotic association was what I'd been told a driver and a *conjure* shared. The man had been talking about their use as draft animals, something rare and confined to the residents in Ogdo. What we all shared was so much more.

Several small stones skittered past my feet. I glanced over my shoulder.

"Sorry," Duncan apologized. "I hope I'm not disturbing you."

"Don't be silly," I answered.

"Me? Silly?" He made an immediate face, crossed eyes, cheeks sucked in. I snorted a laugh. "I was just checking on you. How do you feel?"

"I'm good," I said. "It's a beautiful view, isn't it?"

Stopping beside me, Duncan nodded agreement. "Beautiful, and scary. Like you."

I bit my lip, the cold biting into my heated cheeks. He interlaced his fingers with mine.

"It's been a long road," he said. I nodded. He gave my hand a squeeze. "Feels like we're nearing the end."

"I hope so?" It sounded like a question, the way I uttered the words. I realized it was intended to be a question. Because 'nearing the end' could mean so many things.

"Whatever comes," he said, "we'll be together."

"Yes." I said what he wanted to hear. A hollow promise. So much could happen. So much would happen. We would try, though. All of us. Side by side Duncan and I watched the sun descend and the stars come out. We shivered, but only a little. The *conjures* gave off warmth like heaters.

"What's that?" I asked, pointing.

"Where?"

"There."

He stepped forward onto his right foot, narrowing his eyes at the night sky. "A satellite?"

"No, I don't think so. I think...I think it's the Emerald."

With a gasp, Duncan shuffled forward another couple steps, dragging me with him. "I don't... Crap, I think you're right. It is."

"It's in a weird place. Not where I'm used to seeing it from home. But I hadn't expected to be able to see it at all. Not yet."

He glanced at me and back to the distant object in the night sky, burning small and faintly green. He shivered. I felt it.

"We haven't really been in a position to see it," I went on, trying to sound matter-of-fact. "The mountain ranges have been too high, blocking the sky in that direction. We're at a higher elevation right now and the sky is clear."

"And?" he said.

"And what?"

"It sounded like another 'and' was coming."

Another 'and' had been coming. I just didn't want to say it. I needed to, though. Releasing a breath, I rushed on. "And I think we're closer to the place in my head than I thought."

Duncan's lips compressed. He nodded several times. "Okay."

"Okay?"

"Yes. What else am I supposed to say? We'll do what we have to do, no matter what."

"If the weather were warmer, what I would say is we should stick around here for a bit."

"You'd never say that," Duncan answered in a

dry tone. "Once you set your mind to something, you keep going until it's done."

"Is that really a good thing?" I asked quietly.

He smiled. "So far? Yep."

I snorted and looked away from him, back to the tiny orb among the stars. The stars always filled me with the sense infinite possibility existed. Not so, the Emerald. Emerald was an end. The end. We'd been fortunate to escape, despite all the dangers encountered in the process and since. Despite our lives being "well-maintained" inside the facility. I would have lost my mind up there. Or my will to live.

I wouldn't change what had happened, even if I could. Wouldn't change what had led me to be there. Not now. It was done. It was, in some odd way, necessary. I had Duncan at my side, which wouldn't have occurred otherwise. Mika and Carina were free. Resa no longer lived among the Sisters but with family and friends, and the camaraderie, the consciousness between us, was helping her. I felt sure of that. And she helped us all, too, not only in rescue, but in our everyday lives.

Our bizarre and perilous everyday lives.

My gaze dropped to the *conjures* resting on the ground before us. I watched them breathing, hide-covered abdomens expanding and receding, soft, growling breaths writhing smoke-like in the frigid air. I thought about the Ogdonian driver, the others in Ogdo who'd provided us with supplies. I thought about my companions asleep or preparing to sleep behind me in the cave. I thought about Senta and Enid and the others we'd met along the way, those willing to help us, to stand by us, to shelter us, to share whatever they had. I thought about my family. I thought about Duncan's hand in mine.

My breath went out. Warmth rushed beneath my flesh and through my bones. I felt…blessed. That was something my mother often talked about, being blessed, but I hadn't really understood what she meant until now. And I felt also like maybe I was coming to an ending, too. My end.

I would find out soon enough.

Duncan

Chapter Twenty-One

I had seen ships zigzagging through the sky overnight. Where we had been. Not where we were now. I wondered if the avalanche—Brand's word, not mine—had prevented anything following us on foot. Whatever had happened, for the moment we were safe, untracked, not hunted. At least, I hoped so.

Battered Grace moved slowly, despite the frequent rests since we'd set out in the morning. She possessed quite the shiner and her cheek looked painful. She carried herself carefully, muscles aching. As well they would. At least no bones had been broken, no cuts too deep. Yet she had an air about her, now, of...I don't know. Not melancholy. Acceptance, maybe. Like the fight in her had been pushed deep down. I wasn't sure what the change meant. Perhaps she was merely tired and trying to heal. But it seemed like something more.

The others noticed, too. With exchanged glances, we gathered mentally to reach out to her, to connect. She held back like a wall.

"I'll be fine. Just give me some time," she said

out loud after our third attempt.

So, we walked, oddly separate, heading for the valley below. The *conjures* took point, their huge, lumbering bodies in exposed positions to the fore and either side. Even though the three animals could handle us all on their backs, we had agreed to stay on foot. Even Grace. Conceivably, she thought she would feel better if she kept her body moving. Every stumble, every wince, every sharp breath, made me want to lift her off the ground and stick her on Chauncy's back.

Sure. Like she'd ever allow that. She'd knock me flat with Enid's *lathesa* if I tried, no matter how much she hurt.

I glanced up at the sky, trying to gauge the time. We could all plead a midday need for sustenance, make Grace stop and sit awhile. Trouble was, we didn't do three meals a day. We couldn't afford to rest in the open or consume extras from our supplies. Until we obtained more, our foodstuffs were limited.

At the thought, my traitorous guts gave a rumble.

"For crying out loud, Oaks," said Ren, "you'd think you'd be used to limited eats by now."

"Yeah," I said, declining a comeback, "you'd think."

Shocked into silence by my agreement, Ren trudged on without retort.

I noticed Brand walking with Carina, Mika, and my sister. When not with me, he seemed to like their company best. I don't think he knew what to make of Grace. Sometimes *I* didn't know what to make of Grace.

As for Ren and Hannah, I could tell he wasn't comfortable around them. He often watched them from beneath his lashes. Brand had good instincts, which worried me. Was it only something to do with their attitude, or did he sense more? Those two had been living in an atmosphere marked by distrust. Ren's Gran had sent him to the glass mines, after all, and from what I'd heard, Hannah's mother wasn't much better. The fact they'd been treated badly by their families colored things they said, probably much they thought. The four of us, however—the original four—had gotten used to Hannah and Ren's peculiarities.

Remembering what had happened outside the Sleeping Myth, I realized maybe we shouldn't have. Their behavior then had bugged me, too, especially Hannah's. A little heavier eyeballing was probably in order, from everyone.

I didn't like thinking that way. Enid's insistence we all needed to stay together was not just a whim. She saw a bigger picture, something beyond me to understand. Her ability to teach us to connect the way we now had? Clearly, the woman was something far more than simple me could comprehend. I had to trust her.

Or did I?

Of course, not. I didn't have to believe or trust in anything without first taking full measure. Trusting my instincts the way Brand trusted his had to be the best course, the only trust, because I didn't have the luxury to try anything else.

Suddenly, Carina broke away from her little group and walked back to me, falling in at my side. "Relax, Duncan," she said. "Your thoughts are going in circles."

A breath burst out my nose. How many times would she enter my head, unasked, unwelcome?

"As many times as it takes," she said, "because

you must not falter." With a small smile, she skipped her way back to her boyfriend, to my sister, to Brand.

Skipping, I thought with a frown. White hair flailing side to side, as if she isn't like the rest of us, tired to the bone.

Grace stepped right, took my hand. "She is tired," Grace said. "She manages to hide it better."

"Are you reading my mind, now?" I snapped.

"Nope," said Grace, her tone not altering at mine in any way. "You were talking out loud again. You know, the way you do when you're stressed?"

I closed my eyes, opened them again. How many times had I done this? What made me utter my thoughts aloud? I'd been caught out at it more than once. "Got it. Thanks."

"And 'white hair flailing'?" she added. "When did you get so poetic?"

From her place at Mika's side, Carina glanced back and giggled. I shifted my gaze to the ground, wanting to kick myself. I dropped Grace's hand and strode ahead, past the others, until I was facing Chauncy's rump. The smell of it, of his whole body, was horrendous. I brought a finger up to my nose, hearing limping footsteps hurrying up behind me.

"Grace," I said, "I would have come back to you." I glanced aside at her. She wrinkled her nose.

"I'm sure you would have."

"I just…I just don't know what's wrong with me."

"There's nothing wrong with you," she said. "You're—"

"Don't say perfect. I'd expect some gushing crap like that from the likes of Hannah, but—"

"I wasn't going to. I was going to say worried. We all are. Why wouldn't we be?"

I frowned. Right.

Grace's lip twisted up at one corner. "A year ago, what were you doing?"

"What?"

"Tell me."

I thought about it. Hard. "I'm not sure I remember, exactly."

"I don't think any of us do. What we have been through has driven normal, everyday things right out of our heads. We are…damaged, and yet more and better than what we once were."

"If you say so."

"I do say so. We've become stronger. Smarter. Less trusting and more trusting. Less confident and so confident we can't be shaken. Dichotomies that make us question everything and yet willing to believe the impossible."

Pulling my lips in between my teeth, I considered. "Wow," I finally said.

"What does this mean, 'wow'?" Grace asked. "I've heard you and Mika use it before."

"It's an exclamation, like when you're so amazed you have nothing to say, or so disappointed, or so bewildered, or anything where more words won't do it justice."

She looked at me. Her right brow arched. A slow smile lifted her mouth. "Wow," she said, and laughed.

I kissed her. Possibly the wrong time. But she kissed me back, despite her swollen face. As we had both stopped in our tracks, I figured she'd go right on doing it until the others caught up. Something else happened first.

By Grace's reaction, something bad.

Grace's head jerked skyward. In automatic reflex, her *lathesa* whistled past me as she adopted a defensive position, missing my skull by a finger's breadth. She shoved me back toward the trees, urging everyone else to do the same. The *conjures* had halted, great shaggy heads tipped up, their corkscrew horns pointed like spears toward the sky. Which indeed they were. Spears. I had witnessed firsthand the damage they could cause.

From under the nearest tree, I peered through snow-laden branches, trying to get a glimpse of what Grace had heard or seen, what demanded the *conjures* rapt attention. "I can't see anything," I said.

"Hush."

As if I were two years old. I shut my mouth obediently, however, and loosened a second weapon from my belt. The first hadn't left my hand since we'd woken that morning.

"Grace," I whispered.

She whipped a finger to her lips, then pointed it upward. I followed with my eyes.

"What the hell?"

Things with impossible wingspans circled in the sky. The didn't possess a dragon's bulk or even the strong bodies belonging to the much smaller raptors Grace had pointed out on occasion when she heard their piercing cries. I couldn't tell how big these things were, really, because they remained aloft and black against the high clouds beyond, distance misleading the eye. Not small, was my guess. They dipped and circled and came back again as if searching for something.

Us, no doubt.

A pair broke away, sailed directly overhead, appearing as though they floated on an updraft until they dipped sideways and shot down toward the treetops, wings laid back somewhat against their bodies for speed. Big, yeah, they were big. I could see that now. At the last moment the creatures pulled up, wings stretching wide, and rose into the air again. I glimpsed something odd when they did. A glint. Like metal.

"Did you see—"

Grace nodded wordlessly.

Taking advantage of the creatures' momentary retreat, the others hurried in silence toward us. They gathered close, weapons ready. Brand, whose eyesight outstripped even Grace's, said:

"They're mechanical."

I gaped at him. "What? Like cybers?"

He shook his head. "Only the wings. Those are people strapped to them."

I swore. Just two quick words. Eloquent words. But not pretty.

* * *

I wished those darned *conjures* would get out of sight. To be honest, the trees were too closely grown here. They couldn't. But anyone who knew anything about us as a group would realize the significance to their presence. I hadn't seen any other *conjures* in our recent travels, after all. No wild herds or however they clustered together. If they did. Only these three. Some high-flying searcher would soon recognize they weren't misshapen boulders. Especially not with the single, lengthy horn protruding from each head.

Of course, good luck landing near one. Maybe this was the reason the winged soldiers or whatever they were continued to keep to the air.

"How many do you see?" Grace threw the question out for answer in a general manner. Keen-sighted Brand spoke first.

"Eleven," he said.

"That's it?"

"That's it."

"Doesn't seem like enough," she muttered to herself.

"You mean, because between us and the *conjures* we're not really out-numbered?" I asked. "Wouldn't that depend on how well those airborne folks are armed?"

"Certainly," Grace said. "But it seems to me anyone seeking us has some idea of the stories and they'd come in larger numbers. Much larger numbers."

"So, you don't think they're looking for us?" We couldn't be that lucky, but I asked it anyway.

Grace continued to watch them, her head moving to follow their graceful flight. "I didn't say that. I'm just not quite sure they're a threat, or if they are someone who could help us."

"And how are we supposed to find that out?" Hannah griped.

"We can't," I said. "Even if they came down here with open arms and smiles, there's no way we could know to trust them."

Grace grunted in agreement. "Maybe they'll move on. Otherwise, we prepare for the worst and see what happens. And Carina, if you're able to get something from them?"

"Sure thing, boss," Carina answered with a grin. A decidedly wicked grin, considering Carina's sweet demeanor. The little island mystic was enjoying this for some reason.

"Stretching my mind," she said in response to my inner musing. "It'll feel good."

I bared my teeth at her.

"Three comin' close," Brand cut in.

Everyone stopped talking and looked up.

Three sets of wings spiraled down toward the treetops. Unlike the divebombing pair, the movements weren't quick and aggressive. Instead, it seemed more like lazy reconnaissance. They circled and swept back and forth, dropping a little more with each rotation. Soon, we could see what appeared to be human legs bending at the knees and straightening, as if preparing for a landing on the narrow, rocky track where we'd been walking. I shifted my gaze to the *conjures*. They appeared to be watching, too, but not ready to attack.

"Grace," I said quietly.

"Stand firm."

"Easy for you to s—" Her glance shut me up.

I shifted my weapons in my grip, the smaller one still in my bandaged right hand. Around me, the others made similar preparation. "Is this one of those times we should be linking up?" I asked meaning the connection proving to be so powerful between us.

"I don't think so," Carina said before Grace could respond.

"Why not?" This, from Ren, obviously feeling a little anxious.

Grace looked away from the descending wing-riders, her gaze meeting Carina's, whose eyes had turned as pale as the sky above us. Grace nodded at her, glanced around at the others.

"We wait," she said.

Not even telling us why. I hated this part. The secrets unshared. The not knowing. But Grace had her reasons. Good ones, I told myself. I puffed my cheeks, blew out a breath, and did as I'd been instructed. I waited.

We didn't have to wait long. The figures landed a short distance from the *conjures*, who still hadn't moved. Wings retracted, folded, closed with a whir and a distinct, metallic click. Beneath padded clothing, the figures' bodies appeared to be male. And tall. At least as tall as Grace and I, likely taller. They wore headgear and gloves. Except for the wings, I couldn't see what apparatus they used for flight. The wings hadn't appeared to flap or anything. They must have engines somewhere. Small, lightweight, hidden, powerful engines.

We, on the other hand, were not hidden. Not anymore.

Three helmet-covered heads turned our way, staring straight at us where we stood beneath the trees. The male in the middle reached up, unfastened the full-face covering from somewhere near his throat and lifted it. Yanked off the helmet, too. Beside me, Grace sucked in a breath. A breath like a sob. She started forward. I reached out for her arm. She shook off my hand and the weapon in it. I snatched the fallen blade from the ground.

"Grace?"

Pausing, she turned her head, gazed at me. Her eyes shone with tears. I looked to the unmasked rider and back at her.

"Grace?" I prompted once more. My heart squeezed in my chest like a fist had grabbed it. Grace's lips curved.

"It's my youngest brother," she said. "It's Connor."

Chapter Twenty-Two

I hadn't known Grace had a brother. Or if she'd ever mentioned it to me, I'd forgotten somehow. Looking at them side by side, no one could deny the family connection. His skin was a bit darker, but he had the same shape to his brown eyes, the same brow and cheekbones. The same midnight blue tattoo. The same stance, too, straight, relaxed, but clearly ready underneath for whatever might come his way. And the same smile. The two of them hadn't stopped smiling since he'd taken off his helmet, although Grace's smile had been a bit watery on and off.

He was older than Grace, and apparently there were two more like him, older still. Not with him. I received the impression he had no idea where they might be.

We'd been sequestered in a pavilion with food and drink and otherwise dismissed from mind as Connor took his sister around the camp for introductions. I didn't begrudge him the reunion, but there was something odd about the fact he left us to vegetate. To vegetate with an armed guard in attendance. Granted, it seemed more an honor than to keep us inside, but I still didn't like it.

I didn't like being this far from Grace, either, even if she was now under her brother's protection. Glancing at the others, I could see how uneasy we all were. Whenever we got separated, bad things happened.

I stood up and sauntered over to a tent post. A posted guard moved swiftly to place himself at my side. Maybe I'd been wrong about it being an honor. I pretended not to notice, though.

"How do those things work?" I asked, jerking my chin at the flying apparatus spread across metal triangles in the sun. To dry out after exposure to dampness, I supposed. Or in preparation for some necessary fine-tuning prior to re-use.

Who was I kidding? I'd never seen the like and had no clue how it functioned or what was needed to keep it in operating condition. Under other circumstances, I would have struck up a conversation with Grace's brother about it, but he and Grace were nowhere to be seen. Had he taken Resa and Carina along for the stroll, I would have been much more worried, given past events. Still, I wasn't *not* worried.

"Small propulsion engines. Pretty ingenuous, eh?" the guard answered, grinning at me. Seemed genuine enough. I eyed his weapon. On his belt, not in his hand. Okay. Mine were equally accessible. No one had taken them from me or anyone else. I allowed my shoulders to relax a bit.

"What fuel do they use?" I asked. "I can't imagine anything combustible. That would be dangerous."

"The sun, but I don't really know how," the guard said. "The information is not shared."

I nodded, pointed at the gear with my finger this

time. "May I take a closer look?"

He hesitated before agreeing. We walked over together, where he stood at my side again. I studied the wings, made from thin metal sheets resembling feathers and riveted onto a retractable framework. At a point where a person's shoulders might be in the harness, two cylinders had been attached. I couldn't quite see how, although straps from interwoven metal seemed to provide extra security in their positioning. The engine wasn't visible on the apparatus. Perhaps it had been removed after flight.

I pointed yet again. "Have you ever, you know, flown in these?"

He shook his head. His facial features were blocked by the helmet he wore. Not one like Grace's brother and the other flyers, but something appearing to be both decorative and for protection. A kind of heavy cap, fitted close to the skull and embellished with polished metal wings along each side. The wings at their widest curved around to nearly meet, blocking his mouth and nose from full view. I saw only his eyes clearly. Something about them made me think he might be my age or only a few years older.

"It would be a blast," I said, and meant it. He laughed. "Do you know where Connor and Grace went?" I added, while I had him in a good place. His mood changed in a flash.

"You will call him Commander. Commander Irese," he said.

"Sorry," I said, without the slightest sincerity. "Grace introduced her brother by his name to me and to our friends."

I could tell he didn't quite know what to take from my statement. Was it a rebuke? A reminder regarding Grace's relationship to his commander? He might even have been silently labeling me a troublemaking ass. Having spoken my piece, I waited.

"This is a military encampment," he said sullenly. "You will address the—your friend's brother by his title."

I noticed his stumble. I had no idea what he'd been about to say, but I decided to let it go. Instead, I nodded and turned back to the wings, pretending to admire them still. "I don't know how long we'll be sticking around—"

The guard cut short a word before speaking it. I went on over whatever he'd intended to say.

"—but perhaps you know if we will be camping there, in that tent where we've all just eaten, or somewhere else."

I felt like I was channeling Grace. Speaking in a calm, articulate manner when what I really wanted to do was throttle this guy's head off. Not that I would have. I didn't throttle people. But picturing the act provided a gut satisfaction.

"Accommodations are being made," the guard said. "The girls will go—"

"Nope."

"What?"

"We stay together. You can check with Grace, but I'm pretty sure she'll say the same. She's not going to care how her brother feels about it, believe me."

I didn't give him a chance to say anything else. I turned on my boot heel and stalked back to the tent.

Hannah spoke up first. "What's wrong?"

"Nothing," I said.

"Doesn't look like nothing." Hannah glanced around at the others. "Does it look like nothing?"

"Where's Grace?" Mika asked. "Did that guard

tell you?"

I grunted. "He didn't say much, except I was to refer to her brother as Commander."

"Commander of what?" asked Brand.

"Apparently, we are in a military encampment." I thought my sarcasm evident but Ren, sitting on Brand's left, didn't quite pick up on the tone.

"You didn't notice that before?" he questioned.

"Of course, I did," I said. "Or, at least, I figured it was something like that. I can't say I've actually been in one."

Ren looked past the tent posts to the temporary shelters, the helmeted, uniformed men striding purposefully in various directions, the general bustle. His expression turned ugly. "I have. Nothing like this, though."

Ren's grandmother had maintained a standing army in All Dwellers and yes, not quite like this. Her warriors had roamed the city doing her bidding, keeping peace, maintaining control, guarding her captives, herding others off to the glass mines. My stomach turned in memory. The glass mines had been a horror I never wanted to witness again. I saw the same recollection pass across Ren's face, and Mika's.

"There's no reason to worry," Mika said. "This is Grace's brother."

The reminder served its purpose. After everything we'd been through, paranoia came easily to the mind. Resuming my seat at the table, I pulled my plate nearer, grimacing at the oily slick spreading out beneath my meal's spotty remnants. Normally, I might have licked the plate clean. Seeing the grease, I was glad I hadn't. I shoved the plate away.

Only one person besides Resa had remained silent in the recent exchange. I looked toward Carina and found her eyes on me. I didn't care for the look in them. "What?"

Crossing her arms on the table, she leaned forward. "Where are the *conjures*?"

"What do you mean? They didn't follow us in. And no man of Connor's showed an inclination to make them," I added with a short, sharp laugh.

"But they always stay with Grace, unless she directs them otherwise."

"What are you getting at? Do you think she asked them to remain outside the camp?"

"Maybe."

"Why? For what reason? There's plenty of room inside the boundaries."

"Why, indeed."

Her cryptic answers pricked at my skin. "Carina, if you know something, you need to tell it. In plain language."

"I don't know anything. Not for sure. But I feel…something."

I shot upright, knocking my stool over. Several guards turned and looked my way. I righted the stool with a nod in their direction, sat back down. "Carina?"

"I can't find her. I've been reaching out, but I can't sense Grace. I'm sure she's overjoyed to see her brother, to maybe find out something about her family, and she's blocking me so she can concentrate on those things."

I angled my arms across the tabletop, bringing myself closer to her. "Can people do that? Block you?"

"You can't," she said to me. "If that's why you're asking. I don't know why. You're wide open all the time."

"Well, hell," I muttered. More than inconvenient,

that could be downright embarrassing. "But Grace?" I pressed. "She can?"

"She has in the past. She's probably doing it now. I'm telling myself I don't need to be concerned—"

"She's with her brother." My voice sounded desperate, even to me.

"And she was genuinely happy to see him. As was he, her. Yes, I reached out for what I could sense back there when they found us, just to be sure, as well as after."

"So, then what's your problem?"

Golden iris disappeared in a single blink, becoming like one large pupil, black as night. I thought I'd gotten used to it. How could I have? When her eyes went black like this, nothing good came our way.

"I don't know," Carina said. "It might be nothing."

I scratched my head, sizing up the nearest guards from beneath my fingers, allowing my breath to seep out in a slow, even stream from my lungs. I turned back to Carina. "And it could be something," I said.

"Yes," she agreed. Too quickly. "It could."

Tiny Carina, harbinger of the good, the bad, and the ambiguous. I spent a few seconds thinking about what she'd said, about what we might do about it. Not knowing what or from where any trouble would come was an impediment to planning, for sure. Mika, sitting next to Carina, had heard everything. He refrained from speaking, waiting on me. Beside him, my sister studied the tabletop, not actually seeing it. What she saw could have been anything.

"Okay," I finally said, hoping my thoughts would make sense leaving my mouth. "Connor came looking for us, or at least his sister, so he had to have heard some rumor, yeah? He mentioned something about it when he led us down the mountain to meet the others. Which means he, at least, knows the prophecy and the tales. Whether he believes them is something else. But he would be cautious, on the chance the stories about Grace, Resa, and Carina are true, right?"

As I spoke, the others had slid their seats nearer. They now murmured agreement.

"So, if his intentions are sketchy, he would have done something immediately to separate us, placing us most likely in some inescapable confinement. Not something like feeding us and leaving us in an open-sided pavilion. I think we can assume his intentions, then, are at least not bad. Yes?"

Another agreement around the table, a bit more tentative than the last. I glanced once more at the guards. They remained uninterested in our discussion, talking among themselves. I went on.

"I think we should test the waters, as my Gran says."

"What's 'at mean?" Brand asked.

"Find out if any danger to us exists. And be prepared for it."

Ren wrinkled his brow. "Um…how, may I ask? Do you have something oozing in that mind of yours?"

I knew better than to get riled by Ren at this point. Not this time, at least. This was too important to allow distraction.

"Why don't we all reach out to her, like Enid taught us?" Hannah suggested.

"Based on what Carina said," I reminded her, "I don't know that Grace would be receptive right now."

"Well, what then?" she asked, drumming her fingers on the table, and looking defiant. I sucked in a quick breath and turned to Mika.

"How about a stroll?" I said to him.

"What, you and me?"

I nodded.

"So, are you thinking we ask permission, or just go?"

"Just go," I said.

"But that'll separate us from the others, and I'm not sure we—"

"Oh, hell," I growled.

That quick, Hannah rose from her seat and marched over to the nearest guard. She was about to betray us again.

"Hannah," I hissed.

She glanced back at me and tossed her head. I didn't much care for the smile she shot my way. I rose, too, but didn't follow. Better we stayed together around the table and readied ourselves for whatever mayhem she created.

At the guard's side, she reached up toward his sleeve. For one crazy moment, I thought she had deluded herself into thinking she could enforce sleep, the way Carina could. Not that it would have worked. There were ten guards stationed around the tent. Dropping them one at a time was useless. I saw in the next instant she didn't imagine any such thing. She took the guard's sleeve between her fingertips and tugged it. When he turned to look at her, she swept her other hand in our direction. My teeth ground together. Yes, as I thought. Betrayal. Why had Enid insisted it be all or none? Why had the Universe?

The guard appeared confused. Hannah's whole demeanor changed. I would have laughed if I hadn't been so amazed. She'd never acted this way with me, despite her interest, but she was piling on the charm.

Seeming to plead even, with absolute innocence in her expression.

"What the—" whispered Mika.

The exchange lasted no more than a minute before she headed back our way, a little skip in her walk, a smile splashed across her face. When she reached us, the smile dropped, her expression turning serious.

"Let's go," she said. "Let's take a look around. We've been given permission to 'stretch our legs' and as long as we don't go far, we can go alone. I say, when the time is right, we disappear. Unfortunately, we have to leave our packs here, so I guess we can't run off altogether."

I stared at her with an open mouth.

"And our weapons?" Ren asked.

"He didn't say. Stash the smaller ones in our clothes?"

"Yes," I agreed. "Best to leave the larger ones here, for now."

I could have hugged her. I wouldn't, though. No reason to give her any ideas about us. Any more than she already harbored. Within minutes, with our eyes on the guards to make sure no one paid too much attention, we were secretly armed. I hoped such a precaution unnecessary, but who knew, really? Something felt skewed in this situation.

"Good job," I said to Hannah before we started off. I had to give her something. The move had been a risky one on her part, one that would have been better explained to all involved before operation, but it had worked. I was grateful for that.

"Everybody, eyes open," I said.

"Unnecessary order, Oaks," Ren muttered, but he grinned at me as he headed for the open area beyond the pavilion. We strode out into the brittle sunshine in casual fashion, as though we were, indeed, only looking for a little exercise. Brand, ever watchful, took up the rear position. I walked in front, Hannah on one side, Ren on the other. Mika, Carina and Resa made up the middle.

"Which way?" Hannah asked.

"Carina?" I said over my shoulder. "Sensing anything?"

"No. Not really. Except…maybe we keep going straight."

I nodded. "Straight it is."

Lined up like a fence along our left, more triangular racks held winged gear. I briefly eyeballed the wings, wondered if they might come in handy, dismissed the idea. Since we didn't know how they worked, they'd just be a burden. A weight to be carried while running away. More soldiers existed in this camp than I had seen gathered anywhere else. Many, like Grace's brother, were clearly desert warriors. Easy to spot, despite their heavy clothing. They were taller than most, carried themselves differently, had skin shades darker than those around them. The rest could have come from anywhere. I had no way to tell. I couldn't tell which were female and which male, either. It didn't matter. They were an equal threat to us, if the occasion called for it.

Following the 'straight' path, we left the pavilion behind as well as the guards surrounding it. Although perfectly content with the latter, I wasn't too happy about the former. If something happened, something unexpected, something we had to fight our way out from and flee—not without Grace—all our supplies and Enid's weapons remained there. Yet, we'd been in those straits before. We'd manage. Or so I told myself. Repeatedly.

Tents and several somewhat permanent structures dotted the encampment. Helmeted soldiers tramped through the ice and mud. Others sat before the tents on stumps and makeshift seats, heads uncovered while they ate, talked, cleaned gear. Eyes trailed our movements. I saw no curiosity there. They knew who we were. They'd been informed. No comfort existed in the knowledge. The fact no one tried to stop us walking through the camp unsettled me. Almost like a danger itself.

"I kind of want t'go back," Brand whispered suddenly, catching the same uneasy drift. "To our stuff. To wait for Grace there. An' somethin' about that tells me we shouldn't."

"Agreed," I said.

"We most definitely should not," added Carina.

We continued in grim silence. Looking around more. Trying to find where Grace might be held. Because it felt that way, now. As though wherever she'd gone, she'd not done so freely.

"We have to remember," Carina said quietly, "Connor is her brother."

My mind went to Moros. "Yeah, well, no guarantees there," I said.

She squeaked, suppressing a more vocal reaction to my thoughts. Suddenly, she made a different noise, this time as a shadow stepped in from my right and blocked our path. We all halted. I looked up toward the soldier's face, a head above mine, found it hidden behind a winged helmet.

"Hello," Hannah said. Overly friendly. Overly sweet. I didn't trust the charm thing to work this time, but no reason she couldn't try.

He grunted.

Hannah gave it another go. "What's your name?"

I nearly groaned out loud. He stared at her from beneath the helmet visor.

"Look," I said, "maybe there's a question you could answer for us."

His head turned my way in silence.

"We're trying to find Grace," I said.

His lips moved. I nearly expected them to squeal from disuse. "Good for you," he said. "Aren't we all?"

I couldn't tell if he'd opted for deliberately obtuse, or thought he was being funny. "We all came into camp together," I explained, "but she was separated from us when she left with Conn—the commander. Grace is his sister. A warrior, like him? Pretty girl, with a dark blue tattoo?" At the last, Hannah mumbled something I didn't catch. "Grace Irese," I tried again.

The soldier's gaze slid sideways. I followed it with my own, spotting at some distance a circular fence behind green growth. A steep-roofed tent roof showed above it. "Ah, over there, then," I said and took a step in the tent's direction. The soldier raised his arm, blocked me. Not just blocked me. I hit his extended arm in my forward motion and found myself staggered back a pace or two.

"Is Grace in there?" I demanded.

"That is the commander's tent," the soldier said.

"And is Grace in there?" I repeated.

"Perhaps."

"Good, then so are we." I stepped forward again. With my foot still in motion, I caught peripheral sight of the soldier's fist rocketing in my direction. In the next moment, it was gone. So was he. Well above my head, his body lay prone and moving feebly atop a large branch. His helmet rolled on the ground by my feet. Resa stood on my left, slowly lowering her hands. She looked up at me with a smile. A few seconds later, her expression went long-distance again.

I took her hand in mine. "Let's go," I said to the others. Ren grabbed the helmet off the ground and shoved it on his own head.

"In a pinch," he said, "I could maybe claim to be bringing you all in. At your request, not like everyone's a prisoner or anything. We don't want to assume, right? Might fool someone for a second or two. Enough time to take them by surprise and march in the door."

I took a breath, bit back my initial reaction, and slowly nodded at him. "I've heard worse plans, Ren. Good idea."

Grace

Chapter Twenty-Three

"You're not my prisoner, Grace."

I paced the tent's length and returned, pausing before my brother, fists clenched. He glanced down at my hands with wariness and amusement combined. He shouldn't be amused. Wary yes, but not amused. When we were younger, he often bested me in mock combat. What he'd never realized was that he won because I let him. He'd seemed so fragile to me. Afraid to fail. He fought viciously because of it. I pretended defeat, lest he become damaged somehow by the fact his sister could beat him again and again.

When I viewed our matches in retrospect, after I'd attained my warrior status and they'd ceased, I knew I'd done him a disservice. Yet, now he'd become a leader of men. War had, perhaps, strengthened him in ways life among our family could not.

I opened my fists, stretched my fingers along my thighs. "Then why do you keep stopping me from returning to my friends? With words only, yes. But I tire of them."

"Sit down, Grace. Stop pacing like a wild animal

and sit. We're not done catching up."

"You're stalling. Why are you stalling?" I waved a hand around. "What is happening here?"

He pointed at the chair I'd vacated. "Grace. Sit."

"No."

He blew out an impatient breath, reminding me suddenly of our father. "Suit yourself." Crossing the uneven ground, he snatched fruit from a bowl. Something red and globular and apparently fresh. Where had he gotten fresh fruit in this environment? I didn't ask him, though. I just watched him in silence as he bit into it, chewed, swallowed. Juice dribbled from his lip to his chin. He wiped it away with his wrist, reached behind him with the other hand and grabbed another.

"Have one," he said.

I shook my head. "I've been so long without fresh fruit I'm afraid it wouldn't agree with me."

"Huh," he said, setting the fruit back in the bowl as he continued eating his own. "You're probably right."

I watched Connor from beneath my lashes. I loved my brother, but we hadn't always been the best of friends. Mostly, yes, but there had been moments, minutes, days, when another side came out. Maybe I was so much like him that headstrong meeting headstrong had been destined for the clashes which inevitably followed. I'd always forgiven him afterward. Why would I not? Had he forgiven me, though? I wasn't so sure.

After he'd consumed the aromatic flesh down to the fruit's center, Connor flicked the core and the dark, wrinkled pit out through the open tent flap before wiping his hands on a nearby cloth. "It feels like you don't trust me," he said. "Your own brother.

Why is that?"

Contrary to what I'd said to him, I dropped down into the chair he'd previously indicated. Leaning forward, I folded my hands between my knees, forsaking my more aggressive pacing and glaring. "You must understand. I trust very few these days, except—"

"Your friends. Those who travel with you."

"Yes."

"Why not me, then? We are blood."

So, I thought, are Duncan and his twin brother, but said nothing as to that. I had no idea how much Connor knew, but it seemed like a thing he would have mentioned straight away.

"Blood doesn't always matter," I said. "And anyway, all I want is some answers from you. Your evasiveness is cause for alarm."

"I'm not being evasive," he retorted.

I forced myself to remain visually relaxed, calm. "You are."

"I'm not." His confident demeanor dissolved into something less at his denial, until he caught himself, squared his shoulders, shifted his gaze toward the outdoors as if something had caught his eye. I knew the tactic. Had witnessed it many times as we grew up.

"Connor," I said.

He turned my way again, trying to look as though I'd interrupted a consideration in his head much more important than my own. I released a long, frustrated breath.

"Have you forgotten who I am?" I asked.

Connor's eyes widened. Red splashed his cheeks. I realized he must be thinking I referred to the damned prophecy rather than our familial connection. "I am your sister," I hastened. "I know you. I know when you are hiding something."

"And you're not?" he spat back.

"Like what?"

I held his gaze, calling his bluff, because if he knew—knew even half the truth—he'd either have locked us all up separately or had us all here in his tent. Instead, he'd left my friends in an open-air pavilion with food to eat, their weapons to hand, and only a handful of guards watching them. Resting here, spending time with my brother, knowing he was alive and well, served a purpose. Staying would not. We had to move on. Yet, at this point, Connor seemed reluctant to let me even leave his tent.

Maybe he wanted me near for his own sake, so he could assure himself I was safe. Keep me that way. It couldn't have been easy on him, on our parents, on my other two brothers, when I'd been taken away, threatened with execution, and then ended up on Emerald. They hadn't known the last, and had been told I'd died, but after our escape and return, the stories had started to circulate.

"When was the last time you spoke with mother and father?" I asked him.

"I told you already. Communications are sporadic—"

"So, I've heard. Repeatedly, and from everyone."

He frowned. "Do you think I am lying?"

"No," I said, "I just think you haven't answered my question."

"Yes. Right. Well." He circled around to the table again, stood before it staring down at the fruit in its bowl. I rose, went to stand beside him. His profile was like stone, as if something had petrified his flesh, the muscle and tendon beneath.

"Connor?"

His jaw twitched in infinitesimal movement. Nothing else.

"Connor, what is it? Tell me." I grabbed his arm, shook it. "Tell me!"

The stone cracked. I could barely remember the last time I saw Connor weep. My age had been in the single digits. Without speaking, I put my arms around him. He shook for several minutes in my embrace, the youngest yet the tallest of my brothers, and then abruptly he pushed me away.

"Don't feel sorry for me, Grace."

I had no time to question his statement. A commotion erupted outside the tent. I heard Duncan's voice in it. His voice, and my name. I headed straight for the tent flap, avoiding my brother's hand reaching out to stop me.

Something out there hit the tent's heavy canvas, causing the fabric to shudder. A shadow slid down along it to the ground. I raced to where the *lathesa* leaned against the other wall and snatched the weapon up. I spun it once, splitting the air. Duncan stumbled in through the tent flap with a helmeted soldier right behind him. Forgoing the weapon's use, I rushed in low, caught the guard in the stomach and flipped him over my back. He landed with a grunt, inches from my brother. Oddly, Duncan ran to the fallen man's side. He whipped off the guard's helmet, exposing yellow hair.

I grounded the *lathesa* against the floor. "Ren?"

"Yeah," he said, pushing himself up. "Thanks, Grace. Hello to you, too."

I spun back to the entranceway. Hannah, Carina, Resa, and Mika were inside. Brand stepped in behind them a second later. At his back, looking as though he'd just picked himself up off the ground, came another soldier. The eyes inside the helmet exchanged a glance with my brother.

"Commander," the soldier said.

"Did I not charge you and Whetrush with keeping all from this door?" Connor demanded, pointing at the open flap.

"All?" I echoed. "Even my companions?"

"Yes," Connor said to me, "even them." He returned his attention to the soldier. "Well?"

"We failed, sir," the man answered quietly.

From his position on the floor, Ren sniggered.

"And where's Whetrush?" Connor went on. "I'd like to hear from him what happened."

The soldier said nothing. Duncan extended his hand to Ren and pulled him upright.

"Big guy? Taller than me?" Duncan asked. "That one's up a tree. Pretty high. Might need some help getting down."

Duncan's gaze sought me out, slipped to Resa, and back again. I understood. Connor missed the exchange. His eyes had narrowed, clearly digesting the information he'd been given.

"Well," he said, "you're all here now. Have some fruit. Take a seat."

Ren was the only one who followed up on the fruit offer, but after catching a look from Duncan, he abstained and sat with the rest on the floor. There were only two chairs. Connor took one. I remained standing.

Connor dipped his head sideways toward the other chair. "Grace, please sit."

"I'm fine where I am," I said. I needed to feel

like I had the upper hand, because no matter what, Connor was still older than me. Not the oldest, but my position as the youngest in our family had sometimes proven an advantage to my brothers and an irritant to me.

"I want you to tell me, to tell us, what's going on," I continued. "Because something is, and I don't believe it's good."

Connor glanced to where his guard still stood uncertainly by the tent opening. "You may leave. Take someone with you and find Whetrush. See if he needs any assistance."

He watched the man depart before speaking again in a lowered voice. "Rumors fly like the wind and carry just as much dust and debris with them. Stories become cluttered. Every campaign someone has brought up the tale of the warrior, the witch, and the thrice-gifted child." His brown eyes turned toward me. Except for the color, it was like looking into my own. "Only recently did I hear you are meant to be the warrior in that trio, Grace."

"I have to be honest," I said. "I wasn't inclined to believe it, either."

"But it is true."

"Appears so."

"You don't seem troubled by that knowledge."

"I am very troubled by it."

Connor turned to my companions. "So, who are the other two players in this? The witch. The thrice-gifted child."

No one answered him. I was grateful. If he truly had no idea, we were better off for now. My brother jerked to his feet and started pacing, his hands behind his back.

"You don't really know what this is all about, do you?" he asked the room in general. "You were away—"

"Away?" I echoed, nearly choking on the word. "I was sentenced to die and instead sent to the Emerald for life. Duncan, Mika, and Carina had the same life sentence." I didn't mention Skelly, who was being unusually quiet now, but I did wonder if he might be listening to the conversation. Normally, when I had thoughts such as this, he'd pipe up with some taunt, but he remained silent.

Connor lifted his hand. "I know. I'm sorry. I don't know why I said that."

I folded my arms across my chest and stared at him. "Believe me, the others here with us were imperiled equally."

"Yes. I'm sorry," he said again. His voice cracked, reminding me he'd been weeping only minutes earlier.

"So," I said, "it is common knowledge how we escaped, where we've been since then?

Connor paused, looked at me. "It's difficult to tell embellishment from truth. As I said, there are stories."

I dropped my arms to my sides, my short nails digging into my palms. "Well, think about those stories, Connor, and pick out the most disturbing parts. Because if nothing else is true, those are."

He dropped down onto his recently vacated chair, shoulders slumped, head bowed. I walked over to him, touched his braided hair. His hand came up, pulled mine down to his shoulder and held it there.

"What were you so upset about before everyone arrived?" I asked him.

"I wasn't."

"You were crying, Connor. I was right beside you. I saw something happening to you I haven't seen in many years."

He remained silent, breathing in and out, his fingers loose on mine. I raised my eyes to Duncan, found him looking back at me. Worried. He was worried. As was I.

"Connor," I said, "where are our parents? Are they at home? Are they fighting with the tribes?"

He shook his head from side to side, a wretched noise tearing from his throat. My heart slammed against my ribcage. I swallowed down bile. "Where are they?" I asked again.

"Where I can't reach them," he ground out.

"What do you mean? Are they—"

"Dead? No. They're not dead." He stood in an abrupt movement, looking down at me. "But they may as well be. Because I've been left with a horrific choice. And it's your fault."

"How is any of this Grace's fault?" Duncan. My Duncan. The sudden tenderness I felt mitigated the anger at my brother's statement.

But not the sudden anxiety.

"What is my fault, Connor?" I asked. "You must tell me. Now."

He released my fingers and clamped both his hands together between his knees. "Do you remember how Stone Tiran removed children from each family the night he took you?"

"I'm not likely to have forgotten." My guts twisted, the pain sharp, the memory fresh again. All of them crammed into the ships, brought down into the bowels of the ruined Quadrate to become both hostage and slave, death hanging over their heads should the tribes retaliate. But they had. The tribes had. They'd risen against Stone Tiran and his army. Senta had told me this. Senta, who had worn my likeness around her neck like a badge of honor. Was this what Connor meant by 'my fault'?

"Did he…did he follow through with his threat?" This had long worried me, often pushed from my mind so I could remain focused, but never far from surfacing.

Connor shook his head. "He didn't make it public you had not been executed following the sham trial. No one knew you were alive until there started to be sightings…" His voice trailed off.

"Did he kill them all?" I interrupted my brother's drifting thoughts, wanting to shake him. "Was it because of me? Because we—I—had escaped Emerald?"

His gaze flickered toward mine, his expression harsh. "No. We had already staged an attack on the Quadrate and freed them all."

My legs gave out. I dropped to the floor, knees slamming hard onto the ground.

Duncan stirred where he sat. His brows lowered. "You're not going to say Grace caused this war?"

"Don't be a fool," Connor said. "It started in myriad small ways before Tiran ever sought the alliance with our family and Grace refused him, stood up to him, thwarted his plans. By the way," he added in an aside to me, "smart decision, no matter what came after."

I heard no sarcasm in those words. This, then, was not where he placed the blame. My lips quivered. I bit down on the lower, the small pain keeping tears away. Connor returned his focus to Duncan, determined to answer his question, though he'd not yet responded to mine.

"The unrest was broader in scope than any of us understood," he went on. "Even now, I'm not sure any faction is aware where this started or what continues to drive it."

The others exchanged furtive glances. Duncan deliberately avoided my eye. I leaned toward my brother.

"What is my fault, Connor?"

In a rush, he bolted upright, knocking the chair over. Snatching the furnishing from the floor, he threw it across the tent. The chair bounced from the tent wall and crashed to the ground, one leg snapping off and skidding toward the table. In the ensuing silence, I heard footsteps outside hurrying our way. I raised my *lathesa*. Connor held up a warning hand to me and shouted toward those approaching.

"No worries! Stay away unless I call you."

Grumbling voices retreated. My friends were all standing now, eyeing my brother and me. Even Resa's gaze touched momentarily on our faces before she retreated into her head. Slowly, Connor approached the broken chair, lifted the two pieces into his hands, stared as if he couldn't imagine what

IN DARKNESS WE BREAK

had just happened. We all waited.

"He's taken them," my brother whispered. "Our parents. And I can get them back. In exchange for you."

Chapter Twenty-Four

My heart jolted again in my chest. Duncan swore, shocking even me with the profanities he chose.

"Who has them?" I asked, closing my eyes, fearing the answer. "Who is 'he'?"

"Who do you think? Tiran."

The tension left my shoulders. Only a little. "And how did you come to learn our parents' whereabouts? How did Tiran make you this offer?"

"Grace," said Duncan, "I think you're missing the bigger question here. Why is your own brother even entertaining the exchange?"

"They're our parents," I said.

"And I don't care."

"You should," Connor barked.

I faced him. "He does. Duncan does. But he cares about me more. Surely you understand how that might color his response to your plan."

Connor dropped the broken chair. "I don't have a plan."

"You just said—" Duncan began, but my brother cut him off.

"I told you what had been proposed, not what I intended. Frankly, I don't know what to do. Had I planned to turn Grace over to him, I wouldn't have mentioned it, I would have just done what I had to. And if I believed even half of what I've heard I would have split you all up and put you in chains the instant you were located, rather than leave you free to roam this camp."

"But you were searching for me. For us," I said.

Connor frowned. "Yes."

"Why?"

"Isn't it obvious?"

"Only if you were planning to turn Grace over," Duncan growled out.

Connor's scowl deepened. "You risked death to save your sister. Why would I not attempt to save mine given what she and the rest of you have been up against?"

I studied Connor's wrinkled brow and down-turned mouth, imagining how torn he'd been by the choice he'd made. Because obviously, he did not plan to turn me over. I supposed a chance existed he had in fact intended to betray me to free our parents, but that moment had passed. I couldn't blame him for any fragmentary thoughts he might have suffered. I also wouldn't let him face this dilemma alone. Our parents would never expect us to risk our lives in times such as these to save them from an enemy. But I wouldn't allow Tiran to keep them as pawns, either.

"How did you know where to look?" I asked gently.

"Luck," he said. "Scouts spotted a party making their way down the mountain. I went back with them and a few extras to take a closer look. There'd been rumors, so…" He shrugged.

"Luck," I agreed, grinning at him.

"But wait," said Brand rather loudly, rushing

forward and stopping an arm's length from my brother. "Grace asked you how y' got this Tiran's offer. How? How did he get it to you?"

Connor stepped back, sweeping his gaze over Brand from head to toe and back up again. He glanced at me, then back to Brand, seeming almost amused. I figured my brother didn't quite understand Brand's qualities at first sight.

"He sent a messenger with a small armed escort," Connor answered.

"So, 'e knows where y'are."

"We know where they are camped, too. Not Tiran, himself. A contingent."

"An' the messenger? Still 'ere waiting on your answer?"

"I couldn't very well let him go back with a 'no' yet."

"Locked up?"

Connor's patience began to slip. "Yes. Of course," he snapped.

Brand hopped from one foot to the other. "Tell me you had 'em searched. That you searched 'em good."

Connor hesitated. I sucked in a breath. "Brand," I said, "are you thinking they may have some means for communication on them?"

"Aye," he said. "An' if they do, then anyone interested knows we're here now, too."

My turn to swear. My intemperance put Duncan's recent tirade to shame.

* * *

Connor dispatched several warriors to more thoroughly search the messenger and his escort. We didn't tarry for the outcome. By the time his soldiers left to do as instructed, we had already put distance between ourselves and Connor's tent, making our way to the pavilion for our packs and the weapons. Once there, we each shirked on the former before proceeding to stash the weapons in belts and elsewhere.

"We're either captive or we're running," Mika mumbled, checking the cutter and the glass blade affixed in the holders on his belt. The spear he'd chosen from Enid's ancient arsenal leaned against the table beside him.

"We had time to rest at Enid's," Carina reminded him.

"Well, that rest wasn't nearly long enough. Besides, we did more than rest."

"One day," I said, "this will be over. One day, we'll be home."

"I have no desire to go home," said Mika.

I slid the *lathesa* into the rarely used strips I'd fashioned to hold the weapon on my pack. "Then you're all welcome to mine."

Mika rolled his eyes. "Oh, I'm sure your mom and dad would be thrilled—" He stopped, stricken.

"It's okay," I said. "We're going to get them."

Standing near my elbow, Hannah opened her mouth and shut it without speaking. Beside her, Ren's brow puckered. He paled. "Are we?" he said.

I nodded, determined. "We just have to find out one thing."

"What's that?" asked Duncan, popping around from behind me for a closer look at my face, presumably to check if I still resembled someone with sanity.

I reached out to a plate on the table, where

someone had left behind a half-eaten biscuit. Snatching it up, I took a bite, talked while I chewed. "Whether our position has, in fact, been discovered, or if it remains uncertain."

"What difference does that make?" Ren again.

"The difference is in the greeting we might expect," I said.

Duncan grunted agreement, stepping away from me at footfalls crunching the dead, frozen leaves outside. I grabbed something unrecognized from another plate and started eating that, too, turning to find my brother and several warriors approaching.

"Well?" I asked, taking another bite from what turned out to be a perfectly steamed, now ice-cold, vegetable.

Connor lifted a hand, a small, circular device held between thumb and index finger. "This was taken from one. He denied its use for communication, but would not explain what it is."

I exhaled a frosty breath through my nostrils. "May I see?"

Somewhat reluctantly, he came over and deposited it on my palm. In turn, I extended my arm out to my right. "Mika, Duncan, look familiar to you, at all?" Following a brief examination, they both shook their heads. I looked around. "Anyone else?"

No one expressed any familiarity with the device. I dropped the object on the frozen soil and ground it beneath my boot heel until I heard a satisfying crunch. "Then we assume the worst," I said. "We need to go."

"Hold on," Connor said, glancing down at the damaged apparatus. "I've been in command of this army for months. Let's talk about what you're planning. I don't doubt your abilities. It seems the tales being told likely hold more truth than otherwise.

I...I spoke with Whetrush about the tree incident."

"Is he okay?" Duncan asked.

"Someone among you put him there. Do you really care?" Connor bent and picked up the broken pieces by my foot. "Never mind. My sister would not cherish you so much if you were cruel or vindictive."

I started to protest. "You have no idea—"

A laugh sputtered from his mouth. "What? Do you think I don't have eyes? It took all of two seconds beneath my tent roof for me to notice."

Oh. He meant Duncan in particular. My face heated in the cold.

"Mother and father will not be best pleased," he added.

"I don't see how you can say that. Do we not all possess mixed heritage? Me, you, Ryan, Sean. It seems our parents do not share your prejudice. Besides, Duncan and I are not—we are not—"

Connor looked from Duncan's confused expression to mine and laughed again. "I tease you, sister."

"Is this actually the best time?" Hannah drawled, her own cheeks high in color.

"No," Connor agreed. "It is not." He raised his eyebrows at me. "Your plan?"

"She doesn't usually have one," Hannah muttered. She quickly looked up from the ground where she'd directed the comment. "But things work out."

I sighed. These Wildron were a surly lot. "Hannah is right," I said anyway. "Plans don't really seem to help. Not unless they're flexible."

"Exactly," Duncan interjected. "They need to be revised on the fly all the time. If we forced ourselves to stick to any actual plan, we'd all be dead."

"A good leader recognizes when to alter a course and when to stick with it," my brother agreed, his eyes on me. The others grew silent.

I frowned. "I don't lead—"

"Shut it, Grace," said Duncan. "You do."

At his elbow, Brand smiled. "Aye. Even I know that an' I ain't been with this happy band very long."

Connor studied each one in our group for several moments. The men with him did likewise. "So, the tales are all true, then?" Connor finally said.

"Who knows?" Duncan answered him. "We haven't heard them."

"You haven't?" Connor laughed again, harder than any time since our arrival. Real and from the belly. He wheezed down to a few chuckles and then sobered. "I suppose you wouldn't have," he said. "What do you know, then?"

"That we have to get going," I said. "Now."

"Where? What is your objective?"

"First, to find mother and father and free them. You?"

"To help."

My head tipped to one side. "Meaning?"

"I have an army. Basically autonomous, from communication's lack and otherwise. I decide what it does and where it goes, depending on my plans that also often go astray. There is a common goal, naturally, to end all this. Which I believe is yours, as well? For now, though, there is the more immediate objective."

"I rather thought we'd try to get in unseen, not march up with an army at our backs," I said.

"An army can provide distraction."

Stubbornly, I said nothing.

"Besides, do you know where they are being

held?"

"No," I said. "Not yet."

"Well," he said, "the messenger happened to be quite a tender fellow. I got the information from him without any drastic effort."

My stomach sank a little, understanding his hint. "And you'll provide the location to me? Now?"

"Once we're all ready to move out, you will know."

Connor turned on his heel and stalked away, his men following. I spat a harsh, whispered expletive after him.

"Grace?" Duncan prompted. "Do we wait?"

I stared after my brother, saying nothing. Ren sidled up beside me.

"All those searching for us?" he said. "They're looking for *us*. Not an army. What better way to stay hidden for a time? You know, until we follow you into wherever. Right? And in the meantime, we're safer than when we're alone."

"I hate to admit it," said Duncan, "but Ren is making actual sense."

"I hate to admit it, too," I said, "but yes, he is."

A great deal of sense. And yet somehow it still felt wrong.

Chapter Twenty-Five

We spent the intervening time stocking up with food from the army's stores. I didn't ask my brother's permission. I told him we were doing it. He merely nodded. It didn't seem to irk him, my telling him. In fact, he was rather amused.

Which irked me.

I needed to get past my prickly relationship with Connor. It seemed a luxury, considering where we found ourselves. I couldn't help recalling how not so very long ago my mother expended a ridiculous amount of energy reprimanding us for our behavior. A not-so-long-ago that somehow felt like years.

"Are we all set?"

I nodded at Duncan. "I think so. I suppose we should rest a bit before we're on the move again."

"I don't think this lot will be much longer," he said, jerking his chin at the soldiers readying themselves. They'd been quick about it. Astonishingly so. I supposed they'd dismantled tents, packed up baggage and supplies, loaded those winged contraptions into mechanized carts countless times already.

"Do you think your brother might let me try out

one of those?" Ren asked, pointing at the nearest conveyance and the metal wings piled inside.

I huffed out an impatient breath. "No."

"Why not?"

Duncan turned to him. "Really? How old are you?"

"What? You think I'm too young to handle one?"

"Not the point I'm trying to make," Duncan said.

I pivoted away, pretending to adjust the articles in my pack one more time. Ren and Duncan continued their bantering. Not arguing, just…not letting it go.

Carina appeared at my side. I hadn't seen her coming. Sometimes, I didn't when she meant to move that way. Graceful, slow, she could manage to blend into the scenery around her. When she still possessed the oversized scarf Senta had given her, a gauzy, reflective, silken thing, she'd at times been nearly invisible.

"What will your brother do with the prisoners?" she asked.

"You mean the messenger and his escort?"

She dipped her head.

"Bring them along, I expect."

She gave me a look, an 'oh, Grace, you're so innocent' look, and said, "That seems like an awful amount of trouble for someone they don't need with them."

At her words, my blood chilled. "Carina?"

"Maybe he'll just let me erase them," she said.

Releasing my pack, I straightened. "Let you do what?"

"It's like when I bring sleep, but I can take recent memories away at the same time."

I stared at her. "I don't… Carina, you can do that?"

"I've done it. Before I was arrested. I don't know if I could do it again, but I would try."

A few words escaped me. A sentence from a prayer I'd sometimes uttered at night when I was very little. Carina touched my arm and tossed her head, her fine, straight hair flowing over her shoulder. Her eyes had gone smoky, nearly white.

"Do not be afraid, Grace. I would never do it to you. But I don't want your brother to kill someone coldly. He hasn't yet had to, you know."

From my rounded lips, a breath streamed into the air. "Have you been inside his head?" I whispered.

"Yes."

"Right," I said. "Come with me."

We left Resa to her brother's care. I insisted the others all stay behind. I refused to let them witness what we were going to suggest to my brother, what Carina would do when he agreed. Because he must agree. I couldn't bear to have him execute those men for the sake of expediency.

We found him where his tent once stood. The trampled ground had been emptied and the broken chair left to rot against a tree.

"Connor," I said. He didn't seem to hear me. "Connor!"

He turned slowly. His focus came back from some faraway musing. "What is it? What are you doing here?" He looked past me. "Where are the rest?"

"Waiting still. I need to speak with you."

His stance shifted. He became wary. "About what?"

"About the men you are detaining," I said. "The messenger and those with him."

His posture altered once more. "Why?"

"What are you going to do with them?"

"Again," he said, "why?"

I braced myself for argument. "Are you going to kill them?"

Something in my tone, my face, must have stopped his next words. He closed his mouth, dipped his head to one side, drew a deep breath. "Have you another suggestion?"

"Yes, I—"

Carina grabbed my arm. Her eyes were on Connor. A second later, they turned to me, red as blood. "It is too late."

I gasped. I don't know why I hadn't expected this, but I truly did not. Something broke in me. I threw back my head and screamed into the cold evening air. My arms lifted. My fingers flew wide. The next thing I knew, I was on my knees on the ground, Carina's hand over mine, and my brother lay sprawled on his back across the clearing. I scrambled upright and hurried over to him.

At his side, I dropped to the soil again, patting him, checking him for injuries, for life. He groaned, pushed my hands away and sat up.

"What the hell was that?"

"I'm sorry," I said.

"Did that come from you?"

I bowed my head. "Yes. I can't always control what I am now."

His eyes, the eyes bearing our mother's shape and our father's color, widened. "What you are now? You are…mage?"

I nodded.

"So, the tales are true," he said, as if he'd doubted the other times he'd uttered those words aloud.

I rose and helped him up. "Why did you have to

kill them?"

"As opposed to what? Bringing them along? Giving them the food designated for my soldiers? Risking their escape to reveal our location, our plans? Your presence? What would you have had me do?"

"They were people," I said. "Same as you and me. There were other choices."

"Like what?"

I glanced at Carina, who shook her head slightly. "It doesn't matter," I said. "Not now. It's too late. But in all of this, we must remember who we are. Not…not what we can be made to become against our better selves."

I strode away from him then. When I reached Carina, she nodded once, slipped her fingers into mine. We walked hand in hand back to where our friends waited for us.

* * *

"All right there, Grace?" Duncan greeted me as we approached.

"Yes," I said. Flatly. I couldn't bring myself to sound any different or to say any more. Brand stepped up to me, holding my pack and the *lathesa* I'd left behind.

"Some 'un said we're about to march."

I thanked him and took my gear. Carina went and grabbed her own, then moved silently to stand before Mika. He grasped her hands in his and held them. Neither spoke.

Duncan frowned at their actions, turned back to me. "What happened? Where did you two go?"

"I'll tell you sometime, but not now. Is that okay?"

He stared into my eyes for almost too long before

answering. "Sure," he said. "Okay."

"Thank you."

My brother did not come to us before we headed out. We vacated the camp with Connor's army. Small cries marked by shock, dismay, fear, started at a distance behind us and eventually caught up to those directly at our backs. I didn't bother to look around. I knew what caused the warriors' reactions. A minute later the three *conjures* lumbered up and joined us, Chauncy to my right, Vigor and Bell taking positions to our left and rear. I ran my hand over Chauncy's stinking hide in welcome, eliciting pleasured rumbles from him. After that, the soldiers backed away, allotting ample room between us, the *conjures,* and them.

Prior to nightfall, Connor sought us out. Although he'd seen them when he found us, he stopped short upon sighting the *conjures*. I called him nearer, greeting him coldly, despite understanding in part why he'd done as he had. Everyone in this now silently marching group was his responsibility, after all, and he sought to eliminate danger. Even so...

"We'll be halting soon," he said to me. "When we do, it might be best if you sent your beasts away for the night. They're making the soldiers jumpy."

"That's fine," I said. "We'll go with them and rejoin you in the morning."

"That's not what I meant."

"I know," I said. "But it is what we will do."

He continued to walk beside me, our strides matched, his expression grim. "Grace."

I shook my head. "There's no need to talk about it."

"I wasn't going to. I was just wondering if, at some point, you and your friends might tell me the whole story. The true story. I think there's much more to it than the fanciful tales being thrown around."

My mouth quivered. I reached across the space between us and squeezed his hand. "We'll all gather in front of the hearth at home and talk through the night," I said with a wistful smile. "Home is still there, isn't it?"

"I hope so," he said.

I dropped my hand to my side. "Me, too."

He only stayed a short time longer before increasing his pace and disappearing into the crowd. Duncan took his place.

"Has he told you yet where we're going?"

"No. Carina might know. We'll talk to her later."

"I heard you tell him we would camp with the *conjures* and not with the army. Good idea. We need to be able to talk away from big ears."

With my mind in two places, I glanced around at our companions, specifically Ren, whose ears were a bit on the large side, before realizing what Duncan meant. "Ah, right. Let's see what Carina has picked up on and then figure out what's next. Because unless we can get inside wherever my parents are being held before Connor starts the distraction or whatever he has planned, it could go badly for them. And I'm not going to let that happen."

Duncan's lips curled up. He put an arm around my shoulder and pulled me close, pressing his lips in a quick gesture against my head. I wished he wouldn't do that. No one's hair had received a good washing since we'd left Enid's. You couldn't tell by Carina, though. Her hair always shone and floated and remained tangle-free. It seemed quite unnatural.

I laughed, picturing little magical creatures picking her hair clean every night, combing it out.

And then I stopped laughing. With all we'd seen, it could very well be so. The inhabitants of this world were so much more than I would have believed when I remained safe and snug at home. I told myself over and over that no matter the circumstances, I'd always be grateful for the friends I'd made since imprisonment and escape. Maybe here was something else. Finding out the world held many wonders.

Not creatures caring for Carina's hair, though. That seemed a bit much. Still, I could not help peering back at her and her wondrous white hair glowing in the fading light.

"What's so funny?" Duncan asked, no doubt confused after my last words before my thoughts transitioned.

"Sorry," I said. "I was fantasizing how Carina keeps her hair in such lovely condition."

"Hmm," he answered, "that is a wonder, but, yeah, I don't really give it much consideration. Hair is hair, although hers is particularly...something."

Beautiful, said a voice in my head. I jumped a little. The voice hadn't been Skelly's, nor anyone I knew. My heart sped up.

"Grace? Are you okay?"

I nodded. "I'm fine."

Despite his obvious doubt, I still held my tongue. He didn't need anything else to concern him. He would be worried, I knew, because although the voice's owner was a mystery, I'd heard it before, most recently when the *conjures* snatched me from the avalanche. *Open your eyes, Grace,* it had said when death was near. *Open your eyes.*

Quelling a shudder, I walked on and kept my mouth shut.

Skelly

Chapter Twenty-Six

Don't you know who it is, Grace? Come on. You're slipping. Quick, brave, always-thinking Grace has suddenly gone stupid.

Well, I'm not telling you. Even if I could. Which I can't. Not since you allowed the witch to talk you into sticking that talisman side-by-side with me. Yeah, we're separated by something. Seems like cloth, maybe. But the thing is still close enough. It burns me sometimes. Do you know that? Do you even care?

Of course, you don't. Why would you? I wouldn't, if our situations were reversed. I'd laugh loud and hard knowing what you were going through. But you aren't, are you? Not going through what I am, at all.

You think you're making smart moves, smarter decisions, to bring you closer to—well, to *him.* Not so smart, Grace. Because you'll need me then. You'll set me free.

IN DARKNESS WE BREAK

And it'll be my turn.
Oh, won't you be sorry.

Duncan

Chapter Twenty-Seven

A physical connection made for awkward movement when traversing particularly rough terrain. I'd dropped my arm from Grace's shoulder some time ago. But I stayed close, maintained an eye on her. She carried more weight than the rest of us did. Not in the pack on her back. In her head. In her heart. In her soul. Grace was keeping something from me. Again. Well, okay. I understood the need, having done it myself more than once. I let out a long breath, fighting back apprehension. If Grace broke, we all probably would right alongside her.

A sudden shout echoed down along the trail. Didn't sound like an alarm. More like an order. A few minutes later we received it, relayed from mouth to mouth. Time to hunker down for the night. The sun had already gone low behind the mountain peaks, leaving the track in shadow. Now the shadows spread everywhere.

As Grace had promised her brother, we led the *conjures* away from the soldiers. Led being a relative term. It was more like the *conjures* already knew and plowed ahead and to either side, seeking refuge for themselves, for us.

The trees were smaller here, with more space between. Connor's mixed group of warriors took up positions under them, set up camp. Not like where we had been, a camp which had apparently been in place for some time, but minimum preparations for one night. We set up on the trail's opposite side. The *conjures* disappeared to hunt, a gruesome process I didn't like to think about, and we all gathered close together for warmth and protection and because this was how we were used to spending our nights. The army hadn't lit fires, so neither did we, eating cold rations from our packs. No matter. We were quite used to that, too. The hot meals at Enid's had been nice, though. I missed them already.

"Carina," Grace said, after we'd finished our meager meal, "have you picked up on anything about our destination?"

Carina turned from some silent converse with Mika and shook her head.

"Nothing?" I asked.

"Belane?" she said. "I have sensed Belane. I don't know where Belane is or what it is, but that name comes into Connor's thoughts frequently. There's nothing else. So many people here. It's hard."

"It's all right," said Grace. "And I know Belane. She's a person, not a place. Connor was quite sweet on her for a time, back home. Once they weren't seeing each other, I plotted with my friend Mara to get Mara and Connor together. I guess I shouldn't have bothered, if he's still thinking about Belane."

Grace's voice went all wistful in remembering. I pictured her brother thinking about this Belane the way I thought about Grace and felt suddenly sorry for Grace's brother. I stared at the ground, bit my lip, said nothing. Beside me, Grace whipped back her blanket and stood.

"I'll have to ask him myself where we're heading," she said. "Again."

"Now?" I asked.

"Yes."

"I'll go with you."

She didn't say no. It wouldn't have made a difference if she had. I got up, too, tossed my blanket over a branch with my pack to keep it off the ground until my return. The *conjures* had come back and were hunkered down nearby, keeping watch, their huge bodies barely visible against the undergrowth all around. We didn't even have a torch burning. All was in darkness, the stars brilliant across the night sky.

Together, Grace and I made our way to the encampment. I didn't know how we were going to find Connor until I saw a very small pavilion nearly hidden in a grove. A few guards stood around it, watchful. It seemed a bad move, I thought, to advertise the leader's position, but I figured it was some military protocol. Grace strode straight up to the tent. I had to hop-foot it to keep up.

The two closest to the tent flap—desert warriors, they looked like—stepped in to bar her way.

"I'm here to see my brother," Grace stated. A voice came from within. I didn't hear the words spoken. The guard moved aside. Without waiting for them to fully clear the entry, Grace marched in. I hurried after her.

Gaining the interior, I paused and glanced around. There was nothing inside but a shielded lamp, a chest, a cot, and Grace's brother, seated on the latter in the shadows with his hands folded between his knees. "This is a step down from the other place," I said. I couldn't help myself.

"Quicker to put up and dismantle," Connor said, taking no offense. "I trust you are all comfortable."

"The *conjures* give off a lot of heat. We'll do."

He nodded, returned his attention to his sister. "Why have you sought me out?"

"To find out where we're going. I don't willingly follow anyone blind."

Connor shifted his shoulders. "And yet you are."

Ow. I shot a look Grace's way for her reaction. She hadn't moved. Her gaze held her brother's. Only the raised color along her cheekbones betrayed her anger. I think Connor saw it, too. He didn't acknowledge the slight change in her, though. I don't think he had any idea what to make of it.

Do you *not* know your sister? I wanted to shout at him. Instead, I folded my hands behind my back and watched. Grace had been formidable enough before she'd changed. Surely, he remembered that much. A second later, he dropped his gaze and his head. His muscles tightened.

"Are you going to detonate now? Propel me across the tent?" he asked. "Should I be prepared?"

My eyes narrowed. I looked from Grace to her brother and back again. Grace rushed over to him, dropped to her knees, placed her hands on his. "No. I didn't mean to do that earlier. I would never hurt you."

I stared at Grace, wondering why she'd failed to mention this to me. Connor nodded, pushed himself forward a little until their foreheads touched. I could see the family resemblance more than ever in their profiles. I cleared my throat. Grace lifted her head, gave me an uncertain glance.

"I'll tell you later," she said.

"Okey-dokey," I murmured and lapsed into silence, observing them both. After a few non-verbal minutes, Grace rose.

"I have some idea where I should be now, and this is a deviation," she said to her brother. "One I've chosen, yes, but still a departure from this vague map in my head. I'm sorry, Connor. I don't know how to explain it any better. I am not one of your soldiers, though, not someone to be led into battle by you. And you shouldn't try to test me. That's not a threat," she added, when he lifted his head, opened his mouth. "I would never threaten you. I only mean it is unnecessary. We share the same ultimate goal. We don't share the same path."

"I don't think we ever have shared the same path," he said, and stood. They faced each other. I hadn't realized how much taller he was than his sister. I moved closer to Grace. Connor looked me up and down. Slowly. Like he meant to intimidate me. I stared right back at him. I admired Grace for never backing down. I intended to emulate her. She was my hero.

"Bah," he finally said, tossing up his hands and turning away. He stomped over to the chest on its small stand and threw the lid open. Reaching in, he drew out a rolled paper, dropped the chest lid, and spread the paper out on top. Grace and I moved closer. The paper was a map, an old-fashioned, hand-drawn map, like the one I'd received from the Fiannan warrior. Seeing my expression, Connor snorted.

"Obviously, we can't count on any signal out here. The old ways work best."

"Obviously," I said, leaning close for a better look. Maps have always fascinated me. This one was filled with placenames I didn't recognize, of course.

What interested me more were the symbols. I reached past Connor's arm and pointed at one. "Is that where Tiran's soldiers are? Some of them anyway. Where the messengers came from."

Connor stiffened at my words, but didn't ignore me. He nodded.

"And here?" I asked, pressing my finger down on another, similar marking. "The bulk of his army. Where your parents are being held, yes?"

He nodded again. "I believe so."

Grace bent nearer, her gaze shifting quickly from place to place on the map, possibly trying to figure out where we were on it.

"This is about where we are now," I said, pointing at a marked trail.

"Yes," Connor said.

"And this?" I asked, indicating another symbol. "What's this?"

Connor straightened. "I don't know. The flying scouts located another encampment. They didn't recognize anything about it. Over here, too." He pointed at another symbol, slightly different than the one I'd picked out. "I have no idea who these armies belong to. As I said, there are many fighting under different command."

I grunted. This was something we'd known already. "Are they converging in this general area for some reason?"

"Intelligence is hard come by, but I would expect so," he answered. I exchanged a look with Grace. Her mouth set into a hard line.

"Are you alone here?" she asked. "Is there no one else coming to fight with you?"

"There are, but no word yet of when they will arrive."

Grace faced her brother. "This is why you should not engage."

Sometimes I forgot being trained as a warrior probably entailed more than learning to fight. To fight with elegance and ferocity and an intent to disarm and overcome rather than kill outright. I think this was no longer the case for Connor. This was not the type warfare that would accept such honorable objectives. He stared at the map, his jaw muscles moving, his tongue pushing against his teeth.

"I am in command here," he finally said.

"But not of me," Grace reminded him.

"I could have you and your friends bound and secured."

"Could you?" Grace countered in a voice soft and low. Her tone sent a chill down my spine. "Could you, really?"

Connor's fingers crumpled the map beneath them. Hastily, he smoothed the paper out again. "You have always been headstrong," he said. "I know you're thinking you could rescue them on your own, you and your friends. I couldn't live with myself if I let you do this alone."

Watching her brother's face, Grace chewed her lip for a moment. I held my breath.

"If you engage on all these fronts," Grace said, sweeping her hand from side to side across the map, "we will never see them again. Once a battle begins, you can be sure Stone Tiran will take drastic measures. If you march in there, that will be the only outcome. Think about it, Connor. What is done with prisoners who are a danger to success?"

His brown skin paled, like ash. The cartilage in his throat moved up and down. For a second, I thought he might be sick. His eyes held steady on the map spread across the chest lid as he breathed slowly in recovery.

"What's your plan, then, Grace?" he said. "Tell me what you would do."

* * *

When we returned to our camp much later, no one had fallen asleep. Not even Resa.

"We were worried about you," Hannah said.

"What happened?" asked Mika.

"Did you learn anything?" from Carina.

I held up a hand and dropped down into the rough circle they'd formed on the ground. Grace remained standing. Beyond them, Chauncy lifted his fearsome head, his single, corkscrew horn glittering in the starlight, the white ring around his eye visible in a nearly perfect circle. A low rumble issued from him, repeated by the other two. I wondered briefly what would happen if Grace were taken prisoner while these three were on the loose. Nothing pretty.

"We have a good idea where they are being held," Grace answered Carina. "We also know more than just Stone Tiran's soldiers are out there, but not who these others are."

"So," said Ren, "more than we could hope to fight, even with, you know, secret powers."

My lip quirked at his chosen terminology. Still, it held a basic truth.

"Yer folks wouldn't survive an attack to rescue them," Brand said in his blunt manner.

I glanced at Grace. She acknowledged Brand's words with a tight nod.

"What're we doin' then?" he asked.

"We're going in without my brother's warriors."

"Which is what you wanted to do in the first place," Mika said.

"Yes. The only difference is, Connor and a few of his best will accompany us. The rest will remain here waiting for word to come back to them, or for the others on their way to arrive. There's been no communication for a while, so Connor isn't sure when that will be, if at all."

A momentary silence followed, until Ren's voice piped up with an inane question. "Do you suppose they'll bring enough flying suits for us?"

I snorted. "Doubtful. But that would be a blast, wouldn't it?"

Ren grinned. Grace cut in before we could carry on with the merits of flight.

"My brother is briefing those he's leaving in command while the warriors coming with him get ready. We should rest up a bit more in the meantime. We'll be heading out soon. We'll camp again before we reach the place where my parents are being held, but it was decided we should give the impression Connor's soldiers aren't moving ahead, if they are being watched."

Grace implied she and Connor had reached these decisions, but mostly it had been Grace. I felt none too comfortable about what her brother might be telling his warriors without Grace standing at his side. Hopefully his claim to see the sense in Grace's idea hadn't been false. Yet, the look on his face—an expression filled with shocked admiration for his sister—had seemed genuine enough.

Grace and I took up our former places side by side, blankets wrapped around our bodies, and heads uncomfortably resting on the packs. I knew I wouldn't sleep. I couldn't see how anyone would. I turned my head to say as much to Grace and found her eyes closed and her mouth open, even breaths frosting the air.

The sleep of the gratified, I supposed. She had to be relieved to finally have her brother seeing sense. I still had my doubts, though. Connor seemed as headstrong as Grace. Possibly more so. The plan from a girl who usually made no absolute plans could yet go very wrong.

A short time later, we were on our way to finding out.

Chapter Twenty-Eight

Grace's brother and the three desert warriors he'd brought with him—one female, two male—appeared massive. They were, of course, tall, but the cloaks they wore around their shoulders covered the inactive wing apparatus they'd strapped to their backs, giving them more bulk than they actually possessed. To Ren's verbal and unending disappointment, they weren't lugging any extras.

Connor and Grace walked together, leaving me with the others. Our group took up the middle position, the warriors at the rear. Behind them, and making them decidedly nervous despite their warrior status, came the *conjures*. I didn't blame Connor's three for being edgy. They'd only heard about but never seen the likes before. Besides, any threat to Grace, or even us, and the animals would charge right through them.

There'd been no introductions prior to us setting out. Grace had recognized one man, though, and spoke with him briefly, asking him about his family. After that, we were down to business.

Business. It would be interesting, meeting Grace's parents. I refused to entertain any notion we wouldn't. Grace and her brother were determined. I decided to be determined, too.

"You're so cute," Carina whispered to me.

"What?"

"Worrying what Grace's mom and dad will think of you."

"Shut up," I said, and trudged on. A short moment later, I wondered what Carina's parents might be like. She'd never mentioned them.

"And I won't," she said.

"Stop listening in on me," I griped.

"Stop thinking so loud."

"I can't help it. You know that."

She giggled.

In front, Grace spun around, walking backward over the rough terrain as if she traversed a wooden floor. Her eyes, the whites glowing beneath the stars, went from me to Carina and back again. She raised a finger to her lips, followed by a shushing noise.

"Okay, Gran," I said beneath my breath. Carina snorted.

The strategy was to travel through the night, stay under cover during the day, move on again when darkness fell. The camp we'd left behind would act as might be expected under the circumstances, continuing to send out scouts to verify enemy position, and to wait for word from their commander to advance. We would sneak in somehow—that much would present itself once we got a good look at Tiran's encampment, I guess—and rescue Connor and Grace's mom and dad. After we were clear, Connor's warriors would strike. Or not, if it ended up such a move didn't seem "prudent." Connor's word.

I told myself the plan sounded solid, yet I couldn't stop myself recalling Resa's rescue. Grace hadn't troubled to clue us in on her plans that time. She'd been afraid we wouldn't agree with them, and she would have been right. All hell had broken loose. Still, we'd managed to grab Resa and escape. Barely.

As if sensing my thoughts about her, Resa slipped away from Carina and caught my hand in hers. She looked up at me and away, her gaze losing focus. Funny, her holding my hand so much at twelve years old, and me hers. Maybe it gave her comfort. It certainly did me.

When I'd been twelve, holding hands hadn't been my thing. I'd already been about two years into service with the Grif-Drifs. The only handholding I might have done was for the purpose of completing a dupe.

Yeah, nothing to be proud of, my past. Yet, it had served its purpose. Now I could only hope to be better.

As the darkness started to fade, we looked around for a place to lay low. We had been descending from the mountains, and a valley appeared at a distance before us, misty and gray. It looked like a winding river ran through the center. On the valley's opposite side, more mountains rose, stony and bare except for the snow clinging to their sides. I wondered how far we still had to go. How far we'd deviated from the course in Grace's mind, as well. The one we intended to be following before the change in plans.

"I hear water," Brand said suddenly. Not the river. It was too far away.

"Where?" I asked him. At our exchange, everyone stopped and listened. The *conjure* stopped last, plodding to a halt close to the three warriors, horns swinging slightly around the warriors' heads and shoulders. I thought it possible the *conjures* enjoyed freaking out our traveling companions.

Brand pointed off to his right. "That way. Small stream. Rocky. Probably clean. Good place to refill the containers."

I trusted Brand's instincts. After a quick glance at Grace for confirmation, he started to lead us all into the trees.

"Wait," said Carina, reaching out to grab Mika's arm and mine. "Someone else is in there. I hear them."

I caught my breath, paused to listen, but she shook her head, tapped her temple.

"In here," she whispered.

I looked back at the *conjures*, who had paused, too. Still, they didn't quite appear to be on the alert. Grace made her way to my side, her brother not far behind.

"What's going on?" he asked gruffly. "Why are you all standing here? I thought one of you was directing us to water."

"Carina hears something," I explained.

He listened for a second. "I don't—"

"Not that way," I said. "She senses other people's thoughts. Sometimes even hears them. So, good thing about that, it means what she's picking up on is probably human."

"As opposed to?" Connor demanded, whipping from his belt a weapon very like the *impulse* used by Citadel guards. I frowned at it. Carina reached up, placed her hand over his, pushed it down, weapon and all.

"There is no need," she said in a voice as fluid as her movements. Shocked by her action or perhaps lulled by her tones, he complied.

"Why not?" he ground out. His arm hung motionless at his side with the weapon still clutched in his hand. Oddly motionless. What had Carina done to him? Whatever had happened, Carina or his own response, it was temporary. A moment later, his arm regained movement and he raised the weapon again.

"Don't," Grace said to her brother, stepping in front. "We wait."

Angry, he slammed the *impulse* down against his thigh. "Why? Do you not know how foolhardy this is?"

She ignored him, turning to address us, her companions. "How do you all feel?"

"Feel?" Connor sneered behind her. "You don't coddle an army."

"We are not an army," she said and lifted her hands, extending them to either side. "Are we all clear-headed, or do we connect?" she asked.

No one needed to ask what she meant. We all sought inside ourselves, searching consciousness for any confusion, warped thought, unbidden anger, strange images.

"Clear," I said. Everyone else answered likewise. Connor and his three warriors watched us in bewilderment but held their places.

"Who are they, Carina?" Grace asked. "Can you tell?"

Carina shook her head.

"Then I expect we'll find out." Grace started into the trees. I fell in beside her, Resa and Carina behind us, followed by Mika, Brand, Ren, Hannah. I glanced back at Connor. I couldn't read his expression. After a moment, he and the others followed. Burdened by the apparatus on their backs, they had a harder time making their way between the trees and fell behind. The *conjures* came behind them, reaching a point where they finally stopped, unable to squeeze through without taking the smaller trees with them. We continued toward the water sounds, figuring the four warriors at our backs would do their darnedest to catch up. I had a feeling that deep inside Connor thought his sister was upstaging him. Idiot.

"Just over that ridge," Brand said, pointing. We all heard the water flowing. We also weren't being silent in our approach, by any means. Perhaps we should have been, but too late now. I asked Carina what she could sense.

"Are they still there?" I added.

"Yes," Carina whispered. "Still there. And frightened."

I grimaced. Fear could make a person dangerous, unpredictable. "How many?"

"Not sure."

"More than one?"

"Yes."

Grace had pulled her *lathesa* out, holding it in a loose, ready grip. Despite the unknowns in this situation, we probably needed nothing else. Even so, I released the glass cutter in its holder. Mika had a hand on his, still in his belt. His spear stuck up from the pack on his back. Connor carried his weapon somewhere behind us, which I didn't believe to be the best position for anyone, but we went on anyway. I assumed he'd warn us to duck if necessary.

I had to remind myself Connor was a decent-enough guy. It seemed Grace might bring out the worst in her brother, and he, her. I'd never had a relationship like that with a sibling. Resa was Resa, and my relationship with her had been strained for reasons beyond our control. As for brothers, I hadn't had any—as far as I knew—until suddenly I had two.

I pushed them both from my mind, our parents, too, because we'd drawn near to the stream. Between the trees, water tumbled over stone. The sunlight would catch it soon, but right now it looked like dark, molten silver. On the opposite bank, three people stood. Three strangely thin, delicately built, gray-skinned people. They stared at us with large eyes, their bodies not moving, as if by holding still they hoped to be ignored. The sun rose, light arrowing out of the East and onto the hillside. The rays sparked on water. I lowered my lids against the glare. When I lifted them again, the people were gone. In their place stood three dainty knee-high creatures, each sporting a pair of nubbed antlers atop their heads. They darted away before anyone could speak or move.

Connor pushed forward, knocking me aside, staring after the fleeing animals. He turned to me, as I was nearest. When he spoke, it was more like a shout.

"Where the hell are we? What is this place?"

I didn't bother to hide my derision. "I don't know," I said, picking myself up. "Your guys made the map." Shock prevented him knocking me down again, I guess, because I remained standing.

"That's not what I mean," he said. "What just happened? What were those things?"

"Dunno. But this isn't the first shape-shifting being we've encountered. I'm guessing not the same for you?"

He sat down abruptly, the gear on his back clanking and shifting upward. His head dropped forward between his knees, the draped wings hunching over him. His comrades-in-arms hurried closer. I was pretty sure they'd missed from their vantage point the phenomenon we'd all witnessed.

"Commander?"

He waved a hand. "I'm fine. Step back. Give me some room."

They obeyed. I stuck out a hand. He grabbed it. I helped him to his feet as Mika steadied the apparatus swinging precariously at his back. Connor stood a moment, staring at the ground. Grace joined us. Hunching her shoulders, she grabbed his arm and turned her head to look him in the eye.

"Connor?"

He grunted something. Sounded like it might be in their desert tongue, because she answered him in kind. I'd forgotten Grace's ability with languages. So far, we hadn't really run into anyone we couldn't talk to. We'd been fortunate. Most we'd had contact with spoke the common tongue or possessed some form of it in addition to their own. If not, Grace took the lead in conversation.

"Are they…real?" he asked her.

"As in do they exist? Yes," Grace answered.

"I didn't imagine it?"

"Not unless we all did."

"And you've seen these creatures before?"

Grace straightened, released her grip on his sleeve. "Not these, but we met another."

"Met?"

"Spent the evening with, in humanoid form. They change in the daylight, apparently."

He blinked, said nothing.

Grace jerked her head toward a small, green clearing overhung by branches. "Let's set up camp there. Since we're leaving when night falls, we shouldn't disturb them too much. Hopefully, they won't be afraid to return."

Connor nodded wordless agreement, signaled his warriors to follow. We leapt across the rocky streambed and prepared to bunk down for the day on the grassy soil. No snow. In abrupt recognition, I realized we'd been walking on a clear trail for quite a distance. It would be nice to be dry for a while.

Grace insisted on taking first watch. Connor assigned a warrior from his team to join her. The rest of us rolled up in our heavy blankets to sleep. I thought I'd drop off straight away, but it was odd sleeping in daylight. I covered my eyes with my sleeved arm, hoping to make a difference. The others around me breathed deeply, evenly, as if they'd fallen asleep despite the constant babble from birdsong. And the wind. And water bubbling over rock. The dead leaves rustling in trees. Two branches rubbing together with an unnerving creak.

Then there was Grace's low-voiced conversation with the warrior keeping watch with her. A hum, almost, on hearing's edge, their voices quiet. Intimate. Whatever they talked about didn't sound urgent. More like they discussed memories from home. I even heard her laugh once, quick and light. I tried to ignore the annoying, jealous twinges, slammed my lids shut. In determination, I rolled once again onto my side. Right onto something which drove into my cheek like a dull needle. Yelping, I struggled up wiping the blood from my face.

"Oh, hell, no," I said out loud.

Its point dripping with my fresh blood, a star tracker lay on the ground where my head had just been.

Grace

Chapter Twenty-Nine

Duncan threw his blanket over the tracker. I got everyone up and told them all to check the area, reminding them not to touch the things. Connor insisted on full-blown details before allowing his warriors to join in. As I dug a hole in the ground with a pointed branch, I told him what I could, what I knew. He watched me from beneath a twisted brow.

"What are you doing now?"

"Making a place to bury them. We'll pile stones on top after. I don't know how Enid disarmed them. It was mage craft of some type. I'm doing the best I can. It has to be done fast before any get away."

"Get away?" he echoed.

Oh, yes, I hadn't told him that part. I explained to him their ability to move, as well. He appeared horrified.

"And who is this Enid?"

Impatience got the better of me. "Connor," I snapped, "enough. Grab something and help me."

Without another word, he did so and together we dug a knee-deep hole. His three warriors watched what the others were doing and glimpsing an understanding, joined in.

"Don't touch it," I heard Duncan warn one.

"I have gloves on," said the man.

"Well, okay then."

I stepped out from the hole into the dirt pile around it. "Did you get them all?" I called out quietly.

"I think so," Duncan answered me. "Give me a sec." He and our friends visually scoured the area again. After several minutes, he said, "Looks like we got them all."

Everyone brought their bundles over and dumped the contents in the hole. Blood smeared on the blankets indicated at least some in our party had been tested. Quickly, I kicked the dirt back into the hole and stamped on it, right and left, releasing frustration in the action.

"We'll pile stones and wood on top. Hopefully none escaped before you noticed the one near you, Duncan. We'll have to move to somewhere different to rest, in case they did, and quickly."

"But I'd barely gotten to sleep," Ren murmured.

"Who made these things?" I glanced up at Quin, Connor's warrior I knew from home. Mara's cousin.

"We don't really know," I said. "Someone with significant technology and mage skills manufactured these trackers."

"That's what they are? Trackers?"

I frowned at his tone, speaking slowly in response. "Yes. They take samples of blood and probably skin, tracking a person through the results. They move across the ground, attach themselves to animals for mobility, and according to Enid can also travel briefly through the air." I glanced down at the mound marked by my boot prints. "I can't imagine how, but I'm not questioning it."

"Sir," said Quin, drawing Connor's attention away from the mound and the stones Carina, Brand and Ren had started to pile onto it.

"What is it?"

"We found some of these back at the old camp. At first, no one picked them up, afraid they might detonate or something. Someone tested that theory out, tossing one or two against stone. After they didn't explode, a handful snatched them up and kept them. Until we packed up to move on, there was one hanging as decoration from the tent I shared with Ons and Sousa."

Connor swore. It was good to know Connor, better-than-me Connor, had a vocabulary at least as rude as my own when the circumstances moved him. I wanted to shake Quin. Swearing or not, Connor had more control. He sucked in a deep, angry breath and took no physical action.

"Fools," Connor growled out.

"Sir," Quinn responded, head bowing low to his chest.

"I have no reason to doubt what my sister has said about these things. We are all at risk. You will have to go back to the others and warn them. Hopefully, it is not too late."

Quin nodded. Silent, he retrieved his flying apparatus.

"I want to see how those go on," Ren said.

"Can't," Quin answered. "Not enough room. I'll put on the wings when I get back on the trail."

"Be careful," said Connor. "If these things are tracking any of us, you don't know what's out there."

With a brisk nod, Quin took off at a trot through the woods. Ren looked longingly after him before turning to assist again with covering the dirt mound. Connor called me aside.

"What else are you not telling me?" he asked.

"I could ask you the same question."

"We are not at cross purposes, Grace. Or at least, we shouldn't be."

I heaved a heavy breath. "You told me about the various factions bidding for power in all this fighting. Wanting to have the upper hand, gain control. Of lands and resources and people, yes?"

He nodded, his mouth in a thin line. "What else do you know?"

Before I could answer, Duncan approached. "We're ready to move," he said.

"I'll tell you what we've learned as we go," I said to Connor and hurried to retrieve my things.

It was time he knew what we were up against, that these were not just warring factions. I told him about the mutant creatures Tiran had brought down from Emerald, about the cruelty of the Lyoness and her joining forces with Stone Tiran. I told him we'd encountered others, too, who seemed to be functioning separately from them, but likely with the same goal. To come out on top. All led, or misled, by one person, as he had suspected. But not just a person. Something more.

Even though I didn't quite understand it all, I explained to him as much as I dared. Underlying my explanations was the need to keep him and the others away from direct battle with Moros. This much I knew. I didn't believe they could fight him or whoever he had under his immediate command. I feared Moros would gain control of them all. I'd worried about this from the moment my brother found us, that he and the others with him were under a dark influence, but they hadn't proved to be.

Still, it could happen. I hoped Duncan's brother and whoever assisted him with his mage work—I prayed he needed assistance and this wasn't all Moros' doing—couldn't operate if they spread themselves too thin. The focus needed to remain on us so others could continue to fight. In the meantime, we had more pressing problems. Those seeded trackers had found us. I didn't believe we were lucky enough to have contained them all before they sent a signal back.

In reaction to what I told him, Connor grew quiet at my side. Duncan, walking with his sister at our backs, had interjected his own take on what had been going on but seemed to be following my lead about not mentioning his familial connection to Moros. Behind him came the others, including Connor's two warriors and the *conjures*. Chauncy, Bell and Vigor had rejoined us as soon as we got near. I felt comfort in their company, not only as protectors, but in their ability to sense trouble. Right now, they showed no indication anything immediate existed in the area.

"So," Connor finally said, "if we are able to rescue—"

"When we rescue," I corrected him. I refused to believe any other outcome.

"When," he agreed. "When our parents are safe and away, we'll return them to the camp. I know they'll want to fight with us if they're in any condition to do so, and I won't dishonor them by insisting they don't. I'll send scouts out to find those who had promised to join us and alert them to our new target. You're sure you don't know where this Moros is?"

"I do not." I only half-lied. I truly had no idea where Duncan's brother was, but the compelling sense as to where we needed to go constantly pulled at me. The inner map, I supposed Duncan would call it. Yet, unlike the maps I'd seen, no clear directions existed. "Besides," I reminded him, "you can't just throw all your warriors at him and whatever is with him. If you and the armies you hope will come are affected—"

"The mind control you mentioned."

I nodded. "Yes. And if you're all subjected to it, you could turn and fight for him. Or be surrounded by his armies, unaware, and that would be the end."

I didn't like how absolute my last statement sounded, yet I recognized the disheartening possibility of truth in it, filling me with heaviness and foreboding. I shuddered, contained the movement, lifted my chin.

"You're not the only one who studied history and tactics during warrior's training," I added, trying to lighten my spirit with a prod at Connor. "The course was standard."

"I remember," he said, "and I know. But I command my army, and I will decide."

He already appeared to have forgotten my warning about the mutant creatures and was dismissing my concerns about Moros. He didn't understand. It didn't seem likely he could.

We started out at a quick pace, but before very long the shorter-statured among us began to slow us down. It was a matter of stride-length and with Carina, Resa, Hannah and sometimes Brand having to take nearly two for our every one, we were losing progress. The *conjures* decided the matter.

Connor eyed their sudden push into our midst with distrust and anxiety. His eyebrows arched behind his segmented helmet when the *conjures* lowered themselves to the ground across the trail. "What are they doing?"

"They want us to ride," I said.

"To do what?"

"To ride," I repeated. "We have before, all of us on these three. *Conjures* are very strong."

"Fast, too. And great in a fight," Duncan added, smiling at the animals' huge bodies hunkered nearby.

"Yeah, I...no...I think...I think I'll continue to walk," Connor said, sounding so much like Duncan right then I nearly laughed. His warriors chose to stay with him on the ground. Odd, when they had no compunction about flying high in the air. Of course, I understood it was the *conjures* they feared, not the elevation.

Duncan, Ren, and I decided we'd continue walking with Connor and the other two. I urged Mika to ride with Carina and Resa. To keep them safe, I said, but in truth I didn't like how tired he looked. Although he'd gotten much stronger since our escape from Emerald, his neurological ailment still plagued him. His medication had long ago run out. Somehow, he had remained seizure-free. Only luck, I figured, and luck was always ready to abandon us. Fortunately, Enid had something she had supplied him with, a
remedy concocted from plant matter and magic, most likely, because otherwise I don't know where she would have gotten it. He'd returned to his

regimen only days ago, but he still held strong. He couldn't afford to go without sleep, though. At least on Chauncy's back he could doze.

Hannah and Brand rode on Bell, the gentler ride among the three, leaving Vigor riderless. Being the largest, Vigor would provide defense unhindered if necessary.

I glanced up at the sky through the branches, attempting to locate the sun in the pale sky. Following my gaze, Brand commented from Bell's back that it looked like snow was coming. In the mountains, he added. Likely not as we neared the valley. Brand's gift. Weather and animals. An added boon to our little group. More and more I understood Enid was right. We were meant to be together.

Duncan took my hand. My brother viewed us sidelong, releasing a snort through his nose. I ignored him, reveling in Duncan's warm grasp.

"It'll be all right," he said. He never stopped saying those words. I hoped he never would.

A moment later I looked up again, figuring it didn't matter how many times he said them. That promise wasn't ever going to come true. And I was right. Ships appeared overhead. Not one or two or three, but a whole fleet. Black, these were, like the
Citadel cruisers. I swore and ordered everyone off the trail.

"But slowly," I said. "No fast movements to call attention to anyone who might be watching from above."

Observing the ships for a few seconds, the fact

there were so many reassured me somewhat. At least for the time-being. It seemed to me they must be moving troops rather than looking for us. I said as much to Duncan and Connor, seeking affirmation.

"Agreed," whispered Connor. Duncan seconded him with a nod. Jammed up beneath the trees, we continued to visually mark the ships as they passed into the air above the valley and veered left, disappearing beyond sight. My breath went out in relief.

"Let's go," I said. Duncan's hand slapped down onto my arm, stopping me.

"Where are the *conjures*?"

My gaze followed his. The *conjures* and their passengers were nowhere to be seen. My heart jerked into my throat and hovered there. I could barely swallow.

"I don't see them anywhere," Duncan said, peering ahead and from side to side. "The *conjures* would only leave us for a reason."

"Right," I said. "The others are with them, so they're safe. But we probably aren't."

Duncan concurred. Weapons out, Duncan and I led the way with Connor and Ren surprisingly quiet at our backs. Connor's two warriors came behind.

"We need to be together we need to be together," Duncan kept chanting in a whisper beside me. His fear was palpable, matching mine. I glanced back at Ren, whose eyes were wide. I glimpsed the others' eyes behind their helmets. They appeared calm. Concerned, determined, but calm.

Only us, then.
That probably meant just one thing.
"We need to find them," I said to Duncan. "We need to find them and connect. Now."

Chapter Thirty

We picked up our pace until we were running. We moved in silence, eyes cast upward when we safely could, to see if any ships had returned to the area. Otherwise, we raced on. No one questioned why. They followed wordlessly, allowing Duncan and me the lead.

Reaching a point where the trail split in two, each cutting downhill toward the valley, I stopped. I signaled to the rest to get in under the trees. Duncan pressed close. I stood beside him shaking, feeling the tremors running through him, too. I called Ren over.

"Why have we stopped?" he asked.

"Because I am, quite frankly, an idiot," I answered quietly.

Ren's yellow brows lifted.

"We don't need to be physically with them to connect. Enid had us practice doing it without contact. I'd say we give it our best now, to find them, and to block out whatever is trying to disorient us and make us afraid."

"Oh," Ren said, sounding relieved. "You feel that, too?"

"Yes," said Duncan, an impatient edge to his tone.

"What are you talking about?" Connor asked, having come up beside us.

"There's no time for explanations," Duncan replied, restraint's last thread giving way.

"Please," I said. Connor backed off.

As Enid had taught us, we pushed back the outside world. It took several tries, because right then the outside world posed a threat not kept away by Enid's charm, and we were vulnerable. When it happened though, we felt it, each recognizing the other in that strange, ethereal fashion. It was like floating in total buoyancy without physical limitations. Or bodies, even. We couldn't see anything, or at least I couldn't. Nothing but a vast, white, cloudy stream. We reached out together for the others, our thoughts braided like invisible silky hairs, catching Carina first, followed by Hannah and Mika and Brand. Resa came in last, her presence always confusing because her consciousness could sometimes take us elsewhere. We weren't one entity, but many clinging together following the same path, not readings minds, but...holding them. Until suddenly we weren't. A chaos-filled scene rushed in, knocking us apart, banishing the fear not our own. Instead, we feared for reasons very real. The mutants had found them.

Before losing the connect, I had seen the *conjures* battling the creatures and our friends swinging with the weapons to hand. Somehow, they all managed to cling to the *conjures'* backs, despite the *conjures* lunging and spitting the beasts on their horns. I knew where they'd be found.

"How much weight do those things hold?" I

asked Connor, indicating the inactive wings strapped to their backs.

"Enough," he said. "At least two or three times our own. Why?"

Ren was about to have his wish fulfilled. Partially, anyway. "You need to fly us to our friends."

Connor asked no other questions, giving immediate orders for the wings to be readied. Ren observed every aspect in open avarice.

"We can't leave our supplies behind," I said, when the apparatus was ready.

"You won't have to," Connor assured me.

"How are we doing this? Do you have rope?"

Connor continued preparation. "I thought this was your plan."

"Very well," I said. "You tie each of us to one of you, and we'll hold everyone's packs secure somehow, yours and ours. Does that work?"

"It certainly does," he answered. Several straps hit the ground. He sorted through them. "And you won't need to hold the packs. We have means to secure them. too."

More quickly than I imagined possible, we were in the air. I could never have envisioned flight to be like this. Strapped and clinging to our partners we lifted above the treetops in movements that were alarming, mindboggling, and beautiful. After his first muted whoop of excitement, Ren's mouth remained firmly shut in a slightly terrified, tight-lipped smile. I pointed out the way. I hardly needed to. As we neared, the battlefield was obvious.

The fliers released and dropped us to the ground before descending. We rolled to prevent injury and leaped up again. The first thing I saw was Mika sprawled facedown. Racing to him, I dispatched the nearest creatures and helped him up. Uninjured. I sent a grateful, silent prayer into the sky. The girls and Brand still clung somehow to the *conjures'* backs. Gored mutants lay all around. The *conjures'* pearlized horns glittered with blood.

In short order, the final few met their ends as well. Breathing heavily, I stared in disbelief at their numbers. Far more than had attacked us outside Enid's charm. Had Tiran imported more from Emerald or were they somehow making them? My stomach churned.

"Is anyone hurt?" I asked, spinning away from the decimated beasts. Receiving negative responses from all, I turned to my brother. Mouth and nose wrinkled in distaste, he shoved at a creature with his booted foot.

"So, these are—"

"Yes," I said.

"How are your friends still alive?"

"The *conjures* mostly," Mika said, passing by us to check on everyone's condition.

"But not only them," I said, because I knew better. "The *conjures,* however," I explained to my brother, "are immune to the mutants' ability to affect the mind."

Connor nodded. "That's fortunate. What should we do with these?" He waved his hand to encompass the dead.

I knew what we had done before. This time, however, there would be no disposal. "We'll leave them. As a warning."

"A warning, eh?"

"Yes."

Connor's mouth curved, not quite a smile. "You're angry."

"Getting there," I admitted.

"Good. But take care. You are a warrior, after all."

A footstep sounded beside me. "More than that," said Duncan.

"An even better reason to remember who you are, Grace," Connor said, and walked away to join his two warriors, preparing once more the wings for transport on their backs.

We didn't tarry long. We still had to find a safe place to camp for the remaining daylight hours. Everyone needed sleep. Sleep and then food. After that...

Well, after that, we would save my parents.

* * *

Connor found us a place to camp. Another cave. The mountains were filled with them. Once we'd checked it for animal habitation, we settled in. Duncan and Brand insisted on first watch, for which I was grateful. The last thing I remember were voices, Duncan's and Brand's, discussing what their favorite meals had been at home. I anticipated hearing Duncan's stomach growl at any moment, but was asleep before it did.

Sometime later, I awoke to those same voices, Brand and Duncan, which could only mean I hadn't been sleeping very long. I rolled over, stiff and achy, and looked to the pair silhouetted in the cave opening. Only they weren't a pair. They were three. Connor had joined them.

Without his helmet, the sunlight glinted on his dark, braided hair. They spoke quietly, laughing. I heard Connor say my name before he glanced back my way, smiling. Sharing some of our misadventures, I supposed, mine and his. He didn't see me watching and returned to the conversation. I wished I could hear his words. It would have been nice to know what he recalled with such amusement. Those days seemed so very far in the past.

"Grace."

I rolled back over, finding Carina awake, too. She extended her arm across the cave floor, fingers beckoning. I took them in mine.

"I was afraid," she said.

"So was I."

"I don't want to be afraid anymore. I'm getting tired of it."

My lips curved. "So am I."

We both giggled then, a quiet, almost breathless sound. I wasn't prone to giggling. It felt good, though. I knew it couldn't last.

We spent the remaining daylight hours sleeping and eating in turns. Even the *conjures* did the same, disappearing one by one to hunt, and otherwise sleeping across the cave entrance. As evening closed in, Duncan lit his kinetic torch and together he and my brother studied Connor's map while the rest packed up in preparation to leave. I came to stand over them, staring down at the map, too.

"How far?" I asked.

Connor looked up. "We should be sighting Tiran's sentries about halfway through the night. Hopefully they don't see us first."

"And hopefully that's all he has," Duncan said. "Sentries. Soldiers that can be avoided or overpowered. Not anything more sinister and deadly."

"Like those mutants, you mean."

Duncan met Connor's gaze. "Like them, sure.

But I was thinking about other means for defense. Laser emissions and the like."

Connor grunted and swore. Quietly, yes, but the emotion came through. His brow wrinkled into a knot. "Tiran's been on the move for a while," he said. "Let's hope there's been no time or ability for any setup such as that."

"Where is he heading?" I asked. "Do you know?"

"I don't," Connor answered. "His movements make no sense, which is why it's been so hard to follow him, to anticipate what's next. No enemy troops are behaving as expected. That and intermittent communication is why we're spread out from the provinces and into the beyond. The Halcyon Range, The Wilds... All new territory for us. Even the older leaders have no real memory of these areas. Since running into you all, I've seen some pretty strange things, too."

He glanced aside at the animals still hunkered down by the cave opening, but I knew he meant more than the *conjures.*

"Dragons?"

Connor's head whipped around, finding Hannah in the shadows. "I'm really not in the mood for jests," he said to her. "We have to work out our route and get going."

"I'm not joking," said Hannah. "Duncan saved me from one."

"I didn't," Duncan argued. "Not really."

Connor's head went back and forth between Hannah and Duncan, not certain what to believe.

"You did," Hannah insisted. "It would have killed me."

"You don't know that." Duncan looked away,

returning his attention to the map. A second later he added, "And it was Grace who ultimately saved us both."

"Wait," said Connor. "You're saying this is true."

"Aye," Brand answered for Duncan, having been drawn nearer by the conversation.

Connor folded his arms. "Have you proof?"

Duncan straightened again. "I'm assuming you don't mean proof Grace saved us, but proof dragons exist." Fumbling deep in his pocket, he pulled out the dragon's claw and held it up for my brother to see. "This broke off its foot. I picked it up."

With a whistling breath, Connor raised his eyes to mine. I nodded wordlessly. His lids lowered, lifted. Another breath escaped him, this one long and slow. He turned back to the map.

"You are all much more than I had surmised. I am sorry for not truly believing in the crazy tales and you. Apparently, the stories are not quite so crazy and you all..." He shook his head. "I don't know what you are."

"Don't worry," said Duncan. "Neither do we."

* * *

We headed out a short time later when the sun slid behind the mountains. Deep shadows, nearly as dark as night, filled the thinning forest. Before long, I heard what I thought might be a nighttime bird, emitting a low-frequency, repetitive call, and then I worried it might be something else. Not an animal at all, but a signal, a very human signal, meant to be disguised.

"Brand," I whispered, "do you hear that?"

"Which sound?"

I raised my finger when the *whoooo whoooo* call came again. He smiled.

"It's a strix," he said. "Or some kind o' strix. They hunt like that. Find their prey with their call."

"What size prey?" I asked.

"Small 'uns," he said. "Leastwise, the strix back home only hunt small prey."

"And you can tell the difference between a legitimate call and someone who might be imitating it?"

In the shadows and starlight, I recognized his disdainful look.

"Right," I said, "Thank you."

He waved aside my gratitude. Practical, unassuming, straightforward, our orphaned hunter. After Resa, he was the youngest in our group. He'd been on his own a long time, from what he'd said. One among a dozen hunters who kept meat on Trill's tables.

Ours, too. Not tables, but in our stomachs when he could. He never killed but what would be eaten. If we temporarily had no means to cook the animal, he let it go. He'd added much-needed knowledge to our foraging skills, as well. Every one of us brought some ability into the fold, necessary for our survival and in the dangers we faced.

I really didn't know what I would do when the time came for us to separate, as it inevitably would, for good or bad. I had meant what I said, about all my friends being welcome in my home. It would hurt very deeply to be without them. It would feel like—

"Having your heart ripped out," Brand said.

"What? How did…"

"Ever since Enid showed us how to do that thing—connecting—I catch a flyin' thought every now and then, 'specially if it's a strong 'un."

"I see," I said.

"Don' worry. I try not to listen."

He slipped away then, to walk with Duncan, who was striding hand in hand with Resa alongside Connor. The others were bunched together, including Connor's warriors. Something had changed. I felt a respect, a shared respect between us and them that hadn't been there before.

Yes, parting from my friends would hurt so very much.

Don't be such a sentimental fool, Skelly said, his voice still distant, blocked by the talisman.

Shut it, I shot back at him, without much force. Oddly, I thought I might miss him, too, and wondered at myself for thinking it.

Skelly

Chapter Thirty-One

I don't like hearing her think things like that. It reminds me of other times. Other people. I had friends, too. Well, one friend, if you didn't count Mika. A long time ago beneath the red sky. He died because of me.

Maybe they will, too, Grace and her *companions*. She calls them that sometimes. Like it means something special. Like they share something no one else can have.

In the end it won't matter. They'll break the way everybody does.

Even me.

Duncan

Chapter Thirty-Two

I had difficulty discerning landmarks in the dark. It didn't help I hadn't an exact idea what we were looking for. The place names and sketches on the map had been drawn by the mapmaker in haste and without accuracy. Even Connor grumbled in frustration as we passed the map back and forth between us. Occasionally, we'd ducked into somewhere shielded from the sky and our surroundings to shine a quick light on the map. Not often enough.

We'd entered the valley some time ago and found it uninhabited, unguarded, unmarked. Both Connor and I had agreed at that point how much easier it would have been to be looking at a virtual and highly detailed map rather than a paper one. But wishes were useless. So, we pressed on. Now, we'd come upon a small town, no more than a village, really, and barely visible through the gloom. Smoke drifted on the air. Some inhabitants were still awake then. Crouched down off the road leading into it, Connor and I studied the map again, trying to decide which way we should go to get around the perimeter. Grace and the others waited behind us for the outcome.

Or I thought they did. Brand suddenly appeared heading toward us on the shadowed road. He moved with his usual silence, knees bent, keeping his body close to the ground. If he hadn't announced himself as soon as he became visible, he might have been taken down by Connor's warriors. Or me.

Behind me, Grace swore.

Brand slipped to his knees at my right. He looked pale, eyes wide.

"What the hell are you doing?" Connor demanded in an undertone. Not quietly enough. I shushed him. He was too busy being angry at Brand to take offense.

"The place is empty," Brand whispered.

"Empty?" I echoed. "It's been abandoned, then."

Brand shook his head. He dropped forward, catching himself on the ground. "Suppose some 'ave, yeah," he said breathlessly. "Rest are dead."

"Dead?" I sounded like my Gran's ancient bird, mimicking words.

He nodded.

"Then why don't we smell them?" Connor growled. To be honest, I hadn't thought of that.

"Not the way they died," Brand said. "Burned. What you see 'ere," he added, pointing to the rooftops in dark silhouette against the sky. "All that's left. The rest is rubble."

I heard Mika's voice behind me. "Maybe we should look for survivors. They might need help."

Brand glanced up, found him in the dark, shook his head again.

"Can we go straight through rather than around?" Connor asked.

"Yeah," said Brand. "Likely so. There's only one road."

We gave Brand a few minutes to recuperate before accompanying him back into the ruined settlement. I had no idea the time, but it felt like the midnight hour. According to Connor's earlier calculations, we should be nearing Tiran's encampment. Perhaps the town's condition was the proof.

"Keep a look out for sentries," Connor instructed quietly, his thoughts seeming similar to mine.

"Also, anything that looks out of place," I said. "Suspicious."

"And how are we supposed to tell that?" Ren whispered.

Like everyone else, Ren was tired and on edge, reverting to his usual sarcasm. I bit my tongue on a hasty retort.

"I don't know," I said. "Just be careful."

He grunted and said no more.

Once we passed the buildings still standing, I had an eerie sense of having been here before. Quickly, I realized what I looked at was very similar to the warded village we'd all passed through, although not together. I glanced around at the others, gauging their reactions. I saw nervous, cautious glances, but nothing to indicate anything more.

"Not warded," said Hannah, catching my eye. Right. Grace said Hannah had been the only one who'd recognized the dark magic in place. I nodded at her in thanks and kept walking.

Bodies littered the ground, so badly burned they scarcely resembled people. At Mika's insistence, we performed quick checks in the least-damaged buildings, looking for survivors. We found none.

Small, scavenging creatures scurried past us. They darted from one side to the other, sniffing the burned. Probably more than sniffing. I picked up a stone and lobbed it at a tangle I saw on a nearby, blackened lump. Brand reached out, touched my arm.

"No need," he said. "Not among these. Nobody's comin' back to claim 'em. Let the beasties do their job."

My stomach revolted at the cold truth in his words. I gagged and swallowed and went on, feeling very far from home.

A disturbing silence engulfed the town, broken only by our footsteps, an occasional word. The tiny scavengers scuttled here and there. Every so often a loud noise crashed the hush and made us jump, spinning around with weapons raised. Luckily, it was only damaged timbers cracking, falling to the ground.

"I don't like this," Connor whispered at one point.

"Neither do I," Grace and I uttered simultaneously. We both laughed. A nervous titter, really. Embarrassing. Overloud.

"Shh." I turned, looked at Carina, at the finger pressed to her lips.

"Do you hear something?" Grace asked.

Carina shook her head. "No. I just...please be quiet."

I got it. No one was unaffected. No one unafraid.

"I feel like we're being watched," Ren muttered.

Ah, hell.

We froze where we stood, visually searching the street, the rubble, the mangled rooftops. Shadows shifted beneath the starlight. An abrupt breeze pushed dead leaves along the debris. My flesh shifted. Hairs rose at my nape. Brand hadn't had time to search the whole town. Of course, he hadn't. Grace made a sudden movement with her free arm. Pink illumination splashed across every surface around us, clinging to shattered stone and wood. We all stared into what the light revealed, watched it fade, felt anxiety diminish with it.

"Nothing," Grace said.

My shoulders relaxed.

"Except whoever is approaching," said Brand.

I whipped around. We all did. One of Connor's warriors raised his *impulse*-type weapon. I reached out, pushed it down. For once, I think I noticed something before everyone else. The rest were still staring, guarded, attempting to understand what they saw. "It's okay," I said.

Cericia, Enid's mate, or wife, or whatever they were to each other, pushed a quilted hood back from her head. I'd recognized her white, tufted hair, her eyes. Her size. It shocked me no one else had. When they did, we all hurried forward, Connor and his warriors trailing behind. The *conjures* pushed past them. They greeted Cericia the way they did Grace, with rumbles and thunderous bumps that so easily could have done damage. Somehow, they never did.

Cericia acknowledged them, touching each one on their overly large heads. She addressed Grace after, indicating the *conjures* with her lifted chin.

"I am so glad they found you in time," she said.

"Thank you," said Grace. "They saved my life, and so did you. Was that the mission Enid mentioned? Had she foreseen it somehow?"

"One mission," answered Cericia. "There are others."

"Where did you find them, the *conjures*?"

"Far afield. Hunting. They kept as much of the danger from you as they could while you were with my Enid. Not all, though, as you know."

Grace nodded. Behind us, someone's throat cleared.

"Cericia," Grace said, "this is my brother, Connor. These are two of his warriors, Tik and Freysa."

"Well met," said Cericia in a grave, formal tone.

Connor swept his hand around at our surroundings. "Do you know what happened here?"

"Terror," Cericia said. "Cruelty. If you are asking if I witnessed it, I did not. I felt it, though."

I guess it was a measure of Connor's growing acceptance that he didn't question what she meant. Instead, he asked something else.

"Do you know who did this?"

She shook her head, tossing her shaggy hair. "I do not know who, precisely, did this. I do know who ordered it, though. I have come to lead you there. This is where you need to go, where the man known as the Revered is encamped?"

"Yes," said Grace before her brother could speak. "Why…why did he do this, to these people, to this village?"

Cericia thought a moment. "I am unsure."

"How come you know where we're going?" I asked. "We didn't. We had a temporary change of plans from what we told Enid."

The Singer's Hart-now-woman lifted her gaze to the sky. Wisps of cloud and closer smoke drifted across the stars. "The forest creatures listen and carry word to those who need to hear it."

Mika stepped forward. "Who chooses who needs to hear? Could information be carried to others who command it?"

Cericia lowered her head. Her always sober expression became even more so. Like Gran about to deliver bad news. I sucked in a breath.

"Yes," she said. "Therefore, we must hurry."

* * *

Hurry. Always we hurried. Except when we weren't, which usually meant captivity. I much preferred the hurrying even though it wore me down.

Cericia's gait outstripped ours. When the *conjures* insisted in their awkward, block-the-path manner that we ride, we did. All except Connor and his warriors, who donned the wing apparatus and flew close overhead. And Cericia. Cericia would not ride either. Instead, she increased her pace so as not to slow the *conjures'* loping momentum. Observing her swift, almost leaping strides, I was both awed and slightly enamored.

Eventually, Cericia slowed and stopped. We had crossed the valley and were once again on higher ground. Dismounting, we gathered around her as she pointed into the distance.

"The man you seek is camped there, on that plateau. Between here and there you must take care. He has watchers."

"What, like soldiers?" I asked, hoping she didn't mean anything more sinister.

Cericia nodded. "And others. They are like them, but not real?" She looked a question at me. Grace turned in my direction.

"Replicants?" she said.

"What are replicants?" Connor asked.

It was Ren who answered. "My grandmother creates them. They're nothing to worry about. Their only purpose is to make it look like an army has more numbers than they really possess. I'm surprised they have them here, though."

I frowned. "Why is that?"

"It takes a lot of energy to generate them."

"Right," Grace said. "The Lyoness showed me."

"Maybe Tiran has a mobile generator?" I suggested.

"If so," said Grace, "perhaps he has spread himself too thin and needs to appear stronger."

"Or," Ren said, "maybe my grandmother is here, too. She likes to use them, the replicants. Even before the war, she moved them often into the outskirts around the city, to make those who lived beyond its boundaries afraid."

I grunted. "Yeah. Wonderful lady, your gran."

Hannah moved closer. "I hope she isn't here, because if she is we'll pay a horrible price if we're caught."

I glanced from Ren to Mika. The Lyoness had sent us to die in the glass mines. She'd wanted the girls for their abilities, and had imprisoned them, Hannah separately. We, however, were expendable. More than that, she'd wanted to make sure we didn't live long, only long enough to suffer.

"I have heard of this Lyoness," Cericia said. "Whether she is here, I do not know."

Grace blew out a long breath. "Whether she's here or not, we have to finish what we've come to do. Did you pick up any information about where prisoners are being held?"

Cericia pivoted her head slowly from side to side. "I did not. I did see many…soldiers, you call them? Many soldiers guarding the entrance to a cave in the hillside above the camp."

"Could be armaments, could be prisoners. Either way, I'm thinking we should start there. Grace?"

Connor finished, deferring to his sister.

"Agreed," she said, spinning her *lathesa* in a deft twirl.

"I'm also thinking," he went on, hesitating, "that some of us should stay behind."

"No way," I started, and stopped, clenching my teeth together. I didn't need to say anything. Grace would never approve. We were meant to be together. We had to stay together. Enid had told us—

"Agreed," said Grace again. I nearly fell over.

"No," I said. The others protested right along with me, in quiet, firm negatives. We couldn't resort to yelling. Not here.

"We shouldn't separate," said Hannah.

Carina's eyes turned fiery red, visible even in the dark. "I won't leave you, Grace."

"And I'm not leaving you," Mika whispered to Carina.

I stared in dismay, not sure what to say. From behind me, Brand spoke.

"Let 'er talk. Let Grace speak."

Shocked by how adamant he sounded, we all lapsed into silence. I kept my gaze on Grace's face, looking for telltale signs she might be vacillating or, better still, teasing. Poor joke, if so. Nothing funny about it. At all.

"You're right, of course, we're meant to be together," Grace said. "Yet if we don't succeed, we can't all be caught inside. Someone needs to be clear and planning."

"But—" I started.

"Who goes in?" Ren interrupted. "Besides you, I mean."

"The warrior, the witch, and the thrice-gifted child. Who else?" said Hannah.

I sputtered, anxious to be heard. "I thought we already had a plan."

Grace's eyes slid to mine. Her lips curved, not quite in amusement. "We did. You know how that goes. I've had more time to think. And I know I'm not the last word in what we do, but listen to me, all right?"

I inclined my head, reluctant but assenting.

"Not you," she said, pointing at me. "Connor and his two, and me. We go in, once we're close."

"Wait—"

"The rest of you," she went on, ignoring my blurted interjection, "will wait outside with the *conjures*. I can't imagine anyone else who could rescue us if the attempt fails. We can connect, even if we're not physically together, and that's what I'm counting on."

"I don't—"

"Duncan. Please. You are formidable, all of you. You've proven that again and again. If things go awry, we will be fighting our way out. I need to know you are on the outside, ready to assess and react. It might be the only thing to save us all."

Hannah made a noise in her throat. "You're talking like you lead us."

"She does," I said.

"You would say that," Hannah shot back.

"She does," said Brand and Mika in unison.

Mika shifted his stance, dropped his hand from where he'd placed it on Carina's shoulder. "You know it as well as the rest of us, Hannah. And I really don't think you want to be going into that cave, do you? You're just being..."

"Contrary," I said, using a Gran term.

"Right," Mika continued. "It has always been

Grace we looked to for leadership, and Duncan her second-in-command, if we're giving titles. That's why Grace wants him out here. We are a team. We've gone through so much together. This is it. This is the way it will be. Got it?"

Hannah nodded wordlessly, trying to avoid a sulk.

"Thank you," Grace said quietly to him. To the rest, she added, "We'll all go together until we're as close as we can get and still be safe. Then I, Connor, Tik and Freysa will make our way in. We'll keep in touch, all of us, the way Enid taught us."

We all murmured agreement. I didn't like the plan. I understood the reasoning, though. Still, it made me angry and a little sick. I decided I'd best suck it up and get on with it.

"What about your friend?" Connor asked suddenly. "Cericia. She looks like she'd be good in a fight."

Cericia smiled. Rare for her, I thought. Her face didn't seem to want to form to it. I couldn't remember any smiles back at Enid's, either. Yet here it was, a bright, toothy, rather stiff grin.

"Not this time," she said, "but soon."

After that, she provided us with directions to the cave above the ridge, said her goodbyes and sprinted away into the darkness.

"I suppose it will be dawn soon," Ren said.

"Yes," answered Grace, "so we must hurry now."

Ren waved his hand after the shapeshifter. "I meant for Cericia."

"Oh. There is that, yes."

Grace explained Cericia to her brother in more detail while we prepared to move out, making sure once again nothing on our persons might clank or slip.

Connor gaped at his sister in amazement, shaking his head. Ren sidled up to me.

"Does she go back to where her clothes are left after changing, or does she wander around naked until she finds others?"

"You're an ass, Ren," I said. "You know that, don't you?"

"You've got to admit you've wondered."

I ignored him, but yeah, he was right. I had.

* * *

The sun had fortunately not yet risen by the time we reached the area above the plateau. There had been a few times we'd had to divert from our route to avoid sentries. Brand's insistence he scout ahead as we went had been a smart move. Now, we were all safely ensconced in this weird, stone circle, almost like a dome with two entrances and a wide opening in the top. It had a smell about it. Not exactly unpleasant, but enough to overpower the scent from the *conjures* and to make me wonder what the structure might have been used for in the past. Vegetation storage, possibly, and built, not naturally formed. It looked—or at least felt—very old indeed.

Brand didn't like it. He kept wrinkling his nose and walking around. When I asked him if he thought we should move elsewhere, he shook his head and said it was the safest place to be. It was roomy enough, certainly, fitting even the *conjures* inside without fear we might be skewered.

I watched the warriors, the desert warriors, ready themselves. One could see straightaway why Grace had chosen them to go into the cave. I was reminded again how scary she could be.

They kept minimum weapons for the job, the warriors did. Grace had Enid's loaned *lathesa* and a single blade. The other three carried their own sharp implements. Tik held onto his firearm, too. Just in case, I supposed. They wore their flying apparatus, wrapped against noise, but their packs were piled together against the wall. I saw Ren eyeing the wings on their backs covetously. He had a fascination for them, even though I'd witnessed the frozen expression on his face when we were all up in the air. He might need watching. He could be impulsive. Make stupid decisions.

"Ren," said Grace, pointing to the packs on the floor, "would you mind keeping an eye on those? You may need to load them up quickly for transport on Vigor. Otherwise, see they stay safe right here."

Ren's spine straightened. Distracted, the greedy longing left his face. He seemed oddly proud to have been given the job. "I will," he said. I smiled. Grace so often knew the right thing to say.

Connor strode to the opening, peered up at the sky. He looked back at Grace. "We should go now."

She nodded and came over to me, took my hands in hers, looked me in the eye. Silent. Staring. After a moment, she squeezed my fingers and let go, pivoting away. I took a step after her, unable to believe she wasn't going to say anything to me before she left. Quite abruptly she did without turning back, her words circling through my brain, my very being, loud and clear and pushing warmth into every pore of me.

I love you.

Glancing around, I realized we had all received the same message from her. Connected. Connected in the blink of an eye without demand.

"I love you, too," I said. Out loud and too late. Grace and the other warriors had already vanished into the fading night.

A chill danced like a spirit's touch along my spine.

Grace

Chapter Thirty-Three

In uneasy combination, my heart felt heavy while my nerves flared and sparked like fire. I sensed a milestone coming and yet this could not be the end. Rescuing my parents was a diversion from the path. We would succeed—we must—and then I and my companions would go on. Destiny called us.

How I hated that word: destiny. It implied one had no choices in life. Yet, it had arisen so often since our escape from the Emerald I had come to believe in it, if only a little. After all, my friends and I made conscious choices. We could easily have made others. Such was the ongoing discussion in my mind as I crept through the pre-dawn gloom toward the cave. To a place where we hoped prisoners were being kept. The truth was, we did not know for certain. We had to start here, though, where it seemed most likely.

Tik and Freysa had already dispatched two sentries in a manner that left them unconscious rather than dead. I had argued before we set out that we deal with them as warriors are taught, disabling, disarming, and avoiding the mortal stroke. Even so, dealing in death might come. I had admitted as much to my brother and his warriors, recognizing inevitability, but I prayed it wouldn't be necessary.

I thought about my friends left behind in the semi-domed structure. I had meant every word I said to them. So much had remained unspoken which I tried not to think about, including the possibility we might not meet again. But marching in with my brother's army would have been foolish, would have gotten my parents killed, and my friends, too. This was the right thing to do, what we were doing now.

Repetition does not make truth, Skelly's voice slithered up from my mind's recesses. I growled at him. Literally growled at him. My brother glanced at me with wide eyes. I shook my head, attempted in silence to express reassurance. He didn't look reassured. Nevertheless, he turned away and we continued easing forward toward the cavemouth from above.

When Connor raised his hand, we all stopped, listened, breath held. He indicated the flat ledge stretching out from the entrance. More than a dozen soldiers stood arrayed upon it in a half circle. I narrowed my eyes, saw the tiny shift in all but six, the replicants wavering for an instant like heat above a flame. A dull illumination from within the cave also revealed they possessed no shadows.

"Only those are real," I whispered into my brother's ear, pointing out the few. He passed on the information to Tik and Freysa. Their heads bobbed once in understanding.

Had Carina and Resa been at my side, there would have been little need for combat. They were safer separated from me, however, for were we caught then Stone Tiran and the Lyoness, or whoever accompanied him, would have us all together. That must not happen. Unfortunately, the anger that seemed to muster my ability to throw others around like straw—a power similar in its way to Resa's—was absent. Just as well. I didn't know how to control the gift and had almost hurt the Fianna as well as Connor with it. Enid had hoped for regulation when she taught us to bind together. Hoped my friends would keep me from lashing out too wildly. Although we now had the ability for connection, I doubted it would be the same from a distance. Even as the thought came to me, I understood doubt could be my undoing.

The drop from above the cave to the ledge was less than twice my brother's height. Tik and Freysa would handle the guards while Connor and I rushed whatever might be waiting inside. The two warriors would join us as soon as they'd dispatched the guards. We'd find our parents and get back out as quickly as possible. After, I would reach out to the others still under the connection and have them ride the *conjures* to meet us.

No guarantee existed any part in this plan would work. I reached down inside anyway, deep inside for the germinating seed of hope I'd planted there when I told my friends I loved them. Because I did. With all my heart. And for their sakes, I would return. I would see them again. We would complete our task and go home.

In silence, I leaped down between Connor and Tik, Freysa on his left. Connor's two warriors headed straight for the six I'd pointed out, intent on taking them down before any warning could be given. Connor and I rushed into the damp cave. Two men stood just within the opening. They were unconscious on the floor before they understood their danger. Connor and I spun, searching for any others. The dull gleam I'd noticed on the outside came from several temporary fixtures high on the wall and revealed no other guards within sight. Odd, except perhaps they hadn't viewed them as necessary with the replicants' deceiving numbers outside. That, or it meant my parents were not here. Worried, I headed deeper into the cave, Connor at my heels.

We passed piled containers with unknown contents. Nothing marked the smooth exteriors. Empty crates jammed the passageway, too, and a few cages. The cages didn't appear to have had anything inside them in a long time.

"Wait," I said, grabbing Connor's arm, hauling him to a stop. "Listen."

In the shadows beyond the feeble light, the cave floor sloped downward. I heard water dripping, and in the dripping, voices. A common acoustic illusion, water sounds transforming within the brain to words. Yet, it sounded like a conversation taking place in the darkness ahead.

"If it's anything at all, I can't tell what they're saying," Connor said.

"Then we go in and find out, yes?"

He bared his teeth in a quick smile. "Of course."

Footsteps behind us caused us both to whirl around before we had a chance to proceed. Freysa and
Tik hurried closer, belts hung with the soldiers' *impulses.* Nodding briefly in appreciation, I raised a finger to my lips.

We crept carefully downward, step by silent step. The voices began formulating into something I recognized. Not water at all, and not a language I understood, but I knew it.

"*Prair,*" I hissed.

"Right now?" my brother returned in low tones.

"Not prayer," I said. "There are creatures called *prair*. Intelligent, fast, and dangerous. I'm distinguishing their speech over the water. They could be securing our parents, which explains the need for only two guards in here."

"You've had dealings with them before?"

"Yes, in the caverns beneath the Halcyon Range."

He twitched at the reference. Whatever he wanted to say, he let it go as we moved down toward the water. I raised my palm and called the light onto it. Running up against the creatures in the dark would be most unwise. We left the dull illumination from the cave behind, until only the pink glow on my palm pushed back the blackness. In it, we saw the water rippling, followed by the huge, slug-like bodies surging toward the water's edge. They rose up but didn't leave it. I knew they could, since they had pursued us and the Fianna. I warned the others.

"What are they?" Freysa asked, obviously repulsed.

I had no answer for her. Flicking my wrist, I scattered the light around the walls, looking for my mother and father.

"There!" Connor said, pointing.

In a crevice near the water's edge, I spotted our parents' faces peering out. Ignoring the *prair,* I raced across the cave floor. An appendage whipped out from the water's surface, grasping at my ankle. I slashed at it with my *lathesa*, striking it hard. The creature withdrew. Squelching noises reached my ears as the *prair* climbed from the rippling water. These were followed by the low-hummed blasts from the warriors' confiscated weapons. Ignoring the sounds, I charged up to the crevice and reached my hand out to grasp my mother's. My fingers went right through.

"It's a trap!" I shouted to my brother. The fading pink glow revealed him already at my back.

Turning, we fought our way through the *prair* and up to the surface. Not much of a fight. In fact, alarmingly easy. The *prair* seemed to be letting us depart, slithering and slapping along behind, yet maintaining their distance. Herding us, I realized. Like before. Fierce, bitter words streamed in silence from my lips.

"Be wary," I finally said out loud.

"Doing that," Connor mumbled.

We passed the crates and empty containers, easier to see now. Slightly above us, a cold, foggy sunlight flowed in through the cavemouth, highlighting the congealed silhouette of many soldiers. Their long shadows stretched across the uneven floor, proving they were genuine. A knot stepped away from the others. Before I could say anything, Connor gave the order for his warriors to fire their stolen weapons and run for cover.

"No!" I shouted. I slammed my *lathesa* straight down, the end impacting stone. The noise boomed through the cave with sonic reverberation. Everyone stopped moving. Stopped as if they'd turned to stone. A moment later, the shadowed knot shuffled forward, separating in the light into five. One, I didn't know. The other four I did. My mother. My father. Ella. Stone Tiran. I glanced down for shadows. Real.

"Grace!" my mother cried.

"Let them go," I said in a voice I did not recognize. My voice, yes, but different somehow. It held a certain authority I did not own. A power not solely mine. It surged through me and out my mouth like I was suddenly more. I held onto it even though it felt as if the influence might burst my flesh and burn me to ash.

A muscle in Tiran's cheek danced. He looked far older than the man I had known, a man only a handful of years older than I. He'd aged under hatred's weight.

"Gladly," he said, and his mouth trembled. Not in fear. In temper. He shoved my mother, sending her stumbling toward me. My father shot after her, grabbing her arm before she fell. Ella peered around, expecting to be stopped, and then scurried after them. My brother rushed out and yanked them all into our small, protective circle.

"I didn't even want them," Tiran went on. "I wanted you. You are your friends." His gaze swept the cave behind us. "But it appears they are not with you."

Oh, but they are, I thought. I sensed them all. Sensed their strength and friendship. The power Enid had helped us uncover. And something else. My own anger.

And me, said Skelly. Nearer and louder than I'd heard him in a very long time.

I swore, spitting an order to those with me to get down on the ground. An instant later, I blasted into a million, flaming pieces.

Duncan

Chapter Thirty-Four

The connection had crumbled. Painfully. I took this as a bad sign. A really bad sign. "We gotta go," I said, jumping up from the ground. Everyone else seemed somewhat dazed by what had just happened.

"Let's go, let's go." I urged them all upright, pushing packs and various items in their direction. The *conjures* had shifted their positions and looked ready for action, although still hunkered on the ground. Waiting, I supposed, for us.

"Did you get a message from Grace?" Carina asked.

"No. An absence of one. The connection vanished. You felt that, right?"

She nodded. "I just thought she might have—"

"No," I said. "Nothing. Which is probably a stronger message than if she'd knocked on her skulls and told us to come get her."

"Yeah, yeah," said Mika, fumbling back into his coat. He'd removed it at some point, no doubt swapping body heat with Carina under their shared blanket.

In record time, we were ready. Ren and I stepped

outside first, blinking in the unexpected sunshine. The structure's interior had been shadowed by the vines wrapped around the open top.

"What do you think happened?" Ren asked.

I shook my head. "I don't know."

"So, what do we do? Ride in the direction they went and find them?"

"She said she was counting on us to save them all if she didn't make it back, right? We're going to have to figure it out and we can't wait until night hides us. It has to be now."

Hannah walked up beside us. "Maybe she's on her way and only stopped…transmitting or whatever."

I looked down at her. Transmitting. Interesting analogy. "Well, we can't wait to find out," I said. "Later could be too late."

"I understand." She shifted her pack on her back, then stepped aside as Chauncy came through the opening, his single horn gliding between us, followed by his massive head and shoulders. In short order the other two came through, followed by the remaining companions. Resa broke away from Carina and rushed to my side. I jerked my head down to gape at her. She grasped my hand and tugged, her eyes on mine. I was so shocked by the interaction, I didn't notice her other hand lifting, pointing to the sky.

Brand rushed past me, rising onto his toes. "Look there!"

My heart leaped in my chest. High above, three fliers began dropping down. It could only be Connor and his two warriors. Strapped to each was another person. I ran to meet them as they circled downward. They were still too high in the air for me to figure out which was Grace, but I planned to be there first when she touched down.

I didn't remember Connor's warriors' names, but the female landed first, clutching a woman. Grace's mom. Disheveled and dirty, she still looked so much like Grace, except Grace's skin was darker and her hair blacker, but the eyes staring around with an indecipherable expression were as green as her daughter's. Next came—Tik?—carrying a man with gray streaks through his black hair, a stern expression and a build like Connor's. Their dad. With process of elimination, I hurried over to Connor as he descended, already reaching out to help unfasten the webbing before he fully landed, anxious to release Grace from the restraints.

Except it wasn't Grace. It was someone else.

When Connor unhooked the straps, the woman tumbled sideways. I grabbed her to keep her from falling and found myself looking into a face many years older than Grace's, with no family resemblance.

"Thank you," she said. Righting herself, she hurried over to Grace's parents. I spun to Connor. He shook his head at me in three long, slow movements. For a moment, I couldn't speak, couldn't formulate words. When I finally did speak, the words just wouldn't stop.

"Where is Grace? Where is she, Connor? Let's go. We'll get her. Who is that woman? It doesn't matter. We're ready to ride. Grace is following on foot, right? I mean, you couldn't fly them all out. It would be just like Grace to step aside, let you take— who is that? Damn it, Connor, where is Grace?"

Connor grabbed me by the shoulders, shook me, bent, placed his face close to mine.

"Where is she?" I persisted. Quietly now. As if I feared the answer.

Which I did.

"She's gone," he said.

"NO!" I punched him, hard. He hit me back. I landed on the ground and stayed down, my head between my knees. I thought I might be crying, but not a single tear dampened my face. I wanted to die. Right there in the sun. Grace loved the sun, the daylight. It would be perfect if I faded away into nothing right freaking there.

Connor spoke above me. "Everyone who's not got wings, get on one of those beasts. Now. We don't have time to waste. We have to move."

"Except me," I said. "I'm not going anywhere. Not without her."

Connor dropped down beside me, shook me again. "Don't do this. Grace wouldn't want it."

I shirked his hand off. "Really? Maybe we should ask her and be sure."

He inhaled, containing his emotion. "Not now. We can't do this now. Look, she's gone but maybe not dead, Duncan. At least, I don't think she is. I saw something I've never seen before. I don't—I don't know what it was."

I looked up at him, expectant as a little kid. He stood, yanked me upright.

"We're leaving. Don't make me throw you over my shoulder. You may be tall, but I've got the weight advantage."

"Okay."

His brows lowered.

"No, really," I said. "Okay. She'll find us. You know she can."

He gave me a look, a look that made me think perhaps he'd lied. That Grace wasn't coming back. I needed to know more about what had happened. We all did. For now, however, I clung to the small hope he'd tendered. I refused to let it go.

* * *

Even hours later, when we reached Connor's remaining army, I continued clutching hope close. We would know if Grace were truly gone, me and my friends. Yes, the connection had been severed in a rather fearsome way, but it hadn't felt permanent. I needed to get the others alone, to discuss our next move, but right now Connor was giving the orders. Sure, we didn't have to obey them, but we also needed to rest, regroup, plan.

First, though, I sought out Grace's parents.

I found them, dazed and somewhat the worse for wear, seated opposite each other on the ground, sipping some steaming concoction from a vessel they passed back and forth between them. Blankets hugged their shoulders. I recognized one of them. It had come from Grace's pack.

Controlling an urge to yank it away, I moved closer, cleared my throat. "You're Grace's parents."

Their heads lifted. I reached out and shook their hands, the way I'd been taught to do. Both seemed surprised by the gesture but returned it. "And you are?" her father asked.

"I'm Duncan, Duncan Oaks. Grace's—"

He shoved the vessel back into his wife's hands and flashed upright, the blanket from his back slumping to the ground. His hand shot to my jacket and gripped it, close to my throat.

"I know your name. I know who you are. I know what you did."

"Thar!" Grace's mother cried.

I barely registered the name, or her distress. I

focused instead on the fury in Grace's father's eyes.

"Sir, I…" My voice trailed off. Obviously, he'd heard the tale that shamed me. I didn't want to excuse my behavior, give him the reasoning behind what I'd done. Here was the judgment I deserved, that Grace had failed to provide me with her forgiveness.

"Thar."

I looked down at the woman calling her husband again. Aiofe. Yes, that was her name. Grace had told me. An ancient name. A beautiful name.

"Grace escaped with him, travels with him," Aiofe said, seeming to be reminding Thar something else he already knew.

Thar frowned. "She wouldn't have had to escape from anywhere if—"

"You know that's not true, dear," Grace's mother went on softly. "If not for the sentencing, Stone would have had her killed. You remember his original plan."

It confused me to hear the woman refer to their enemy by his first name. Casually, like she knew him. Then I remembered negotiations for some bonding between Grace and Tiran had been taking place. That is, until she refused him. War had broken out, not because of her refusal, but providing the barbarous lunatic excuses for retaliation.

Thar's hand dropped to his thigh with a mighty slap. He sat back down, snatched the cup away from his wife and drank from it, expression still thunderous. Aiofe took my fingers, squeezed them, let them go. Just like Grace would. I took a deep breath.

"I can only imagine," she said, "what coercions took place to make you do what you did."

"It's no excuse," I answered her.

"But it is time you forgave yourself."

My head dropped forward. I wanted to bawl

like a baby. I fought it back, blinked away stupid, useless tears.

"See what you've done to the boy?" Thar muttered. "You should have just let me hit him. He would have felt better." I had a feeling he was not the type to jest but I very nearly laughed.

"You're right, sir," I said. "Forgiveness I've had, from Grace, and now from your wife. Yet, forgiveness doesn't seem right, somehow."

He grunted, went back to whatever still steamed in the cup. "Anything else you wanted?" His voice echoed inside the container.

"I...I just wanted to ask what happened to Grace. What you saw."

He raised his eyes, stared at his wife, slowly shifted his gaze to me.

"We didn't see much. We were face down on the ground."

"Do you think she—" I began, and stopped. "I'm sorry. We have a mission to fulfill and I...I want to go after her, if you don't think she..." I halted again, respiring in short bursts. Thar lifted his brows and said nothing, but Aiofe leaned close to whisper.

"What we were able to see was—"

"Frightening," Thar stated in a flat tone.

Aiofe smiled at him. "Yes, dear, it was." She turned to me. "But it was also amazing."

That was my Grace. Amazing. Their Grace, as well, although if I possessed any credit with which to bet, I would have happily wagered the last of it that Thar and Aiofe didn't quite know the Grace I did now.

"You and your friends go find her," Aiofe continued, whispering again. "Do what you are meant to do. Because I've heard the tales, too, and now I believe them."

* * *

I hunted down Connor next to ask him what he'd meant when he said Grace was "gone."

Ren insisted on accompanying me. I wasn't quite sure why. "Do you think she's—"

"Dead?" I finished for him. "No."

"Good. I don't either. I think we would know, somehow, all of us. Plus…"

"Yes?"

"I don't think they would have left her there, even if she was, do you?"

"I wouldn't have. I know that much," I said. "And yes, I don't think her family would have either."

His eyes tightened, his mouth, too, the effort from thought showing on his face. "So, what do you think happened?"

I threw up my hands. "Ren, that's what I'm trying to find out. I'm hoping it'll give us a clue where she might be now."

He shut up then, trudging along beside me in silence. When we reached an area filled with increased activity, I spotted Connor at its center. Pushing past his warriors, I strode up to him, Ren on my heels.

"Connor, I need some answers."

He turned away, addressing someone nearby.

"Connor," I repeated.

He whipped back around. "I don't have time for this. We'll talk later."

"Later won't work. We won't be here."

His expression hardened. He didn't like my answer. "You're going after her, then? Chasing ghosts?"

I huffed out a breath. "Not ghosts. You said so yourself. What I need is for you to explain to me exactly what you witnessed before she was gone."

He stared at me for several seconds, blinked, glanced around, then jerked his head. "Over here."

We followed him, Ren and I, to a secluded area beneath the trees. He paced in a circle while we waited, his hands behind his back working together, fingers twisting and pulling at each other.

"I couldn't stop her," he said. "I couldn't…save her."

"Save her from what? Just tell me what happened."

Finally, he stopped moving, settling with his hands at his sides. His head dipped forward. "I don't know. She warned us all to hit the ground and then she—she exploded."

"She *what*?" Ren nearly shouted.

Connor looked up. "It wasn't as though she went to pieces. But there was a huge, percussive force. It flattened those creatures from the water behind us and Tiran and his army in front. Rock cracked and fell. Containers and crates tumbled over. And it came from her. From my little sister." He went quiet a moment, troubled by memory. No surprise there.

"And then?" I prompted him.

"She...she didn't appear to be alone. Someone, or something, was there with her. She looked to be battling with it. This took place in the blink of an eye after everyone and everything crashed down to the ground. She succeeded I think, in overpowering it. She even turned and met my eye, but..."

"Out with it, man," Ren growled in impatience.

"A dark wind came. A literal wind that blocked the sun."

Ren and I exchanged glances. "And?" I whispered.

Connor's hands clenched into fists against his thighs. "And it took her."

Moros. It had to be some wretched mage work of his. I didn't need any more information. I had enough. I rushed forward, grasped Connor's hand, shook it sharply. "Whatever you're planning next, good luck. Keep your parents safe. Make this all worth it."

He pulled his hand away. "You're leaving?"

"Immediately," I said. "We need a few supplies, if that's all right?"

He nodded, stepped closer, grabbed my sleeve. "Where are you going?"

"To where we were headed originally. To meet my brother."

I didn't give him time to ask more. In fact, I thought it best he didn't know more than he already suspected he did. Ren and I hurried away, pausing only long enough to gather from the army's stores what we could carry. When we reached the others, we passed around the foodstuffs for distribution into everyone's packs. I picked up mine and Grace's with what remained inside, determined she would need it. I wasn't about to accept anything different.

Grace

Chapter Thirty-Five

My head hurt. I figured more from what I'd performed back in the cavern than my transport here. Wherever here was, and whatever the transport had been. Wind it had felt like, but not merely wind. There had been a certain solidity to it. As I'd been buffeted around, I kept hitting a continuous barrier, neither hard nor soft, but definitely there. Like flesh.

Shuddering at the comparison, I studied my surroundings, listening, breathing the air. I wasn't underground. The air came through a small, barred opening about head height on a wall constructed from nearly black stone blocks. If a door existed, the night didn't reveal it in the stone walls surrounding me. Sounds echoed from somewhere, though, echoed strangely, making me unable to determine from which direction they came or from how far away. In that, the construction was like the Quadrate, before its ruin and after. I had no idea how far I'd come. Depending what had carried me here, distance might not matter. I had begun to recognize spell work when I met it. I didn't know if that was good or bad.

After a few minutes, I pushed myself up off the

floor. Every muscle ached. I slicked my hair back from my face. The strands felt damp. The clothing against my body, too. Most likely sweat. I still wore my heavy outer clothing. The air in here was warm. Too warm. I'd been dressing for the cold a long time now, a cold that hadn't been fully dispelled no matter where we found shelter. A building built from stone always held the chill. Yes, my breath frosted in the air. But something had made me sweat.

Unfastening my coat, I removed it, noting my blade was gone. And Enid's *lathesa*. I walked the room's perimeter, garment in hand, running my other hand along the stone surfaces, checking the corners for the weapon. At the barred opening I stopped, rose onto my toes, grasped the metal framing to steady myself and peered out into the night. How long had I been here, unaware? When last ☐ognizent, the morning sun had just risen. I had been with Connor and our parents, his two warriors in the cave above Tiran's encampment. And—

Yes. Me.

My teeth ground together. I stared out at the mountains, white at their peaks, steeply sloping sides blanketed in gloom. Still far from the desert, then. Still far from home.

We took them down, Grace, those others, just like you wanted. I'd at least expect a thank you.

I didn't respond.

But you still managed to put me back in here. That's gratitude. The talisman is gone, though, he added with glee. *Did you notice?*

Dropping my coat, I reached up and prodded the bag beneath my shirt where the Crone had lain as protection. Skelly wasn't lying. I could feel the fragments broken into little more than dust. I didn't know if shape mattered. The material from which it had been constructed remained. The enchantment imbued within might yet hold some power.

Don't count on it, Skelly said, but he didn't sound so sure.

Where are we? I asked him. *Do you know?*

So, now you want to talk to me?

No, I said rather callously, *I don't.*

I dropped down flat-footed and continued my stroll around the chamber's walls. Tentatively, I reached out to Duncan and the others, seeking the ruptured connection, and quickly withdrew when I sensed something else there. Like something on the opposite side of a door, tapping to get in.

Yeah, you don't want him getting in, Skelly whispered. *I, however, would welcome the opportunity to get to know the dolt's brother better.*

A chill sliced into my abdomen. *Moros is here?* I asked. *It that where we are? With him?*

I thought you didn't want to talk to me? But yes. That's exactly where we are. And I'm touched by the 'we'. How sweet.

I began searching in earnest for the door. There had to be one. Didn't there? I supposed if Duncan's brother could pick me up in a whirlwind and transport me here, a door didn't necessarily need to be involved. But common sense—

Common sense? Come now, let's be realistic.

In sudden fury, I grabbed the bag with Skelly's crystal inside and squeezed it, as if I might muffle him somehow, or perhaps crush the crystal and him into oblivion. An instant later I relented, let out a breath, released the bag.

That actually hurt, he said with genuine surprise.

I'm sorry.

I'd spoken automatically but also honestly. Skelly went silent, perhaps as stunned as I. Recovering from the momentary shock, I continued feeling for the door, finally locating a wooden barrier in the stone. I felt along it for a knob or latch, finding none, and swore.

Skelly snickered. *Language.*

I don't care about my language, I said. *I need to get out of here.*

But do you?

I paused. *What?*

Do you? he repeated. *I mean, you're pretty strong in your own right. He could be looking for a partnership.*

Not interested.

I went back to the window and pulled myself up, working a leg out between the bars. My body would never fit. From my wedged angle, I could now see nearly straight down. I stayed there, with my boot toe jammed into a space between stones inside and my head leaning against the barrier. I heard a call in the distance from some night-prowling animal. Probably something that would tear me to pieces given half a chance. Or I, it. I wouldn't want to, though. Not if I could avoid it.

But the thing would be trying to make you into a meal, Skelly said, patently bewildered.

I hope it's a scavenger then, I answered, *because from this height I'd be a dead one.*

He laughed. I did, too. Laughed like friends sharing a joke. I suppose I felt scared. A little lonely. Desperate.

Well, thanks, he said. *Thanks a lot.*

I forced myself not to apologize to him again. The odd thing was, I wanted to.

I tried to be your friend, Skelly, I said. *Back there on Emerald.*

He said nothing in return. Very well. I couldn't afford to be soft or melancholy. I had to get on with things. I needed to find a way out.

I know, he mumbled, sounding like water swirling down a drain.

Know what? That I need to find a way out? Can you—

No. That you tried to be my friend.

I climbed down from the window, pondering his tone. He was silent until my feet hit the floor.

That was your first mistake. I'm not a friendly guy.

"Enough talking," I said out loud. "Or would you prefer I dump the powdered remains from the other bag into yours?"

Silence. A telling answer. I made my way over to the door once more. Running my hands over the surface again, I wondered if I might use the power that had felled Tiran and his soldiers to force the barrier open. I doubted it. The surge didn't appear to be able to move fixed objects, only those with no physical union to the place where they stood. The difference between actions would be like tossing a ball at a *kondar* pin or throwing the same ball at a wall. I tapped my chin in thought.

It wasn't you alone who took down the army, Skelly whispered in reminder.

My finger stilled. "I know that. But in the caverns under the Halcyon Range, it was. I don't really need you, Skelly."

He grunted without retort. Still, I felt his mocking doubt. Recognized a tiny truth in it, forcing me to recall the escape from the City of All Dwellers. I hadn't yet gone through the Sleeping Myth. Releasing him then, albeit not purposefully, had saved us all. And it had nearly cost me my life to return him to the crystal. Not this time, though.

Why might that be? I asked him.

No comment.

Mentally pushing him down and away, I pressed my ear to the door, listening for any sign someone stood on the other side. After a moment, I dropped to the ground and peered underneath, searching for shadows. Seeing none either stationary or mobile in the flickering light beyond, I leaped upright, settling my hands on my hips. A minute passed, and then another. In frustration, I threw myself at my impediment to freedom and hit the wood hard. Picking myself up, I kicked the door before storming back across the room where I leaned against the wall, sliding down until my hips touched the floor. I pulled my knees to my chest, wrapped my arms around them and glared into the dark.

Tantrums will get you nowhere, Grace. I should know.

"Shut up."

Maybe you can will it open.

"Shut up," I said again. I'd always been instructed telling someone to shut up was rude, and yet I did it quite often, especially with Skelly. Maybe for the wrong reasons. Maybe this time he was right.

I concentrated on the door until the sweat ran anew on my face and I heard something click in the corridor. The door opened, only a little, but enough to let the light flood through the room, pushing back the darkness. I jumped up, started forward and stopped, realizing my foolishness. I hadn't opened the door. I didn't have that gift. Dark and formless, something slipped inside.

* * *

Heart pounding, I glanced around again for the *lathesa,* forgetting it was gone. The thing came forward, draped with weightless garments, flowing as it moved. I struggled to find the shape inside, a human shape, or something like one. I adopted a defensive stance. Skelly cried out in my head.

Let me out! Let me out now!

But I couldn't. I wouldn't. I had no idea what I faced, but if the being came to me in innocence, I refused to harm it.

"Who are you?" I demanded. My speech wavered. I swallowed, steadied myself, pushed the tension from my muscles so they would obey me when needed.

The being stopped. "Follow me," it said in a genderless voice. It turned, pulled the door wider, and headed into the corridor beyond without waiting to see if I complied. I decided I had a better chance to escape outside the room than in, retrieved my coat and exited, keeping my distance. The hallway was wide, made from the same black stone, as was the floor beneath my feet. Lumi-discs of the type used in the detention facility lit the corridor at intervals. I faltered, looking at them. Had I been taken back there? No. That place had been sterile, metal walls and floors and the view outside this barred window didn't match the sinister darkness on Emerald. Fighting to steady my heartrate again, I went on, trailing two steps behind the flowing robes and eyeing my surroundings for a place to dart away. In between seeking an escape, I studied the figure before me, glimpsing boots beneath the robes, soft-soled to minimize noise as it moved. It seemed broadly built, its back nearly twice as wide as mine. The head beneath the hood rested at a height somewhere well above my own. I picked out the approximate placement of its knee should its form be humanoid, and estimated what a well-placed kick from behind would do when the moment was right.

The moment never came. The figure stopped suddenly, lifted a black-gloved hand. A hand with five fingers, one of them pointing.

"In there."

An arched opening revealed three steps leading upward. I drew a deep breath, exhaled, squared my shoulders, and set my foot on the first one, listening. In the slightly elevated room above I heard a whirring noise I couldn't define, a fluttering, a tapping, something that sounded like wood scraping across the stone floor, and a heavy sigh.

"Hurry up," someone said from within. "I haven't got all night."

The deep timbre didn't have to be male, yet I

suspected it was. Sensed it in my bones, too, in a prickling warning. Despite the command, I took my time climbing, preparing myself for a visage that would likely rip a hole in my heart.

"There you are!" Moros said as I stepped into view, quite as though he greeted a welcome guest. I didn't answer him. Although I expected what I saw, I experienced a strange, bitter betrayal at finding the features I loved on Duncan's brother's face.

"Moros," I said, coldly, studying his completely black attire, from boots to trousers to the long-sleeved tunic with an ornate vest over it. If Duncan could see this, he'd no doubt pass a comment about 'the darkness vibe.' Probably not out loud, considering the hazardous position we'd be in. I had a feeling his twin possessed none of Duncan's irreverent humor.

"I have a title," Moros said.

"The Darkness?"

"Yes." He stared at me for a long moment, waiting. I kept my mouth shut. "I don't suppose you're going to use it?"

"No," I said, noting his dark brown hair, Duncan's tousled dark brown hair, had a habit of falling into his eyes, too.

One brow lifted. He shrugged. "As you wish. I'll feed you anyway. You must be starving." He waved his hand to the table near where he'd been standing. I knew now where the whirring noise came from, as well as the flutter. A device on the table circulated the air. The caged, spinning blades lifted and dropped the pages in a nearby book. A very old book. Between the two objects sat a tray laden with various food items, as well as a clear container filled with water, and two glass cylinders.

I had been subject to such gracious welcome before by the Lyoness back in All Dwellers, supplying my friends and me with a meal before her guards ambushed us all. I declined the offer.

"The water, then? Hydration is essential to one's health." Without waiting for an answer, he poured the water into the glasses, took one for himself and held the other one out to me.

Still frowning, I took the cup and backed away, but didn't drink. Not until I saw him do so first. Reassured, I swallowed several mouthfuls. The water was cold and soothed my dry throat. I realized only then how parched I was. While he helped himself to something from the tray, I shot a look around the sparsely furnished room.

A large and rather comfortable-looking chair had been positioned by the window, perhaps to catch the natural light during the day. Or fresh air. A second table stood near the window, as well. Large and square and heavily-built, it possessed a huge dome on top. Beneath the rounded, half-circle of glass I saw what appeared to be a topographical landscape, almost like a three-dimensional map. Glass in hand, I walked over to it. Beneath the transparent cover, I could now see an impression of snow-covered mountains, lower hills and trees, valleys, waterways, making me think of the areas in which I and my companions had been traveling. A miniature building stood at its epicenter. All around, tiny flags marked various points here and there.

"Like it?" he asked from behind me. "It helps

me keep everything in order. I enjoy knowing where things are."

Things? It resembled a war map.

Not wanting to show too much interest or ask any questions about the display, I turned, intending to make my way over to the cases lining one wall. I paused, spying Enid's *lathesa* leaning against the window sill. I remembered how the Lyoness had also taken my weapon, displayed it in her office like a trophy. I'd taken that one back. I would this one, too. Given time.

Moving on to the cases, I studied the shelves. There were many, filled with books. Real books and, like the one on the table, worn with age.

"Do you read?" he asked.

"Of course," I said. "Do you?" I had no idea why I baited him. I didn't seem able to contain the urge. Nerves, perhaps. Or anger that the boy who'd turned the world upside down possessed Duncan's face and build and hair. Or the fact that looking at him, he seemed sane and not dangerous at all.

He strolled over to stand next to me. Something akin to an electrical charge lifted the hair at my nape.

"I've read every single one," he said. "Multiple times. Sometimes, I had little else to entertain me. I learned a lot. Things I might never have known if I'd ignored them calling to me."

"Calling to you?" I echoed.

"Figure of speech. But you know exactly what I'm saying. The unknown calls. Knowledge is always waiting."

I made some non-committal comment, walked

closer to the wall. I saw words on the books' edges, some so faded I couldn't read them. I ran my fingers over several, feeling the symbols debossed into the material.

"This one is my particular favorite," he said, reaching for a volume and pulling it out. He handed the book to me. In my single-handed grasp, the tome opened to a page. I nearly dropped the book and my glass.

On a parchment page, sewn into a book marked by its antiquity, the somewhat faded depiction of a long-haired desert warrior in a defensive posture greeted me. She stood beside two other, smaller females, one with hair nearly as white as snow and the second with dark, braided locks, all surrounded by symbols I didn't understand. They were not direct portrayals, and if not for the other two also in the illustration, I would have dismissed the taller one as referencing me. But they were three together and the prophecy everyone kept throwing up at us lurched foremost into my thoughts. I found I couldn't breathe.

"Yes," Moros said. "That's you." He waited for a response that didn't come. "The warrior, the witch, the thrice-gifted child," Moros chanted, tapping the page on each head as he spoke.

I closed and shoved the book back into the case. "No," I said. "It isn't."

I had come to believe the prophecy, truly I had, but seeing it like this, the illustrations in a book clearly more than a hundred years old? This made me ill.

"Maybe you should sit down," he suggested

solicitously, taking my arm. I wanted to push him away, but I allowed him to steer me toward the oversized chair. I sat. He stepped back, eyeing me with his head cocked to one side. "Are you telling me you didn't know?"

I said nothing.

"That's very odd. The whole world knows and yet you don't."

"I didn't say that."

Giving me a calculating look, he returned to the table and poured himself more water, drinking it down. I glanced at the cup still wrapped in my fingers and took a few more sips myself. Good thing I did. My hand started to shake so badly I would have spilled the contents had it been full. Hastily, I lowered the cup to the floor and then folded my fingers together in my lap.

"Where are we?" I finally asked when he had filled his cup again and taken a mouthful. "What is this place called?"

"This building, or where we are geographically? Not that it matters. They have the same label. Gabrilon."

Gabrilon. I'd heard the name, back in Trill. Only when Duncan and Brand caught up with us again did I learn about his paternal grandmother, and the fact his parents and his little brother together with the people of Trill had fled the town and sought refuge at her court. I didn't really know what a court was, except a different governmental form.

"Where is your grandmother?" I asked. "The Lady of Gabrilon?"

"She's gone," he said. "Some time past. No one let me know until later. This was her study. It's mine now. Everything is mine now."

His matter-of-fact tone tried for nonchalance, but something in his eyes said differently. I decided not to ask after Duncan's other family members. Caution held my tongue in that regard. There would be time later to find out how they fared. In the meantime, it seemed prudent Moros didn't realize I knew about them.

Wise move, Skelly whispered, so unexpectedly I jumped.

Moros didn't seem to notice. Not my sudden movement, anyway. He did, however, glance around before turning a sharp gaze on me. "Did you hear that?"

A chill passed over my body. I looked where he had, pretending befuddlement. "What did it sound like?"

"Like we are not alone." He rushed to the stairs and down them, into the corridor, returning a few moments later with a slower tread.

I pointed at the window. "Maybe it was a noise from outside." I hated playing stupid, especially when my mind was circling around various actions I could be taking.

Like throwing him out that window?

I schooled my face to show nothing. This time, Moros' eyes shifted toward the shadows in the corners.

He's afraid.
Shh, I said. *Be quiet now. Please.*
Since you said please...

With one last look, Moros snatched something else from the table and popped it into his mouth, talking around it. "You really should eat something. I only wanted to introduce myself. Did you enjoy the ride, by the way?"

I stared at him in silence.

"What happened to your face? Did I do that?"

I reached up, prodded the bruised skin around my eye, my swollen cheek. "Avalanche," I said.

"Avalanche?" he echoed, disbelieving, and somehow amused. "You are very interesting, indeed."

I drew a deep breath, let it out, made no comment.

He laughed. "It doesn't matter. Remain silent, if you choose. You will be returned to your room now. I've had a bed and a few others niceties brought in for you. You'll remain there until your friends arrive. Because they are coming for you. You know that, don't you?"

Odd, how he didn't mention his brother's presence among them. Possibly, he didn't know as much as he thought he did.

"What is your plan?" I asked him. "What are you trying to accomplish?"

His lips curved. "You mean we, don't you?"

"We? Who is helping you?"

He laughed again. The sound rang false. "You are," he said. I said nothing, tried to act as though he hadn't shaken me with his statement. His fake amusement faded away. "I've been waiting for you. You, and the others. We'll do it together."

My hands clenched into fists. I forced my fingers

open, lay them flat along my thighs. "Doing what together, exactly?"

"Grace," he said, "we're going to change the world."

Duncan

Chapter Thirty-Six

"How do we know we're even going the right way?" Ren asked me.

"Shut your mouth and open your mind," Carina snapped at him while I was still working on a response. Carina, usually so patient, had lost her ability for tolerance a day ago. I felt her worry like a coating on my skin. We all did, which could account for Ren's increased sullenness. It was like being covered in electrified honey. Much more of this and I would start sounding like a testy five-year-old, too.

"I'm sorry," Carina said to me, to everyone. "But we can't break the connection now. It's leading us where we need to go, no matter what Ren's doubts are." She gave him a reproachful look before leaning back against Mika, closing her eyes. She and Mika rode on Bell. Ren, Hannah, and Brand on Vigor, leaving Resa and me on Chauncy. In the recent past, I would have worried about the separation between Carina and my sister, but as Grace had pointed out, Resa had changed. I watched her changing each day.

Riding side by side now the trail had widened, we

stayed connected despite the mental discomfort. We followed a calling which had nothing to do with Grace. We'd had no contact with her. Most likely, my brother attempted to lure the company in. The two he feared, anyway, if not all of us. We accepted this, figured it worked just fine for now. Besides, as usual, the *conjures* knew where to go. So far, we'd met with few obstacles, the *conjures* having dispatched several mutants in the early morning. Maybe luck was with us. Doubtful, though. Yeah, so very doubtful.

"Doesn't anyone else think this might be a trap?" Ren persisted.

"O' course it is," said Brand. "We just have to make sure not t' fall into it."

Behind me, Resa remained calm. I took this as a good sign, but tried not to allow myself too much complacence. All hell could break loose at any moment. We all knew this.

"Wish Grace was here with us," Ren muttered, "instead of wherever she is now."

"Me, too," I said under my breath.

He heard me, though, and glanced in my direction with a small, commiserating smile. I smiled back. Not grudgingly. We were all friends, our friendships forged under fire. Still, I did sometimes want to smack that yellow-haired individual upside his head.

Once again, we descended toward a valley, leaving the snow-peaked ridges behind. Evening was falling as the *conjures* trotted with their uneven gait out from the heavy forest for a sparser tree line. The temperature had risen during the day enough for us to loosen outer gear. Apparently, the direction Grace had foreseen when first we passed through the Sleeping Myth was holding true. The sun disappearing behind us indicated our somewhat easterly heading.

Hannah lifted her hand and pointed. "What's that? On the mountain?"

I followed her finger, squinting. A portion of the mountainside across the valley looked to have been blasted away, revealing steep, sharp sides. The jagged cliffs disappeared into something brown and smoky, most likely leafless trees draped in fog. A black, rectangular construction stood nearly atop a peak.

I reached out with my right hand, the bandages grimed and shredded along the edges. "Where's the…whatever it's called. Telescope. Somebody give me… Mika?"

Reaching inside his coat, Mika removed the device he'd taken along with the weapons Enid had offered us. Leaning across the space between the *conjures,* he managed to press it into my fingers without dropping it. I raised the conical tube with its magnifying lenses, and pressed it to my eye. With two hands, I steadied the apparatus against the bouncing from Chauncy's gait and peered out across the valley to the structure.

Not a product of nature, even though it seemed to grow out from the ragged mountain itself. The sides were too linear to be natural, all corners perpendicular, the width exceeding the depth as far as I could tell. On each corner atop the perfect rectangle stood raised elements, squared off, like towers.

The *conjures* halted. Mika dismounted and hurried back to me, reaching for the telescope. "Here," he said, "let me see."

I handed the device to him and he looked, too. After a few seconds, he let loose a nasty, quiet expletive. I rarely heard Mika swear.

Ren also slipped from Vigor's back, rushing to Mika's side. "Can I?" he asked, hand extended. He, too, observed the structure for a time. A low whistle escaped his lips. "This isn't good."

"What are we looking at?" I asked Ren.

"A fortification of some sort, I think."

"Abandoned?"

"Nope," he said, handing the telescope back to me. "Lights are coming on inside."

Fixing the instrument to my eye again, I saw the lights, too. The upper floor was coming to life. Yet things were clearly much worse. As the sun descended below the mountain behind us, the valley lit up next, dotted with various luminants beneath the barren trees from one side to the other.

I shoved the telescope back at Mika and leaped off Chauncy's back. Spinning, I yanked Resa off to stand beside me.

"We need to take cover," I said. "Now. We've got to figure this out."

* * *

We ate our evening meal in the dark, without fire or kinetic torch. Resa sat beside me. I leaned close so she could see my lips move and asked her how she was doing. I had no guarantee she'd even notice me with my face planted so near hers, but she did. She smiled and went back to eating.

Grace and Carina were the reason for this change in her. I couldn't claim any part in it. I knew I couldn't. I wondered if before the traumatic period with Stone Tiran, Resa had been more responsive among the Sisterhood than I'd known her previously. In other words, was it only me she couldn't relate to?

"Not true," whispered Carina, from Resa's other side. "She is always aware of you. But her visions take her elsewhere."

I didn't protest Carina reading my thoughts. What she said was comforting, even if not exactly an answer to my inner question.

"It looks like the whole world is camped down there," Ren said quietly, his head turned toward the valley below.

"Not quite," I muttered. "But that's someone's big army. I'd like to know whose."

Ren grunted. "It might help if we knew where we are."

"A sat map would have come in handy," Mika said. "I thought about taking the one from the ship when we crash landed, but I knew there'd be no way to power it."

"Crap, good thinking, Mika," I said. "I didn't even consider that. It really would have come in handy if we'd been able to keep it running."

Brand lifted his head from contemplating the food in his hand. "You can navigate by the stars, you know. Grace used to do it. I saw 'er."

My stomach rolled at Grace's name. "But the

stars won't tell you where you are, only the direction you're going."

"True," he said, and bit a piece off what he held, chewing hard. The dried meat sticks provided by Connor were difficult to get through.

Hannah stirred. "Do you think Grace is in there? In that fortification place?"

The thought had occurred to me, to all of us, I think. But I would have expected to know, somehow.

"Unless we're being blocked," Carina said.

Beside me, Resa scrambled upright and turned to face the valley and the structure on the mountainside. A second later we felt what she had, a blast immediately cut off, but not before we were filled with static charge and the essence of two separate words. *Help me.*

"Grace!"

Carina grabbed my hand. "You don't know that's her," she said. "Would Grace ever cry out for help like that? It didn't even sound like her."

I stood, breathing hard, gazing toward the fortification, invisible in the night but for the distant lights. "No," I agreed, "it didn't and she wouldn't, unless—"

"Unless things were that bad," Ren cut in, standing, too.

Right. Unless things were that bad.

"Even if it's a ruse," Mika said, already beginning to methodically re-fill his pack, "we can be assured one thing."

"What's that?" I said.

"She's close, Grace is. Probably in that place,

and Moros, too. I'd wager his army is down there, and like everyone else he would want the three of them, yes? Resa and Carina and Grace. He might not have any idea the rest of us are here, likely doesn't care. It was a distress beacon of sorts, to catch anyone's notice."

"Like casting a wide net for fish," Brand said, "hoping t' get the ones ya want and any others, well, they get tossed back in or—"

"Or not," said Ren.

"Aye," Brand said. "Or not."

Rubbing my eyes, I thought, hard. "We'll never make it through this valley undetected," I said. "We're going to have to come at that building the long way around and hope…and hope Grace is holding her own." My guts burned as if at a knife cut. "Maybe the place won't be as well guarded, given its position. Carina and Resa will have to stay outside in hiding."

"No," said Carina.

I shook my head. "We can't all go in. If he has the three of you together—"

"And if he has any of you, he has the means to lure us out. Because he can hurt you. I'm not going to stay in hiding while that happens."

"But—"

"Listen to me!"

I sucked in a breath. Mika reached for Carina's arm. Carina spoke again, lowering her voice.

"Resa and I will go in by ourselves," Carina went on.

"No," Mika and I said in unison.

Carina shook her head, her hair flowing in that

freaky way it had. "Let him think we're alone, that he's gotten what he wants. He's not going to do anything to risk our abilities. So, we pretend whatever we need to, like we did before, at All Dwellers. You all wait in hiding until you receive a signal that we're either on our way out or need rescuing. And you must keep blocking him. You can't afford to be compromised."

Her plan made sense. Even so, I didn't like it at all. Neither did Mika. His scowl would have put anyone off but Carina ignored it.

"And the signal?" I asked.

She tapped her temple. "In here. And if not in there, it'll be something a lot more obvious."

"Like blowing a wall out?"

Carina smiled, the playful smile I'd rarely seen since we'd escaped the Emerald. "Sure," she said. "Blowing walls out would be fun."

Despite her light tone and her smile, I felt her fear. I'm sure we all did. But she was also determined.

"I wish we had, I don't know, an army with us," Hannah murmured.

So did I, but that would only bring more danger on Grace. "It's just us," I said, "and it'll be all right."

Did I believe it? Did I absolutely, one hundred percent believe it? I told myself I did. The stakes were too high to allow my emotional misgivings to override what my logical bit of brain recognized as the most sensible, though nerve-wracking, plan.

The quickest way around the valley, and hopefully up the mountainside, would be with the *conjures'* assistance. As always, they understood without command what we needed, lowering themselves to the ground for us to climb on. In short order we'd mounted to ride.

"Chauncy," I said, patting his stinking neck before I climbed on, "to think I was afraid of you." He growled, reminding me I still should be. Whether due to the discussion among ourselves or the animals' innate understanding, the *conjures* headed off in a direction that would circumvent the valley. Chauncy took the lead. The beasts traveled at stop speed, increasing the urgency I felt. We rode hunkered down against each other to avoid being swept off by branches.

Halfway through the night, they slowed their pace and began picking their way up the slope on the valley's far side. Glancing back over my shoulder, I saw the valley below still lit with lamps and campfires, but there seemed to be fewer now as the hour grew late. The closer we came to the structure the jumpier we all got. The building seemed to be protected by something more than guards, which we hadn't yet come across. The syrupy, electrifying unhappiness Carina had been projecting had been replaced now by something designed to fray the nerves. It didn't come from Carina. Not anymore.

The *conjures* took a path beneath the last trees before unbroken land met the rockfall on our left. They plodded slowly upward, taking care where they placed their feet. We stayed low on their backs, trying to project lumpy, unrecognizable shadows to anyone spotting our movements. Spying two large, rock slabs leaning against each other, I pointed them out to the others.

"Looks like a good place to keep out of sight," I said.

The *conjures* had other ideas. They continued past the place where the rocks formed nice, deep shadow. Figuring we had to trust their visceral reasoning, we hung on. At the ridgetop, they stopped. Halted right in the open where by daylight we could easily be seen from the towers on the building below. We scrambled off to the ground, crouching low.

"How is anyone going to get in there now without notice?" Ren grumbled, shooting accusatory glances at the *conjures*.

Brand, who had wandered off a short distance, came scurrying back. "This way," he said.

"What is it?"

"A tunnel o' some sort. I peeked over the ledge. Looks like it comes out down there." He pointed to a craggy, narrow opening three-quarters of the way down the barren slope. The distance between the lower opening and the stone structure was about thirty long strides. Even at this distance the breach looked like a tight squeeze, but manageable. Neither my father nor my uncle could have made their way through, but it looked like I could, as well as the rest of us.

I turned to Carina. "If you're really set on going in alone with Resa—"

"I am," she said.

"I want to go with you," Mika said quietly, firmly.

She took his hand. "You can't. I don't want to lose you and if you're with me, I will." She turned back to me. She'd spoken with unnerving certainty. I wondered what she might know that she wasn't telling us. "Go on," she said.

"The tunnel Brand pointed out seems the best bet for getting down there. We'll all make our way down, and we five," I said, jerking a thumb at those who would remain behind, "will stay inside. You and Resa will sneak in. Or march through the front door, whichever seems best." I gave a nervous snort and immediately sobered. "Are you sure?"

Carina nodded.

"What is it that you know?" I asked.

She touched my face, my hand. "Nothing I can tell you."

With that, we left the *conjures* behind and followed Brand to the upper opening. Bending over it, I wondered if we'd make it down without breaking our necks. I quickly flashed the kinetic torch down inside and turned it off. There were protrusions to hold us in descent. At least as far as the light had reached.

"I'll go down first, I said. "Ren, can you take the rear? We can offer help from both ends as we go down."

Ren nodded his agreement. Nothing guaranteed we wouldn't reach a point we could go no further, or that we might not all tumble into a very painful heap at the bottom. But the *conjures* had seemingly pointed us in this direction and I was going to clutch that straw with all my might.

I blew out a heavy breath and threw my leg

over the edge. "Here goes nothing," I said. I didn't know exactly what the expression meant, but I'd heard Gran use it more than once. Good enough for Gran was good enough for me.

Grace

Chapter Thirty-Seven

So far, I'd been treated reasonably well. I had been made comfortable, provided with food and water, was only subject to Moros' false pleasantries and casual conversation in brief intervals. It seemed Moros was waiting, that he had some foreknowledge my friends would come. Or perhaps not foreknowledge, but another means to lure them here.

Breaking out through the chamber door had proven impossible, even when I placed a broken stone in the latch to keep it from securing properly. The stone had been discovered. The strange, lumbering guard who escorted me to and from had tsked at me like I was a child, popped the stone out, shoved me across the floor, and then shut and re-locked the barrier.

My intent now was to try to loosen the bars in the window. Not with the objective to climb out. That would have been foolish. But the bars were long, easily as long as my absent *lathesa*, and would come in handy as a weapon.

Hearing the door latch rattle, I abandoned my

attempts at the window and rushed across the floor to sit on the bed—having no chair—pretending innocence.

The door swung inward. A hulking shadow fell across the floor. I crossed my arms over my chest.

"What is it you want now?" I demanded. "It's the middle of the night."

"The middle of the night," said the guard, "and yet you do not sleep."

"That's correct," I said.

"Then you will come with me."

"Very well." I got up and followed. I had grown tired of my own sullenness, yet it was the only defense I had right then against worry and fear. Again, as with every time I entered the corridor, the only ones in it were the guard and me. We walked to the study, I with long strides, the guard still seeming to float before me even though I could see boots touching the floor. The hood never revealed a face.

The entire floor where I was housed appeared to be empty except for us three. Any noise I heard filtered in from outside, occasionally from inside, but very little from below sounded substantial. However, with the stone block construction, I supposed there could be an entire army down there, unheard.

This time when I entered the study, and despite the ridiculous hour, food was spread across the tabletop with two plates and utensils at either end.

"Sit down," Moros said. "We will eat while we talk. Very civilized and all that."

"It's the middle of the night," I said, repeating my words to the guard.

"And yet you do not sleep," he answered, mimicking the guard's response. I glanced back, wondering if Moros controlled the guard somehow, or merely had set up some listening device in the room where I was being held. The hulking figure had silently disappeared. I made my way over to the chair nearest the short staircase, slid it out and sat.

"What would you like?" Moros asked, waving his hand above the offerings in congenial fashion. I was in no mood to be deceived.

"Water," I said.

"You're not hungry?"

"I've grown used to eating very little." I stared at him, trying not to betray how unnerved I felt every time I witnessed the similarities to Duncan. I would have said they were identical, but Moros sometimes carried himself differently, spoke with a distinct inflection not Duncan's. They'd been raised on different planets, so I supposed the latter was inevitable.

He passed me water in a glass and I drank, watching from beneath lowered lashes while he ladled food onto his plate. I had eaten earlier, before nightfall. I truly had no appetite for more, and especially not in his company.

What I did desire was to find out more about him. Strengths and weaknesses. Plans. Powers. Intentions. He'd regaled me with his sorry history, his upbringing in a household which seemed little better than what Ren had had to deal with. His anger at his parents for letting him go. His hurt and his contrary gratitude because, as he said, had they kept him, he would have missed out on so many opportunities. When I'd pushed him about those opportunities, he'd change the subject. Thus far, I'd succeeded in saying very little about myself, and nothing about my friends or where they might be.

"Moros," I began.

"The Darkness," he said, releasing at that moment a little power, like an animal its scent. It drifted across the room, enveloped me in tangible display.

I managed to ignore it. "Mm, yes," I said. "Anyway, I have a question." I put myself in danger with my insolence, but hoped to draw him off his guard, perhaps force him to reveal something he did not want me to know about himself.

"Go ahead," he stated after a brief hesitation. Hard-toned, unsmiling.

I took another sip from my glass. "What are your plans for me?"

He leaned back in his chair. "You mean, for you and your friends."

"No," I countered, "just me. My friends are safe and will remain that way."

Good bluff. You don't even sound like you're lying.

I didn't allow my face to change at Skelly's words, merely drank again.

"You're wrong," said Moros. "They are on their way here."

"I'm afraid you're the one who is wrong," I said. "My friends and I have certain abilities which enabled us to make sure you believed they were on their way. This, of course, is false."

Oh, you are so good at this. No wonder I thought I might come to like you someday.

I had never been good at pretending, not really, but when my life depended on it—and my friends' lives—I managed my heretofore unknown talent well. Moros leaped from his seat. I tensed, ready to defend myself. He strode past me, though, and pounded down the three steps to the corridor. As he had before, he returned grumbling. And frightened, I thought.

He looked at me, eyelids twitching. "You don't hear that?"

"What does it sound like?" I asked. "Maybe I do, but I wouldn't know unless you tell me. In my chamber I heard an animal outside. Is it something like that?"

"No, it's not anything like that!" he shouted.

I stared at him, waiting.

"It's—it's nothing," he said, and slouched once more into his chair.

Reaching forward, I pulled what appeared to be a bird's leg from a platter, coated with bread crumbs, perhaps, and baked, brown and glistening. I set it on my plate, pierced the meat with a fork and placed a tiny portion in my mouth. I wanted to vomit. Not from the taste, but from nerves, nerves I couldn't let him see. I chewed and swallowed.

"What do you want with my friends, anyway?" I went on, taking another bite, chewing slowly, swallowing again, rinsing the part stuck in my throat down with water.

"I thought you weren't hungry."

I shrugged. "I changed my mind. It smells good."

He jerked his foot up onto the chair seat, knee bent nearly to his chin, and studied me over black fabric. "You're quite a bit colder than the tales say."

I glanced at him and back to my plate, as if unaffected by his words. "Colder? I suppose. I've learned to be that way. A skill hard won. It helps me. Every day."

Skelly remained quiet, for which I was glad. Unnerve Moros too much and I might get no answers. Worse, he might lash out in the same way I could. I had no idea what powers he possessed beyond whatever he had done to bring me here, his ability to control others, and his attempts to alter from a distance our thought processes, mine, and my companions. Enid believed he'd been performing the latter, and I trusted her to know. He wasn't doing it now, though. I wondered if he couldn't any longer, if we'd somehow permanently disabled that link with Enid's assistance.

"Your friends will come for you," Moros said, as if there had been no break in our conversation.

I set my fork down on the plate's edge. "No, they won't," I insisted. "Besides your futile hope, why would you even think that? We discussed the possibility something might happen to me and they are under strict orders not to look for me. Only to keep you misled."

"Orders? So, you do command them."

Reaching for the pitcher, I poured myself more water. He watched me, the air around him starting to hum.

"I need you all here, including the expendables," he said. "Rumors fly about how close those you've gathered beside you have all become. The others,
well, their lives are my guarantee you, the witch, and the powerful child will do as *I* command."

In that moment, I envisioned throwing him across the room with such force he would shatter. Realizing I could do that very thing, I reined in my emotions, my temper. Moros was Duncan's and Resa's brother and though I hadn't yet figured out if he even knew or cared about the relationship, I determined there had to be a better way than destruction.

Are you serious?

At Skelly's question, Moros' gaze delved into all the shadowed, cobwebbed corners. I stood. If Skelly was to go on unnerving him, I would get no more answers.

"Thank you for the meal," I said. "I'll return to my room, now."

"No!"

The dishes flew across the chamber, slamming, shattering, against the barren wall. Spattered food and water dribbled over stone. Cutlery, glass, and porcelain, all very fine, glittered in shards on the floor. My exploded heart reformed in my chest. Silently, I counted back from ten, calming its racing rhythm.

"You've made quite the mess," I said. I managed not to flinch as I anticipated a violent reaction to my words. Nothing happened. Nothing at all. I cut my gaze in his direction. Moros stood, arms at his side, head bent, staring at the empty table.

"I didn't mean to do that. I'm sorry."

My eyebrows rose.

He's lying, Skelly whispered.

Perhaps not, I said.

You're an idiot.

"I can help you clean up," I suggested.

"No, Valard will do that."

I assumed he meant the person who escorted me. I wondered how frequently Valard cleared up the aftermath from Moros' tantrums. Despite his powers, Moros seemed more troubled than anything else. I couldn't imagine how he accomplished control over the intricacies related to war. War was an ugly tapestry whose threads were infinite and he had not the skill to weave.

"Why are you alone?" I asked suddenly.

"I'm not!" A quick and aggressive response and an obvious lie.

"I've not seen anyone else," I said, "except for—Valard, is it?"

"You know nothing," he ground out.

"Probably not," I answered in an agreeable tone and headed for the truncated staircase.

He took a step in my direction. "Where are you going?"

"Back to my cell." I set my foot to the first tread.

"It's not a cell!" he shouted after me.

"My mistake," I said, stepping down another. My hand on the railing shook. The other I shoved in my pocket so we wouldn't see.

"Wait. Wait!"

I did, holding my breath, hoping my attitude wouldn't drive him to attack but to open up. I knew he was alone. In the time I'd been here, I had not heard or seen anyone but him and this Valard. Moros might be coerced to share his secrets for the sake of conversation.

Moros hurried across the floor and down the stairs until he stood beside me. "I'm not alone. Really, I'm not. May I show you something?"

I released my held breath. "All right."

"This way," he said, and bounded down the last step to the floor below. In the corridor, he waited for me and walked by my side. I didn't want to be reminded of Duncan, and yet I couldn't help it. They possessed the same stride, the same height. The same face.

"Where are we going?" I asked, prudently preparing for danger while trying to ignore the fact I had expected a certain amount of hatred and evilness to emanate from Moros. I felt none.

May I say again you're an idiot?

I ignored Skelly, and Moros seemed unaware of him in a corridor where our footsteps echoed off the walls. We took several turns through into smaller, dimly lit hallways, finally halting before a door similar to the one which sealed me into my chamber. The building was far larger than I'd assumed. Yet, in all our walking, we'd passed no one else.

I stopped Moros before he could manipulate the latch. "Who else lives in this building? I assume that's who you want to show me. Sometimes, I hear vague noises from below, but I don't know what they are."

"Are you afraid?" he asked, almost hopefully.

"Curious," I said.

He didn't want to believe me. I could tell he didn't. But as I exhibited no over fear, he found himself forced to accept what I said. Throwing open the door, he stepped aside so I could precede him. I did, striding out onto a protected ledge, a balcony perhaps. The air felt frigid. We were higher up than I'd been able to tell from the small window in my room. Perhaps the structure had been built into a mountain. That would account for the shorter distance to the ground in back and the unnervingly high perch where I stood now.

The stars overhead shone brightly, revealing mountains opposite a valley. The stars seemed to shine there, too, in the vale among the trees. I realized with a start they were lights, but not from a town. I saw no structures. The scene appeared more like a vast, sprawling encampment. I moved to the carved railing, curled my hands over it tightly, looked down.

Moros came and stood beside me. "You see," he said, "not alone. What do you think?"

What did I think? I thought about my friends, trying to make their way through that valley, undiscovered. I thought about my family, the desert tribes who'd taken up arms to battle forces they likely didn't fully comprehend. I thought about everyone I'd met in the course of our journey, ally and enemy. I thought about the elusive reasons for this war, motives steeped in confusion, misinformation, self-interest, darkness. I thought about Moros, wanting to change the world. What did that even mean?

He took a sliding step closer. Beneath his vest, the hem on his tunic-length shirt snapped in a sudden breeze as he indicated the lit valley with a sweeping finger. "Look at them. More than I would ever have expected."

"Whose are they?" I asked, gripping the railing more tightly. I needed to know.

He chuckled, an intimate sound reminding me of quiet moments with Duncan. I shivered.

"They are here for me, Grace," he said. "And

now, they are here for you."

I backed away from him and from the railing, the dizzying height, resisting the urge to put my hands over my face. The entire army below commanded by a boy no more than a year older than me. It was not unknown. History spoke about them, leaders of such an age and, I suspected, a different caliber. Yet, Moros held sway over more than those encamped in the valley. He had somehow managed to influence others to help achieve the chaos he desired. To what end?

"What do you mean, they are here now for me?" I asked him.

"When your friends arrive, you will know."

"They aren't coming. I told you that."

He shrugged. "I don't think I believe you anymore."

"Then you'll be disappointed. How often have you been disappointed, Moros? Is that why you seek destruction? Pandemonium?"

His expression altered. A twitch, a hardening, transitioning from calm to anger. "You don't understand," he said. "No one understands."

I braced myself. "Explain it to me. I'm listening."

The floor vibrated beneath my feet. Lightly at first, but soon much stronger. The buzz from it coursed through my head, causing me to stagger back.

"Afraid now, are we?" he called over the sound. "Go ahead, Grace, you can admit it."

"I'm not," I said. "Not afraid. But that noise—what is it?"

As if you don't know, Skelly's voice slithered in response.

Moros jerked his head from side to side. "You don't hear that?"

"No," I said.

"You lie!"

Run.

Moros had left the door slightly ajar and I darted through the narrow space, stumbled off balance, righted myself, bolted away. The door cracked in two with explosive force behind me, the segment not attached to the wall rocketing past and slamming to the floor. I leaped over the wooden slab and kept running.

Racing down side halls, seeking a door or a stairwell, or a window with a ledge where I could climb out, I quickly lost my way. I could hear him behind me, never getting any closer, as if he toyed with my nerves or knew I had nowhere, really, to run. Every so often, stone would crack and fall. Nothing too large. I could tell that much. More like rubble. Enough to keep me moving and to not impede his progress.

I had no idea if Moros' strength surpassed mine. In physical combat, he'd likely be hard put to beat me, yes, but he had mage gifts, too. Gifts he'd had longer to master, to learn their extent and how to control them or, as with the damaged door, permitted emotion to override restraint.

"Grace!"

I didn't falter.

"Grace, listen to me!"

Turning a corner, I heard sounds at a distance.

Not voices. Something different. I couldn't change my direction. No side passages existed here, and he was coming. The oddly empty corridors provided nothing I could use as a weapon.

You don't need a weapon, Skelly whispered.

I frowned. *I can't take the chance.*

Don't be a sentimental fool.

Not troubling to answer him, I hurried on. The voice-like murmurings seemed louder, as though they echoed beneath an elevated ceiling somewhere.

"Grace!" Moros cried out in a sudden, desperate screech. "Stop! You must stop!" He skidded around the corner behind me and halted. I had reached a stairwell. I paused, too, glanced back, found him standing stock-still at the corridor's far end, his eyes wide. Amber eyes. Duncan's eyes.

"What do you want to change in this world, Moros?" I asked him. "Why do you want to rule it?" Skelly prodded me, wanting out. I pushed him back down.

"This world was once beautiful," he answered.

"It's still beautiful."

"Not like it was," he said. "I've seen it." He took a single step, stopped, looked past me with fear in his eyes, and then back again. "It's all in my grandmother's library. In all those ancient volumes. The stories that are no more."

I started walking again, backward. He held up a hand. I jerked mine up, too, a powerful surge rushing through me, but I kept it inside. It hurt, the power did, cut off in that manner. He'd lowered his hand, though, against his thigh. I did, too.

"What was can be again," he said.

He wasn't making sense. He sounded sad, and desperate, and not quite sane.

Didn't you think that once about me, Skelly whispered. I paid him no heed.

"What makes you think your way is the right way?" I yelled at Moros as I spun toward the darkened staircase.

"Don't! Don't go down there!"

I did anyway. I shouldn't have.

Duncan

Chapter Thirty-Eight

There had been another low-voiced argument, a last-ditch effort for us to stay together. It was so hard to let them go, even though Carina's plan made far more sense than anything I tried to come up with instead. Mika and I had watched from just outside until darkness took them, Carina's white hair covered by a blanket to decrease the chance they might be spotted. Now, Mika sat in the flume opening, arms around his updrawn legs, staring into the night. I could barely see his face. What I could see tore me up inside.

Brand slid down from his rocky perch to stand beside me. "Now they're gone, I should head out an' track 'em, yeah?"

I turned sharply, looked at him. "What?"

"Some 'un should make sure they get inside, see where they go in, come back with word if things go wrong. Ought t' be me. I'm not as important to this group as the rest o' you. If I get caught an'—you know—it won't matter as much. Won't influence anyone to give in."

"That's crap," growled Mika from the ground.

"I can keep an eye—"

"No," Mika said, pushing himself upright. "There are two things wrong with what you said. One, we're not gambling their lives. Until we hear from them, we do nothing. This is a big risk and it's killing me, but I understand Carina's reasoning. And two…"

We waited. Mika cleared his throat. "And two, you're one of us, just as important as anyone else."

Brand turned his head away, likely so we wouldn't see his face. What Mika said had moved me, too. Mika stepped forward, halting right before the ledge dropped off to the broken ground below. I saw his hands, the shadowed shape they formed rolling into tight fists.

"It'll be okay," I said. He didn't answer. He believed it about as much as I did. Yet I clung to the words as if to truth. I had to.

Mika slid over and I moved in next to him, staring up into the night sky filled with stars. I'd never had a best friend, let alone this many friends, period. I'd had pals, cohorts, eventually the like-minded Grif-Drif members as companions. Until I'd gotten locked away in a facility meant to break me, maybe even end my life, and was saved by meeting Grace, Mika, Carina.

I recalled the first time I saw Grace. Not the images I'd been made to study in order to give my false testimony. I'd been so miserable at that point I hardly noticed what I observed except for the particulars I was meant to remember. Even in the courtroom, I hadn't really looked at her. I couldn't. It would have been too much.

When I'd followed her down the corridor in the facility, half hoping she would kill me then and there,

I'd been gripped by the way she walked. Like I expected a warrior would. Proud. Confident. Refusing to be broken.

Her expression had reflected the same, despite her rage and disgust once she learned my identity. I had deserved her contempt, but instead, once she'd calmed down, she'd offered compassion, concern, friendship.

Forgiveness, too. I wouldn't ever forget that.

I bit my lip, blinked several times, trying to flap the idiotic moisture from my lashes. Beside me, Mika sniffed, trying to stifle the noise. We were in similar states, thinking about similar things. I knew how he felt about Carina. We all did, even though they'd never been really obvious with their relationship. Like an old married couple. Yeah, that was them.

Grace and me? That seemed to be something for later. I understood why. But I very much feared there wouldn't be a later.

Thinking about Grace and my sister and Carina in that big, ugly, foreboding building made my heart pound. Thinking about the danger we were all in made it pound harder. I wished I had even a portion of the power my siblings possessed. Why had I been passed over? It seemed decidedly unfair, given what we were all facing.

I glanced back into the blackness behind me. I listened to the sounds made by rustling clothing, indrawn breaths, a few whispered words between Ren and Hannah I couldn't quite make out. I didn't think anyone here knew how much they meant to me. Even Ren. Even Hannah. They were different than the rest of us, sure. Different didn't necessarily mean bad. It was sometimes hard to take, though, and yet I knew I'd give whatever I could to keep every single companion safe. Every friend.

"You okay now?" Mika whispered.

"Yeah," I said. "You?"

"Uh-huh."

"Liar," I said and laughed, just a small noise. He echoed it. After a moment, I asked in a voice I hoped didn't carry to the others, "How long do we give them? Really?"

"As long as it takes," Mika answered. "We have to."

Yeah. Okay.

I folded my arms across my chest, inhaled and filled my lungs, then let the air out slowly, as if my frustration deflated me. In a way, it did. Imagining myself a hero, when all I could do was stand around and wait.

"Brand," I called quietly over my shoulder. He appeared behind me. "You have the best vision. Can you see where they are now?"

I stepped aside so he could move past me. "Mika," he said, "could I borrow that thing o' yours? What d' you call it?"

"A telescope," Mika answered, handing the instrument to him. "And it's not mine. It's Enid's."

Even without it, I distinctly saw light burning on the building's top floor, as well as the structure's shape against the sky. The fortification's base remained lost in darkness. Brand fitted the telescope to his eye, gazed down along the mountainside. Suddenly, he sucked in a quick, tight breath.

"Do you see them?" I shifted my position until I stood at his shoulder, narrowing my eyes to follow the line formed by his head, his eye, the telescope.

"No," he said. "They're not anywhere. I see somethin' else."

I almost grabbed Enid's device from him. "What do you see?" I barked quietly.

"Hold on." He fiddled with the lenses. "Shadows. Moving up the slope."

I swore, scrambling for the blades on my belt. "Mutants?"

Brand snapped the telescope down, shoved it back at Mika. "Not unless they started carryin' weapons," he said.

* * *

We did the only thing we could. We hid.

As quietly as possible, we scrabbled our way back up the flume. The tunnel's narrow dimensions would work to our advantage. If those outside were fully outfitted and possessed any girth at all, they'd be hard put to get inside. Their entry would be limited to one at a time. Disabling the first to stick his head in would hold up the entire contingent. Of course, if they had no real idea we were here, we only had to remain silent until they moved on.

A sweaty tang filled the cramped space. We'd been wearing the same clothes for days. More than days. Bathing since Enid's had once again been, well, non-existent. Like pack animals, we'd gotten used to our own scent, but it suddenly seemed overwhelming.

The warriors advancing outside made little noise. I worried this meant they did know we were here, after all, and were trying not to alert us to their approach. My muscles tensed. I had taken up a position closest to the bottom, nearest the opening onto the mountainside. This had been accepted without argument. I'd had to repeatedly debate my leadership with Ren early on, but when Grace had been hurt, I had stepped into her role without complaint. I supposed they all remembered this. Or perhaps they sensed the change in me since leaving Trill. Sensed the fact only I, among all of us, had seen true battle.

My experience meant little. That day had been filled with action and reaction, automatic at best. I had been determined afterward to never repeat it. Unless I had to. Perhaps, this was the moment.

I hoped not. I really did. But I would do what needed to be done.

Listening to sounds from outside, we conversed with touch and the smallest whispers. Brand indicated by passing the message that he would make his way up top to check the area above, just in case we had to make an escape that way. He was the stealthiest among us. As a hunter for Trill, he could track and move in total silence. I sent back my agreement by a thumb pressed into Mika's hand, which continued through each person behind him. At what point Brand departed, I had no idea. I didn't hear him. I wasn't meant to.

I'd never been the most patient person. Not impatient with people so much as with myself, my own forward motion. Ants in my pants, Gran used to say. Whatever that meant. Always on the move, I supposed. Unable to sit still. Wanting to discover and learn and accomplish without the steps in between. I insisted I didn't need the various steps, and often found out the hard way how very wrong I could be. Except for Ren and sometimes Hannah, my friends weren't like that. They were considered, careful, occasionally impetuous when the need arose, but otherwise being among them kept me grounded. I needed them. I didn't know what I would do when we went our separate ways. Like Grace had recently admitted to, I didn't want us to ever be apart.

Such a strange development. Even among the Grif-Drifs each of us acted alone. It wasn't a team sport. We met for certain purposes, but otherwise our lives were lived among our marks. No camaraderie, no cozy, homey feelings. Nothing like my life with Gran. She'd grounded me, too.

Mika bumped my shoulder. I looked at him.

"You're dozing off," he whispered against my ear.

"Nah," I whispered back. "Just thinking."

He pointed, then, toward the opening. I realized I could see his finger, his hand, his sleeve. My own legs and the blade in my grip. The sun would soon be up. I signaled to the others to carefully move back, away from the growing light.

We'd barely retreated into the darkness when a shadow shifted across the opening and onto the rock inside. I slipped the glass cutter from my belt, too, but didn't activate it. However, I now had a blade in each hand. We'd only been able to bring the smaller weapons down into the hole. The bulkier ones supplied by Enid had been hidden above with our packs.

With breath held, I watched, hoping whoever stood out there would move past. Although the opening could be easily defended, if the soldiers or whoever they were had already headed up top, we'd be trapped in here, blocked from either end. Chances for survival would be...well, not in our favor.

After several lengthy minutes, the shadow moved away. Sunlight sparked on the mica in the stone. Just a glint, quick and hopeful, before the shadow returned. From the shape, a man. He dropped to his knees and shoved shoulders and head inside, allowing the daylight to filter in around him. A long blade extended up from his hand, pointing directly at me where I'd been hunkered down.

"Come down out of there now," he said. "All of you."

A dry chill coursed along my skin. I recognized the voice. Draig. My traitorous uncle.

Grace

Chapter Thirty-Nine

A sound rose up from a place so black I couldn't see into it. A sound like my name. My thoughts went straight to the mimicry in the mammoth forest on Emerald, causing my breath to catch. I paused on the stairs, my hand on the railing, straining to see what lay hidden in the dark. Behind me, daylight seeped in from above, somehow not penetrating to the lower floor, as if the blackness was somehow solid.

Moros is right, said Skelly suddenly. *Don't go down there.*

Cold enfolded my veins like frost at the terror in Skelly's voice. He feared very little, disembodied and protected within the crystal. In fact, only one thing. The thing that had killed him.

More than one, he said, a bare whisper.

I knew. Of course, I knew. I had that tragic day waded into the fiendish gathering to rescue Duncan. It had already been too late for Skelly Shane.

"Are they down there?" I asked, aloud.

A surging tide.

Moros was a fool. Exactly like Stone Tiran. How did either one believe they could control these creatures? This would explain why Duncan's brother was calling me back. He'd never be able to use me as planned if I got myself torn to shreds. The way Skelly had been, I thought, and felt him writhe in remembered agony. I hated that he possessed the memory. No matter what I might feel about him, the recollection of his brutal demise was not something I wished him to suffer.

Grace, he said so unobtrusively I almost didn't hear him, *thank you.*

I slammed a sudden tear from my lashes with the heel of my palm and started back up the stairs, away from the swirling chaos I sensed in the dark below. A small landing broke up the staircase between the lower floor and the upper where I'd left Moros and I paused there. Moros had ceased calling me, but I heard other noises now. Like someone suffering. I took another step in his direction, placing my hand on the wall. My fingers hit a latch. I lifted it, turned the handle sharply on a small door. I expected to find it locked. Instead, the door swung toward me—with force. I threw myself backward into a defensive stance, narrowing my eyes against the piercing light that followed. Almost immediately, the glare was shielded.

"This way," said a voice.

Carina.

A relieved breath tore from me. I followed, pulling the door closed behind. Once inside the narrow passage, I called the mage-light to my palm, a gentler illumination than the kinetic torch in Carina's hand. Resa stood behind her, wide-eyed and watching us both.

"Just the two of you?" I asked.

Carina nodded. "I got your message, loud and

clear."

"How are the boys?"

"Pissed off," she answered, using a term I'd never anticipated hearing from her mouth. "Worried."

"It can't be helped," I said.

"And the mutants? That's what I feel, isn't it?"

I nodded. "They're on the floor below this one. I can't imagine how they're being contained, but they must be, or they'd have been up those stairs the moment they sensed me. Or sensed Moros, for that matter. It's not like they care who they destroy, even if he fancies himself in control of them."

Carina's mouth settled into a very thin, un-Carina-like line.

"What's going on?" I asked.

She shook her head. "Nothing."

"Carina?"

She took Resa's hand and turned, leading me away from the closed door.

"Carina?" I prompted again.

"There's something wrong here," she finally answered. "In this place."

I could have told her that. But I knew she meant something more than the obvious. Something I'd vaguely detected, too. Something that didn't quite make sense, even in the present situation.

"I think I feel it, too," I said, "but I don't quite understand—"

"There's no one else here," Carina cut in, speaking quickly. "In this whole, vast building, we've come across no one else since entering. The mutants could be a reason why, but as they seem to be confined, that makes no sense either."

"Besides Moros," I said, "I've only had contact with the one guard. I've haven't seen his face yet. Or anyone else."

"I assume that struck you as odd."

I arched a brow at the slight sarcasm in her tone. "It did."

"I wonder if he is being held here. Moros."

My eyes widened. "You mean by someone else?"

"Perhaps," she said.

"Carina, do you know something I don't?"

"Only what I feel, and what I'm feeling is making me very unhappy."

Carina's Tansi accent could become emphasized when she was stressed, as it did now. Still, I'd understood her well enough. "Can you describe it?" I asked her.

Releasing Resa's hand, Carina raised hers to either side, palm out, reaching toward the walls in the narrow corridor. Her head dropped back. Her pale hair tangled in the blanket around her shoulders. The strands gleamed pink from the mage-light in my hand.

"Deception," she said, "and sorrow. Pain. Confusion. Anger. A salted wound."

That was enough to be getting on with. It seemed to me exactly what Moros might feel, were he imprisoned here. I touched Carina's arm, thanked her.

"What's next?" Carina whispered. "Are we leaving?"

"I'm not sure," I said.

"What is it you're thinking?"

"I need to find out more."

With a nod, Carina led the way again. I didn't question how she and Resa had found me. I had no need to. Between the two, they could see and hear and know more than anyone else could even guess.

We exited the passage at the far end, not through a door but through a shattered opening in a dead-end wall. Upon stepping into the area beyond, I saw similar destruction on all sides.

"He has a temper, Moros does," Carina said. "I mean, this is him, isn't it?"

"Probably," I answered.

"And what does he want from us? Has he said?"

"Like the others, he wants to use us. To change the world. To make it beautiful again."

Carina huffed an unfamiliar word, possibly a Tansi expletive. Although I didn't recognize it, I gleaned the meaning from Carina's tone. A repetitive boom began as we stood there. It sounded like a distant and very large drum. A distinct and even beat, one loud, one louder, rolling back and forth over and over. I raced to a misshapen, blasted window where the bars had been bent and broken. Avoiding the sharp edges, I latched onto two, pulling myself up to peer outside.

"It's coming from out there," I said, glancing behind me at Carina and Resa. "I don't know what it is, but it seems to originate across the valley, not in it."

"It sounds rather martial," Carina said, after listening for a moment.

"Yes," I agreed, dropping down onto the floor, "it does. War drums. I didn't think anyone used those except in ceremony."

"Whose are they?"

I shook my head. "I don't know."

Not my brother. He'd never announce an arrival in that way. Yet, now that I found myself in the place where I'd been led since the Sleeping Myth, I finally recognized one thing. This was or would be the epicenter of chaos, the point where war converged.

"Grace?"

"We have to fix this."

"What?"

"We have to fix this," I repeated, recognizing I'd made a grave error. "We were meant to stay together. To *stay together*."

Swearing, I ran from the room into the next hallway, Carina and Resa at my heels. I raced up the stairs leading to the top floor where Moros lived restrained by powerful mage work, and not his own. Mage work that also kept in check the mutants guarding him from below. Because that's what they were. A vast guard to keep him contained. Afraid. Haunted by a threatened and horrible death every single day.

I couldn't imagine it.

Duncan

Chapter Forty

My knees banged down hard. I gritted my teeth, glaring up at my uncle from the rock-strewn ground sloping down from the fortified building looming above us. He'd hit me before, Draig had, during the battle in Trill. I remembered that incident. Not fondly. I really hadn't expected to ever see him again or I might have been better prepared to reciprocate.

I recognized my father in his thinner, younger face. A man I also did not know well and hadn't cared to see again either, until those last minutes before I left Trill and he fled with the rest of my family to Gabrilon. We'd had…a moment, I guess you'd call it. I still wore his ring on my right hand. He said it might come in handy at some point. Might help me. Yeah, it would come in handy about now if I stood up and punched my uncle in the face with it. But I wouldn't. Draig had my friends rounded up nearby, surrounded by his warriors.

To be honest, I'd started this particular

altercation. Kind of. Probably because I still stung from our last meeting. At this point, the man was about half again my weight and all of it muscle. I hadn't cared, but I could see now I should have chosen a better tactic in response to his questioning.

I clapped my hands on my thighs, rocked back onto my heels and stood. He took a step away, somewhat wary, yet a muscle began twitching in his jaw in what I thought might be amusement. Either that, or respect. I doubted the latter, though. He didn't seem to have much respect for anything except his own life choices.

Turning my head, I spat blood on the ground. My molars had crunched my inner cheek rather nastily. In the distance, from the mountains, I heard a rolling drumbeat. No one reacted to it, so I didn't either.

"Are we finished here, Duncan?" Draig asked in a deliberate drawl. He shook his braided, beaded hair from his face. When he did, I spotted with some satisfaction an expanding welt on his cheekbone.

"Depends," I said.

Wordlessly, he lifted a hand and signaled. My friends were dragged forward. All except Brand. He was out there somewhere, having made his way up the flume before Draig's arrival. I worried less about him than us. He knew how to stay hidden, avoid detection, stay alive.

"Leave them alone," I growled.

"I only want to question them," Draig said. "I expect after what they've just witnessed, they'll be happy to respond."

Hannah shook off the hand on her arm and marched up to my uncle, her red hair bobbing like a bird's tail and her pale eyes flashing fire. "We're not afraid of you," she said.

If he went after her, I'd take him on again, no matter how slim my chances. She'd be in love with me anew, I supposed, but I'd deal with that later. Draig eyed her up and down. I could see him thinking, wondering perhaps how to handle her, what he could get away with.

"You don't need to be afraid of me," he finally said. I gaped in surprise. "Who is it you think I am?"

"A bully!" she cried.

I brought my hand up to my mouth, covered it so my uncle wouldn't see my crooked, painful smile.

Draig glanced around at the warriors nearest him, then returned his attention to Hannah. "A bully?"

"You heard me," she said.

I couldn't help it. I laughed. Immediately, I held out both my hands in a placating gesture as Draig swung my way. I shrugged.

"You are the one who tried to separate my girlfriend, Grace, and Resa from us," Mika added, moving to stand next to Hannah. "Or are you going to deny that?"

Draig's eyebrows shot up. He looked around at his warriors again, wagged his head from side to side. Disbelievingly, I thought, as though he doubted the nerve of us.

"I needed to bring them to Gabrilon," he said, "and they were determined to continue west with the rest of you."

"Do you even know why we were heading into the west?" Hannah demanded. I shot her a look and she clamped her lips shut.

"I didn't really care," he said. "We needed them. All three of them together."

At the word 'together,' I glanced at Mika, Hannah, Ren, wondering if we should try to get a message to the girls somehow, let them know this latest development. No one was meeting my eye.

"Like everyone else," I said, hoping to draw their attention to me again, "with that damned prophecy. Needed them to help you in this war, so, you'd come out on top. That's what everyone wants. To triumph. Conquer. Or am I wrong?"

"You're not wrong," Draig admitted, sounding resigned. I frowned. He waved a hand at his warriors. "Let them sit."

He indicated I should sit also. I eased down on Mika's right. Ren lowered himself beside me. Hannah remained on Mika's opposite side, still looking defiant. I gave her an encouraging nod before turning to watch Draig's long legs pacing before us. We didn't plan to stick around. I could see that intent in everyone's eyes. We needed to get back to Resa, Grace, and Carina, or they to us.

I noticed the distant drumming had stopped, asked Draig what their purpose had been.

"They are not ours," he said. "Armies are converging on Gabrilon. They are being drawn here."

I swore silently, shooting a look at the black structure shining now in the sun. "This is Gabrilon?"

"You didn't know?"

I shook my head. It made sense, though. Of course, it did. We were all drawn here for a reason. Perhaps not the same reason, but it was meant to be.

"How are Mom and Dad?" I asked, flippantly. Recklessly. The last I'd seen them they'd all been fleeing to Gabrilon. "And Toma? How about the rest of the residents from Trill? Imprisoned, are they?"

Draig paused, brows lowering over his dark eyes. "Why would you think that? No, they are preparing for battle."

My stomach dropped. "Even Toma?" My little brother who barely reached my ribcage. What could he do? And why? How had Draig coerced any of them to fight with his warriors? I knew the answer to that. Moros. Moros had control.

"Toma is safely hidden away with the others who are not fighting," Draig answered, studying me.

"In there?" I jerked my thumb toward the fortified building, wondering if Grace had come across them yet. Maybe she was freeing them all, preparing to take them elsewhere. We needed to connect, to get some sense what was going on. But Mika, Ren, and Hannah seemed too intent on Draig and his words.

Draig crouched down, meeting my eye. "No. Far from here. You really don't know anything, do you?"

"I know I can't trust you," I said.

"As I said, you know nothing."

I held his gaze.

"I am a warrior. A nomadic warrior. It is not the easiest life. I often act with expedience, rather than refinement. But I am not your enemy, Duncan."

My mouth twisted. "Until recently, what did you do as a nomadic warrior?"

He appeared to take my question literally.

"Protected the law, settled disputes, helped when needed, no matter the task. Ever built a dam? It's a pain in the ass."

Releasing a slow breath, I searched his face, searched for the lie. I found none.

"And now?" I asked.

He dipped his head forward, his gaze even more intent. The beads in his hair clacked together. Disturbingly like tiny teeth. "We are trying to end this madness."

I chewed my lip a moment. "By siding with my brother? With Moros? By doing his bidding?" I did my best to sound adamant, accusatory, but failed.

"You know about him, then?"

I nodded.

"That's why you're here. The prophecy is holding true." He stood, reached a hand to me, yanked me to my feet. "Moros is secure, but we have not yet found a way to break the hold he has on the various factions. He is very powerful, your twin. My mother—your grandmother—was able to help him maintain a balance, but she also allowed him too much free rein, encouraged his fantastic and sometimes destructive views. She practiced the art of the dark mage and I believe she had plans for Moros. She passed away long before any of us knew what was going on. I didn't find out she'd died until I physically returned to this place. Even with maintenance, Moros still wreaked havoc in places beyond our borders."

My friends had clambered upright when I did. They listened in silence to Draig's explanation, eyeballing each other.

Draig jerked his chin at the edifice. "The Lady's warding still holds, though. He can't physically get out, although his mage-work can. There is one who guards him, who cares for him, who reports to us. He possesses a gift that makes him immune to what Moros is. Before she died, my mother added an extra deterrent."

"What do you mean?" I asked.

"Beyond those doors," he said, pointing to a huge portal, barred and chained on the lowest floor, "are housed creatures Moros fears more than anything. They were brought down from the prison planet. Not by us. By that fool, Stone Tiran. It is said the Lady purchased dozens from him, housed them here. Moros sees them in his nightmares. The black dreams started about the same time the stories of the prophecy began to circulate. The creatures are contained to the lower floor by the same warding that keeps Moros prisoner. The same that keeps us hidden in this valley—"

He checked, turned, looked at me, at Mika, as we snatched our weapons off the ground, taking our first running steps away from the rest. Several warriors moved in, blocked our path. I shouldered one aside, but the other two had Mika by the elbows. I waved the arm holding the glass blade, nearly slicing the swinging hair from a warrior's head.

"The valley is not hidden," I shouted at Draig. "We saw your lights last night."

Draig stared back at me, stricken. "This is grave news. If what you say is true about the valley being visible, the warding has started breaking down—"

I placed my right foot behind my left, walking backward. "Resa and Grace and Carina are inside. We're getting them out."

Draig lunged at me, missed. I knocked aside the warriors holding Mika. He and I dodged away.

"I order you to stop." Draig called after us. "Now!"

I made a rude gesture in his direction and started up the hill.

Grace

Chapter Forty-One

"Something's wrong, something's wrong," Carina kept whispering under her breath. I didn't stop her. It seemed to ease her mind a bit, expressing herself in this quiet way. It was very unlike her, though, and it unnerved me.

We walked with Resa between us, each clasping a hand, passing the chamber where I'd been kept. The door stood open, as it usually did when I was not there. The single guard had not made an appearance, nor had Moros. The convoluted hallways remained empty.

"He's not gone, is he?" Carina said in a low voice, breaking off from her chant.

"I don't know that he can leave," I said. "As you pointed out, he might be imprisoned here, himself."

Carina nodded, her eyes as red as blood, pupils huge in the dimness. The sunlight from outside barely touched us. The shadows appeared uninhabited, but I didn't quite trust them. Although the mutants seemed contained below somehow, I walked with the mage-light cupped in my palm, banked down to a low glimmer.

This is my life, now, I thought, *expecting death at every turn.*

And it may soon be your death for certain, Skelly muttered. *I want you to release me.*

I frowned at his words. *Why?* I asked. *Would you die with me?*

That's not what I meant.

He went silent, though. I could feel his contemplation, weighted and uneasy. I hadn't thought about it before, but now I'd questioned the possibility, the scenario curled through my mind, too. In the end, would this be the only way? I'd hoped—well, I'd hoped to somehow give him ease, despite the torment he presented. In this, no one had been able to give me an answer. No one could tell me what I needed to do.

"Grace."

I glanced at Carina.

"Is that you?" she asked.

I felt it now, too. A slight tremor beneath our feet and running through the walls. Not the threatening blast when Moros broke the door in two, but a different vibration, more pervading and, in its way, more sinister.

"Hurry," I said, and broke into a run.

As we neared Moros' study, I slowed again, approaching the abbreviated staircase cautiously. I
heard a voice inside. Moros, his tone agitated. Talking to himself? I didn't know. Below us, on the lower floor, a rumbling shook the structure's foundations. I raced up the three steps, skipping two. Carina followed directly behind with Resa

clinging to her hand. In the study, I skidded to a halt. Carina and Resa paused just out of sight.

Moros stood by the table with its domed scene. Keeping track of the armies or something darker? At the very least, I figured he'd want to know how battles were progressing, confirmation his machinations were working. At the worst, I supposed he could be using the objects inside to aid in manipulation through dark enchantments. I fought down the urge to blast the thing apart. If the domed scene was indeed mage-work, then any disruption I caused could be brutal, for both sides.

"Moros?" I called.

The nearly identical similarity between he and Duncan made me pause, even as I spoke his name. Yet I could see in his eyes he was nothing like his brother. Genetically, they might be the same, but his heart was not Duncan's heart. In Moros' amber eyes I saw a coldness I'd never seen in Duncan's. I saw anger, too, and confusion and deep-seated fear he fought with all the bluster he could manage. Because of this, his mage powers made him more dangerous than they might otherwise have done, but was he truly dark mage? The old being, new again? I didn't believe it. In my heart, it seemed Moros in loneliness and isolation had been influenced in ways that had warped him. Yet, we would have to stop him somehow. Stop him cold. I wouldn't hurt him, no matter what he'd
become. He was still Duncan and Resa's brother. Something else had to happen. Something had to be made to happen.

Oh, please, Skelly groaned. I paid him no heed.

"Moros," I said again.

His slowly curving smile made me wince. "You came back."

"Yes."

"Why?"

"To save you." I don't know why I said those words. They were the very worst I could have spoken to someone who thought he possessed the power to remake the world. Remake it into something he'd imagined from his grandmother's books. But I meant them. For Duncan's sake, for Resa's sake, for the sake of their parents and little Toma. For Moros himself, I realized.

You are a fool, Grace.

He wasn't wrong. Moros turned and sent a pulse our way like a raging storm. A thunderous crack filled the air. Stone fell and glass shattered. The violence broke against the counter measures we'd immediately formed around us, Carina, Resa, and me. Moros' eyes flew wide upon seeing them at my side.

"Don't fight me. You're not supposed to fight me," he ground out, teeth clenched, spittle flying from his lips. "You're on my side."

Shock caused me to falter. The counterforce wavered and he stumbled forward. Quickly, we got the shield up again, expanded it around us. Here and there, bits of ceiling rained down. One larger piece struck his arm. He gaped in surprise at the place it had torn his dark tunic. A bloody trickle ran over his skin.

"No," he cried. "No!"

He seemed horrified by the small wound and

dropped his attack, clutching his forearm and swinging his head to blindly stare about the chamber. The shadowed gaze in his ashen face finally rested on us. He held up his arm. "This can't be. I don't get hurt," he whispered.

The injury didn't look that bad. Though bleeding, it appeared superficial. Nothing to warrant the utter dismay in his countenance.

"We can help you," I said, lowering our defenses. "We'll tend to it." Carina shot me a look like I'd lost my mind.

Abruptly, he straightened his spine, started to laugh. "You know what this signifies, don't you?"

"That you're *lacethnea*," Carina hissed at him. I didn't know the word, but could guess the meaning.

He frowned at her but wasted no time puzzling over what she'd said. "I don't know what that is. I don't care. What I do know is the warding has collapsed. And I am free."

My flesh shifted over bone. Power tingled in my palms. I envisioned a violence I knew I could not contain and fought it. Carina touched my hand. I drew a breath, a deep, deep breath, watching Moros, waiting.

"I'm free," he said again, his gaze drifting downward to alight on Resa. Resa, moving toward him. I cried out and took a step in her direction, but she was already beyond my reach and nearer his.

Moros dropped to one black-clad knee. He draped his wounded arm across the other, observing her approach with a strange expression, apprehension tinged with wonderment, I thought.

His eyes followed
her hands as they lifted. I took another hesitant step. The shattered window gaped wide and dangerously close behind him. Resa's arms stretched toward Moros, her hands so much closer. My bowels churned. I pictured Duncan's brother—Resa's brother—cast out through that window and broken on the ground far below.

Instead, Resa pressed her fingers against his face. Moros closed his eyes, his eyes so much like Duncan's, and not like his at all. It occurred to me Resa might think Moros was Duncan. I wondered what would happen when she realized her mistake. Then I reminded myself this was Resa. She knew the difference. She had *seen* him.

In an abrupt movement, Moros grabbed Resa's hands away from his face and jerked upright. Anticipating the price he'd pay for his sudden reaction, I readied myself. Despite my expectation, he didn't whirl away through the window to debris and broken bones.

"I have a sister," he announced. My breath caught. Reaching up, Moros pressed two fingers to his temple, winced. "Two brothers, as well." His voice rose. "Why was this kept from me?"

I had no answer for him. Moros glanced down at Resa and back up to Carina and me. "A family I never knew."

"Yes," I said, filled with pity. Why, indeed, had no one told him the truth?

He stared around at the damaged room like he hadn't seen it before. Carina and I moved closer, slowly.

"Living in this terrible, terrible world," he said.

I couldn't tell if he referenced himself and his existence alone here, or once again the world he wanted, in his altered perception, to change.

"Why did they all lie to me?" he snarled. The air hummed around him. Resa looked up.

"Moros," I said in warning.

He raised a hand. I tensed, lifting my own, prompting a humorless laugh from him. "Give me time for this fight," he said. "I'm still sorting through the things she released into my head." He pointed at his sister beside him. "How did she do that?"

"I don't know," I answered.

"The thrice-gifted child," he whispered.

I exchanged a glance with Carina. She nodded almost imperceptibly. We took another step nearer. Beneath our feet, the floor shook.

"Moros," I said, "don't."

He recalled himself from his inner thoughts, looked all around with a perplexed twist to his brow. "That's not me," he said. "But I told you the warding is collapsing, so..." He sucked in a sudden breath. "It is collapsing!"

"Yes, Moros," said a voice behind us, "and the beasts are loose."

I spun to find Moros' guard filling the space at the stairhead. For the first time, I saw the face beneath the hood, a man's countenance as brutally scarred as the Lyoness had been. Ancient injuries from some other war. The worst were only partially concealed by a short, grey beard.

"They are almost here," the man said. "We

cannot stop them."

Wordlessly, Carina reached one hand to mine and extended the other toward Resa, who had come back to Carina's side. Our fingers connected, hands folding together. Power surged between us, a power to keep the mutants at bay. What happened next, however, was not our doing.

Duncan

Chapter Forty-Two

We were caught again before we'd gone very far and dragged back before Draig. I struggled against the hands clutching my arms. "Why are you giving up?" I screamed at my uncle.

Draig scowled at me. "I'm not giving up. But I'm not letting you go on a fool's errand. We need every man out here now. If the three have survived, they don't require rescuing anyway. Not by you and your friends. And if they haven't... If they haven't, may the gods help us."

He turned away from me, instructing his warriors to stand ready to attack the beasts if they exited the building. Obviously, he knew very little about the mutants to believe the warriors could face them unprotected. I tried to explain, but he cut me off.

"You will do what you are told. This is a military camp. We are at war. Orders will be obeyed or there will be consequences."

I nodded my head and relaxed my body, as if I yielded. What I really wanted was for Draig's warriors to believe me compliant and release my arms. They did, a moment later. Not due to any playacting on my part. A cascading sound like thunder filled the air. Everyone looked to the sky, still brilliant and clear, and then jerked around to face the black walls behind us on the mountainside. Huge cracks had appeared in the stone.

I took off running again, glancing back for pursuit, and finding instead only Ren, Mika, and Hannah close behind. Ahead, huge stone chunks dropped from the building, smashing into the ground. Displaced dirt and shattered rock plumed into the air like smoke. Draig's warriors abandoned any ideas as to our detention and hastily withdrew.

"How do we get in?" Mika panted beside me. "The door's barred."

"I don't know. We'll figure it out."

Hannah pushed up on my left with Ren. "What about those things? Those mutant things?"

"We block them out," I said, "the way we learned, and fight like hell."

"I'm scared," Hannah said.

I touched her on the arm. Lightly. "So am I."

She smiled at me, a sickly, wavering gesture. I turned away, scanning the wall for windows. None existed at ground level. The ones on the second and third floors were all barred, the space between upright metal too narrow for entry.

"Do you think Carina and Resa actually got in?" Ren asked, eyeing the windows, too.

"Brand didn't see them anywhere outside," I answered. "Draig and his warriors don't have them so, yeah, they have to be in there."

Mika loped ahead, his face pale and sweaty. "I'll check the back," he called over his shoulder.

"We'll all check the back," I said. "No one goes anywhere alone."

We headed to our left, where the least damage showed. Climbing the rough terrain as fast as we could still wasn't fast enough. I feared the building would collapse before we got everyone out.

Suddenly, I felt cold touch me. It ran over my skin like ice water. Pressed into my skull. I faltered, forgetting for a moment how to move my feet. The others had stopped, too. I froze, dazed, struggling for awareness. My weapons were in my hands, but I couldn't hold onto why.

Now, said a voice in my head. Grace's voice. I sucked in a breath, lurched around toward the others. As though electrified, they all seemed to react to the same call, eyes wide, consciousness stirring. We connected, blocking out the mutant's mind control. Responsiveness returned. Hurrying around the building, we searched for the way in Carina and Resa had used.

"Look!" Ren cried, pointing an extended finger. "Do you think we can fit?"

A small door stood partially open low on the wall. Drawing closer, I saw where the wood had been marked with a sharp object, maybe to let us know they'd entered here, Carina and my sister. Spotting the quickly incised letters, **C + M**, Mika made a desperate noise behind me.

"I don't think it's big enough," Hannah said to me. "It was probably a tight squeeze for Carina and your sister. And what if those things are waiting on the other side?"

Backing up several paces, I gazed up at the wall, looking for another way. The only option was the tiny door. My shoulders dropped. My jaw clenched.

"Okay. The packs will stay out here. Hannah—gods, Hannah, you're the smallest of us four. I'm sorry, it has to be you. I'll stick my head in for a looksee and if it's clear, you'll go in. We'll have to pass our weapons in to you, then wriggle in behind and—"

"Pray," Ren said.

I swore. Why had we ever agreed to let the girls go on alone? First Grace to rescue her parents, where she'd been seized, and then Carina and Resa?

"Because they gave us no choice," said Mika.

I groaned. "Was I talking out loud? Again?"

All three nodded. With another first-rate word, I shirked off my pack and rushed to the tiny door, my glass blade drawn and the kinetic torch in the other hand. Sliding onto the ground at the opening, I tossed the torch in first so it would illuminate the space inside. Light and shadow careened around. The hand with the weapon went next, followed by my head. My shoulders barely made it through. I twisted my neck, searching the area as far as I could. The empty passage sloped upward. Although the dimensions were wider than they were tall, the girls had to have gone on hands and knees. What the hell purpose did the door and channel even serve? Still, if I squeezed all the way in, I could possibly turn enough to take the weapons instead of Hannah and move on for the others to get inside.

I left the torch where it continued to roll and wrenched myself back out the opening to let everyone know.

"It's doable," I said. "I'll go first—"

Something tossed me like an untethered leaf. I crashed to the ground. I wasn't the only one. Everyone staggered and fell. Rolling, I swung my blade defensively. The ground heaved again. I heard a thunderous crack, worse than before, followed by Grace's voice.

Run!

We did. Behind us the stone blocks fractured like glass. When gravity took over, huge chunks shot out from mounting pressure caused by collapsing weight. They slammed the mountainside. We took shelter behind a large boulder. I didn't realize I was screaming the girls' names until Mika shook me hard. His face was gray with shock. Behind him, Ren and Hannah huddled together, guarding their heads with upflung arms.

The destruction seemed to last for hours, yet when the noise dissipated to a few, solitary thuds and we realized it was over, I looked up the sky. Dust filled the air, but I could still see the sun. It hadn't moved. However, Gabrilon, the fortified stronghold of Gabrilon, had been reduced to rubble. Again, I shouted the girls' names, less in hysteria than resignation. Nothing could have survived this.

Yet, I should know better than to think in absolutes.

Stone shifted atop a nearby debris pile, fell away. I leapt up and started running toward the movement, my heart in my throat, strangling my voice. While still several strides away, I saw a large slab tumble from the mound. A hand reached through the gap, followed by a head. Neither were human.

Pebbles rolled beneath my boots as I skidded to a halt. I shouted a warning, scrambled around on my belt for another weapon. A second head appeared above a semi-intact wall segment. The beast clambered over, leaped down. A third made an appearance. Still connected without conscious effort, I felt no ill effects. Neither did the others as they retreated to higher ground, calling me to follow. When a fourth and a fifth grappled their way free from the destruction, I realized higher ground would do us no good, and prepared to fight them.

Something flew past my head with a whine. A rushing mutant jerked backward and fell, close enough for me to see the hole where its eye had been. It didn't get up. The next met the same fate, rolling over the first and sprawling nearly at my feet. The last three hesitated, possessing enough intelligence to recognize a threat. On Emerald they'd fled Grace, too, after she'd killed so many. I looked over my shoulder, spotted Brand with his deadly aim fitting another rock into his slingshot.

Shouting, we all scrambled down to meet the

beasts. Without their mind control, they stood little chance to disable us before we reached them and in minutes, they were dead. I stared at the bodies, my limbs shaking, the beasts' stinking, hot blood spattered across my clothes. The rest, I hoped, had been crushed beneath the fallen building's weight. I gasped, even as I thought it.

"They're dead," I whispered.

"Them beasts?" Brand said. "Nothin' to cry over."

"No," I said, struggling for breath, for composure. "The girls. Resa and Carina and Grace. They were in there. They couldn't have survived. Could they?" I asked of no one. The cosmos, maybe. My brother had been in the building, too. I found I couldn't ignore his loss, no matter what he was or had been made to be.

Brand issued a noise from his throat, pushed past us. He paused, looking up at the intact wall, lifted his hand, pointed. "Nah. I saw 'em leave, from right there before the roof come down. In a black swirl like smoke. They weren't alone."

My breath rushed out. The dark whirlwind description was already familiar to me. Moros had taken them the same way he'd grabbed Grace before. This time, though, he had all three. I was grateful, yes. And I was afraid.

Grace

Chapter Forty-Three

I reached over to Carina in the dark and shook her gently awake. Not that she was sleeping. Not restfully. She'd been tossing in a struggle with nightmare. I recalled that from last time, the unsettled sleep, the physical and mental imbalance, the sense of falling without end. It didn't last long, though. I remembered that, too. Resa slept undisturbed on Carina's other side. Enid had said Resa was immune to her brother's gifts. Finding this proof before me filled me with relief. I didn't know how Resa would have reacted if she'd experienced what Carina and I did.

Carina mumbled something and rolled over. Mika's name, I thought. Her breathing regulated, evened out. Her limbs stopped thrashing. I wrapped my arms around my drawn-up knees and returned my attention to the window. We appeared to be in a house, an abandoned house, without illumination or furnishings. The sun had gone down while I'd been sitting in attendance on Carina and Resa, a soft glow filling the sky before nightfall. As darkness descended, the air came alive with tiny lights, like the firemites at home. While the sun still shone, I had seen trees and mountains. Now I saw nothing but the insects flitting with their lovely bioluminescence beyond the glass.

Peace settled over me while I watched the miniscule creatures. A conscious peace. An intentional frame of mind. The urge to yank Resa and Carina from the floor and run had been strong. But I had no idea where we were. We had no supplies. No weapons—although an argument could be made that we didn't need them. No direction calling me on. No reason to move.

It's like you've given up.

I drew a deep breath, ignored Skelly, continued my vigilant study through the window glass. My thoughts drifted from calm to unsettled. I wondered if Skelly prodded me that way, trying to bring me back from the peace to which I was desperately clinging. I found myself recalling the night I'd been taken from my home by Stone Tiran, followed by the trial and Duncan's false testimony. Then on to my imprisonment and our return to a world seething with war. To the many times, like now, when I'd been separated from my friends. From Duncan. I closed my eyes, pushed away all those distressing thoughts, determined not to remember. After a while I lifted my lids to view the flashing insects again. But they had gone.

Yes, I reminded myself, so it was with the firemites, too. Their brilliant, strobing dance always a brief one.

Perhaps this is my lot in life, too, I decided. Perhaps my brilliance is spent and my time is done.

"Grace?"

I pretended not to hear. Carina sat up, placed a

hand on my arm. I considered shaking it off, but decided I didn't care that much.

"Grace," she said again. "I can feel you. You have to come back from where you've gone."

"I'm right here," I murmured.

"You know what I mean. Don't give up. You never give up."

Don't I? I thought. Perhaps once this was true, the not-giving-up, but that Grace seemed to be slipping away.

Carina shook me, hard. Needlelike anger jabbed me, growing inside. The window started to vibrate in its frame.

"Please, Grace."

I stood in one fluid movement. My heart pounded. Emotion, many emotions, surged into a blood-red swirl behind my eyes. I couldn't see anything anymore. Not the window, not the insects, not my friends on the floor beside me. My chewed and tattered nails dug into my palms. My muscles tightened until they felt more like bone, my bones like fire. Suddenly, I heard Duncan's voice in my head, his connected, ethereal voice: *It'll be all right*.

I dropped to my knees and wept. Carina threw her arms around me. A moment later, Resa was there patting my face, looking me in the eye. Right in the eye.

"Sorry," I gasped out, pulling free from them both. I swiped both palms across my face, smearing tears.

"Nothing to be sorry about," said Carina in a crisp, cheery tone. Too cheery and too crisp. She wasn't fooling me. "Where are we, anyway? Do you know?"

"I don't."

"What about Moros and that big guy? Have you seen them?"

"Not yet," I said. "But Moros is here. I feel him."

Carina glanced over her shoulder. "I think I do, too," she said in disgust.

I flicked a few more tears from my lashes. "He saved us," I whispered.

"Because he needs us," said Carina. "And it was more like he stole us. But at least we survived," she added begrudgingly.

With the moments before we were whisked away from Gabrilon rushing back into my consciousness, I recalled something else. "The others were trying to get into Gabrilon just before the collapse. I warned them in time."

Carina's eyes narrowed. "Idiots. I told them to stay put." Her affection for them was as obvious as her dislike of Moros. I couldn't blame her. Perhaps the only reason I had any sympathy for Moros was due to his relationship to Duncan.

"I didn't feel them," she added. "How did you?"

I shrugged, unsure, and rose. I strode to the window, looking out with my arms crossed over my chest. Nothing looked familiar and yet everything looked familiar, the landscape seeming identical in the dark to what we had been traveling for many days. Not a single rock or tree or mountain hinted at where we might be, though. And me, with the map in my head no longer.

Carina came and stood beside me. Resa did too, pressing her face to the glass. Her gaze wasn't on the outside world, but on something beyond our sight.

"The walls were starting to come down before we got—whatever happened to us. Do you think the mutants were killed?" Carina asked.

"I hope so," I said. "If not, our friends are going to be in trouble." Carina bit her lip. I went on. "As for whatever happened to us, that was how Moros transported me the first time."

"Ugh. Twice for you, then."

My mouth twisted into a crooked smile. "Yes. Twice for me. Not a competition I meant to win."

Carina shorted. "And now?"

As if summoned by her question, the door flew open. I spun, flicking my palm out to cast mage-light into the shadows. Pink illumination highlighted the person standing in the opening. For a fleeting, insane moment I thought it was Duncan. Of course, I did. I had to stop letting that happen.

"Come with me," he said.

I was inclined to refuse. Instead, I took Resa's and Carina's hands and started toward the door. There seemed no point in refusing.

"Not you." He pointed at Carina and Resa, and then at me. "Just you."

"It's all or none," I said, standing my ground. After a short-lived standoff, he agreed.

"Fine. All of you, then."

We followed him out and along a corridor toward a lit room. "Where are we?" I asked. "What is this place?"

"This is Valard's home," Moros answered in a conversational tone. "He has not had need of it in a long time."

Carina stared at his back, trying to get a read on him. "Is he dead, this Valard? Is that why he has no need of his house?" she asked.

Moros laughed. "Dead? You met him. In Gabrilon."

I listened for signs anyone else moved about in

the small dwelling. "Is he here?"

"He went for supplies," Moros answered, sounding uncertain. I wondered how long the man had been gone. If he held no loyalty, he might not be coming back. I realized we must be close to a settlement, a military camp, or even a mountain village, if hope existed to find provisions. I stored this information for discussion with Carina later.

"In here," said Moros, signaling we should enter the lit room. We did, walking into an empty, high-ceilinged square. A torch, something like the kinetic torches we had carried, stood on each windowsill, power waning. They wouldn't last the night. Two other things were in the room. One, the *lathesa* Enid had given me. It leaned against the wall beside a cold fire well. The other I recognized straightaway, too, and strode over to it, Carina and Resa on my heels. Lifting my palm, I held the mage-light above the table, identifying beneath the dome the edifice that had been Gabrilon. It lay now in a tumbled mass. I recognized, too, the valley below, the mountains stretching out in all directions. The three-dimensional depiction didn't extend far enough to show Landing, The Wilds, Odgo, the desert provinces, but I had a good idea where they all lay.

Abruptly, I bent for a closer look. The tiny flags I had seen before appeared to be moving. I thought I imagined it until Carina stepped forward and gasped, pointing.

"Grace, do you see?"

I looked at Moros, asked the question I had not before. "Is this how you keep track of the armies?"

"Yes," Moros answered.

"And how you control them?"

He didn't reply right away. His gaze followed the

barely miniature movements beneath the glass for several seconds before glancing my way. "Yes."

I sucked in a quiet breath, my facial muscles tightening. "How?"

Moros shifted his position, cocking his head to one side. Duncan possessed that habit, too. I wanted so badly to stop noting the similarities between Moros and his brother. They confused me.

"Before you get the wrong idea," Moros said, "the representations only help me to focus. They are not the control itself. The variables are too many for that. I manage the control. In here." He tapped his head. "Still, when the warding broke, I couldn't leave this special treasure behind."

I moved my hand, bringing the light closer to the dome and the small movements within. He nodded toward my raised palm. "How do you make that light, by the way?" he asked. "Teach me."

Surprised, I held my hand out to him. "It's just mage-light. And I don't believe I can teach you."

His brow knotted. "What do you mean?"

"From anything I've ever heard, if one doesn't have an ability, it can't be given or taught." But was this true? The Sleeping Myth appeared to have given us far more than we'd expected.

"You mean, certain gifts are yours and the rest aren't?"

"Yes," I said. Enid had said so, too, and I had no reason to believe otherwise.

"I can't have them all?"

Slowly, I shook my head. He stared at me through Duncan's eyes, but it wasn't Duncan who lived behind them.

"But this can't be true," he said. "All gifts are meant to be mine."

I gazed back at him, willing myself not to flinch. Carina's breath whistled out through her nose. Moros didn't appear to hear it.

"A silly light doesn't matter. More important things require my attention."

"Of course," I said, feigning a deference I certainly did not feel. He squinted at my tone. I trod an uneasy path, trying to get information from him. If we were going to disable him, however, I needed to know his strengths and his limitations. "Who taught you in all this?" I persisted. "Who was your teacher?"

His eyes shifted away. I knew his next words would be a lie.

"I had no need of one," he said.

Oh, yeah, said Skelly. *He lies.*

Moros' head snapped up, turned toward the opening to the hallway. "Valard?" he called. I stilled and waited. He looked back at me. "Did you hear him come in?"

"I didn't notice anything," I said.

He glanced at Carina, who shook her head, and then at Resa.

"She doesn't hear," I said. "Not like you or me."

"Oh," he said, much like a revelation, and let it drop.

The dolt is as clueless as his brother, Skelly chuckled.

Moros hurried to the hallway in three quick strides. He stood in the opening looking first one way, then the other. I moved closer to the table.

"If he managed to bring this with him, undamaged—" I whispered to Carina.

"Then who knows what he's capable of," she finished for me.

"This is mage work beyond anything I might

have imagined. And yet—" I stopped, hearing him return.

"Impressive, isn't it?" he commented, pausing at my shoulder.

"Did you make this?" I asked.

His hands slipped behind his back. He rocked a little on his heels. "Yes," he said.

Another lie.

Moros startled again, but this time he didn't go running off to see if Valard had returned. Instead, he looked straight at me. I pretended I didn't notice his study, wondered if he thought I might be tricking him somehow.

"How do you control all these armies?" I asked.

Distracted from me, he made a dismissive noise and bent over the glass, his hands fidgeting behind his back. "You really don't understand, do you?" he said, impatient.

"You're right," I admitted. "I don't."

He straightened, still looking down. "I have no need to control the armies. I get into the minds of those who lead them. Their followers do as they are commanded in turn. It's easier, really. I only require control of a small number."

I exchanged a small, sidelong glance with Carina before returning my attention to him. He was erratic, was Moros. I began to see him as overwhelmed, especially with his admission about control. His statement that he possessed all gifts seemed extreme, and likely impossible. I suspected those gifts he did possess were more than he knew how to handle. In this, he likely felt as alone as I did. And as inherently dangerous.

"All the leaders," I asked him, "or just the aggressive few? The ones already inclined to war?"

He became quiet, the restless action of his hands behind his back growing still. "Does it matter?"

"It all matters," I said. "How could it not? But are you forcing people to fight who would otherwise choose not to?"

Eyes narrowing, Moros waved his clasped fingers in an odd gesture. "Those who are inclined will destroy each other. Those who are left...well, they will live their lives."

"Under your rule," I said.

He gave me a sidelong glance I couldn't read. "Maybe now Gran is gone."

He called his grandmother "Gran" like his brother. Two different people these women, yes, but odd how Moros and Duncan picked the same appellation. Or maybe not so odd. Twins shared many commonalities that had nothing to do with physical composition.

Snuffing the mage-light, I strode away from him to the window, where due to the fading lights on the sill I saw only myself and the room behind me. "What about those who fight only to defend their homes? What about them? Those people who are not inclined to war but are only caught up in what you started?" My thoughts went to the Ogdonians, the Kanon, the citizens of Citadel, the many others who had been peacefully living their lives until this.

In the reflective surface, he watched me, face shadowed. "I didn't start it. Others did. I stepped in after my grandmother went away."

"Died, you mean. That's what you said."

"She died after, not before."

I grunted, trying to assimilate what he was telling me. It seemed he left something out. Many somethings out. Maybe they were beyond him. Maybe he didn't remember. Maybe he just didn't understand.

I pivoted on my heel to face him again. "Everyone speaks about 'The Darkness.' I had no idea until recently the term referred to a person. To you."

"Everyone?" he echoed as if delighted.

"Don't let it go to your head," Carina mumbled.

Moros clenched his hands into fists. With effort, he straightened his fingers along his trousers. His belief he needed us appeared to be preventing rash behavior. For now. As for me, I was rapidly losing patience, which could be a risk to everyone in the room. I struggled against anger. I did not want to call forth the frightening power that had previously dashed everyone to the ground. Carina and Resa were standing too close to him. Besides, I had more questions.

Ignoring my tense stance, Moros pointed at the dome-covered map. "My grandmother used to observe the comings and goings of outsiders through this," he said. "To ensure Gabrilon remained unnoticed. To ensure its peace and security. But once she became ill, I found I could see what she didn't. Not under the dome, but in here." He tapped his temple again. "I saw and felt and knew so much. Things far away. Actions. Intentions."

Like Resa. My eyes swung in her direction. I spotted her crouched beside the table, staring into the dome. Her hands lifted. Moros' gaze followed mine.

"What are you doing, girl?" Moros demanded.

"Resa," I said, recalling how many times Duncan had been forced to say these very words in explanation. "Her name is Resa. And she can't hear you."

But perhaps she read his lips, because it seemed she responded in some way only he could perceive, something slipping into his mind the way he slipped his will into others. "Don't!" he screamed.

Before the echo of his cry died away, the domed table with all its various representations flew straight up into the air, smashed against the ceiling, and spun back to the floor in more pieces than could be counted. Moros fell with a shrill keen to his knees among the wreckage.

Inside my head, Skelly stirred. *Big mistake, little girl.* He sounded almost gleeful.

Duncan

Chapter Forty-Four

"Let me see your hand!"

Holding it between my thighs, I continued to swear with abundant imagination, refusing to let Mika check. A stubborn ass, yeah, I was, but it really hurt, and I really, really didn't want him telling me I'd broken it again. In fact, I didn't need him to tell me. I knew.

Hannah watched with her mouth set crookedly and her hands clasped beneath her chin, as though trying to keep from reaching out and grabbing me. Good idea, Hannah. No touching. Brand stood to Mika's right, an expression on his face hinting at some ridiculous consideration to wrestle me down. Ren, on the other hand, looked only like he might be sick. It must be bad. I hadn't had the nerve to eyeball my fingers yet myself.

"Duncan, man, come on," Mika persisted.

"It'll be fine," I hissed out through clenched teeth. A thumping footfall landed beside me. All heads turned toward the sound.

"What's going on here?" Draig demanded. A man usually lacking in patience, the last few hours relocating his warriors to higher ground in preparation for battle had drained him of any he might have left.

"Duncan's hurt his hand and Mika wants to fix it," Hannah told him, jerking her head at Mika.

"And you're a doctor?" Draig asked, looking Mika up and down.

"His father is," Ren volunteered. "So, Mika knows his stuff."

Grunting, Draig raised his left eyebrow. "Show him then," he said to me. "Now."

I inhaled a lungful of dusty air and lifted my fist above my head. The bandage's final remnants fluttered to the ground, torn and bloody. Mika stretched his hand toward mine. Before he could make contact, Draig grabbed my wrist and yanked me upright.

"What the hell?" I yelped, too stunned and in too much pain to attempt to pull free.

"Where did you get that?"

"My hand ended up in the way of a runaway cart. One of your guys let it go," I added, in case he thought I'd done something stupid.

"That," he said, pointing. "That! Where did you get it?"

Angrily, I followed his finger. Because it had been stashed behind a perpetual bandage for so long, I'd nearly forgotten what I wore. I frowned at the ruby ring, the stone colored like fresh blood in the night. Huffing out a breath, I raised my head to Draig's.

"From my father," I said.

"Your father? Did you steal it?"

Jerking my hand away, ignoring what surely seemed to be grinding bone, I took a step back. "Did I—are you kidding me? No! He gave it to me when we parted, back in Trill."

Draig's face went cold. "He wouldn't."

"He would and he did. Go ask him yourself." I hadn't yet had the opportunity to speak with my father, but Draig had said he was with the warriors, readying for battle. "It shouldn't be too much trouble for you to locate him."

Draig's expression altered yet again. Unable to grasp the emotion it revealed, I waited.

"I haven't been honest," he said.

My heart did a funny little jump and then seemed to go still. "About what?"

"Your father. My brother." His head bowed, his long, dark, beaded, braided hair swinging forward across his face. "Aeron is not preparing for battle. He already met his end in one."

Shock rushed through my veins like tiny blades. "No," I said, quietly. "You're lying now."

He shook his head from side to side. "I'm not. He died, fighting beyond these lands. Side by side with me. I hadn't thought to have him there again."

Grief I never expected to feel seared through me. I wanted to lash out, to punch Draig, hard. To fall to the ground and wail like a baby. Why? Aeron had never been anything to me. But once met, I couldn't take back the bonds of blood. And in our last conversation, he'd revealed to me a different man. One I'd been oddly proud to know, however briefly.

I swore again, a single, potent utterance.

"Duncan, listen to me," Draig rushed on. "He gave you that ring. I cannot doubt you when I cannot ask him. But I do believe you are speaking but truth. To be absolutely certain, there are those among us who have the small gift of truth-sensing. I would ask you to submit to them."

"Wait. This is stupid. Does it matter that he gave

it to me?" I took my damaged hand into the other, staring down at the ring. The pressure from the fingers on my left against my right reminded me the pain had not gone away. The momentary shock was wearing off. So was my urge to weep. Instead, I felt...betrayed. Betrayed by the short time I'd had with my dad, by his choice and now by his death. Betrayed by Draig, who'd lied to me for some reason I didn't comprehend. Betrayed by Grace, who had made the decision to rescue her parents without us, giving Moros opportunity to take her away. Now, the very three he wanted were with him and I was left here with a broken hand, my desperate need to get them all back, and the fear I would never see Resa, Grace, or Carina again. Oh, and my uncle's weird behavior over the ring my father had given me. I was tempted to yank the thing off and throw it at him. Except I couldn't. My fingers were too swollen for the band to pass over my knuckle.

Anger took me. My emotions were all over the place. I began pacing in a circle, clutching my right arm against my chest.

"Sit," said Draig, waving at the ground. "Let— Mika, is it?" Mika nodded. "Let Mika examine your hand."

Glowering, I lowered myself back down. To my surprise, Draig crouched down beside me. Mika began prodding and poking my damaged fingers. Gently, I supposed, but it sure as hell didn't feel that way. I bit back a hiss and another profanity.

Draig spent a moment observing Mika's examination before speaking again. "When Aeron was killed, I assumed the ring had been lost on the battlefield," he said. "That ring was our father's, Aeron's and mine. Sometime before Father passed away, he gave the ring to Aeron in a ceremony, proclaiming him heir to Gabrilon. His successor. But your father already had a position in Trill he wished to maintain. Plus, he'd had a falling out with our mother over…over something I will not dwell on here."

Wincing as Mika worked, I frowned at Draig. I knew why my dad had fallen out with his overbearing mother. Because of her, he'd been forced to keep his marriage to my mother secret. A secret apparently discovered when my newborn brother had been taken away before Mom gave up her second and third child to Gran, to keep them away from the woman. What had that been about, anyway, making off with the first born? Was Moros being raised to take my father's place? Or was it his gifts they'd been after? How could anyone possibly know about Moros' powers at his birth?

Whatever, I thought with an inward grunt. I wouldn't pretend to understand. In the end, it appeared my father remained the heir and, once gone, it seemed obvious Draig would take his place, not Moros. I assumed this was the point Draig was trying to make. So, what? Water under the bridge, as Gran often said. Gabrilon and its goings-on were of no concern to me.

I gasped from the pain of having a joint popped back into place, and turned back to Draig. "He gave me the ring. I'm not lying. He told me it was his ring of office, that it might serve as a token to get me through trouble, or to trade if I found myself in need. Why would he say that, if it meant so much to you and your people?"

Draig moved his head. "Perhaps, he cared so little after all."

"That's crap," I snapped. "I didn't know him, but

even I could see he cared a lot about the people of Trill. And maybe even cared a little about me."

Brand muttered agreement.

"But Trill is not Gabrilon," said Draig. "And the ring is to be passed on for only one reason."

"And that is?" I drawled.

Hannah sucked in a breath at my question, her pale eyes wide. I would have said she feared Draig's reaction, but she'd recently walked right up to him and called him a bully. Took guts, that did. Not like someone who is afraid. She watched Draig though. Expectant. I wondered what she thought she knew.

Draig glared into the distance contemplating his answer. Deciding what to tell me, no doubt. Something close to the truth would be nice. Something to explain why he seemed so ticked off about the fact my father had chosen to give me a family heirloom. I was family, whether Draig liked it or not.

Clapping his hand on his thighs, Draig rose. He stared down at me for a long, silent moment. Finally, he blew a frosty breath into the cold air.

"If he truly gave you the ring," he said gravely, "even without any ceremonial attendance or the proper words, you are now heir to Gabrilon. And with my mother gone, you are its ruler."

I gaped up at him in stunned silence.

* * *

I suppose, in times of peace, a fuss would have been made over the news. In time of war, the significance fell by the wayside. To be honest, I wanted to pretend the conversation hadn't taken place. Therefore, the latter suited me just fine.

JO ALLEN ASH

I sat in the chilly dark beneath the stars. My friends slept around me, the way we always did. We'd talked for quite a while, whispering. Not about the ring's significance, but about the girls. Where they might be. How we were going to find them. Whether we ever would, as Hannah had determinedly pointed out.

I took first watch, even surrounded by warriors. It was what we did. The habit could not be broken. Nor should it be. Not until…well, not until.

Turning my wrist, I rolled by hand from side to side. The new bandages glowed pale in the shadows, the lump beneath revealing where the ring remained firmly on my finger. There'd been no getting it off, even if I'd been inclined. After submerging my hand in ice-cold water for a time, the swelling had receded, but not enough. Mika had reset the broken middle finger for the third—or maybe fourth—time. It had broken slightly higher up than the last. Mika said bone scar was stronger than the bone itself. Pretty soon, that middle finger was going to be invincible. As for the pinkie, it had not, after all, been broken. The way it felt after being manipulated back where it belonged made me almost wish it was. The ripe-berry bruising covering most of my hand I could live with. I could live with it all. The alternative didn't bear thinking about.

A shadowy form moved through the night in my direction. Two, I realized, as they separated and drew near.

"Draig," I said. I had never called him uncle, despite my knowledge of our familial relationship.

He stopped a few feet away. A woman was with him. Unlike most among Draig's warriors, she had bi-colored hair, gold and brown mixed. She looked vaguely familiar. She might have been with him in the Guardsman that night which seemed to long ago now. The night Draig and his warriors had come to our aid in the mountains beyond All Dwellers.

"Duncan," he said, "this is Becca. She will determine the legitimacy of the ring."

I released a sigh. "Fine. What do I have to do?"

"Just tell her what you told me. She will know lie from truth. She is one of the gifted I mentioned."

Becca sat down before me. Without hesitancy, she reached out to my unbroken hand and pressed three fingers against the veins in my wrist, her thumb on the opposite side. "Tell me now," she said. "I am ready."

Okay. No messing around. I leaned forward and repeated what I had told Draig. Quietly, so as not to wake my companions. When I had finished, she looked up at Draig and nodded her head. Draig blinked once, rather slowly, before he dropped to one knee. He bowed his head. My good hand shot up.

"Whoa," I said. "Don't do that. This is ridiculous."

Draig lifted his head. "In what way?"

"What if I don't want this. To be…whatever I would be. Heir."

"Why wouldn't you want it?" Draig asked with a baffled expression.

I frowned, yearning for Grace so I could discuss this strange occurrence with her. "Maybe you could just leave me alone for a bit, okay?"

"I can't do that," he said fiercely. "Protocol deems that you be protected now. You will have to come with me."

"Was my father protected? He's dead."

Draig reeled back. "Aeron refused protection," he nearly shouted. Beside me, both Ren and Brand grumbled in their sleep. I lowered my voice, hoping my uncle would, too.

"Then I refuse as well," I said.

"No," Draig responded. "I won't let you."

I straightened my shoulders, glared back at him, eye to eye. "Does this whole heir thing require you to obey me?"

He sucked in a deep breath, causing the leather across his chest to creak. "Yes," he admitted reluctantly.

"Good." I gripped his arm, gave it a small shake. "Then please, leave me alone."

He looked very much like he wanted to argue, might even have enjoyed knocking me back over the ground. Instead, he rose with a strange, silent refinement, bowed his head again and strode away without another word. Becca followed.

Hearing a noise nearby, I glanced over at Ren lying on his side. With a smirk, he gave me a thumbs up. I swore at him, ignoring his muffled laughter as he rolled over. A short time later, I exchanged places with him, curling up in my blanket to sleep while Ren took next watch. I counted on the pain in my hand to keep me awake, but the ordeal had apparently sapped my energy. The last thing I heard before sunlight touched my lids was Ren grumbling about a stone he'd sat on. I opened my eyes to a call to arms.

I jetted into a sitting position, forgetting about my hand, and slammed it down hard trying to free myself from the blanket. It hurt too much for any vocalization beyond the breath whistling through my teeth.

"What do you see?" I managed to ask Mika, who was standing at a short distance, looking in all directions through the telescope. The other three were near him, straightening clothes and scrabbling for weapons.

"I don't know. Something's got them excited, but I can't see what."

I clambered to my feet, holding my battered fist momentarily against my gut. Suddenly, I spotted something up at the ridge and directed Mika's gaze there. He frowned through the telescope for several seconds and then passed it to me.

"I can't tell what I'm looking at. Can you?" When Mika didn't answer, I glanced over at him. He seemed focused on a place much nearer. I turned to follow his gaze. Several of Draig's warriors headed our way at speed. I handed the telescope back to Mika and went to meet them.

"Are you Duncan?" one shouted at me.

"Yes," I said, eyeing him up and down.

"Somebody's asking for you."

All three promptly turned around, returning up the hillside. I trotted after, wondering why they needed three. In case I required coercion to accompany them? This was all getting a bit irritating. A moment later, I heard footsteps following. Mika fell in alongside, carrying both our packs and weapons. I slung my pack over my left shoulder, then took the weapons one at a time and stashed them in my belt.

"The others?" I asked.

"They'll be along momentarily," he said.

Nodding, I increased my pace to catch up with the three warriors, who'd only glanced back once to see if I followed. "I don't think it's the girls, do you?"

"They would have come to us," Mika answered.

Yes, I thought. No matter who stood in their way.

We reached a point where we had to climb, finding handholds on rocks. We'd originally come down through the flume thing Brand had found, but obviously Draig's troops weren't going to squeeze through there. In following these three, we weren't either. With me traveling one-handed, we soon fell behind. I swore soundlessly, trying to contain my language and my exasperation. Mika hooked my elbow a couple times, assisting my passage. I knew he only wanted to be helpful. Knew it, yet bit my tongue to prevent shouting at him to stop. I would have felt awful yelling at him. Worse than I felt not yelling.

Draig met us at the top. He grabbed my good arm, hustling me along. Mika jogged to keep up. The temptation was strong to ask Draig if such treatment of Gabrilon's ruler was permitted. I didn't, though. I had no real desire to bring that conversation up.

Draig's warriors stood in a large, uneven circle, shoulder to shoulder, preventing me seeing past them. Two parted upon a word from my uncle, making way for us. As soon as I stepped through, I was attacked, a body impacting mine as I fought for stability and pushed it away with one arm. The body stumbled a few steps backward.

"Duncan!"

"Oh, crap," I said. "Alwyna. Were you hugging me?" Alwyna, the girl who'd thrown a knife at my eye.

"I...yes." She shifted her weight from one foot to the other. The heavy cloak she wore danced from side to side. Her exhausted, worried expression lifted a little. I recognized in astonishment it was relief at seeing me.

Mika pressed close to my side. "How is your mother?" he asked her.

Alwyna shook her head. "She still lives, but she is very poorly. We had to leave her with Enid."

We? I glanced around the circle, only now noticing the area filled with the Fianna, far more than we'd met. I wondered if the others who'd previously departed had flocked to follow Alwyna now. Draig's warriors eyed them as though not quite sure what to think about the all-female company or their vast numbers. The Fianna glared back at them. I recalled Neala's words to Grace. *When the time comes, the Fianna will join you.*

"Alwyna," I said, "is this the time your mother

spoke of? Is this why you came looking for us?"

"Yes." She jerked her head in Draig's direction. "I tried to tell that one, but he refused to listen. He said Grace isn't here, but he wouldn't say where she is, so I asked for you. Where is Grace, Duncan? Has something happened?" Her voice betrayed her anxiety. As did her hands, suddenly twisting together.

"The three of them, Grace, Resa, and Carina, are with Moros. The Darkness," I said, not sure if she had learned about my brother.

"What?" She stumbled where she stood. I reached out my good hand to steady her. She shook it off. "How can that be?"

"They are not with him voluntarily," I explained. "It's a long story and I don't know all the details, so it's not worth me trying to tell it. We'll get them back, though, I promise you that."

She gave me a look as desperate as the emotion I held inside. Draig came close, right up beside me, and frowned at Alwyna.

"What do you know?" he demanded. "Tell me everything."

I half-expected Alwyna to toss the thin blade at him. Belatedly, I remembered I had it in my belt. Fortuitous, that, given the murderous expression on her face.

"Alwyna," I said, "what word do you bring?"

She tore her gaze away from Draig and back to me. "Enid said to tell all of you—you and Grace and the others—that this…" She faltered.

"Go on," I said.

She lifted her chin, stared me dead in the eye. "That these are the last days."

Grace

Chapter Forty-Five

These are the last days...

I sucked in a breath as the unknown voice rammed through my brain. Not Skelly's. This voice was soft. Unknown, but familiar. I had heard it several times now. A stranger in my head. I didn't enjoy the knowledge someone else, a voice I did not know, reached out to me this way. The message itself chilled me to my very core. I glanced aside at Carina.

"Did you hear that?" I whispered.

She nodded, her eyes a strange hue in the risen sun. "It came from Duncan," she answered me quietly.

"It wasn't him—"

"No, but it came from him somehow."

That made no sense, but our discussion ended there, because Moros had turned toward us on the back of the beast Valard had returned with. The animal greatly resembled a shaggy version of the equines kept in Citadel. He'd brought two, Valard had. One for himself and one for Moros, securing them outside his former home at the very moment Moros destroyed the residence.

We'd been prepared, somehow, we three, and were able to keep the debris from striking us. Moros had managed to put himself within that bubble.

Perhaps not intentionally, but thus had he survived his own stupidly reckless behavior after the destruction of his bewitched table.

I raised my eyes and met his in challenge as we trudged along behind him on a wide track. The guard rode at our backs.

"What are you talking about back there?" Moros asked in a liquid tone. He was feeling quite powerful right then, I could tell.

"The fact we're hungry," I shot back, shifting Resa's unconscious weight in my arms. He had caught us off guard once we'd managed to get outside and threatened Resa if she made another move. Carina had enforced sleep on her. For now.

Moros nodded at Valard, who rode forward and tossed a small packet at Carina. She caught it, opened it, gave the contents a sniff, and then doled out a piece to herself and placed another in my mouth, as my hands were otherwise engaged. I chewed the substance, swallowing it with difficulty after. We needed water.

Moros turned back around. I stared at the hood he'd pulled up over his head, wondering why he heard only Skelly's voice and not this other one.

"Where are we going?" I shouted up to him.

"You'll know soon enough. But if you'd like a hint, we're going to observe certain people," he said with a dramatic flair.

I rolled my eyes at his back, wanting mostly to drag him off the beast to the ground. I didn't dare, though. In the commotion of our escape from the collapsing house, the two bags around my neck, the one containing Skelly and the other the dust from the crushed talisman, had slipped free from my collar. Moros had ripped both off my neck. The bag filled with dust he'd cast aside, but he'd taken a liking to the crystal. Having managed to come away from the destruction with my borrowed *lathesa,* he had tied the crystal to one end, the way I had done with the orb's other shards back on Emerald. Moros called me foolish for holding onto something so nastily sharp just because I thought it pretty, right before he'd claimed the crystal for his own. He had no idea what power he carried around now in ornamentation. I couldn't risk him finding out. And if my actions or Moros' resulted in the crystal breaking, it would release Skelly once and for all with no hope he might be contained again.

Carina poked another bread-like bit past my lips, took one herself, then folded and stored the rest away for Resa. I worked up as much saliva as I could inside into my mouth before forcing the masticated lump down my throat.

"Is it far, where we're going?" I called out to Moros again. "Carina and I might need a little rest at some point."

He glanced back. "Oh, don't you think you're sly? But I don't mind telling you. We're on our way back to Gabrilon." He paused, watching me. "Are you surprised?"

"A bit," I said. He turned front again, clearly dissatisfied with my blasé response.

"Gabrilon?" Carina whispered.

As I couldn't comfortably shrug, I arched my brows at her.

"And what did that mean, 'the last days'?" she asked.

"I don't know."

"You're still talking," Moros threw over his shoulder.

I decided to stop trying to figure things out for a while. I needed to conserve my energy and my breath. Resa was heavier than I recalled, or perhaps my stamina had lessened. Either way, if we had much longer to travel, I'd have to wake her. While we remained calm, Resa might, too. It would benefit Moros to keep himself in check. He wasn't likely to be convinced of that, the all-powerful Moros. The more I watched him, the more I doubted this to be true. He had multiple gifts, yes, and strong ones, yet even with possible training over the years, he seemed little different than who I was now. Troubled, though, in some strange and morbid way. I tried envisioning what his upbringing had been like, stolen away from his mother for who knew what reason. Because he would be powerful? How had they known? And then locked away. He seemed tormented by many things I would never understand.

And why would you want to?

Skelly. Definitely Skelly this time, still reaching out to me. Ahead of us, Moros glanced from side to side.

I didn't intend to let you go, I said to Skelly. My words felt like an apology.

He didn't take it as such. *I bet you didn't,* he barked back. *But this is exactly where I'm meant to be.*

I bit my lip. His statement boded no good. I had to find a way to get the crystal back, intact.

Carina touched my arm. "Are you all right?" she whispered.

"I will be."

"We're almost there."

With a start, I looked around. I didn't recognize anything, wondered what Carina saw that looked familiar to her. Carina jerked her head toward the guard behind us.

"I got it from him," she said.

"Then we were never far from the boys," I said, "and Hannah." Somehow, this news made me feel better. In my arms, Resa shifted and started to wake. I lowered her to the ground, pausing while she got her bearings. Valard on his mount nearly ran into us. I turned and glared at him. I couldn't read his expression through the misalignment caused by his old injuries. I felt his annoyance, though. His impatience, his anger. Or was that someone else?

I glanced to where Moros had halted, his face clearly marked by these emotions.

"I feel it, too," Carina said. "I think Resa enhances what is around us. It could be why she destroyed the table. Something she sensed or knew or had seen."

Valard brought his beast closer, forcing us to turn and follow Moros. I took Resa's right hand and Carina her left. As soon as our fingers touched, something powerful coursed through us. Coursed through and out, searching for the others, Duncan and Mika, Hannah, Ren, and Brand. Seeking strength and hope and deliverance. But then that other voice broke through and quietly said: *Not yet.*

Not yet. *Who are you?* I asked and received no reply.

I had first heard this voice after we went through the Sleeping Myth. Had it something to do with our passage? It seemed Carina heard it sometimes, too, although she gave no sign right now. Instead, she walked with her head held high, watching the sky, her movements as graceful as ever despite the rough track underfoot. I glanced up, too, wondering what had caught

IN DARKNESS WE BREAK

her eye. There. I saw them. Far above and mere specks against the blue, winged creatures circled in the updraft. I had seen birds do that before, take joy in the wind beneath their wings, but these were not birds. Knowing what to look for, I spotted body shape, and the precision with which they circled. Not joyful, this. Martial.

My brother was up there.

I closed my eyes and lowered my head, an actual smile curling my lips. I could almost hear Duncan saying, "It will be all right." Because he did so often say that, always reassuring me, and always, through some peculiar and unanticipated event, true.

As we walked, the trees thinned out, revealing a surprising vista. We were quite high up. Moros halted on a bare, rocky escarpment, allowing his mount's head to lower toward the ground, where it tore at sparse, tufted grasses. The straps used for control lay slack in his hands. We walked up beside him, Valard moving in our right. My breath caught.

"Oh, no," Carina whispered, her words snatched away by the buffeting wind.

Below us lay Gabrilon. I saw the fresh ruins, the sharp incline behind, the river in the valley, where I had witnessed hundreds of campfires. But now the valley, the hillsides, the mountain slopes, teemed with movement and reflection. Countless numbers covered the landscape, probably far more hidden beneath trees and shadow. Toward the southeast, Citadel ships hovered, dropping down wherever a clearing afforded them access. I recognized the dark shapes. They had never possessed weaponry and I hoped they did not still.

Here and there, colorful banners likely marked by traditional heraldry flapped in the breeze. Voices rose and fell, indistinguishable at this distance and mingling into a sound oddly like music. A throbbing, muffled, dangerous music. More ships came, ones I did not know, landing on a distant ridge. Behind the ruined structure, more folk spread out along the crest above. Except for those arriving in Citadel ships, I hadn't a clue whose armies crowded in from all sides. However, I possessed no doubt as to their intent.

These are the last days...

I bowed my head and whispered.

Praying?

Yes, Skelly, I said. *I am.*

He laughed, but said nothing more to taunt me. Hearing something of Skelly's words and his derision, Moros gazed down at me from the beast's back. I shielded my eyes, looked up at him.

"Are they gathered here for you?" I asked.

"Who else?" Moros answered. His face, Duncan's face, held a profoundly smug appearance. I wanted to smack it.

Lying again, Skelly said.

Who, me?

No, he answered. *Lover boy's twin.*

Are they not all under his command?

I heard his bitter laugh. *They are none of them under his command. Only those who lead. He told you this. Don't you pay attention? You surprise me, Grace.*

I bit back an irritated reply. *Are there other armies gathering besides those he influences?*

This is what he fears. I can feel it, Skelly said, his tone indicating he enjoyed the intimate knowledge. *He's vulnerable. He's scared. Sound familiar?*

Skelly—

He snorted. *Bye, now. I have more important things to do.* His voice drifted away.

I looked up again at Moros. A blow came quickly, and not from him.

I picked myself up, whipping around to face my attacker. Valard stood before me.

"A coward's move," I said, "attacking from behind."

On his mount, Moros laughed, and kept laughing. Valard shuffled sideways until he stood between me and Duncan's brother. To my left, Carina clutched Resa, backing away with her. I adopted a defensive stance, lifted my chin.

"Next one," I said, "not so lucky."

He made a quick feint at me, and when he did, he hissed, "Run."

I faltered.

"Now," he said. He spun in Moros' direction. I didn't wait. Snatching Carina's and Resa's hands, I raced away, dragging them along. Grunts and curses filled the air behind us. In moments, the ground began to vibrate. The destruction Moros could command still fresh in my mind, I pushed harder to get away from the rocky overhang. Swiftly, I realized the tremors came from in front, not behind. Yanking the other two nearly off their feet, I veered from the path. Several huge shadows appeared on the trail, moving at speed.

"Chauncy!" I cried. The three *conjures* skidded to a rumbling halt, cloven feet digging into the dirt, spewing tiny rock and debris. Sprinting toward Chauncy, I tossed first Resa and then Carina up on his back, my strength borne from adrenaline. I followed, leaping up behind. With our fingers dug into his fur, Chauncy and the other two galloped on. Not away from Moros, but toward him.

"No!" I cried. It didn't matter. They were on their own course. I had to trust them. The two scruffy equines pounded by us, heading in the other direction. Before we reached the cliff, a high-pitched scream savaged the air, dying away in a long, fading wail. Someone had fallen from the clifftop. Or been pushed. When we thundered past the crag, a dark, spiraling mass in the sky told me who had fallen. Moros was headed into battle.

Skelly

Chapter Forty-Six

Grace is far from me now. I never expected to feel the loss. It hurts a bit, I can't lie. But not enough.

The last days. Yep. The last days. I'd heard that, in her head. If I want out, it has to be soon. I just need to make this Duncan lookalike hear me. Properly hear me.

And then it will be time for some fun.

Duncan
Chapter Forty-Seven

A warning shout went up. It sounded like a warning, anyway, yet, no one reacted in a manner I would have expected. Instead, words passed from mouth to mouth, words I didn't understand, rushing like water. Heads turned, warriors backed up, moved aside, looked expectant, as if something had come into our midst. Alwyna and the Fianna, who had opted to settle into a space around me and my friends, stood up quite hurriedly. We did, too.

"Look!" Hannah cried, pointing.

I tried, but only glimpsed a dark mass moving swiftly through the crowd, causing a hurried exodus to either side. A mere moment later, it broke through, charging right toward us. The Fianna scattered. My friends and I stood our ground. The grin on my face felt like it would shatter my jaw.

Chancy veered at the last moment and halted, his horn kept clear from skewering range. Grace launched herself off the *conjure's* back and straight into my upraised arms, limbs wrapped around me. I held onto her like the end of my life. I think we were both weeping. Through my definite tears and Grace's dark, tangled hair, I saw Mika help Carina down, followed by Resa. Resa raised her eyes, met mine, and smiled. Truly smiled. With Grace still pretty much attached to me, I hurried over to my sister's side.

"Never again," I said. "Never again." I couldn't get anything more than those two words to leave my mouth, over and over, but it didn't matter. No one questioned what I meant.

Our emotional reunion was cut short, however, by Draig's arrival. He yanked Grace away from me. Before I could object to his actions, she tossed him back with frightening ease. Regaining his footing, he stood a moment, stunned.

"Grace," I said, "you remember my uncle. Draig?"

"Yes. A traitor, as I recall. At least to us."

"Long story," I said, "but not entirely a traitor."

Grace scowled at him. She hadn't noticed Ren and Hannah and Brand, yet, or Alwyna and the Fianna. Her eyes had been only for me. I smiled a little in recollection.

"Is he dead?" Draig finally asked.

Grace's brows shot up. "Pardon me?"

"Don't play games. Moros. Is he dead?"

Grace took a step toward him. He took a wary step away. "Duncan's brother, you mean? His family and yours?"

I heard a few gasps behind me. Apparently, Enid had not mentioned this fact to all the Fianna.

"Yes, that's exactly who I mean, and you know it." I didn't like Draig's tone to Grace, or his coldness regarding someone who was, indeed, family. I had never dwelled overmuch on how we would stop Moros. Not by harming him, I figured. Most definitely not through his death. I'd always thought there would be another way. I stared at Grace, waiting for her answer.

"He is not dead," said Grace. My breath rushed out. "He is also not to blame for the entirety of this mess. He took advantage of the evil intent of others, yes, and that influence must end, but otherwise, this is the choice of men. And women," she added. "Free will."

Leave it to Grace to never back down from what she believed to be the truth. To defend it, even.

"What of the prophecy?" Draig demanded. "The prophecy would destroy the danger. Instead, you set it free."

Slowly, Grace's head moved from side to side in denial. "Prophecies are subject to human interpretation." I wondered what Grace had learned. What she hadn't yet had the chance to tell us. What she might be holding back.

"Bah," spat Draig. "You are a coward, not a warrior."

I lurched forward. Carina grabbed my sleeve.

"It's all right, Duncan," she said, lifting her hand. "He's afraid."

Draig heard her. He spun in her direction. "How dare you?"

She tapped her head. "I feel you," she said. "I hear you, in here."

Eyes widening, he slashed his hand down in dismissal. "I have an army to ready for battle. You can all cower here." He looked at me, his mouth lifting in a sneer. "My brother made a mistake, giving you that ring."

He stormed away. Carina watched him go. "He believes too much in portents and prophecy and not enough in cold, hard truths," she said. I grunted, not too sure what to believe, myself.

Grace returned to my side, took my hand, frowned at the bandages as she stroked the ring beneath. "What about the ring?"

"Draig insists that by my father giving it to me, he made me heir to Gabrilon," I said. "Tradition, despite the lack of 'ceremonial trappings.'"

Grace's lips twitched. In a moment, she was laughing. I followed suit, trying to get words out between.

"It's serious, Grace," I stammered. I swept my left arm out dramatically. "This is all mine."

We both fell to laughing again. Hysteria, more likely than not. The others watched with crooked smiles, confused. Grace quieted down first.

"Do you want it?" she asked. "Gabrilon."

Shaking my head, I leaned toward her. "No."

"Then, at some point you must figure out what to do and how to do it, because I don't think you can just turn your back on what your father intended. Is he here? Have you spoken with him?"

I sobered. Completely. "He's not and I can't. He's dead."

Before Grace could express the shock and sympathy in her eyes, Ren moved in. He grabbed Grace's sleeve between thumb and forefinger. Yanked on it like a kid. "Is what you said true? We don't have to worry about Moros?"

Grace took a deep breath. "That's not exactly what I said," she replied. "He's even more dangerous than before." She turned her gaze back to mine. "Duncan, he has the crystal. He has Skelly."

* * *

All but Brand understood the implication. However, he could tell by our faces a very bad thing had happened.

"So, what's next?" he asked. "Now we're all back together, this is better, yeah?"

I looked at Grace. We all did. Alwyna, who had been listening, came closer.

"What should we do, Grace?" she asked. "Fight with these here, or set out with you? Because you're not finished with The Darkness yet. I know that."

"You're right. I'm not. We're not," Grace said. "But Moros is not The Darkness, despite his fascination with the title." She looked out over the valley below and to the mountains all around. I followed her gaze. The area had been filling with armies overnight. "The last days" was a true statement. It seemed we were headed to the final battle.

"The Darkness is what we see," I said, "isn't it? The state of the world we live in."

"You sound like your brother," said Grace. "He believes he and the three from the prophecy can bring about a change to the world, make it beautiful again. He doesn't want to rule it, Duncan," she added. "I don't believe he embodies absolute evil. I truly don't. Your brother is not a monster. He has suffered depravation. Isolation. Ridiculous expectations. And he is gifted. Very much so, and possibly left to his own devices with that. You know how scary that can be. You've all seen it in me."

"What about Valard?" Carina went on. "Was that on purpose, or a horrible accident?"

I had no clue who Valard was, or what had happened, but by Grace's expression I reckoned something unpleasant had occurred.

"I don't know," Grace answered her. "We'll ask Moros when we see him. Because we will see him. I can still hear Skelly. He'll lead us there."

In that statement, the decision was made. No one was going on alone this time. We would go as one, fully as one, the way Enid had shown us. I didn't like that Grace could still feel Skelly, still hear him, but if he—it?—could take us to my brother—

"Grace," I said on a sudden thought, "what happens if Moros, you know, lets him loose or whatever?"

"Then the gods help us," she said.

"Right," said Brand. "We'd best be prepared."

I didn't know how he meant to do that, prepare for the deadlist release of power, but Brand was always practical. He had something in mind. Behind him, Ren gave a brief squeal. We all jerked around to gape at him. Poking Hannah with an elbow, he pointed with his other hand toward the sky. Shielding my eyes, I followed where he indicated and spotted great winged things spiraling down from the sky. Not things. Warriors. I turned to Grace.

"Your brother?"

"Either him, or others with him," she said.

"I suppose we should gather our things and get out of sight then." Our packs had been located when Draig's warriors took the hill. They'd lumped them into a communal pile. Determined, I led the way to where I'd last seen them. I heard many footsteps in pursuit and glanced back to find Alwyna and the Fianna following. I'd forgotten them. "What are you doing?"

"Coming with you, of course," Alwyna said.

I glanced around at their number, and then looked beyond them for Chauncy and the other two *conjures*.

I hadn't seen Vigor and Bell at all, and wondered what had happened to them. Only then did I recall how Brand and I had 'borrowed' them from Draig and his warriors. Perhaps they'd claimed the animals as soon as they appeared in their midst.

"There are too many of you," I said. "We'll never be able to pass unseen."

She seemed ready to argue, but her gaze slipped past my face. Grace appeared at my side.

"What Duncan says makes sense," Grace told her. "His decision is valid."

"Very well," Alwyna said with surprising compliance. She called one of her warriors to her side and spoke with the woman in a low voice. The woman nodded, returned to the others. "Leah is my second-in-command," Alwyna explained. "She will take the warriors to that oaf—what is his name? Draig. They will offer to fight with him. If not accepted, they will fight on their own. But I am coming with you."

Grace glanced at me. I nodded. "Thank you," I said to Alwyna.

Now, we were nine. I liked odd numbers better, anyway. Perhaps from growing up on Riley. Odd numbers always seemed to win more at the games. I know in terms of probability that wasn't likely, but I'd snuck around quite often to watch the play, and I knew what I had seen.

We made our way to the supply cart without being noticed. Imminent battle had everyone too busy to pay attention to what we were doing. So long as we avoided Draig, I figured we'd be fine. Our packs lay in the dirt beside the wagon and had clearly been rifled through. Still, enough remained inside to get us through this day. We'd break our fast on the move, and scrape together remainders for whatever else might be needed. After that, well, depending on the tide of war and our personal success or lack thereof, sustenance could be a moot consideration.

As we headed toward the tree line, Grace paused, looked back. "Where's Chauncy? And the other two?"

"I didn't see Vigor and Bell, but Chauncy probably wandered off," I said. "You know them. They'll be there when needed."

Grace looked at me with a nod and a smile, but her eyes remained troubled. She always took the *conjures'* absence hard, especially Chauncy's. He'd been with us a long time now. I wondered if Chauncy would follow her home. He seemed to miss her as much as she did him. I knew I would. Miss her. I'd also follow her home. She'd made the offer. I hoped she meant it.

Grace

Chapter Forty-Eight

An iron tang filled my nostrils. The air hung heavy with blood-scent. Beneath our feet, the soil was stained. Someone had recently died where we crouched. No, not died, or they'd still be there. They'd been taken away, or somehow managed to get up again, unlike the many we could see from our hiding place. The slope below was littered with bodies, some still animate. In a struggle visible to everyone, Mika grappled the urge to go down and help them.

Among the distant, moving masses in the valley the fallen were not as evident, yet the river's currents flowed dark with the wounded, the dead, the dying. I had no idea to whose army the combatants belonged. Most of the fighting was hand-to-hand, or at least deadly proximity, and identifying the participants from this height impossible. Far above our heads, uncaring about identity, birds circled—real birds, not my brother's army—anticipating the outcome below. Carrion eaters. I didn't want to picture it, these winged creatures doing what they were meant to do, yet the image crept into my mind and lurked there, unwilling to depart.

I glanced down at Duncan's fingers curled around my own, then looked up at his face, trying not to see Moros in it. Duncan's mouth opened.

"Don't say it'll be all right," I whispered, cutting him off. "Please."

"I wasn't," he said, just as quietly. "I was going to say I love you. I might not get the chance again anytime soon."

My heart, my pounding, angry, despairing heart, cracked a little around the edges. I fought to pull it back together. "I love you, too, Duncan," I said. "I love you all."

Because that was the reality of it. In this connected state, there was no differentiation between one person and another. Not for me, anyway. I sensed them all like the roots in the forest, entangled, intertwined deep beneath the soil, each rising into the core of the other thriving trees. I, desert dweller, clung to an image of the previously unfamiliar to explain what I felt. But it didn't need explaining. It just needed for me to let it be.

"Grace…"

"Shh," I said to Duncan, closing my eyes. I reached out, beyond us, searching for Skelly, and again found him. This time, though, the others, those who had known him, reacted differently. Mika, with remembered friendship. Carina, with sadness. Duncan, with tolerance.

Skelly turned within his crystal prison in surprise. *Well, hello, Grace.*

I could tell by the slight gasps around me that we'd all heard his response. Even Ren and Hannah and Brand. The only one who had not was Alwyna.

Don't look for me. It's too late.

"What does he mean?" Hannah asked, disrupting

the link between us and him. She apologized for doing so.

"It doesn't matter," I said. "I know where they are now." Leaning forward, I pointed through the closely woven branches screening us from view. Moros would not expose himself to the fray. He had no desire to fight, only manipulate those who did. In mountains riddled with caves, one showed raw and new on the hillside above and to our right. It looked to have been blasted open like the Gabrilon fortifications. "He's in there."

Hannah leaned over my arm, looking where I pointed. "And if we stop him, all this is done?" she asked.

That would be too simple. I dropped my hand. "No. You see, Moros is not the cause, only the impetus that keeps them going. This is what he told me, that he is driving those who lead the armies. Coercing them to win, even though only one can. They won't be dissuaded from that goal even if he no longer pushes it. To come out on top was what they wanted anyway, how this all started before Moros stepped in, so they'll still strive for that."

Hannah frowned, disturbed by my words. "Then why are we—"

"Hannah," said Duncan, "enough."

I saw the hurt in her eyes. I knew Duncan didn't mean to be cruel. If not for her feelings for him, she would have shrugged him off, and her attachment was not something he could control. Still, we faced a perilous situation. She deserved honesty.

"Right now," I said, "he's more dangerous than ever. He has Skelly, or whatever Skelly is. Remember how scared you were during our escape from All Dwellers? How frightened everyone was? That wasn't me causing all the destruction. It was him."

Hannah watched me with a peculiar expression, her eyes trailing down to my coat, to the place where until recently the bag holding the crystal had been safely stored. I recalled the way she'd looked as she'd attempted to take the crystal from me outside the Sleeping Myth. I determined to ask her why before we took another step. It felt important, suddenly. Imperative.

"Hannah," I said, "do you remember the night we stood before the Sleeping Myth?"

"Before you shoved us through," Duncan added. I shot him a look. Hannah's gaze shifted until she stared at the ground.

"You tried to take the bag from around my neck," I said. "Do you remember?"

Slowly, she nodded. Her lip trembled.

"Why? Why did you do that?"

"Maybe because she wanted whatever power she could get from it for herself," Duncan said.

Hannah's head jerked up, eyes shining. "That's not true!"

I rushed her, pulled her against my shoulder, whispered for her to be quiet. To be quiet, and tell me.

"It was nothing like that," she sobbed in an undertone. "The Far-Seer—the Far-Seer," she repeated, gulping air, "k-k-knew. She said all who passed through the Sleeping Myth would be forever changed. She gave me the talisman to make sure you would survive. That's why I pushed you through when you were all touching each other. It was the only way you would all live."

I gazed at Duncan over Hannah's head, horrified at the thought what would have happened if anyone had let go and satisfied her words were truth. Touched by it, even. After a moment, I asked, "And why didn't you come with us?"

"I was afraid," she whispered.

"Afraid of what?"

She hesitated. "Of what the change in me might be," she said after a moment. "I thought I might become worse than I am."

"What do you mean?"

Hannah didn't answer.

"She's never liked herself very much," Ren explained softly.

Grimacing at the sadness of that, I stroked Hannah's tangled hair. "But why did you try to take the crystal, Hannah?"

She sighed, pulled away, wiped her eyes with her palms. "Because—because I was sure he—it—would change, too, and kill you all."

We all looked at one another, wondering at her statement. At the truth in it, or the lie.

She's not lying.

It wasn't Skelly speaking. I heard the other voice, Soft, oddly-voweled, the sounds rounded and clumsy, almost childlike. We all heard it. Heard it and looked around. Every eye fell on Resa, even Alwyna's, who had no idea what was going on. Resa looked back at us all.

Hello, she said inside seven heads.

* * *

Duncan dropped to his knees with a muffled cry into his cupped hands. Amazed, we gathered in a half circle, silent, waiting for him to get himself together. Resa remained immobile, studying—truly studying—her brother crouched on the ground. Duncan finally scrubbed his face and looked up, meeting his sister's gaze. For the first time in twelve years, he and his sister possessed an ability, no matter how sporadic, to share words, to understand one another. Tears blurred my vision. Duncan turned his head in my direction.

"Enid said passage through the Myth changed

everyone. I just wouldn't have imagined this. Gran will be so—" He stopped, left the sentence unfinished. I held out my hand to help him up. He latched onto my fingers and stood.

"I wonder what other surprises await us," Carina muttered. Ren snorted, as though she were joking. We all knew she wasn't. Taking Resa's hand, Duncan tucked her fingers into his bandaged, splinted, right. With the left, he checked his belt, then swung his nearly empty pack onto his shoulder.

"I have something to say," he announced in a low, oddly emotional voice.

Biting my lip, I looked at him. After what we'd all just witnessed, it could have been anything.

Duncan brushed his sleeve beneath his nose. "We don't have an actual plan. We never have any plan. But I'm suggesting one."

"Go ahead," I whispered.

"My brother lives," he said. "We save him."

A crooked smile lifted my mouth. I touched his knuckles. "I don't think any of us intended otherwise."

He studied the others, searching each face, then huffed out a breath. He sounded like he'd been holding it a while. In a metaphorical manner, he probably had been, since first learning his brother existed. He nodded. "So, we're agreed."

"Yeah," said Mika. "What else would you think?"

After that, we abandoned our hiding place and headed up the hillside, keeping under cover. The high-pitched whine from *impulse*-type weapons rose up as another skirmish broke out not far below. It had taken us nearly all day to make our way along the slopes, avoiding the major battling in the valley. The sun would soon slide behind the mountains, casting deeper shadows I hoped would keep us concealed and not hide others from our notice.

Resa had reverted to the faraway look in her eyes, but regularly glanced around, caught someone's eye, expressed recognition, connection. We could all feel Duncan's happiness. Maybe Resa's, too. Sometimes I couldn't grasp how Duncan, with his wonderful heart, had ever managed any success with the con artists guild. It seemed incomprehensible to me now. But I'd found we'd all done things which ran counter to who we really were, deep inside. Circumstance, I supposed.

Night fell and darkness folded over the valley like a shroud. The only light existed in the stars overhead and in the bright trails from decreasing *impulse* fire. The armies drifted into fallback positions, hampered from fighting by their inability to distinguish opponents in the gloom. Soon, I heard the wind in the trees again. Throughout the day I had witnessed the branches moving but could not hear the sound over vicious battle. This was not something they could teach us, our mentors—the horrendous, brutal noise obliterating all else.

"Are we still headed in the right direction?" Duncan whispered to me.

"Yes," I said. Short. To the point. I wasn't in the mood for speech. I fought a sudden and unnerving perception the darkness would swallow us hole. Nearby, Mika paused, jerking Carina to a halt. He looked up at the sky, then around us into the shadows. Brand stopped, too, reaching out to Ren and Hannah, yanking them back. Resa and Duncan shuffled to a halt, looking at me where I stood, frozen.

"What is it?" Ren said in a voice I barely heard.

"The creatures from Emerald?" Mika asked. "We haven't seen any since the building came down."

"No," I said. "It's not them. It feels like—" I gasped. "Hurry, hands together!"

We'd learned how to connect without touching,

yet this seemed a time for physical action. Arms lifted and stretched, fingers grasped fingers. We steadied ourselves against a powerful, rushing force. Treetops cracked and plummeted, shaking the ground beneath our feet. We brought forth the shielding, Carina, Resa and I, more reactive than true summoning. Debris battered the defensive dome, skidded across its lightly lit surface and spun away into darkness. We leaned into the onslaught despite the protection, to prevent being rolled like a cup filled with tea leaves. All the while, I kept pushing away at a single, shared, damaging thought before it took us over, tore us apart: *Hide.*

As abruptly as it all started, the bombardment ceased. Bent forward, my hands on my knees, I struggled to get my breath back. "Is everyone all right?" I asked.

Through nods and verbal cues, everyone let me know they were unharmed. I straightened, pivoting to study the damage all around.

"That wasn't good," Mika said.

Duncan jerked to face me. "Seriously, Grace, what the hell was that?"

I inhaled. "I don't know."

"Yer best guess," pushed Brand.

Swearing, I looked toward the place we were headed, the direction still delineated in my brain.

"Best guess?" Duncan answered when I didn't. "Moros just let Skelly out to play."

Duncan

Chapter Forty-Nine

I knew I was right. What else could it be that had Grace looking so worried? She wouldn't say, though. Maybe she didn't want to scare us. What did she think we were already? Scared, yeah. But resolute. Like always. Maybe more so. We were coming to the end of our journey. I didn't like the way it felt. My imagination had shown me a happy ending for so long, but right now it showed me nothing. I walked between Resa and Grace, their expressions fierce, even Resa's. My original happy endings. Neither one looked at me.

Soon I would come face to face with my twin brother for the first time in my life. I had meant what I said. I wanted to save him, not let him be hurt by anyone. I should have known my friends didn't hold such intent. It had probably never even entered their heads. Only mine. Mine, because I had been in battle before. To be honest, I didn't know if anyone I fought had died. I told myself I should hold onto that uncertainty, find hope in it.

Fat chance.

Without turning her head, Grace reached over

and squeezed my wrist through my sleeve, avoiding my broken hand. "Fat chance? Is that a gambling term?"

I'd been talking out loud again. I groaned, yet since she'd picked up on those two words, perhaps the remaining conversation had taken place only in my head. "Yeah," I said. "Sort of."

She dropped her hand, a flickering smile loosening her clenched jaw. "I'll have to remember that one," she said. A moment later she sobered. "We're here."

I could tell. We all could. We stopped dead, at a momentary loss what the next step should be. The very air around us fizzed like those carbonated beverages they served in the gaming houses. Gran frowned upon them, wouldn't serve the drinks at home, but occasionally I'd snag a few to share with the other Grif-Drifs. Not friends. I could never call them friends, but at the time they were all I had.

The fissure—less than a cave, after what we'd seen and been in—emanated a strange, nearly purple light, a dark illumination as far from sunlight as it could possibly get. It made everything it touched look…well, odd. Shadows appeared translucent and pale objects touched by it took on a ghostly hue. Movement shattered, almost like it broke down into individual frames of sight rather than smooth, uninterrupted motion. I blinked several times, trying to clear my focus, but it didn't help.

"Grace?" I said softly, not daring to speak louder. The light unnerved me. I think it did everyone.

"What is that?" Alwyna. She'd come up beside me. Her breath frosted the air in rapid puffs.

"Dark mage stuff, maybe?" I answered, still whispering.

"And really, what is it you all are planning?"

"We don't know what we're facing, so we'll figure it out as we go." I met Alwyna's eyes. She didn't look reassured. Truthfully, I hadn't intended to ease her mind. There was no point.

Grace shushed us, moved forward. We followed on her heels. I found myself pushing the hair at my nape down again and again. Beneath my clothes, my skin shifted over muscle and bone as if trying to shake tiny embers off my flesh. A buzzing started inside my head. Glancing around at the others, they seemed to be in similar distress. And this, with the connection to keep Moros out. Remembering Alwyna lacked protection, I turned my head to look at her. Her eyes were squeezed shut. Her step faltered. I reached out and grabbed her hand, attempting to will some of what we all were into her. She tried to pull away. I wouldn't let her.

"Let go," she mumbled.

"Shut it," I said.

A face flashed on her left side as Hannah strode up next to her. She took Alwyna's other hand, weapon and all, and looked at me, nodding.

"We've got this," Hannah whispered. "She'll be okay."

I hesitated marginally before nodding back, then returned my attention to Grace. In the unnatural light, the pale garments she wore appeared to be glowing. Mine, too. Carina's white hair shone like a lantern.

"Crap," I said beneath my breath. "We're visible to anyone who wants to take a shot at us."

No sooner had those words departed my mouth than something whizzed past my head and burned into the darkness beyond. Everyone dropped to the ground. Several long moments passed without repeat.

IN DARKNESS WE BREAK

"A stray?" suggested Mika.

"I don't want to stand up and test that theory," Ren responded.

Grace continued forward, bent low. Crouching likewise, we followed her, shielded only by the sparse undergrowth. I had to release Alwyna's hand to make my way along. She seemed okay. Not great, but not any worse at that point than the rest of us. Within a short distance, we reached the entrance.

Grace glanced back. "I'll go in first—"

"The hell you will," I said. "It's all or no one. We stay together. Remember that?"

I didn't wait for an answer. Neither did anyone else. Resa needed no prodding. She darted silently past me and grabbed Grace's hand, Carina right behind her. They stood first, those three, as if they thought themselves invincible. Could be they were right. We rose immediately after, feeling something like warm liquid envelope us. I believed we had just moved into the spell or whatever one wanted to call it wrapped around Grace, Carina, and my sister. Beside me, Alwyna gasped.

"The warrior, the witch, the thrice-gifted child," she murmured. Like a chant.

"It occurs to me," I said, undisguised amazement in my tone, "those titles are interchangeable between them."

Our conversation ended there. Propelled by mage work, we left where we'd been and ended up in an unfathomable and frightening elsewhere.

* * *

We were on our knees, all of us, except the three from the prophecy. A ringing filled my head. Beyond the protective bubble, where a small cave should have been, I looked instead on a vastness so immense it snatched the air from my lungs. It was like space had been above Emerald, limitless and bleak. Except here apparent movement existed not on a vast, interplanetary scale, but smaller, somehow personal, no less frightening. The purple light—black really—came from it. So many things spun within. After a moment, I made a connection to one, watched it spin away.

"Thoughts," I said, my voice overloud. "Not mine," I said a second later. It seemed someone else spoke, not me. Yet, I knew my voice. I'd heard my words inside my brain. It was me. It had to be.

I bowed my head, squeezed my eyes closed, opened them. Another thing went winging by. I recognized it but didn't. Someone else's thoughts like phantoms in a whirlwind.

Don't you know me, Oaks?

"Skelly Shane," I said.

He cackled and his thoughts swirled again in infinite space. Among those on our knees, only Mika looked up when I spoke Shane's name. He stared around, eyes wide, mouth agape. I turned my eyes to trail another thought, another memory, and caught sight of something else.

"Moros!"

Yes, Moros. Or me. In this confounding, altered state, what I looked at could have been either one. But then I noted the clothes. They were different. Different from mine. He sat slumped in nothingness. When I blinked and looked again, I glimpsed a stone wall at his back. Reality.

"Don't hurt him, Shane," I said. "Please."

His thoughts eddied, swung close. I saw Skelly's

face, enormous and wavering, yet not quite like his. I wondered if this was how he remembered himself. Or perhaps I recalled incorrectly. I shut my eyes, opened them again, and gasped.

He appeared to be standing before me, Skelly did, whole and unbloodied and solid. Well, not quite solid. I could still see thoughts or whatever the images represented, spinning behind and through and around him.

I would think you'd be happy, Shane said. *Isn't this what you traveled so far to do? Destroy him?*

"No!" I shouted, the single syllable echoing like a bell.

No? You're a fool, Oaks. I can take what he is. I can take what all of you are. I can be...

His voice trailed off.

"Be what?"

More.

Pain ripped through me, ripped through us all. I heard the whimpers and moans from the others and struggled to stand but the weight on my shoulders, in my mind, wouldn't let me.

"He's my brother! Let him go."

Your brother. And what was I to anyone? Ever? Nothing.

The agony strengthened, tore at every fiber. I realized what I felt, what we all felt, was Skelly's own torture. Soon, it would rip us apart.

"Not true," said a voice. A real voice. Hannah's voice. What?

Somehow, she'd managed to stand. I saw her from the corner of my eye. Although already upright, the other three, Resa, Carina, and Grace, did not move.

You, said Skelly. *The one who wanted the idiot*

boy for your own. Yes, Grace, he said, in a weird aside, *I read your thoughts on that. How could I not?*

Silent, Grace watched. She still held Carina and Resa's hands. I turned my gaze back to Hannah. My head wouldn't follow, but my eyes caught her coming nearer.

"Think," Hannah said. "Think back to when you were really young. Don't you remember me?"

You?

"We are family. Back before our colony was torn apart. We played together, you, me, our kin."

Shane's confusion was palpable.

"My mother and yours were related by blood," Hannah went on. "She looked for you, your mother. We all did, for you and the others who were stolen away. Your mother died still searching for you. And the rest of us scattered."

A resounding silence filled the ether following her words—words that explained so much. I caught a glimpse, a mere resonance from the memory she invoked in Skelly. Enough to let me know she spoke the truth. Enough for Skelly to recognize the same.

He sighed. The air shifted with his breath. Somehow, I rose. Praying I would find stone beneath my feet and not an infinity of emptiness, I ran to where my brother sagged. Threw my arms around him, pulled him close, checked him for life. "He lives," I shouted out, for no one's particular benefit. Except my own.

Skelly Shane's memories began to fade, the vastness of a mind unfettered either compacting or drifting away. The dark illumination vanished. Scarred and burned rock walls, the uneven floor, the returning mobility to all my friends, revealed themselves in its absence, though. But he was not gone, Skelly wasn't. I still saw him, the almost solid him, the ghost of him, staring at Hannah. Trying to gauge the truth, even after what he'd been made to recall.

I saw this all very clearly. Uncounted time had passed in what seemed no more than a few minutes. Morning had come, its soft light rushing in.

Grace

Chapter Fifty

I spotted the *lathesa* on the floor, the crystal at its tip cracked but still intact. I picked it up, turned to face Skelly's apparition.

I won't go back in there.

"I'm not asking you to," I said. Out loud, because now I could. "I'm sorry for what happened to you. You know that. You always have."

You wanted to be my friend.

"I tried."

I wanted to be yours, too.

My heart squeezed. "I know. You just didn't understand how to be one. Not your fault."

Someone was crying. Hannah, I thought.

My chest rose and fell as I drew a deep breath, let it out. I nodded to where Duncan sat beside his twin, holding him. "What did you do to Moros?" I asked.

I took his pain. It made me stronger.

"Will he be all right?"

He can be, Skelly said, enigmatically. But I understood.

I turned toward the fissure's opening, narrowed my eyes against the sun's glare and walked forward, close to the edge. Carina and Resa followed, stood at my side. Together, we watched the movement in the valley, heard the escalating battle sounds as fighting began anew. Ren had passed a remark yesterday, about how the war engines were quick to start and ran hard. He hadn't been wrong. Moros bringing all these armies here hadn't been wrong, either. If they could be stopped right now, it would be so much better than the war escalating, going on and on. A definitive end.

Behind me, Skelly spoke again.

It's time, isn't it? For me to leave.

"Perhaps," I said over my shoulder. "I can't explain what kept you here. I don't know how you became what you are. But I think the choice is yours whether to be done with it."

He said nothing. I realized how risky it was to speak to Skelly so openly about this. How easily he could revert to something dangerous and malignant. But I didn't think he would. Unless I offered it to him. I closed my eyes.

"We have been sought by those who would use us to gain the upper hand in this war. We have been sought by those who thought we could stop The Darkness. We have been hunted and tracked and hounded for too long," I said. "I want to go home."

Carina's and Resa's hands slipped into my own, one to each side.

"But we can't," I said. "One thing has held true in all we've been told. We can end the fighting. But not alone. I think this is why I carried you with me for so long, Skelly. Why you stayed."

I felt him strangely near, like a frothing chill between my shoulder blades. He didn't speak. Outside, shadows passed overhead to our left. Ships, heading toward the valley, with wicked protrusions at the fore. Weaponized ships finally making their entry. My stomach bolted into a knot.

"You've been with me everywhere I've gone, Skelly. You know what I have done, what the three of us are capable of. Yet, there are too many fighting here. I don't think we can do it alone. We need our friends. *All* of them."

Beside me, Carina sucked in a breath. Her lips turned up in a small smile as she looked at me and nodded.

Okay, Grace, Skelly said. *Okay.*

It was so odd, hearing his voice in an atmosphere beyond the brain inside my skull. "I don't want to kill anyone," I clarified.

I'll need your help for that, Grace. I might not be able to stop. Will you help me?

"I've always tried my best."

Mika strode up to Carina's other side. "We need to be down there, in the worst of it," he said. "I'm not sure how much you can do from up here."

"And I don't know how we're going to get past the soldiers on the hillsides," Ren added.

Brand stepped in front, frowning at the growth spread below us. No doubt, he thought to scout a quick, concealed path. The cumbersome ships continued forward at a slow speed, preparing for deadly employment.

A footstep fell behind me. "There's no time."

I turned, expecting Duncan. It had been his voice for a moment, until I recognized the small difference in tone. Moros. I met his eyes. Duncan's eyes. Yes. The shadow in them had gone.

"I'll take you all," he said. "We'll work together. To end this. That's all I ever wanted."

"Eh, not quite," I said.

He smiled, a lopsided, Duncan-smile. "I know. But it is now, I think. We'll still have a chance, those who want to live in peace."

Clutching his brother's arm, Duncan frowned. "Peace? Really? You're saying this?"

I stared hard at Moros. Peace had been his claim, in a convoluted, somewhat violent, not quite rational manner. Had it all been pain? Could Skelly's consumption of it really make that much difference? But we needed help. We had to trust. I had one more question, though. "Valard?" I asked.

"He fell," Moros answered. "I couldn't catch him."

Truth, said Resa's voice.

I don't care whose brother you are, Skelly hissed to Moros. *You harm them and I'll stop you. For good.*

Behind Carina, Mika stared at the pale specter of his old friend, his game-playing companion. "Skelly," he said. "I'm so sorry for what happened to you."

Skelly nodded in silence. His gaze shifted to Alwyna, lighted on her with an expression I couldn't read. She gasped and he laughed, still the same Skelly. And yet somehow not.

Moros stepped forward. What he did next, I didn't see, as I had not before, but a second later we were gone, spiraling through a dark, curling mist.

When we touched down, Enid was there, dressed in a garment I could only view some type of flexible, natural armor. Cericia was with her, in her hart's phase, as well as other animals I suspected shifted to humanoid form at night. One, a huge and ferocious creature, dripped blood from its maw. While I stared, it loped away into the fray.

"Where's my mother?" Alwyna demanded upon seeing Enid. Enid turned to her. Alwyna's voice softened. "Is she…has she gone?"

"Not yet," Enid answered. "She is in a tent above, guarded by several of your warriors. Go to her. Protect her in what is coming."

Alwyna hurried up the hillside past the fallen, black stone toward a small pavilion. A crest adorned it, perhaps belonging to the Fianna.

"What do you mean, protect her in what is coming?" I asked.

Enid smiled. "You know the answer to that better than I. I'm only here to help you all. You, Carina, Resa, and your steadfast companions."

"Bloody hell," Duncan muttered. Beside him, Moros chuckled. Not the harsh, humorless laugh I'd heard from him before. He seemed genuinely amused by his brother's expletive. Enid looked him up and down.

"A quick conversion, that one," she said.

I bear his pain now, Skelly whispered around us. Enid turned her head, following the path his voice took. Although I, and perhaps my friends, could still see him, I wasn't sure Enid could. However, she answered him readily.

"You will have peace soon, young man." She looked at me, leaned forward, tapped the crystal on the staff I still held. "You won't need that anymore."

"No," I agreed. "But I'll keep it until I find a place so green and beautiful I won't be able to stand it, and I'll bury it there, in his honor."

"That will be well done," she said.

I raised my head to the ships above us. Some of the fighting had paused, as the combatants noted them, too. I didn't know whose airships they were, who they sought to kill, or if their operators would differentiate any on the ground as theirs. Perhaps, I mused, everyone below was expendable. Even us.

It didn't matter, though. Our time was up.

"Hands," I said, lifting my arms out to either side, fingers spread. One by one, everyone linked together to my left, Moros between Duncan and Resa. I expected trouble from him yet, but right now, his intentions seemed genuine. Enid stepped up to my right, held her hand, palm up, near my own.

"May I?" she asked.

"Of course." I twisted my neck, searching the area behind us. "Skelly?"

Right here, he said, at Enid's back. His incorporeal fingers closed over both hers and mine, cold as ice. Ice that burned.

"I don't want to harm anyone," I said, recalling the way I'd laid low the Fianna beneath the mountains, and later, Tiran's soldiers. "I just want them to stop. But I've never done this without anger."

The burning cold worked its way up my arm. Skelly spoke in my ear. *I have an abundance. I'll share some of mine. Gladly.*

Too late for me to wonder if I'd made a mistake. Too late for anything. The world exploded around us all.

Duncan

Chapter Fifty-One

I struggled to get off the ground. I couldn't tell how long I'd been there, face-down in the dirt. A hand appeared and grasped mine, yanking me to my feet. Moros stood before me, pale and shaken.

"It's over," he said.

Gasping, I looked around. I located my friends close by, either on the dusty ground or already upright. Carina crouched next to Mika, wiping trickling blood from his face. Brand helped Ren and Hannah to sit. Some distance beyond them, Enid stood next to Grace, Resa at her side. I sprinted over to them. My steps slowed the closer I got, my head pivoting from side to side on my aching neck. Moros hadn't lied. It was over.

Bodies covered the ground from the valley to the hillsides. Some dead, but obviously too long ago to have been at our hand. Most were stirring, sitting up with or without aid. Dazed. Unnerved. I recognized some as Draig's warriors. Many more wore accoutrement I didn't know. Strangers, all. Mangled, useless weapons littered the ground. In the distance, the three, armed ships lay in crumpled heaps, looking as though they had nose-dived from the sky. Smoke plumed into the air. I halted completely, spun on my heel to stare at Grace.

Had I said before she scared me? Right now, fear filled me like it had replaced my blood. I wanted to throw up.

"Duncan!" she cried. When I didn't move, she raced over to me and threw herself against my body. Her arms tightened around me to keep me from falling over.

"Are you all right?" she whispered.

"Are they?" I croaked back, indicating the fallen with a chin jerk.

Grace stepped back, looked around. "Yes. Yes, they should be. You were a long time waking up. Most were. Those who weren't have already set about taking the…ringleaders, someone called them. Seems a strange name. Anyway, they are being taken into custody or will be hunted down. The war is ended, but there will be skirmishes to finalize it. Not everyone converged here, but for the most part, it's done. Or so I am told."

I swallowed, my mouth dry and oddly gritty. "How long have I been out?"

"A while," she said, with a look marked by apology. "I checked on you all, frequently, rearranged you for comfort, but I didn't dare wake you up before you were ready. Enid's warning."

Nodding, I stared down at the ground, shuffling my boot across the dirt. Tiny pebbles grated beneath the sole. "And the ringleaders?" I asked, using her newfound word. "Tiran. The Lyoness. I suppose there were others?"

"Yes. According to my brother and your uncle

and a score more I heard talking. It is being promised they will be tried and sentenced. Very likely, they will live out their lives on the Emerald."

"Fitting, I suppose." I managed a weak smile at the irony.

Grace took another step away, dropped her hands to her side. "You're not okay," she said.

I shook my head. "How can I be?"

"We stopped the bloodshed, Duncan. Stopped others who were not in this for gain and glory and senseless reasoning from being hurt, imprisoned, killed, without hurting anyone ourselves. It's over."

"That's what Moros said," I mumbled. "His words, too."

"And?" she prompted me.

I thought a moment. "I don't know."

She slipped her hand around my bandaged one, lifted it, tapped the ring beneath the bandage with a finger. "Your uncle has been checking on you, wanted to be told when you woke up."

My head dropped forward, bouncing a little. "Well, crap," I said.

"We can all sneak away," she suggested. Almost cheerfully, as if what had taken place here this day had somehow lifted a weight from her shoulders. I supposed it had. For me, it felt different. I couldn't explain why.

"Is Skelly…gone?"

She nodded. Even that hurt, somehow. I left her then, and with some direction found Draig. When he spotted me approaching, the whites showed around his eyes in a wide, startled stare, as though he thought I might do something unexpected and frightening. I didn't really care. Raising my right hand, I shook it at him. He actually flinched.

"I don't know what I'm going to do about this," I said without preface, indicating the hidden ring with my other hand. "That's a conversation for another day, okay?"

He nodded wordlessly. I stalked away. He called me back. I turned.

"Thank you," he said. "Thank you, and your friends."

With a shrug, I walked on, heading for a tent where the Fianna stood at attention outside. Alwyna stepped out as I approached. "Is she—" I began.

"She's gone," said Alwyna. "We were together at the end. Once we've prepared the body, we'll be taking her home." Her eyes were dry, though red-rimmed. It appeared she'd made her peace. "Thank you," she said, "for everything."

Her arms lifted and dropped. She had possibly been thinking about hugging me, but she stood and faced me instead in an awkward stance. Preventing herself from doing something so foolish as sharing emotion with a lesser, I guess. I didn't give a jolly good crap. I grabbed her and hugged her tight, told her how sorry I was about her mother, and then stepped away, grinning at her astonished face. After, I wished her a safe journey and headed back to where I'd left my friends. Taking the long way round. I didn't want to bump into any more gratitude.

When I'd circled the wrecked building, I found Moros with Enid and Grace. Resa stood beside him, clutching his hand. His posture indicated relaxation. Had she had close contact with him before? A bit jealous, a lot confused, and still feeling oddly wretched, I marched over to join them.

Moros released Resa's hand and took mine, shaking it without crushing my battered digits.

"I'll be leaving soon," he said. "I wanted to say thank—"

"It's okay," I interrupted him. "No thanks needed for me. I'm your brother. But I should thank you anyway. You did your part here, too."

He cocked his head to one side. His dark hair—dark hair like mine—swept down across one eye. "You haven't asked where I'm going."

"Into custody, I assume? Don't worry. I'll do what I can for you. We all will."

He glanced at Enid. She stepped forward, whispering like a conspirator.

"He's not being taken into custody yet," she said. "But he and I will have to leave quickly with Cericia and the others before he is. There is a place where I will take your brother, where others of my kind reside in secret. He will be safe there. He will relearn. He will heal. We will care for him and he will return into the world, unbroken."

I staggered back from her. This was all too much. A hundred different questions raced through my mind. I blurted out the most persistent.

"For crying out loud, why didn't you do this a long time ago?"

Her nut-colored face creased in a smile, that smile she had. The one to make me blush. She tapped a finger against my chest. "Because he hadn't met you, yet, Duncan. He needed you, to show him the lighter side of himself, the fact he is cared for, that he has value. This is your power. The power you don't think you possess. Because it is your gift, your goodness. It affects everyone you meet."

* * *

They left a short time later, Enid, Cericia, and my brother, surrounded by the other shapeshifters. No one stopped them. No one seemed to notice their departure. I figured this was Enid's doing. I hugged my twin before they slipped away. Really hugged him.

"Heal well," I whispered, "because I want you back."

No sooner had they disappeared than Grace's brother showed up. He strode straight over to Grace.

"I've made arrangements," Connor said, "for Tik to lead you back to our camp. Mother and Father are there, waiting for you. I'd take you myself, but…" He waved his hand toward the many hundreds still being sorted out all around. "Your friends are welcome to go with you, accompany Mother and Father back home. We'll make arrangements for their transportation to their own homes, after."

A muscle twitched in Grace's cheek. I knew what it portended. So did we all, I think.

"You're assuming we can't find our way on our own," she said. "Have you forgotten how far we've come without being led by you or one of your warriors?"

I had noted their prickly relationship early on. Typical brother and sister, I'd been told. I wouldn't know, though. Resa and I hadn't had any of that. But with the changes in her, possibly we now would.

Connor raised his hands, palm out. "I didn't mean anything by it. It just seemed expedient. It's not far. Yes, you could have found it on your own. But there's food waiting, and I figured some of you—" he glanced back at me, "might want to get started on it sooner rather than later."

At food's mention, my stomach roared. Everyone

laughed but me. I couldn't shake my abnormally deep gloom. After gathering what little property remained to us, we met Tik on the slope above and followed him over the ridge into the forest. Connor's statement about returning us all to our homes stuck with me the whole way, repeating in my head. Yeah, sure, I had Gran waiting for me, but no one else had a home to return to or which appealed or where they'd be welcome. Or was that just the impression I received, held onto, once Grace had invited us to all remain together? Maybe that had only been all the stress, the long months together, the yearning for normalcy talking.

Aiofe and Thar greeted Grace with tears and gruff sentiment, neither alarmed or wary of their daughter. I wondered what they had heard or had not about those final minutes on the battlefield. I followed Grace's lead and said nothing. Thankfully, they promptly fed us, as Connor had promised. I ate in silence, listening to the conversations around me.

"When we get back home," Grace said, wiping juice off her chin from a bright little fruit, "my friends will be staying. For a while, at least, because except for Duncan, they have nowhere to go."

She looked at me with a smile, not noticing her parents' silence.

"We're perfectly happy to sleep under the stars," Mika hastened. "We've been doing that for a while. Just until we find somewhere else."

"Nonsense," Aiofe answered, recovering. "You are all welcome to stay as long as you like. I'm sorry I didn't speak up sooner. It's dreadful you have nowhere else." Her green eyes drifted to me, sensing, I supposed, my attachment to Grace.

"We'll help out with whatever you need doing,"

said Carina. Hannah mumbled an agreement around a mouthful. Brand shifted where he sat, his gaze on the forest.

"Your home is in the desert, yeah?" he asked.

"Yes," said Aiofe. "It might take some getting used to."

Brand nodded, returning in silence to his meal. Ren thanked them. I did, too, but my delay did not go unnoticed. Grace's eyes lifted to mine. I avoided looking back.

"Duncan?"

Abruptly, I stood. "I'm sorry," I said. "I'm really sorry. My...my heart is breaking, and I don't know why."

I ran from the low table and out into the forest, stopping only when I nearly collided with the three *conjures*. Chauncy, Vigor, and Bell clustered together on the ground in a clearing. Chauncy turned his white-ringed eye my way and let out a gentle rumble. Something in the sound caused tears to erupt. I didn't bother to check them. I stood there with my head down, letting them flow.

Fallen leaves rustled behind me. A hand touched my arm. Grace's fingers curled into my sleeve.

"What's wrong, Duncan?"

"How can I return to my old life after all this?" I asked her. Asked myself. "I don't want to give this up. I don't want to give *us* up. Any of us."

"Enid was right," Grace whispered. "Goodness is your gift. It has affected us all. What is it you want to do, Duncan? Tell me."

I thought for a time, wiping the embarrassing tears from my face. "I want...I want to find Toma and my mother, spend some time with them. And then I'd like to go to that secret place where Enid has taken

Moros, be with him, learn with him, maybe even learn from those others of Enid's kind, you know? I want to see more of the world without being hounded, hunted, chased. I want to do it with you, Grace. And with Resa and Mika and Carina. With Brand and Ren and Hannah. We belong together, me, you, our friends, for better or worse. I mean, we'll likely run into things that are bad, I'm sure. And we might have to get jobs intermittently, just to…just to make ends meet. Maybe learn a trade that doesn't involve duping people. But we can't do any of that. It won't be allowed."

Grace was silent. Perhaps I had said too much. Revealed too much. She started to shake beside me. I'd made her weep. Swearing, I spun to face her. She wasn't crying, at all. She was laughing.

"What? Did I say something funny?"

She grinned at me, her face, after all, quite wet as she laughed through her tears. I'd driven her to that.

"Only one thing was funny," she said.

"Go ahead. Spit it out."

"It won't be allowed," she quoted me. "Truly? Do you hear yourself? Have you forgotten all we've been through? All we've done? Won't be allowed," she repeated. "Bah."

I looked past her. The others had trailed after Grace and all stood behind her, watching in silence. Finally, Mika and Carina stepped forward.

"We're in," they said in quiet unison, hand in hand.

"Me, too," said Brand. Ren and Hannah chimed in with their own agreement. Resa stared at me, smiling.

And me.

I smiled back at her.

"But first," Grace announced, "I want a bath.

They've got to be able to heat up some water in an old tub in the camp somewhere, I would think. Girls?" Carina, Resa, and Hannah joined her, clasping hands in a line. Grace glanced back, looking suddenly carefree, despite our conversation. Or maybe because of it. "The warrior, the witch, the thrice-gifted child and friends," she said.

We watched them go, Mika, Brand, Ren, and I.

"I could use a little more food," I said to them. "Just putting that out there." The other three agreed, no hesitation. We knew what it was to be without. Knew, too, we might find ourselves in those circumstances again. But it would be all right.

The *conjures* rumbled, telling us in their way they'd be there waiting when we returned.

AUTHOR'S NOTE

As the final book in the series, *In Darkness We Break* tended to prompt mixed emotions in me while writing. I have, quite honestly, fallen in love with these characters (as many of you have also professed) and am sorry to see them go. But they'd also reached the tale's end and…well, as an author, it's my job to escort them there and then let them get on with their lives.

However, as so many have also asked to know more about the wonderful companions in the Shadow Journey series, I am in the process of writing back story about each, a series of short tales which will be released in 2025 in its own volume. I think that's a proper send-off for all of them, even those who did not have their own voice.

Again, I want to thank you all for sticking with me and my imaginary friends (lol) through all their trials and successes. I do so hope you enjoy this, the latest and last volume in the series. Feel free to reach out to me on social media or through the contact page on my website with any questions, comments, or, perhaps, theories (because those abound, too).

Take care, dear readers!

Robin (aka Jo Allen Ash)

More in The Shadow Journey Series by Jo Allen Ash

THE SHADOWS WE MAKE, BOOK ONE

THE THRICE-GIFTED CHILD, BOOK TWO

THE SLEEPING MYTH, BOOK THREE

Where to find out more about the author, her works and her interests:

www.joallenash.com

Facebook.com/JoAllenAsh

YouTube.com/@JoAllenAshWrites-2024

Instagram.com/joallenash

Milton Keynes UK
Ingram Content Group UK Ltd.
UKHW020738071024
449371UK00014B/927

9 798987 068191